Hot Blooded

Hot Blooded

Lisa Jackson

HODDER &
STOUGHTON

First published in the USA in 2001 by Kensington Publishing Company

First published in Great Britain in 2011 by Hodder & Stoughton
An Hachette UK company

1

A CIP catalogue record for this title is available from the British Library.

Hardback ISBN 978 1 444 71350 3
Ebook ISBN 978 1 444 71354 1

Typeset in Plantin Light by Hewer Text UK Ltd, Edinburgh

Printed and bound by CPI Group (UK) Ltd, Croydon, CR0 4YY

Hodder & Stoughton policy is to use papers that are natural, renewable
and recyclable products and made from wood grown in sustainable
forests. The logging and manufacturing processes are expected to
conform to the environmental regulations of the country of origin.

Hodder & Stoughton Ltd
338 Euston Road
London NW1 3BH

www.hodder.co.uk

To John Scognamiglio, who was not only the editor of this book, but a major player in the creative process, just as he was with all my books for Kensington, especially during the writing of If She Only Knew. *Always sane, with infinite patience and brilliant ideas that push me farther than I might dare to go, John has so inspired me that I'm paying him back by naming the villain in this book after him. Thanks, John!*

ACKNOWLEDGMENTS

First and foremost I would like to thank the City of New Orleans Police Department for their help and courtesy, even though I bent the rules a tad to accommodate this story.

I would also like to thank the following individuals who offered their support, knowledge, and expertise, without which this book would not have been written. Thanks to Nancy Berland, Eric Brown, Ken and Nancy Bush, Matthew Crose, Michael Crose, Alexis Harrington, Jenny Hold, Richard Jaskiel, Michael Kavanaugh, Mary Clare Kersten, Debbie Macomber, Arla Melum, Ken Melum, Ari Okano, Kathy and Bob Okano, Betty and Jack Pederson, Jim and Sally Peters, Jeff and Karen Rosenberg, Robin Rue, Jon Salem, John Scognamiglio, Larry and Linda Sparks, Mark and Celia Stinson, Jane Thornton, The LO Rowers, and, of course, Pliney the Elder.

If I've missed anyone, my apologies.

Prologue

'You want something special?' she asked, running the tip of her tongue over her lips provocatively.

He shook his head.

'I can—'

'Just strip.'

There's something wrong with this guy. Seriously wrong, Cherie Bellechamps thought, a drip of fear sliding through her blood. She thought about calling the whole thing off, telling the john to get lost, but she needed the cash. Maybe her imagination was getting the better of her. Maybe he wasn't a creep.

She unbuttoned her dress slowly and felt his eyes upon her, just as hundreds of other eyes had stared in the past. No big deal.

Over the noise of the city, music played from her bedside radio. Frank Sinatra's smooth voice. Which usually calmed her. Not tonight.

A hot June breeze, heavy with the dank breath of the Mississippi, blew through the open window. It ruffled the yellowed lace curtains and cooled the beads of sweat collecting on Cherie's forehead, but didn't ease her case of nerves.

The john sat on a three-legged stool and fingered a rosary in one hand, the blood-red beads catching in the frail light. So what was he? Some kind of religious nut? A priest who couldn't handle celibacy? Or was this just another weird fetish? Lord knew in New Orleans there were thousands of oddballs, all with their own sexual fantasy.

'You like?' she asked, conjuring up a slightly Cajun accent as she ran a long-nailed finger along the cleft of her breasts and pushed aside any lingering trepidations.

'Keep going.' From the stool in the little room, he wiggled a finger at her bra and panties.

'Don't you want to?' she asked, her voice low and sultry.

'I'll watch.'

She didn't know how much he could see. This second-story room on the fringes of the French Quarter was lit by a single lamp, the shade covered in a black-lace mantilla so that intricate shadows played upon the walls and hid the cracks in the old plaster. Besides that, the john was wearing Ray-Bans with dark lenses. Cherie couldn't see his eyes, but it didn't matter. He was good-looking. Athletic. His jaw was square, his nose straight, his lips thin and secretive in a day's worth of stubble. He wore a dark shirt, black jeans and his hair was a thick, coffee brown. Unless there was something hideously wrong with his eyes, this guy was Hollywood handsome.

And spooky as sin.

Already he'd asked her to scrub her face and don a red wig to cover her short platinum hair. She hadn't argued. Didn't care what got a trick off.

She flicked off the front clasp of her bra and let the scrap of red lace slide to the floor.

He didn't so much as move. Except to rub the damned rosary beads.

'You got a name?' she asked.

'Yeah.'

'You're not going to share it?'

'Call me Father.'

'Father like . . . my dad . . . or' – she glanced at the dark beads running through his fingers – 'like a priest?'

'Just Father.'

'How about Father John?' It was her attempt at a joke. He didn't smile.

So much for levity.

Time to end this, get paid, and send him packing.

She wriggled out of her panties and sat on the edge of the bed, giving him a full view of every part of her.

Okay, so some guys got off on watching a woman strip. Some even just watched, never touched as she fondled herself, but this john was so cold and emotionless – eerily so – and what was with the glasses? 'We could have some fun,' she suggested, trying to speed things up. He was well into his hour, and so far nothing much was happening. 'Just you and me . . .'

He didn't respond except to reach over and drop a hundred-dollar bill onto the nightstand. Sinatra's voice was cut off as Father John switched the radio station. From 'When I Was Seventeen . . .' through a series of beeps, chirps and static until he found the station he wanted – some talk show she'd heard before – a popular one with a female psychologist giving advice. But Cherie wasn't listening. She was staring at the C-note on the nightstand. It was marred. Ben Franklin's eyes had been blacked out with a marking pen, as if he, too, like the man in shades, was hiding his identity.

Or didn't want to see.

Odd. Creepy. Weird.

Father John had picked her up a block off Bourbon Street, asked her for a date, and she'd looked him over, thought he'd seemed all right and named her price. He'd agreed and she'd brought him here, to the seedy apartment she and a couple of other girls kept just for this purpose. Her other life was in another parish . . . across the lake . . . and for a second she thought of her five-year-old daughter and the ongoing custody battle with her ex. No one in Covington knew she turned tricks to help make ends meet; no one could ever, or she'd lose custody and any contact she had with her only child.

Now she was second-guessing her actions. The john was too edgy, his calm masking a restlessness that was evident in a small vein throbbing near his temple and the movement of finger and thumb on the beads. She thought of the pistol she kept in the top drawer of the nightstand. If things got dicey, she'd reach over, swoop up the hundred-spot, yank open the drawer and pull the .38. Scare him off. Keep the C-note.

'Why don't you join me?' she suggested, lying back on the chenille bedspread, smiling and not expecting him to move. God, it was hot.

'Take off my clothes.' He stood. Walked to the bed.

His command seemed out of sync, but at least it was a common one. So he was going to get down to business. Good. Voyeurs usually didn't touch. The minutes were ticking off, but she took her time, standing so that she could slowly unbutton his shirt. She shoved it off shoulders that were muscular and a chest without any flab, just a wall of rock-hard muscles covered with dark, coiled hair. She unbuckled his belt, and he fingered the cross she always wore as it dangled just above her breasts.

'What's that—?'

'It – it was a gift from my daughter . . . last Christmas.' Oh, God, he wouldn't steal it, would he?

'You need something more.' He slipped the rosary beads over her head. Over the red wig. Yeah, maybe he was a priest. A freaky one.

The sharp beads were warm from being fondled. They fell into the cleft between her breasts. It was creepy. Too creepy. She should tell him to get out now. 'There. That's better.' One side of Father John's mouth lifted, as if he was finally satisfied with the scenario. Ready to get down to business.

About time.

'What's with the rosary?'

'Touch me.'

His body was perfect. Honed. Tanned. Hard.

Except for his cock. It hung limp, as if he wasn't getting off at all.

She ran a finger down his chest, and he pulled her against him. Kissed her hard with cold, unfeeling lips and dragged her onto the sagging mattress of her iron bed. She had a rule – no lips on lips, but she let it slide, just to end this.

'That's a boy,' she cooed, and reached for the sunglasses. Strong fingers circled her wrist.

'Don't.'

'Afraid I'll recognize you?' Maybe he was famous – God, he was good-looking enough. Maybe he was some kind of celebrity and didn't want her to recognize him. Or maybe he was married. More likely . . .

'Just . . . don't.' His grip was like steel.

'Fine, fine . . . whatever.' She kissed his cheek and ran her fingers along the ridges of his well-toned muscles. He moved against her and she worked hard, touching all those erotic spots guaranteed to cause an erection. To no avail. No matter how much she kissed, licked and purred, he was only going through the motions, not turned on at all.

Come on, come on, she thought, *I haven't got all night.* She was vaguely aware of the radio, the psychologist, Dr. Sam, was close to signing off, giving her signature spiel about love and lust in this city on the Delta, and Father John, too, turned to listen to the radio shrink.

Maybe he was being distracted and that was the problem. She reached for the radio dial—

'Don't touch it,' he growled, every muscle in his body flexing.

'But—'

Smack!

Blinding pain exploded in the left side of her face as his fist connected.

She squealed. Tasted the metallic flavor of her own blood. This was not good. Not good. 'Wait a second, you son of a bitch—'

He raised his fist again. She saw him through a rapidly swelling eye. 'Don't mess with the radio or my shades,' he growled.

She tried to squirm away. 'Get out! Get the hell out!'

He tried to kiss her.

She bit him.

He didn't so much as flinch.

'Get out, you bastard! No one hits me. Don't you get it? It's over.'

'Not quite yet it isn't, but it will be.' He pinned her to the sheets. Kissed her again. Hard. As if he was getting off on her pain. Cheek throbbing, Cherie tried to wriggle out from under him, but he held her fast with his athletic body.

She was trapped.

Frantic. Hitting him, clawing at him, shoving him.

'That's it, you sinner, you cunt,' he growled. 'Fight me.' His hands were rough. He nipped at one breast, twisted the other.

She screamed and he stopped her by grinding his mouth against hers. She tried to bite him, flailed at him with her fists, but he was strong. Incensed. Turned on. Oh, God, how far was this going to go?

Fear congealed her blood. What if he didn't stop? What if he tortured her all night?

Pain shot up her torso as he bit her breast.

Writhing, she spied the radio, the digital display glowing over the hundred-dollar bill, Dr. Sam's voice cool and collected and savvy.

Help me, Cherie thought, scrabbling for the drawer and her gun, knocking over the lamp, kicking wildly, feeling his suddenly rock-hard erection.

So it was rape.

He wanted to rape her. If he'd only said something, she would have played along, but now she was scared. Scared as hell.

Just do it and don't hurt me!

He yanked her head off the pillow and she cried out just as he tightened the rosary around her throat, the sharp-edged beads slicing her skin, the dark facets winking malevolently.

Oh, God, he's going to kill me. Fear screamed through her blood. She looked into those shaded eyes and knew it.

He twisted the rosary as he thrust deep into her. Cherie's eyes bulged, she couldn't breathe, her arms flailed and she scratched, but to no avail. Blackness . . . all around her there was blackness . . . Her lungs burned . . . her heart felt as if it would explode . . . *Please God, help me!*

He wrenched the beaded noose. She gasped. Got no air. Something rasped and gurgled inside her. Blood, oh, God, she tasted her own blood . . . Again . . .

Blackness crawled from the outside in and she thought fleetingly of her daughter . . . sweet, sweet baby . . .

He was sweating, grinding against her, his breath racing and as she let go she felt him stiffen and heard his guttural, primal roar. Dimly over the sound of his labored breathing and the roar in her brain there was another voice. Far away. So far away.

'This is Dr. Sam, with a final word . . . Take care of yourself, New Orleans. Good night to you all and God bless. No matter what your troubles are today, there is always tomorrow . . . Sweet dreams . . .'

I

July
Cambrai, Louisiana

There's no place like home, there's no place like home.
Now, click the heels of those ruby slippers three times and . . .

'That'll be thirty-seven dollars,' the cab driver muttered, breaking into Samantha's thoughts. He pulled the cab around the circular drive and as close to the front door as possible while she dug deep into her jacket pocket for her money clip.

'Would you mind taking the bags inside?' she asked.

The driver, twisting his head to get a better view from the front seat, slanted her a curious look. His eyes were dark. Suspicious. As if he expected some kind of come-on. Finally, he lifted a big shoulder. 'If that's what you want.'

'It is.' Using one crutch, she crawled out of the cab into the sultry Louisiana night. A fine, steamy mist shrouded the live oaks surrounding her rambling old house in this unique community tucked along the southern shore of Lake Pontchartrain, a few miles west of New Orleans. God, it was good to be home.

Some vacations were dreams, others were nightmares. This one had been worse than a nightmare, it had been an out-and-out disaster.

But at least she knew she would never become Mrs. David Ross. *That* would have been a mistake.

Another one.

A heavy breeze riffled through the clumps of Spanish moss dripping from ancient, gnarled branches. The flagstones of the front walk, slick with rain, shimmered in the frail illumination cast from the porch light. Wet weeds that had the nerve to poke through the cracked mortar tickled the bare toe of her injured leg as she hitched her way over the uneven stones. Sweat ran down her spine. Barely July, and the Louisiana heat closed in on her. Gritting her teeth, she hobbled up steps to the broad porch that skirted the front door and swept around all sides of her lakefront cottage. Wind chimes tinkled out their lonely tune. She propped her crutch on the arm of the porch swing, then found her spare key tucked in the cobwebs behind the shutter of one window. Quickly, she unlocked the door. As the cab driver lugged her bags, she flipped on a switch. Immediately the foyer was illuminated, two-hundred-year-old hardwood gleaming with a fine patina, the air inside the ancient house stagnant, hot and still.

The driver dropped her three bags near the hall tree, then retrieved her crutch.

'Thanks.' She handed him forty-five dollars and was rewarded with a satisfied grunt and a quick nod of his head.

'Welcome back.' Dark eyes flashed from beneath the bill of his Saints cap. 'Have a good one.'

'I'll try.' Shutting the door behind him, she pocketed her house key and called over her shoulder, 'Honey, I'm home.'

No response.

Just the soft ticking of the clock over the mantel and the drone of the refrigerator from the kitchen. She flipped on the switch for the overhead fan, another for the air-conditioning.

'Aw, come on . . .' she called into the darkened rooms. 'You're not mad because I left you here all alone, are you? You know, that's *so* typically male.'

Finding the spare set of keys in the pantry, she waited, listening for the distinctive click of ID tags or the light tread of paws upon the floor. Instead she heard a soft meow and then Charon slunk out of the shadows. Pupils dilated, his eyes were as dark as his inky coat, just a tiny ring of gold visible. 'Don't tell me, now you're going to play hard to get,' she accused as he eased around the edge of the foyer, feigning disinterest, his tail twitching. 'Oh, yeah, you're a real cool dude.' She laughed, and he sauntered closer, doing a few quick turns around her ankles and rubbing up against the fiberglass shell surrounding her left calf and foot.

'Like the cast? Compliments of that fiasco in Mexico,' she said, plucking his near-liquid body from the floor and holding him close to her chest as she scratched his chin. Charon, a stray she'd named after the ferryman in Dante's *Inferno*, began to purr instantly, his aloof routine forgotten, his wet nose brushing the underside of her chin. 'So what went on here while I was away, huh? Did Melanie take good care of you? No?' Smiling, she carried the feline into the den and cracked a window, waiting for the house to cool.

She set Charon on the bookcase, where he slunk through her tomes on psychology and her stacks of paperbacks, then hopped onto the desk where her mail had been stacked neatly, sorted carefully by envelopes, junk mail, magazines and newspapers. Melanie, Sam's assistant, who had not only watched the house and seen to Charon while Samantha was vacationing, but had commandeered her radio show as well, was nothing if not efficient.

Samantha pulled out the desk chair and plopped onto the familiar seat. She glanced around the room. It felt different somehow, but she didn't know why. Maybe it was just because she'd been gone so long, over two weeks. Or maybe it was because she was jet-lagged and a little on edge. Though the flight hadn't been that long, she'd spent too many hours without sleep in the past few days, and the trip had been emotionally draining.

Ever since touching down in Mexico two weeks earlier, things had started to go awry. Not only had she and David had the same old fight about her giving up her job and moving back to Houston, but there had also been the boating 'accident' that had dumped both her and her purse into the shallows of the Pacific. She'd ended up with a sprained ankle and no ID – the purse had never been located. It had been a nightmare trying to get out of the country, and when she'd finally persuaded the authorities to let her back into the USA, she'd been sporting this god-awful, bulky cast.

'These things happen,' David had said with a shrug, as they'd finally boarded the 737. He'd offered her a smile and a lift of his eyebrows as if to say, *Hey, there's nothing we can do about it now. We're in a foreign country.* He'd been right, of course, but it didn't help her bad mood and suspicion that the fishing-boat captain had been drunk or under the influence of some other drug and that somehow her purse, along with a couple of others in the tour group, had been found by local divers, the credit cards, cash and other items of value now being used or pawned up and down the west coast of Mexico. According to the captain, the tiny fishing boat had lurched, avoiding a rock – for God's sake. It seemed implausible. A stupid mistake from a captain who daily patrolled the waters off Mazatlán. Samantha hadn't bought it and had wanted some kind of compensation, at the very least an apology for crying out loud. Instead she'd landed in a tiny hospital with an elderly doctor, an expatriate American who looked as if he should have retired in the seventies. He probably had, or been run out of the States for malpractice.

'Sour grapes, Dr. Sam,' she chastised herself, as Charon settled into his favorite spot on the window ledge. He stared through the watery glass, his eyes following something in the darkness. Probably a squirrel. Samantha looked through the panes and saw nothing but the dark shadows of the night.

She pushed the play button on her answering machine while grabbing her letter opener and slicing through the first envelope – a bill. No doubt the first of many. The recorder went through a series of beeps and clicks before playing.

The first call was a hangup.

Great.

She tossed the bill onto the table.

The second was a solicitor asking if she needed autoglass repair.

Better yet. She thought of her red Mustang convertible, couldn't wait to get it on the road again. But she didn't need a new windshield. 'No thanks,' she said tearing into several letters – offers of credit cards, requests for contributions to worthy causes, the sewer bill.

Finally a voice.

'Hey, Sam, it's Dad.' Sam smiled. 'I forgot you were out of town . . . You give me a call when you get back home, okay?'

'Will do,' Sam said as she scanned her most recent Visa bill and was grateful that she'd called Melanie who had assured her that she would cancel all her credit cards immediately.

Two more hangups and then she heard her boss's voice boom from the recorder. 'Sam, I know you're probably not home yet,' Eleanor said, 'but call me the minute, the *minute* you get in. And don't give me any crap about you not going to work because of your leg, that's just not cutting it with me. I got your message from the hospital, but unless you're hooked to an IV *and* a heart monitor *and* strapped to a hospital bed, I want you back at the station pronto. You got that? Melanie's doing a decent enough job, I mean it, but since you've been gone, ratings have slipped and Trish LaBelle over at WNAB is picking up your market share . . . not good, Sammie, definitely not good. Your listeners want you, girl, and they aren't in the mood to accept any substitutes, no matter how good they might be. So don't you go bringin' me some note from a hunk of a doctor, y'hear? Uh-uh. You all haul your ass down to the station. Okay, I'll get off my soap box now. But call me. A-S-A-P.'

'Hear that, Charon? I am loved after all,' she said absently to the cat, then felt the skin on the back of her neck prickle. Some noise, some shift in the atmosphere, some intangible *thing* caught her attention.

The cat sat on the sill, his body frozen except for the barely perceptible twitching of his tail. 'You see something?' she asked, trying to shake off the feeling. She dropped the rest of the mail and moved to the window, searching the darkness through the steamy drizzle on the windowpanes.

The live oaks stood like bearded sentinels, unmoving dark shapes guarding her two-hundred-year-old house.

Creeaaak.

Sam's heart nearly stopped.

Was that the wind in the branches, the house settling, or someone shifting their weight on the porch? Her throat went dry.

Stop it, Sam, you're jumping at shadows. There's nothing sinister here. This is your home. But she'd only lived here three months, and after she'd moved in, she'd learned the history of the house from a gossipy old neighbor across the street. According to Mrs. Killingsworth, the reason the old home had been on the market so long and Sam had gotten it far under its market value was that the woman who had previously owned the place had been murdered here – the object of an enraged boyfriend's vengeance.

'So what's that got to do with you?' she said now, rubbing her arms as if she were chilled. She didn't believe in ghosts, curses or the supernatural.

The recorder spun. 'Hi, Sam.' Melanie's voice. Samantha relaxed a bit. 'Hope you had a good trip. I called the credit-card companies, as you asked, and left the mail on the desk, but you've probably found it by now. Charon was a pill while you were gone. Really out of sorts. Even sprayed on the piano, but I cleaned it up. And the hair balls. Gross. Anyway, I bought you a quart of milk and some of those fancy French vanilla coffee beans you like. They're both in the fridge. Sorry to hear about your leg. What a bummer. Some romantic getaway, huh? See you at the station, or you can call if you need anything.'

Sam hobbled back to her chair. She was imagining things. Nothing had changed. She glanced at the picture of David on her desk. Tall and athletic, with gray eyes and a square jaw. Good-looking. Executive vice president *and* director of sales for Regal Hotels, she'd been reminded more often than not. A man with a future and a quick, if cutting, sense of humor. A catch, as her mother would have said had Beth Matheson still been alive.

Oh, Mom, I still miss you. Sam's gaze moved from the five-by-seven of David to a faded color portrait of her own family, both smiling parents flanking her in her cap and gown at graduation from UCLA. Her older brother, Peter, stood just behind her father's shoulder, frowning, looking away from the camera, not even bothering to remove his sunglasses, as if making a statement that he didn't want to be there, wasn't interested in sharing any of Sam's glory as her parents beamed beside her. Beth had believed in marriage and would want to see her daughter with an ambitious man; successful David Ross would have been just such a man.

And a man with a dark side.

Too much like Jeremy Leeds. Her ex.

She sliced open another piece of junk mail and wondered why she was always drawn to control freaks?

'Hey, Sam. Dad again,' her father's voice said. 'I'm worried about you. Haven't heard anything since you called from Mexico trying to get out of the country. I assume you made it . . . hope so. So, how're you getting along with the leg? Call me.'

'I will, Dad. Promise.'

Several other calls came through with well-wishes for her recovery. She listened to each as she continued opening the bills. Celia, her friend who taught first grade in Napa Valley; Linda, a college roommate who had settled with her cop husband in Oregon; Arla, a friend she'd kept in touch with since grade school. They all seemed to have gotten the word that she'd been hurt, and they all wanted her to call back.

'It's great to be popular,' she muttered to the cat, as the receptionist for her dentist called to remind her of her six-month cleaning. The next call was from the Boucher Center, where she did volunteer work, reminding her that her next session was the following Monday.

She reached for the final envelope – plain, white, legal-sized. No return address. Her name typed on a computer label. With a slit the envelope opened, and the single page dropped onto the desk.

Her blood froze.

She stared at a picture of herself. A publicity shot she'd had taken several years ago. It had been copied, then mutilated. Her dark red hair swung around a face with high cheekbones, pointed chin and sexy, nearly naughty smile, but where there had once been mischievous green eyes with thick eyelashes there were only jagged-edged holes as if whoever had cut them out was in a hurry. Across her peach-tinged lips was a single word scribbled in red pencil:

REPENT.

'Oh, God.' She pushed herself away from the desk, repelled. For a second she couldn't breathe.

She heard a scraping sound on the porch.

As if someone had been watching through the window and was hurrying away. Footsteps.

'Oh, no, you don't,' she said, whipping around in her chair and stumbling to the window only to look out at the dark, lonely night. The tick of the clock was barely audible over the beating of her heart, and as she stared through the steamy glass, the recorder played the next message.

'I know what you did,' a male voice whispered in a low, sexy tone.

Sam spun around and glared at the machine with its flashing red light.

'And you're not going to get away with it.' The voice wasn't harsh, not at all. In fact it was seductive, nearly caressing, as if the caller knew her personally. Sam's skin crawled. 'You're going to have to pay for your sins.'

'You bastard!'

Charon hissed and jumped from the sill.

The recorder clicked off and went silent. The house seemed to close in on her, the shadowy corners of the walls, darkening. Was it her imagination, or did she hear footsteps running across the yard?

She took in several deep breaths, then, using her crutch, checked all the locks on the doors and the latches on the windows. *It's a prank*, she told herself, *nothing sinister*. In her line of work she was a quasi celebrity, one who invited the public to contact her, to help them with their problems, to get to know her. As a radio psychologist she dealt with people's problems and phobias every night while she was on the air. And this wasn't the first time that her private life had been violated; it wouldn't be the last. She thought about calling the police or David or someone, but the last thing she wanted to appear to be was a hysterical, paranoid woman. Especially to herself.

She was a professional.

A doctor of psychology.

She didn't want to risk public disdain. Not again.

Her heart thundered, and she slowly let out her breath. She'd have to call the police whether she wanted to or not. But not yet. Not tonight. She double-checked all the locks and told herself to remain calm, go upstairs, read a book and tomorrow, in the morning light, reassess what had happened to her. There was just no reason to panic. Right? No one would seriously want to do her harm.

Repent?

Pay for her sins?

What sins?

The guy was psyching her out. Which was probably his point. 'Come on, big guy,' she called to the cat, 'let's go upstairs.' It was her first night home; she wasn't going to let some anonymous creep ruin it.

2

'If you ask me, she's faking it,' Melba whispered to Tiny, then gave Sam a friendly wink as Samantha hitched her way past the receptionist's desk at the WSLJ offices a block off Decatur Street. Wasp thin, with mocha-colored, flawless skin and a thousand-watt smile that could turn to cold, angry disapproval if anyone tried to get past her, Melba guarded the doors of WSLJ as if she were a trained rottweiler. Behind her was a glass case lit by soft neon lights and filled with everything from celebrity photos and awards for the station to a voodoo doll and stuffed baby alligator, memorabilia to remind any visitor that they were definitely in the heart of New Orleans.

Sam rolled her eyes. 'You're right. I've been wearing this—' She tapped her cast with the rubber tip of her crutch, '– just to get out of work and gain sympathy, yeah, that's it. And that's why I'm popping ibuprofen every couple of hours. I kinda get off on the masochistic thing.'

'Psychobabble,' Melba accused.

'What can I say? It's my job.' She relaxed. It felt good to be back at the station, at work. After a fitful night's sleep, she'd woken to the new day, told herself to quit being a chicken, checked the yard for footprints, found none, then eyed the mutilated picture of herself as a professional, from a distance. She'd listened to the ominous call again and decided not to freak out. There would be time enough for that later.

Melba propped one hand under her chin. A dozen bracelets clinked and caught in the light. 'You know, I have a theory about all shrinks – er – psychologists.'

'Do tell,' Sam encouraged.

'I think every one of you got into the field because of some basic character flaw. Most shrinks I know are nuts. And you radio types are the worst. I mean, who would want to sit in this damned studio all night, listening to other people's problems, when you know you don't help 'em? They just call you cuz they're lonely.'

'Or horny,' Tiny added as he passed through the glassed-in reception area. He dropped a package onto Melba's desk as light jazz whispered from hidden speakers.

'Right. Or horny. Get your rocks off by calling Dr. Sam at 1-800-Dial-A-Shrink, New Orleans's own private late-night couch. Confess and be healed.'

Sam's head snapped up. She felt the smile slide off her face. 'What did you say?'

'Get your rocks—'

'No, no, what's that about confession?'

'Well that's what you are,' Melba said as the phone rang. 'Kinda like a priest, or preacher or whatever. And this whole place turns into a late-night, high-tech confessional. Even the name of the show, honey. *Midnight Confessions*. Need I say more?' She punched a button and studied her glossy pink nails. 'WSLJ, New Orleans's heart of smooth jazz and talk radio. How may I direct your call?'

'Don't mind her,' Tiny said. 'You know she's always got a bug up her butt. She loves you.'

'And it's great to be loved,' Sam muttered, still wondering about Melba's remarks. Maybe she was just jittery, looking for hidden meanings. She hadn't gotten much sleep, her leg had ached while her mind had spun reviewing the damned taped message and the scarred publicity shot. Her cast had been heavy and cumbersome, making getting comfortable impossible, and so far the day had been nerve-stretching. First she'd dealt with the Cambrai police, talking to an officer on the phone, then waiting for him to show up. He'd assured her they would patrol the area more often and had taken the tape, envelope and publicity shot with him. Later, still edgy, she'd called credit-card companies to make sure they'd gotten Melanie's message from Mexico about her lost cards, driven with difficulty to the DMV to get a new driver's license, gone to a locksmith and asked him to come over to replace all of the locks in the house and make a duplicate set for her car. Then she'd finally stopped by the Social Security Administration to stand in line for nearly an hour to ask that a new card be issued. She hadn't yet replaced her prescription sunglasses, but that was the last item on her list and for a while she'd settle for contacts and over-the-counter shades.

'. . . I'll give Mr. Hannah the message,' Melba said as she clicked off the telephone and scribbled a note. 'Why we don't have voice mail around here is beyond me. It's like we're in the damned dark ages or somethin'.' She glanced over at Tiny. 'You're the computer genius, can't you hook us up?'

'I'm working on it, but it's the damned budget.'

'Yeah, yeah, always the budget, the ratings, the market share.' She rolled her expressive eyes, and her curly hair shone under the fluorescent tubes that passed for lighting in the reception area. 'Well, I hate to admit it,' she said to Sam, 'but, from the stack of fan mail in your cubby, it looks like you were missed.'

'Surprising.'

Another call came in, catching Melba's attention, as Tiny walked with Sam down the central hallway known affectionately as 'the aorta.' The station was a virtual rabbit's warren, a maze of offices and hallways linked together fitfully as the ancient building that housed WSLJ and its sister stations had been remodeled over and over again in the past two hundred years, the nooks and crannies incorporated into closets, studios, offices, and meeting rooms.

'Check your e-mail as well,' Tiny advised as he stopped at the door of his office – a small room that had once been a walk-in windowless closet placed smack-dab in the middle of the offices. Inside was a single desk chair, benchlike table and laptop computer. Tiny's only nod to decorating was a large poster of an alligator, which Sam guessed, from the multitude of tiny perforations on the slick surface surrounding the gator's snout, Tiny used as a dartboard. Where he hid his darts was a continuing mystery that no one in the station had unraveled.

Tiny seemed to know what was going on in the station at all times. A part-time communications student at Loyola, he designed and maintained the station's web site and was a whiz when it came to any computer glitch. In Sam's opinion, Tiny was invaluable, if slightly out-of-sync with the rest of the world. He was still gawky, a computer nerd in serious need of braces, Scope and Clearasil, but a hard worker who just happened to have a crush on Sam. A crush she pretended didn't exist.

'Lots of e-mail?' she asked, and the kid visibly brightened.

'Tons. All of it about the same – the listeners want you back.'

'You *read* my e-mail?' she asked.

The tops of his ears turned bright red. 'Some of it was addressed to the station in general, but it was mainly about you and when you'd be back. I, uh, I didn't look at any of the personal stuff.'

Oh, right, she thought sarcastically, but before she had a chance to question him, the program manager's deep voice assailed her. 'So the prodigal has returned!' Eleanor's words ricocheted down the hallway.

A tall black woman who had brass golf balls fashioned into a paperweight that she kept forever on her desk, she strode down the hallway and smiled wide enough to show off a gold-crowned molar. 'And oh, look at you . . .' She motioned to the cast covering Sam's leg. 'High fashion if ever I saw it. Well, come on, haul yourself down to the office, where we can talk.' She preceded Sam down the aorta and took a right near the back of the building, across from the glassed-in studio where Gator Brown was pretaping some smooth jazz favorites that he planned to play on his shift. Earphones covering his bald spot, Gator saw Sam, grinned and raised a freckled hand, never once interrupting his velvet-voiced patter as he started to play another CD for the tape.

'Okay, so tell me,' Eleanor said, waving Sam into a chair crammed between bookcases stacked high with files, disks, tapes and books, 'how long are you gonna have to put up with that?' She waggled a finger at Sam's left leg as she sat behind her cluttered desk.

'Less than a week more, I hope. It's just a sprain. Nothing broken. I can still work, you know.'

'Good. Cuz I want you back in that booth. Your listeners are clamoring for you, Sam, and WNAB is getting more aggressive with your audience. They've moved Trish LaBelle from seven to nine, to get a jump on your show, then go head to head with you when you come on at ten. I'm considering moving you up an hour, and Gator's screaming bloody murder, claiming his audience will stop listening, that his style of jazz *has* to be played late at night. He'd rather you be pushed back from ten until midnight.' She reached into the top drawer of her desk and found a bottle of Tums. 'And my husband can't understand why I have high blood pressure.'

Sam wasn't buying all the competition. 'WNAB is AM, we're FM, entirely different format, demographics and audience.'

'Not so different.' Eleanor was all business. She popped two pills. 'Look, we've all worked hard to make this station the best, and we don't want to lose our audience now. I don't begrudge you your vacation, of course,' she said, holding up her hands, palms outward, 'but I've got to be practical. It's my job. We can't let WNAB or anyone else muscle in on our ratings.' She managed a smile that seemed false and when the phone rang, took the call. 'This is Eleanor . . . yes . . . I know.' Stretching the cord, she rolled her chair back and searched in a stack of files that was piled on top of a credenza. 'Okay, let me see. Did you talk to the sales department?' Her voice was tight. Strained. 'I understand . . . we're working on it. What? Yes. Samantha's back, so late night's taken care of . . . Right. Just give me a minute.' Turning back to the desk, she grabbed her computer mouse with her free hand and signaled to Sam with her eyes that the discussion was over. 'Listen, George, just sit tight. I said I'd handle it.'

Samantha hobbled out of the room, but Eleanor's voice drifted after her.

'I'll come up with something. Yes, soon. For God's sake, don't have a heart attack. Just calm down. I understand.'

Negotiating two corners, Sam entered the hallway that opened to the glassed-in studios and recording rooms. She glanced through one window and saw Gator still leaning into the microphone, talking to the tape as if he were actually speaking to the audience and every listener were his personal friend. He'd cut this tape into his regular program. On the air his voice was a soft drawl, inviting, a real down-home boy. In person he was much more animated and lively. Sam waved, Gator gave her a cursory nod and she wended her way past several more studios, an editing room, the library and finally wound up at the communal office she shared with the other DJs. Her mail was, indeed, stuffed into her cubby. Remembering the ugly missive she'd received at home, she sorted through the envelopes carefully. Telling herself that the prickle of dread crawling up her spine was totally out of line, she slit open each envelope and scanned the pages.

Nothing was out of the ordinary.

Nothing was the least bit suspicious.

Offers to speak at or host charity functions, well-wishes from listeners who had found out she'd been in an accident, advertisements, more bank-card offers . . . nothing sinister. She'd told herself that she wasn't going to bring up the letter and crank call to anyone at the station, but she would talk to the police again. The letter and voice on her answering machine were probably just pranks. Nothing more. Some guy getting his perverted jollies at her expense.

Then what about the footsteps on the porch?

How about the way Charon had reacted?

What about the way you felt *last night, as if unseen eyes were watching your every move?*

Gritting her teeth, she reminded herself for the hundredth time she was letting a couple of stupid, malicious pranks get to her. She'd dealt with crank callers before. As long as she changed the locks, fixed the faulty alarm system that had come with the house and made sure that the Cambrai police were true to their word and increased their patrols of the area, she'd be fine.

Right?

A few hours later, after most of the staff had gone home for the night, Sam was tossing the trash into a wastebasket when the click of high heels caught her attention. Turning, she spied Melanie breezing into the room. Her hair was windblown, her cheeks pink from the heat of the summer night.

'Welcome back,' Melanie greeted with a grin. All of twenty-five, Melanie had graduated at the top of her class at All Saints, a small college in Baton Rouge, where she'd majored in communications and minored in psychology. She'd worked at the college radio station, then landed a job in Baton Rouge before accepting a position with WSLJ not long after Sam had hired on. Melanie, like Sam, was one of Eleanor's recruits.

'Thanks.'

'I'm gonna run down to the shop on the corner and pick up coffee and something totally fattening and sinful . . . Probably a beignet smothered in powdered sugar. Want one?'

'Tempting, but I think I'll pass.' Sam set the mail aside and rolled her chair back from the long counter that served as a desk. 'And thanks again for taking care of the cat and leaving me the coffee and milk. You're a lifesaver.'

Melanie beamed under the compliment – in many ways she was still a kid. 'Just remember that when it comes time for my review and raise, okay?'

'Oh, I get it. You bribed me.'

'Absolutely!' Melanie was blocking the doorway, a hand on either side of the jamb. In a gauzy purple dress, thin black cape, platform shoes and fresh makeup, she looked ready to go out on the town, rather than work.

'Hot date?'

'A girl can hope.' Melanie laughed and lifted one shoulder. 'Maybe I'll get lucky. And—' she held up a finger, '– no motherly advice about being careful. I'm a big girl now.'

'And I'm *not* old enough to be your mother.'

'Then no friendly or even professional advice, okay?'

Sam knew when to button her lip. Melanie's past relationships had been less than stellar, and the girl was waiting to get her heart broken again, but Samantha didn't argue. After all, she wasn't exactly batting a thousand in the love department herself. 'When are you off duty?'

Melanie looked at her watch. 'After the show, same as you. Now, what can I get you from the coffee shop before it closes for the night? Tea? Perrier?'

'You don't have to wait on me.'

'I know. It's only because of the cast. Once you're on your feet again, you're on your own, so make a slave of me now, if you feel so inclined.'

'You asked for it. Okay, get me a Diet Coke.'

'Will do.' Melanie glanced ruefully at Sam's leg. 'Does it itch?'

'Like crazy.'

'I'll be right back.' She left as quickly as she appeared. Sam did a cursory look over her e-mail, her pulse elevating a bit, her palm sweaty on the mouse, but no one had sent any notes that could be construed as threatening. A few notes from fans asking about her return, two dozen jokes she deleted immediately, interoffice memos that were outdated, an offer to speak at a local charity event, another reminder from the Boucher Center about her next appointment and several quickly dashed thoughts from friends. One from Leanne Jaquillard, a seventeen-year-old girl she worked with at the Boucher Center where she volunteered.

There was nothing out of the ordinary in her letters from cyberspace. Nothing sinister. She began to relax.

By the time Melanie returned sans cape, with a little bit of powdered sugar still clinging to her lips, a can of Diet Coke in one hand, a cup of coffee in the other, Sam had answered those she could, saved the ones she wanted and deleted the rest.

'Thanks,' she said, as Melanie handed her the drink. 'I owe you one.'

'More than one – maybe a dozen or so for taking care of that persnickety cat, but who's counting?' Melanie took a sip of her coffee and the remaining bits of sugar vanished from her lips.

Sam pulled the tab on her Coke just as Gator poked his head into the room. 'You've got about fifteen minutes,' he said. 'I've got two pieces taped, then the weather and ads will follow. After that, you're on.' He started to leave, then thought better of it. 'Hey, it's good to have you back.' There wasn't much sincerity in his words.

'Thanks.'

'So what happened?' He jabbed a finger at her cast.

'It's a long story. Basically, the captain of our fishing boat was an idiot and I'm a klutz.'

Gator's grin was tight. Forced. 'Tell me something I don't know,' he said, then added, 'Gotta run, somewhere in this city there *has* to be a woman dying to meet me.'

'I wouldn't count on it,' Melanie whispered as he left.

'Remind me again why I wanted to get back here so badly,' Sam said.

'He's just pissed because they're talking about cutting his show to expand yours. It's jealousy.'

Sam wasn't sure she blamed Gator. He used to be the morning DJ, was pushed to the afternoon 'Drive At Five,' then eased back to the early evening. It didn't take a crystal ball to see that he was slowly, but surely, being phased out. Right now, with the popularity of her *Midnight Confessions*, she took the brunt of his misaligned anger.

'I guess I'd better get back in the saddle.' Sam struggled to her feet, felt a painful twinge in her ankle and ignored it. Melanie stepped out of the doorway to let her pass. 'Thanks for pinch-hitting for me while I was gone,' Sam said.

'*No problem.*' Melanie's gold eyes darkened a bit. 'I liked it.'

'You're a natural.'

The girl sighed as they started down the corridor. 'I just wish the powers that be recognized my talents.'

'They will. Give it time. And finish getting your doctorate. A bachelor's degree in psychology isn't enough.'

'I know, I know. Thanks for the advice, *Mom*,' she said with just a trace of envy. Melanie was great behind the microphone, she just needed seasoning, more life experience as well as the educational credentials before she could regularly hand out advice to the thirty- and fortysomethings who called in. Pinch-hitting was one thing; her own show was another.

'Any big news happen while I was gone?' Sam asked, changing the touchy subjection.

'Nothing. It's been soooo boring around here.' Melanie shrugged and took another sip of coffee.

'New Orleans is never boring.'

'But the station is. It's the same old, same old. There's gossip about the possibility of WSLJ being sold to a big conglomerate or merging with a competitor.'

'There always is.'

'Then there would be major reformatting. All the DJs are freaked because they'd be replaced by computers, or syndicated programs from Timbuktu, or God knows where.'

'That never stops,' Sam said.

'Right, but this time there's more to it. George is talking about spending big bucks on more computer equipment, cutting staff, doing more of the taped stuff. Melba's thrilled – practically orgasmic – at the thought of voice mail, and Tiny, he loves the idea. The more high-tech stuff, the better.'

'It's the wave of the future,' Sam said cynically. Computers were rapidly replacing disk jockeys just as CDs had replaced tapes and vinyl. The library of LPs and 45s in the station was collecting dust in a locked glass case that only Ramblin' Rob, the crusty oldest DJ in the building, played upon occasion. 'I catch hell for it,' he always said, laughing, his voice raspy from years of cigarettes, 'but they don't dare fire me. AARP, the governor and even God Himself would shut this place down if they did.'

Melanie followed Samantha along the hallway. 'Doing the show was the only thing that was interesting around here.'

'Liar, liar,' Melba said as she cruised past and grabbed her jacket from the rack in an alcove near the offices. 'Don't let her give you any of that bull.' Her elegant eyebrows lifted a notch. 'There's a new man in our girl's life.'

Melanie blushed and rolled her expressive eyes.

'True?' Sam asked as she turned a corner and slipped through the door to the studio. The information about her assistant wasn't exactly a news flash. Melanie had a new boyfriend every other week, or so it seemed.

'This one's serious.' Melba tucked her umbrella under her arm. 'Believe me, the girl's in loooove.'

'It's only been a couple of dates. That's all.' Melanie fiddled with the chain around her neck. 'No big deal.'

'But you like him?'

'So far.'

'Do I know him?'

'Nah.' Melanie shook her head, then slipped into the adjoining booth. 'I'll start screening the calls,' she said, as Sam settled into her chair and adjusted the mike. She checked the computer screen. With a touch of her finger on the appropriate button on the monitor, she could play a pretaped advertisement, the opening music, or the weather. She placed headphones over her ears as Melanie nodded, indicating that the phone lines were working and connected to the computer.

Sam waited until the thirty-second advertising spot for a local car dealer had finished, then pressed a button and the first few notes of 'Hard Day's Night' by the Beatles soared, then faded. Sam leaned into the mike. 'Good evening, New Orleans, this is Dr. Sam. I'm back. And this is *Midnight Confessions*, here at WSLJ. As you probably know, I was out of town for a little R&R in Mexico. Mazatlán, to be precise.' She leaned her elbows on her desk and kept one eye on the computer screen. 'It was a beautiful place, very romantic, if you were in the right frame of mind, but rather than give you a blow-by-blow travelogue, I thought I'd settle in with kind of a light topic, just to get back in the swing of things.

'As this is my first night back, I thought we'd open the discussion tonight by talking about vacations, how stressful they are, how relaxing they're supposed to be, what's considered romantic. Call in and tell me where you've been and how it turned out. In Mazatlán, the weather was hot, hot, hot, the sunsets to die for. Plenty of hot sun and sand, lots of couples strolling along the beach. Palm trees, white sand, piña coladas, the whole nine yards . . .'

She talked about romantic vacations for a few minutes and gave out the phone number, again asking for callers, waiting for a response. Glancing through the plate-glass window she saw Melanie, headphones in place, nodding as the phone lines began to light. *Here we go.*

The first caller's name, Ned, appeared on the screen beside line one, while someone named Luanda was on two. Sam pushed the first button and said, 'Hi. This is Dr. Sam. Who's this?'

'Yeah, this is Ned.' The guy sounded nervous. 'I, um, I'm glad you're back. I listen to your program all the time, and . . . and I gotta say I missed ya.'

'Thanks.' Samantha smiled slightly and tried to put the guy at ease. 'Well, Ned, what's on your mind? Have you been on a vacation lately?'

'Yeah, uh, I, uh, took the missus on a trip down to Puerto Rico, it was about two months ago, and . . . well, it was kinda to make up . . . y'know.'

'Make up for what?' she asked.

'Well, I'd been seein' someone else and me and the wife, we split for a while, so I decided to surprise her with a trip to the Caribbean, you know, to try and get things back together.'

'And what happened, Ned?' Sam asked, as the guy haltingly poured out his heart. Another midlife fling. His second, he admitted, but he loved his wife, oh, she was the best, a good-hearted woman he'd been married to for twelve years. However, his wife got even with him in Puerto Rico. Found herself a Latin lover and rubbed Ned's nose in it. Ned was offended. What had she been thinking? The romantic vacation had turned into a catastrophe.

At least at that level, Sam could relate.

'So how do you feel about it?' she asked, and noticed that Luanda's name disappeared from the screen. She'd gotten tired of waiting and had hung up. But someone named Bart was on line three.

'I'm hurt and mad, I guess,' Ned was saying. 'Mad as hell. I spent two thousand bucks on that trip!'

'So you lost your money and your wife. Why do you think you got involved with the other women in the first place?' Sam asked.

The phone lines began to light up like a Christmas tree. People couldn't wait to comment on Ned's story or offer their own, asking Sam's opinion. Kay was on two, Bart on three and, oh, there was Luanda, again, on four.

Sam talked to Ned a while, explaining about the age-old double standard, then switched to Kay, a vicious woman who was ready to rake Ned and any other cheating man through the coals several times over. Sam imagined her foaming at the mouth in her rage. From there, she listened to Bart, whose girl-friend had gone with him to Tahiti and refused to come home.

The stories, anger, laughter and despair sizzled over the airwaves. Sam interrupted the calls by playing advertising bits and updating the weather with promises of news as soon as it broke, but the time sped by and she felt more at home by the minute. Fleeting thoughts of the letter and mutilated picture she'd received faded as she talked with her listeners.

She'd been at it for nearly three hours, had finished her soft drink, was on her second cup of coffee and was close to signing off when she answered a call from someone, who the computer screen displayed as John.

'This is Dr. Sam. How're you this evening?'

'Good. I'm good,' a smooth male voice intoned.

'What's your name?' she asked for the viewers.

'John.'

'Hi, John, what would you like to talk about?' She reached for her coffee cup.

'Confession.'

'All right.'

'That is what you call your show.' It wasn't really a question.

'Yes, now, John, what's on your mind?'

'You know me.'

'I know you? How?'

'I'm John from your past.'

She played along. 'I've known lots of Johns.'

'I'll bet you have.' Was there a hint of disapproval, or superiority in his voice? Who was this guy? Time to get on with the show.

'Do you have something you want to talk about tonight, John?'

'Sins.'

She nearly dropped her cup. Her blood ran cold. The voice – the same voice on her recorder. The blanket of security she'd felt all night unraveled. 'What kind of sins?' she forced out.

'Yours.'

'Mine?' Who was this guy? She needed to get off the line and fast.

'People are punished for their sins.'

'How?' she asked, her pulse pounding hard as she glanced at Melanie, who was shaking her head. Obviously John had asked her a different question when she'd screened the call.

'You'll see,' he said. Sam signaled Melanie, hoping the girl understood that she needed to get off the line. Fast. She was certain this was the same creep who'd left the message on her personal recorder.

'Maybe I'll have to repent,' she said, her nerves strung tight as she stalled for time.

'Of course you will. Confession, Samantha. Midnight confession.'

Oh, God, this *was* the guy. 'I'll take it under advisement.'

'That would be wise, Sam. Because God knows what you did, and so do I.'

'What I did?'

'That's right, you hot-blooded slut. We both know—'

Sam cut him off. From the corner of her eye, she saw Melanie on the other side of the glass, frantically motioning toward the clock. Only twenty seconds until her program was over. The phone lines were blinking like flash lightning. 'That's all we have time for tonight,' Sam said, trying to compose herself, somehow recalling her signature sign off. Her heart was pounding like a drum as she pressed a button to start the music that ended her show, the Grass Roots singing, 'Midnight Confession.' As the first few lines of the song faded, she said, 'This is Dr. Sam, with a final word . . . Take care of yourself, New Orleans. Good night to you all and God bless. No matter what your troubles are today, there is always tomorrow . . . Sweet dreams . . .'

She pushed the play button for a series of commercials, shoved her microphone out of the way and rolled back her chair. Stripping off her headset, she found her crutch, climbed to her feet and, nearly hyperventilating, hitched her way out of the booth.

'How'd that guy get past you?' Sam demanded, as she and Melanie entered the hallway from their separate booths.

'He lied, that's how!' Melanie's face was flushed, her jaw tight, defensive. 'Now, where the hell is Tiny?' She stormed up and down the hallway. 'He's got less than five minutes to set up the *Lights Out* show!' She searched the hallway with her eyes.

'Forget Tiny. What was the deal with that last caller?' Sam was shaking inside. Furious. Scared.

'I don't know.' Melanie threw up her hands in exasperation. 'He – he tripped me up. Said he had a comment about . . . paradise and paradise lost . . . I screwed up, okay? So crucify me!'

Sam cringed at Melanie's choice of words. 'Let's keep all biblical references out of this!'

'It's over, okay? It won't happen again! I said "I'm sorry."'

'No . . . you didn't. And you fouled up. Those calls are supposed to be screened and . . .' Samantha let the sentence drop, realizing she was unleashing on her assistant for no good reason. Taking a deep breath, she forced herself to calm down. 'And I'm overreacting.'

'Amen . . . oops sorry. Didn't mean to get "biblical."' Melanie made air quotes with her fingers around the word, and Sam, despite her fear and anger had to chuckle.

'Forget it.'

'I'll try.' Melanie was still searching for Tiny as she stalked along the narrow corridor, poking her head into the rooms that were unlocked and rattling the knobs of those that weren't. 'Tiny had better show up—'

'Paradise,' Sam said to herself as the impact of the caller's words to Melanie hit her like the proverbial ton of bricks. She leaned heavily against the glass wall encasing the old LPs, Ramblin' Rob's shrine. 'He wasn't talking about a romantic paradise . . . it was a reference to Milton's *Paradise Lost*.'

'What?'

'The caller, he was referring to Milton's work. About Satan being cast out of heaven.'

Melanie stopped dead in her tracks. 'You think?' She lifted questioning eyebrows. 'You mean like he's into old literature, or something?' Clearly she wasn't buying it.

'Yes . . . I'm sure. It's all about sin and redemption and punishment,' Sam said, not liking the dark turn of her thoughts. Glancing down the hallway to her assistant, she decided to come clean. 'This isn't the first time that guy has contacted me. There was a message left on my answering machine while I was gone.'

'What?' Melanie's thoughts of locating Tiny were momentarily forgotten. 'You mean when you were in Mexico?'

'Exactly.'

'But . . . wait a minute. I thought you were unlisted – not in the phone book.'

'I'm not, but there are ways around that. This is a high-tech world. Anyone can hack into computers, get records, anything from credit cards to social security number and driver's licences. It wouldn't be too tough to find a phone number if you knew what you were doing.'

'Just like there are ways to get around the call screener here.' Melanie's eyes clouded a bit. 'I'm sorry, Sam,' she finally said. 'He tricked me.' Shoving her hair off her shoulders, she asked, 'So what have you got, your own personal nutcase? Oh, excuse me, I know that's not PC these days, but this guy sounds waaay off his rocker.'

'My speciality. I'm a shrink, y'know.'

Footsteps clomped closer, and Tiny rounded the corner, nearly careening into Melanie.

'Hey, watch it,' she said, then skewered him with a typical Melanie glare. 'We've only got a couple of minutes to start *Lights Out.* Where the hell were you?'

'Outside.'

'Jesus, you're supposed to have the recording ready to go.'

'Don't worry,' Tiny said over his shoulder. His coat was damp, and the smell of cigarette smoke followed him as he made his way to the booth Sam had just vacated. 'I've got it handled.'

'You're going to give me a heart attack.'

'Why? You're not the station manager.'

'I know, but—'

'Lay off, Melanie, I said it's under control.' Tiny shot her a hard glare, and Melanie, always quick to anger, opened her mouth to say more, then added, 'Fine, just do it.'

Sam took that as her cue to leave. She was tired, edgy and her ankle was beginning to throb. 'I'll see you both tomorrow,' she said as she made her way back to the shared office, grabbed her raincoat and new purse and headed through the maze of WSLJ offices toward the bank of elevators. Her nerves were still strung tight, and she imagined that the old building with its narrow, labyrinthine hallways, musty smell, and tiny cubicles was more sinister than she remembered. 'Stop it,' she growled, as the elevator car landed on the first floor. 'You're imagining things.' At the front door she swiped her card through the automatic lock, then stepped into the humid New Orleans night.

The air was cloying, damp and sticky. Hot and oppressive. A few cars drove through the narrow streets, the smell of the river was heavy in the air, and the streetlights glistened off the fronds of the palm trees in Jackson Square. There were still people wandering the city streets, and Sam couldn't help wonder if any of them was the caller, her 'own personal nutcase,' a man whose smooth voice caused her blood to congeal.

Rather than try to walk with the damned cast the few blocks to the parking structure, Sam hailed a cab and, during the short ride, watched the pedestrians, who never seemed to disappear no matter what time of night it was.

One of the denizens of this city seems to have a personal vendetta against you. Why, Sam? Why does he want you to repent? Who the hell is he? And more importantly, just how dangerous is he?

She leaned back against the seat and hoped that this was the end of it. The caller, 'John,' had finally made contact with her. Maybe now he'd leave her alone.

And yet as the darkened streets of the city passed, she thought of the mutilated publicity shot of herself someone had mailed to her and she knew with mind-numbing certainty that this was just the beginning.

3

The moon was blocked by thick, night-blackened clouds. Rain slanted from the sky, and the wind kicked up, causing whitecaps to foam on the usually calm surface of Lake Pontchartrain as the summer squall passed over. Ty Wheeler's sailboat bobbed wildly at the mercy of the wind, sails billowing, deck listing over dark, opaque water. He ignored the elements along with the certainty that he was on a fool's mission – definitely in the wrong place at the wrong time. He should take down the sails and use the damned engine, but it wasn't reliable, and a part of him liked daring the fates.

The way he figured it, this was his chance, and he damned well was going to take it.

Bracing his feet on the rolling deck, he stood at the helm, legs apart, eyes squinting through the most powerful set of binoculars he could find. He focused the glasses on the back of the rambling old plantation-styled home Samantha Leeds now occupied.

Dr. Samantha Leeds, he reminded himself. P H damned D. Enough credentials to choke the proverbial horse and more than enough to allow the good doctor to hand out free advice over the airwaves. No matter who it harmed.

His jaw hardened, and he caught a hint of movement behind the filmy curtains. Then he saw her. His fingers clenched over the slick glasses as he watched, like a damned voyeur, as she walked unevenly through her house. He checked his watch. Three-fifteen in the morning.

And she was beautiful – just as she was in the publicity shots he'd seen – maybe even more so with her tousled red hair and state of undress. Dr. Leeds wore a nightshirt buttoned loosely, its hem brushing the tops of her long, tanned thighs as she walked unevenly through a room lit by Tiffany lamps and adorned with a lot of old-looking furniture – probably antiques. He caught a glimpse of the cast that encased her left foot and half her calf. He'd heard about that, too. Some kind of boating accident in Mexico.

Lips compressed, he anchored the wheel with one hip and felt rain slide down the neck of his parka. The wind had snatched off his hood and tossed his hair around his eyes, but he kept the powerful glasses trained on the house nestled deep in a copse of live oaks. Spanish moss clung to the thick branches and drifted in the wind. Rain ran down off the dormers and down the gutters. An animal – cat, from the looks of it – crept through a square of light thrown from one window. It disappeared quickly into dripping bushes flanking the raised porch.

Ty concentrated on the interior of the house – through the windows. He lost sight of Samantha for a second, then found her again, bending down, reaching forward to pick up her crutch. The nightshirt rode upward, giving him a peek at lacy white panties stretched over round, tight buttocks.

His crotch tightened. Throbbed. He ground his back teeth together, but ignored his male response just as he disregarded the warm rain stinging his face blurring the lenses of his binoculars.

He wouldn't think of her as a woman.

He needed her. He intended to lie to her. To use her. And that's all there was to it.

But, God, she was beautiful. Those legs—

She straightened suddenly, as if she sensed him watching her.

Turning, she walked to the windows and stared out, green eyes wide, red hair tousled as if she'd just gotten out of bed, skin without a hint of makeup. His pulse jumped a notch. She squinted through the glass, her eyes narrowing. Maybe she saw the silhouette of the boat, his shadow at the helm. Eerily, as if she knew what he was thinking, she met his stare with distrustful eyes and a gaze that scoured his black soul.

Wrong.

She was too far away.

The night was dark as pitch.

His imagination was running wild.

There was a slight chance she could see his running lights or the white sails, and, if so, make out the image of a man on his boat, but without binoculars there was no way she'd be able to see his features, would never recognize him, and couldn't, not for a minute, guess what he was thinking, or his intentions.

Good.

There was time enough for meeting face-to-face later. For the lies he would have to spin to get what he wanted. For a half a second, he felt a twinge of remorse, gritted his teeth. No time for second-guessing. He was committed. Period. As he watched through the glasses, she reached up and snapped the shades of her window closed, cutting off his view.

Too bad. She wasn't hard on the eyes. Far from it.

And that might pose a problem.

In Ty's mind, Dr. Samantha Leeds was too pretty for her own damned good.

'. . . so you're sure you're okay?' David asked for the fifth time in the span of ten minutes. Holding the cordless receiver to her ear, Sam walked to the window of her bedroom and looked into the gloomy afternoon. Lake Pontchartrain was a somber gray, the waters shifting as restlessly as the clouds overhead.

'I'm fine, really.' Now she wished she hadn't confided in him about the caller, but when David had phoned, she decided that he would find out soon enough anyway. It was a matter of public record, and sooner or later the news would filter across state lines. 'I've talked to the police, and I'm having all the locks changed. I'll be okay. Don't worry.'

'I don't like the sounds of it, Samantha.' She imagined the tightening of the corners of his mouth. 'Maybe you should look at this as some kind of . . . warning . . . you know, a sign that you should turn your life in a different direction.'

'A sign?' she repeated, her eyes narrowing as she stared at the lake stretching from her yard to the distant shore. 'As in God is trying to talk to me? You mean like the burning bush or—'

'There's no reason to get sarcastic,' he cut in.

'You're right. I'm sorry.' She balanced her hips on the arm of a wing chair. 'I guess I'm a little edgy. I didn't sleep well.'

'I'll bet.'

She didn't mention the boat; she was certain a sailboat had been drifting just off her dock, that in the barest of light from the shore, she'd seen running lights and the reflection of giant sails with a man's contour against the backdrop. Or maybe it had been her imagination running wild . . .

'So where are you, again?' she asked, reaching to the night-stand and retrieving a knitting needle she'd found in the closet, part of the personal items she'd inherited from her mother. Feeling a twinge of guilt, she slipped the needle between the cast and her leg and scratched. Her doctor would probably kill her if he knew, but then he was the crusty old guy down in Mazatlán, the expatriate she'd never see again if she was lucky.

'I'm here in San Antonio, and it's a deluge. I'm standing at the window of my hotel room looking over the River Walk and it's like a wall of water – can't even see the restaurant across the river. The sky just opened up.' He sighed and for a second his cell phone cut out, the connection was lost, only to return. '. . . wish you were here Samantha. I've got a room with a Jacuzzi and a fireplace. It could be cozy.'

And it could be hell. She remembered Mexico. The way David had smothered her. The fights. He'd wanted her to move back to Houston, and when she'd refused, she'd witnessed a side of him she didn't like. His face had turned a deep scarlet and a small vein had throbbed over one eyebrow. His fists had even clenched as he'd told her that she was an idiot not to take him up on his offer. At that moment, she'd known she never would.

'I thought I made it clear how I felt,' she said, watching a raindrop drizzle a zigzag course down the window. She gave up on the knitting needle and tossed it onto the bureau.

'I hoped you'd changed your mind.'

'I haven't. David, it won't work. I know this sounds corny and trite, but I thought you and I, we could—'

'—just be friends,' he finished for her, his voice flat.

'You don't have to put the "just" in there. It's not like being friends isn't a good thing.'

'I don't feel that way about you,' he said, and she imagined his serious face. He was a good-looking man. Clean-cut. Athletic. Handsome enough to have done some print work while he was attending college, and he had the scrapbooks to prove it. Women were attracted to him. Sam had been, or thought she'd been, but in the two years they'd dated some of the luster had faded, and she'd never really fallen in love. Not that there was anything specifically wrong with him. Or nothing she could name. He was handsome, intelligent, the right age, and his job with Regal Hotels was certain to make him a millionaire several times over. They just didn't click.

'I'm sorry, David.'

'Are you?' he asked with a bite. David Ross didn't like to lose.

'Yes.' She meant it. She hadn't intended to lead him on; she'd just wanted to be careful, to make sure this time.

'Then I suppose you don't want me to be your escort at that benefit you've been talking about?'

'The auction for the Boucher Center,' she said wincing when she remembered she'd brought it up to him months ago. 'No, I think it would be best if I went alone.'

He didn't immediately answer, as if he expected her to change her mind. She didn't and the tension on the line was nearly palpable.

'Well,' he finally said. 'I guess there's nothing more to say. Take care of yourself, Samantha.'

'You too.' Her heart twisted a bit. She hung up and told herself it was for the best. It was over, and that was that.

All of her friends thought she was nuts not to marry him. 'If I were you, I'd set my hooks in him and reel him in faster'n you could say prenup,' her friend Corky had confided over shrimp bisque less than a month ago. Corky's eyes had twinkled mischievously, almost as brightly as the three rings she wore on her right ring finger – prizes from previous relationships and marriages. 'I don't know why you're so uptight about the whole thing.'

'I've been married before, and I believe in the old once burned twice shy routine.'

'I thought it was once bitten.' Corky had broken off a chunk of bread as she glanced out the windows of the restaurant to the slow-flowing Mississippi, where a barge covered with gravel was chugging upstream.

'Samey-same.'

'The point is you'll never find a better catch than David, believe you me.' Corky had nodded, her short blond curls bobbing.

'Then you take him.'

'I would. In a heartbeat. But he's in love with you.'

'David's in love with David.'

'Harsh words, Sam. Wait 'til you get back from Mexico, then you tell me,' Corky had said with a naughty smile. As if hot sand, even hotter sun, and, she implied, far hotter sex, would change how Samantha felt. It hadn't. The sand had been warm, the sun hot, the sex nonexistent. It had been her problem, not his. The fact of the matter was that she just wasn't in love with the guy. Period. Something about him grated on her nerves. An only child, a brilliant scholar, David was used to having things his way. And he always wanted them to be perfect.

Life wasn't supposed to be messy, which, of course, it always was.

'All men are not Jeremy Leeds,' Corky had said, wrinkling her pert nose as she mentioned Samantha's ex-husband.

'Thank God.'

Corky had signaled to the waiter for another glass of Chardonnay, and Sam had absently stirred the soup while trying not to conjure up images of her ex-husband.

'Maybe you're still not over him.'

'Jeremy?' Sam had rolled her eyes. 'Get real.'

'It's hard to get over that kind of rejection.'

'I know about this,' Sam had assured her. 'I'm a professional, remember?'

'But—'

'Jeremy's flaw is he falls in love with his students and doesn't take his marriage vows very seriously.'

'Okay, okay, so he's yesterday's news,' Corky had said, waving the air as if she could push the subject of Jeremy Leeds out the window. 'So what's wrong with David? Too good-looking?' She'd held up a finger. 'No? Too eligible – never been married before, you know, so there's no baggage, no kids or ex-wife.' She'd wiggled another digit. 'Oh, I know, too rich . . . or too ambitious. Too great a job? Lord, what is he, CEO of Regal Hotels?'

'Executive vice president and director of sales for the eastern United States.'

Corky had flopped back in her chair and thrown her hands over her head as if in surrender. 'There you have it! The man's too perfect.'

Hardly, Samantha had thought at the time. But then she and Corky, friends since second grade in LA had always had different views on boyfriends, courtship and marriage. One lunch hadn't changed anything, and the trip to Mexico had convinced her – David Ross wasn't the man for her, and that was just fine. She didn't need a man, didn't really want one right now. She shook herself out of her reverie and stared through the sweating windowpanes to the lake . . . where she'd imagined a mysterious man on the deck of his sailboat, binoculars trained on her house in the middle of the night, no less. She grinned at her folly. 'You're jumping at shadows,' she told herself, and with Charon trailing behind her, hitched her way to the bathroom, where she tied a plastic sack over her cast, sent up a prayer that the damned thing would be cut off soon, and climbed into the shower. She thought about David, about the man on the sailboat in the lake, about the seductive voice on the phone and about the mutilated picture of herself – the eyes gouged out.

Shivering, she turned the spray to hot and closed her eyes, letting the warm jets wash over her.

4

'What the hell happened here last night?' Eleanor's voice shook with rage, her face was set in a hard mask, and as she followed Sam down the aorta of WSLJ, she was hell-bent for an explanation.

'You heard about the caller?' Sam set her dripping umbrella in a corner of the compact room, then placed her crutch over it.

'The whole damned town heard about the caller, for Christ's sake. It was on the radio! Remember? Who was he, and how in the hell did he get past screening?'

'He tricked Melanie – we were talking about vacations and he said something about Paradise—'

'This much I know,' Eleanor said, her lips pursing, as Sam shrugged out of her raincoat. 'I have it all on tape, and I've listened to it half a dozen times. What I'm asking you' – she pointed a long, accusing finger at Sam as she tucked her coat into a closet – 'is do you know who this guy is and what he wants?'

'No.'

'But there's something more.' Eleanor's dark eyes trained on Sam's face. 'Something you're not telling me. Does this have anything to do with your accident in Mexico?'

'I don't think so.'

'What about your ex? I remember him from when we worked in Houston together.'

'I don't think Jeremy would bother with crank calls. It would be beneath him.'

'But he still lives here, right? Got that professorship at Tulane.'

'Give it up, Eleanor, okay? Jeremy's remarried – what we had was over a long, long time ago,' Sam said.

'Well, *some*body around here made the calls, and I want to know who. Don't I wish we could trace calls from here. I've suggested it, you know, but George is so damned tight he squeaks.'

Sam smiled with more than a trace of cynicism. 'Maybe we'll get lucky. Maybe John will call back.'

Eleanor chased her down a jagged hallway to the kitchen area, where coffee was brewing, and the lingering smell of chili from someone's lunch permeated the air. The room was utilitarian, remodeled half a dozen times in its two-hundred-year history, with three round tables, a few scattered chairs, microwave and refrigerator. Whatever charm the area once embraced had long ago been covered with layers of Formica, vinyl, and glaring white paint. The only hint of the building's original charm was in the French doors, surrounded by original, ornate grillwork that once opened to a small verandah seven stories above the street. Now the doors were locked and double bolted.

Sam clomped her way to the coffeepot and poured herself a cup.

'When do you get the cast off?' Eleanor asked, her temper seeming to be under control again as Sam poured coffee into Eleanor's favorite cup, one that read, I *hear* what you're saying, I just don't *believe* it!

Sam wasn't lulled into thinking the subject of the crank caller had been dropped. It wasn't her boss's nature. Eleanor was like a pit bull with a bone when something bothered her. She never gave up.

'I should get rid of this thing' – she lifted her leg and cast – 'tomorrow morning, if I can convince the doctor that I'd be better off without this extra five pounds to lug around. I have an appointment with my orthopedic guy at eleven.'

'Good.' Eleanor scooted out a chair and waved Sam into a seat. 'Now, I've got to tell you that ever since that nutcase called last night, the station has been besieged with calls and e-mails.

Be-frickin'-sieged. I mean, we've had listeners call in all day.' Her dark eyes gleamed as she wrapped long fingers around the chipped ceramic cup. 'George is going bananas.'

'George would,' Samantha said, thinking of the owner of the station as she slid into her chair. Tall, dark and handsome, born with a silver spoon shoved decidedly between his teeth, George was forever worried about the bottom line, about losing a dime. He would do anything to increase the audience and the ratings. Sam considered him one step up from pond slime.

Leaning on the small of her back, she cradled her cup, blowing across the steamy surface. 'I guess I'd better come clean with you,' she said, wondering if she was making a major mistake.

'What do you mean?'

'Last night wasn't the first time the guy contacted me.'

'Come again.' Eleanor's coffee was forgotten. She pinned Sam in her gaze.

'He left me a message on my recorder; I thought Melanie would have told you.'

'She hasn't come in yet.'

'Okay, well, he did. And then there was this letter and a marred publicity shot.'

'What letter?'

She gave Eleanor a quick update and watched as the animation left her boss's dark face. When she'd explained about returning home and discovering the message and letter, Eleanor reached across the table and wrapped bejeweled fingers around Sam's wrist. 'Tell me that you called the police.'

'Didn't I say I did? Don't worry.'

'It's my job to worry. So what did the police have to say?'

'They said they'd send more patrols around the area.'

Eleanor's eyes narrowed. 'Did they come out to the house?'

'Not yet,' Sam said.

'Why not?'

'I haven't been home much.'

'Jesus H. Christ . . .' Eleanor sighed loudly. Her neatly plucked eyebrows slammed together. 'Since the Cambrai police don't have jurisdiction here in the city, tell me you're going to haul your ass into my office and pick up the phone to tell them about the calls coming into the station here, cuz, honey, if you don't, I sure as hell will.'

'I will.'

'You bet you will.' Eleanor wasn't taking any excuses. 'As soon as you finish your coffee, you use my office.'

'I'd planned to call tomorrow,' Sam said.

'Why wait?'

'I just want to see if the creep calls back tonight,' Sam said. 'Make sure it's not a onetime thing.'

'I doubt it. Considering what's gone on at your home.'

'You said yourself that the station was being inundated with calls. That should mean a larger audience,' Sam argued. 'Isn't that what we all want?'

Eleanor tapped a fingernail on her cup. 'Yes, but I think you're playing with fire,' she said, but she was warming to the idea.

'Maybe. It's true, he's scared me. But I'd like to find out what makes him tick. So far the threats have been pretty vague. And I'd like to find out what's going on with him.' She finished her coffee in one swallow. 'Bet my listeners do, too.'

'I don't know about this—'

'If I get another call, I'll run straight to New Orleans's finest, I swear,' Sam said, raising two fingers as if she were a Boy Scout.

'Promise?'

'Cross my heart and hope to die—'

'Don't even say it,' Eleanor cut in. 'And for the record' – she thumped a finger on the Formica table – 'I don't like this. Uh-uh. Not one little bit.'

'Don't like what?' a gravelly voice demanded. Ramblin' Rob, dressed as if he were planning to attend a cattle drive rather than sit in a booth with a presorted stack of CDs, swaggered in. He smelled of smoke and rain, the brim of his Stetson dripping.

'Sam, here, wants to go on the air again without talking to the police about her own private nutcase.'

A grin stretched across Rob's weathered features. 'Not so private. Seems like half the damned city was listening to her last night from the number of e-mails. I'm surprised the cops haven't called you.' He laid a leathery hand on Sam's shoulder.

'I think they have more on their minds,' she said.

'Okay, okay, enough of this.' Eleanor glanced at her watch. 'I've got a meeting in ten minutes. Just promise me you'll be careful.'

'Always am.'

Eleanor rolled her large eyes. 'Yeah, and I'm Cleopatra. I mean it, Sam, don't bait this guy. Who knows how dangerous he is. He could be hopped up on drugs, or have a hair trigger on his temper. Just, please' – she spread her hands expressively – 'take it easy.'

'I'm a psychologist, remember? I'm used to this kind of thing.'

'Yeah, right,' Eleanor muttered under her breath as she bustled out of the room.

'She's right, kiddo.' Rob sat down. Tipped the brim of his hat back, pinned Sam with blue eyes that had seen it all. 'Don't do anything foolish, okay?'

With mock severity, Sam said, 'I'll try my best, Cowboy Rob. Honest I will.' She said it lightheartedly, but the truth of the matter was that she intended to be very careful with the guy should he phone in again. If she got any hint that he was danger-ous, she'd phone the police. Pronto.

That night as she walked down the hallway, a cup of coffee in her hand, the offices seemed darker than usual. The shadows in the corners, deeper, the corridors more crooked than before. It was stupid, of course. The old building in the heart of the city hadn't changed at all, but despite her bold words to Eleanor earlier, Sam was edgy. She'd gone home last night and nothing had happened. She'd thought she'd heard someone outside, but as she'd stepped onto her back porch, she'd seen nothing through the curtain of rain and only the whistle of the breeze and the clink of wind chimes had disturbed the night. Later, she'd spied the lone boat on the choppy waters, or at least thought she had. She'd shut her blinds and pushed him out of her mind. What was happening to make her so jumpy?

It wasn't as if she was alone, for God's sake. Melanie was manning the phones, Tiny was about, making sure that the equipment was working and that the preset programs for later in the night were ready to roll.

Nothing was out of the ordinary.

Except that someone out there – in the city – wants to scare the devil out of you.

And it was working.

Big time.

She was tense, her stomach in knots as she closed the door to the soundproof booth, slid into her chair and settled behind the microphone.

Eleanor and George had been right, she thought as the intro music played through the speakers mounted over her desk. The e-mail and calls the station had received in the last twenty-four hours had far surpassed any other similar span of time. The conversation last might between Dr. Sam and 'John' had spurred interest in the program, and she could feel a new sense of electricity in the station, through the headset, in the voices of the callers as they phoned in.

'Good evening, New Orleans and welcome . . .' She started out her show with her usual bit. Then, knowing she was dancing with the devil, said, 'I thought we'd pick up tonight where we left off. Last night a caller phoned in, bringing up the subject of forgiveness, repentance and sin.' Sam's fingers were a little shaky as she leaned into the mike. 'I thought it was worth exploring tonight as well. I know a lot of you were listening, and I'd like to hear your interpretations of sin.' The first phone line was already blinking. Lines two and three lit up almost simultaneously. Once the program was over, Eleanor would probably kill her, tell her that she was inviting trouble, but though her hands were sweaty and her pulse elevated, she wanted to connect with

John again . . . to find out more. Who was he? Why had he called? He had to be the same man who left her the voice message on her machine and was the same guy who had sent her the muti-lated publicity shot. Why was he trying to terrorize her?

The computer screen showed that Sarah was line one and Tom on two. Three belonged to Marcy. New Orleans was eager to talk about sin, redemption, quote Bible verses and express opinions vociferously about the wages of sin. Two men named John called – neither being the one who had phoned the night before. The hours rolled by into morning and Sam felt a mixture of relief and disappointment. She didn't believe he would just go away.

But there was tomorrow night.

'Take care of yourself, New Orleans. Good night to you all and God bless. No matter what your troubles are today, there is always tomorrow. . . . Sweet dreams . . .' she said, signing off over the sound of music. She yanked off her headset and pushed the appropriate buttons so that the advertisements would flow into the opening for the *Lights Out* program, then met Melanie in the hallway.

'I guess my personal creep didn't have the urge to call.'

'Disappointed?' Melanie asked, eyebrows elevated.

'I just want to know what he's thinking.'

'Maybe it's over. He got his jollies last night and he's given up . . . gone on to greener pastures.'

'Maybe.' Sam wasn't convinced. In fact, silly as it seemed, she thought he was playing a game with her. That he was listening, knowing she expected him to call, and was trying a new tactic to freak her out.

'Forget him. You all but begged him to call what with the subject tonight,' Melanie said. 'He's probably bored.'

'Or he might be more cautious. He doesn't know that I haven't talked to the police yet. He could have thought the cops could trace the call.'

Melanie yawned. 'You know, Sam, maybe you're not as important to him as you think.' She seemed irritated, and added, 'It was probably just a kid with a deep voice playing a prank.'

Sam didn't think so.

'You really expected him to call, didn't you?' Melanie asked, as they walked toward the locker room and Tiny, hurrying in, sped past them.

'I thought he might.'

'You *wanted* him to.'

Did she? That was kind of a sick thought. 'I just figured he might and I could get a little insight into what it was he was talking about last night.' She leaned on one crutch as a sudden thought struck her. 'What about when you were hosting the show while I was in Mexico? Did he call you?'

'Me?' Melanie laughed but the sound seemed brittle. 'No way. This one, he's *all* yours.'

'Maybe.'

'Samantha?' Tiny's voice called down the hallway. 'You've got a call on line two. Says his name is John.'

'What?' She froze for a second.

'I said—'

'I heard you.' She twisted around and hitched her way back to the darkened studio, where line two was blinking ominously.

'It's your guy,' Tiny whispered, though no one could hear him until she clicked on.

'Make sure you record this.' Tiny nodded, restarted the tape. Sam grabbed Melanie's headset and leaned over the console, pushing the flickering button.

'This is Dr. Sam,' she said.

'It's John.' His voice was breathless, yet smooth – as if he was trying to pretend a calm he didn't feel. '*Your* John. I know you were expecting me to call, but I was busy.'

'Who *are* you?'

'This is not about me,' he said, and his calm seemed to snap.

'Sure it is. What is it you want?'

A pause. 'I thought you'd like to know that what happened is all because of you. It's your fault. Yours.'

Her blood turned to ice.

'What – what happened?' she demanded.

'You'll know.'

Click.

'What – what will I know?' she asked. The line was dead. 'Damn.' She tossed off the headset and stared at the console, willing a light to blink again. But the phone lines didn't illuminate. In fact the room seemed strangely dark and when she looked through the glass to the studio where she worked, she saw her own thin reflection as well as the translucent images of Tiny and Melanie in the clear glass – ghosts inhabiting the empty building.

'It was him, wasn't it?' Melanie whispered.

'Oh, yeah.' Sam nodded.

'You'd better call someone.' Tiny rubbed the stubble on his chin and bit his lip as he stared at the blank console.

'The police?' she asked.

'No! I mean, not yet.' Tiny shook his head and thought so hard he squinted. 'I mean, maybe you should call Eleanor or Mr. Hannah.'

'I don't think I'll wake George up,' Sam said, thinking of the owner of the station. George Hannah didn't like any ripples in the water. He wouldn't appreciate a call in the middle of the night. 'I think he cherishes his beauty sleep.'

'Well, *some*one should know.'

'Someone does,' she said, thinking of the smooth voice without a face. He knew what she looked like. Where she lived. What she did for a living. How to contact her. And she was at a distinct disadvantage. So far she knew nothing about him. Nothing at all.

5

'We've got ourselves another one.' Detective Reuben Montoya leaned a muscled shoulder against the doorjamb to Rick Bentz's office in the weathered stone building that housed the precinct. His black hair was glossy as a raven's wing, his goatee trimmed and neat. White teeth flashed when he spoke, and a gold earring caught the bluish glare from the flickering fluorescents overhead.

'Another one?' Bentz glanced at the clock. Three-fifteen; he'd been on duty since 7 P.M., was about to call it a night. A fan was whirring behind him, pushing around warm air that the old air conditoner hadn't found a way to chill.

'Dead working girl.'

The muscles in the back of Bentz's neck tightened. 'Where?'

'Around Toulouse and Decatur. Not far from Jackson Brewery.'

'Hell.' Bentz rolled back his chair.

'Her roommate came home and found her on the bed.'

'Have you called the ME?' Bentz was already reaching for his jacket.

'He's on his way.'

'Has the scene been disturbed – the roommate, did she do anything?'

'Just scream loud enough to wake everyone in the building, but the super swears he's closed the door and kept everyone at bay.'

Bentz frowned. 'You know, this isn't really my baby. You should call Brinkman.'

'He's on vacation and besides he's a dick, and that's not meant to be a compliment.' Montoya's dark eyes flashed. 'You've got experience with this kind of thing.'

'That was a while back,' Bentz admitted.

'Not that long ago, and just cuz you're not officially working homicide here, doesn't mean jack shit, okay? Now, are you in or not?'

'Let's roll.' Bentz was on his feet and out the door, the lethargy he'd felt seeping into his bones half an hour ago replaced by a jolt of adrenaline. Through a room filled with beat-up desks and down one flight where their boots clattered on the old metal and linoleum, they hurried into the street, where Montoya's unmarked was parked illegally. Bentz didn't think about the consequences. Brinkman would probably be pissed, but then he always was, and Melinda Jaskiel, in charge of the Homicide Division, had pretty much given Bentz carte blanche.

Despite what happened in LA.

If she didn't like him taking charge, she could pull him off the case and call Fred Brinkman back from Disneyland. Bentz had always believed in asking for acceptance rather than permission. More often than not it got him into trouble.

Montoya snapped on the ignition as Bentz climbed into the car. Though nearly twenty years Bentz's junior, Montoya had earned his stripes, hurtling over barriers of racism, poverty and attitude to land, at twenty-eight, as a full detective with the NOPD. He wanted to work Homicide and sometimes did a double detail just to be involved in murder investigations.

He also drove through the dark city streets as if he were at Daytona. As the police band crackled, he managed to jam a Marlboro into the side of his mouth and light up while negotiating the sharp turns and keeping the wipers at the right tempo. The misty night clung, like a shroud, to the corners of the old buildings and mingled with the steam that escaped from the manholes in the street.

Within minutes they skidded to a stop in front of the building. Montoya flicked his cigarette onto the street, where some of the beat cops were keeping a small crowd at bay and crime-scene tape was used as a shimmering yellow-and-black barricade. A couple of news vans had pulled up, and Bentz cussed the reporters under his breath. 'Jesus, if they'd just give the cops a couple of hours to do their jobs before descending like vultures, it would help.'

A microphone was pushed close to his face but before the pert Asian reporter could spout her first question, Bentz growled, 'No comment,' and in tandem with Montoya took the front steps two at a time to a door tucked by the side of the deli, where a uniformed street cop let them inside.

'Third floor,' the cop muttered, and Montoya was a step ahead of him as they took the stairs to a cramped hallway that reeked of marijuana, mold and incense. People had gathered in the corridor, craning their necks, talking and smoking, all the while casting curious glances toward the door marked 3F.

Montoya flashed his badge to a cop Bentz had seen around the precinct, but then the young buck got off on showing his ID. It gave him a 'rush,' the younger cop had admitted on more than one occasion. Bentz had long since given up on the authority trip. If LA had taught him anything, it was humility. There just weren't a helluva lot of reasons to be an asshole. A cop learned more from subtlety than intimidation. Though, at Montoya's age, Bentz, too, had thought differently.

Standing in the doorway, Bentz took one look into the tiny room and his stomach clenched. Bile rose up the back of his throat as it always did when he viewed a murder scene, but he wouldn't admit it to a soul, and it immediately disappeared as he assumed his role as detective. He smelled stale coffee and blood, the stench of death, even in the early stages, noticeable, and heard muted conversation over a radio tuned to some soft music, an instrumental piece.

'I want to talk to the roommate,' he said to no one in particular.

'She's in the next room – 3E – pretty shook up.' The uniform, Mike O'Keefe, nodded to a door with chipped paint that was slightly ajar. Through the crack he caught a view of a pale, rail-thin woman with bags under her eyes, kinky brown hair and bad skin. Her lipstick had faded, her mascara had slid from her eyelashes to darken the natural circles under her eyes. She was smoking, swilling coffee and looked scared of her own shadow. Bentz didn't blame her.

'Keep her there. I'll want to talk to her.'

'You in charge?' O'Keefe asked, questions in his eyes.

'Until someone says differently.'

O'Keefe didn't argue.

Careful to disturb nothing, Bentz walked past a small kitchen alcove where a glass pot was half-full of yesterday's coffee and crumbs from the toaster had scattered over a counter that hadn't seen a sponge in quite a while. The chipped sink was piled with dishes. Cobwebs hung near the ceiling light.

The living area was small, occupied almost entirely by a double bed shoved into one corner. Upon the crumpled sheets the victim lay, half-dressed in a black teddy, eyes staring glassily at the ceiling where the blades of a fan moved lazily. She was around thirty, he guessed, white, with short dark hair and little makeup. Her throat was bruised and cut with tiny nicks where blood had crusted, as if she'd been garroted by some kind of kinky noose that cut into her flesh – like barbed wire or one of those S/M dog collars turned inside out. While her legs were spread wide, her arms had been placed together, fingers inter-locked, as if she were praying. The perp had taken time to pose her.

Bentz's gut tightened. 'Time of death?'

'Best guess – sometime after midnight, from the looks of her. The medical examiner will know more.'

'Name?'

'Rosa Gillette according to the roommate and the super.'

'One bed? Two women?'

'They just use the place for tricks. Rosa, here, and a couple of friends. The third, a woman named, oh get this – Cindy Sweet, sometimes known as Sweet Sin – she hasn't been located yet. They're independents, no pimp.'

'Check this out.' Montoya pointed to a small table. Tucked beneath a candle was a hundred-dollar bill that no one had swiped. Odd, he thought. The roommate would have taken the cash or the perp would have retrieved it . . . then he noticed the mutilation – someone had taken a black felt pen to Ben Franklin's eyes. It wasn't the first time. His gut tightened.

'Look familiar?' Montoya asked, dark eyes gleaming. The kid really got off on all this cop shit.

'Yep.' Bentz nodded. There had been another murder, much like this one. The victim, a prostitute, had been strangled with some unknown noose – one that bit into her neck in a distinct pattern like this one. 'The hooker near the French Quarter . . . A few weeks ago. Cherise Something-or-Other.'

'Cherie Bellechamps.'

'Yeah. That's it,' Montoya said.

An odd case. A waitress and loving mother by day, a hooker at night, a woman involved in a custody suit that her ex-husband, by default, had won. 'Shit,' Bentz muttered under his breath. He'd seen enough. 'Make sure nothing's disturbed for the team. Let's talk to the roommate.'

As he crossed the hallway the ME and crime-scene team clattered up the stairs. While they entered 3E, Bentz introduced himself to the frail-looking, tense woman, who, guardedly, said her name was Denise LeBlanc and after being assured that the cops weren't out to bust her admitted that she'd come back from a trick in the Garden District, to the apartment and found Rosa on the bed. Obviously dead. She'd started screaming, the super, Marvin Cooper, a beefy man of mixed race with few remaining teeth and a shaved head had taken charge, bolting the door and calling 911. Marvin, who occupied this studio alone, was leaning on the cabinets of the kitchen alcove, huge arms crossed over a black T-shirt while Denise chain-smoked and drank cups of coffee laced with cheap whiskey.

'I know this is tough,' Bentz said, as Denise lit a cigarette while the last was burning in an overflowing ashtray.

'It's freaky, that's what it is. Fuckin' freaky.' Denise's hands were shaking, her eyes wide.

'Did you notice anything missing?'

'How the hell would I know? I walked in and . . . and saw . . . Oh shit.' Her head dropped to her hands and she sobbed. 'Rosa was a nice kid . . . She had dreams of gettin' out of the business . . . oh, God . . .'

Bentz waited, then said, 'Was anything taken? Disturbed?'

'The whole fuckin' place was disturbed! The guy who did it is *disturbed!* Shit, yes, it was disturbed.' She was sobbing, and Bentz could coax little out of her.

'I just want to find out who did this to her, and you'll have to help.'

'She's scared out of her mind,' Marvin said gruffly. He sat next to Denise on the couch, and she curled up under one of his muscular arms. 'I saw that C-note under the beside lamp. When Denise started screamin' I ran over there and I saw that hundred-dollar bill all messed up. Man, whoever did this is weird, I'm tellin' ya.'

'Did you notice anything else?' Bentz asked. 'You saw the body.'

'Hell, yes, I saw her.' His lips folded in on themselves, and absently he patted Denise's shoulder. 'I saw the way that freak messed with her, leavin' her all spread-eagled and . . . crap.'

'So did you see anything you thought was odd?'

'Everything, man!'

This was getting him nowhere. 'What about your other roommate? Cindy. Where's she?'

'Dunno,' Denise grumbled. 'She and Rosa had a fight a week or so ago. Cindy split. Haven't seen her since.'

'She hasn't called?' Bentz asked.

'No! Hasn't paid her share of the rent, either. I say "good riddance to bad news." She was a real pain.'

Bentz asked more questions and didn't learn anything new.

For the most part, Marvin's story matched Denise's. As the night hours crept quickly toward dawn, Montoya and Bentz interviewed the other denizens of the Riverview Apartments. They discovered that no one admitted seeing Rosa enter with any man, nor had any person noticed a lone man leave. Bentz suspected so many people came and went that unless this guy was extremely unusual, none of the tenants of the building would take note.

It was broad daylight by the time they headed back to the station. The streets were crowded with the rush of eight-to-fivers, only a few clouds drifting across the sky. Sunlight glared against the pavement and bounced off the hoods of other vehicles. Horns honked, engines thrummed and pedestrians filled the crosswalks, spilling around parked cars as New Orleans woke up. By necessity Montoya drove with a lighter foot, barely breaking the speed limit.

Once in his office, Bentz yanked off his tie and took the time to check the files of open cases. It didn't take long to come up with the folder and computer information on Cherie Bellechamps, the prostitute who had been found a few weeks earlier. She, too, had been strangled with something causing a peculiar ligature around her neck. Cherie had been posed as well, in mock prayer in her seedy apartment. Left with a marred C-note on the bedside table, a loaded gun in the drawer, all the lights blazing and the radio playing. The crime-scene team had collected dirt, hair, semen and fingerprints. Whoever had offed Cherie hadn't been careful not to leave other evidence.

The ex-husband, Henry Bellechamps, who lived on the other side of Lake Pontchartrain, had been the primary suspect, but with an ironclad alibi and no evidence linking him to the crime, he'd been questioned and let go. The local PD in Covington was supposed to be keeping an eye on him, but so far, nothing. Henry Bellechamps had suddenly become a model citizen.

Bentz rubbed the stubble on his chin and twisted a kink from his neck. He'd have to check the guy out, see what old Hank had been doing earlier this evening, but it was his guess that the truck driver was clean. At least as far as the murders were concerned. And the third roommate – Cindy Sweet – he wanted to hear what she had to say, know where she'd been.

In the Bellechamps case, the crime team had collected dozens of fingerprints that had turned up some other suspects, all of whom said the last time they'd seen Cherie Bellechamps she'd been very much alive. Their alibis confirmed that they hadn't been in the apartment at the time of death. The hair samples and blood types hadn't matched those of the perp.

So much for a break in the case.

He glared at the computer monitor where a picture of Cherie's dead body was displayed and posed. So similar to the dead woman tonight. The murders had to be linked. Had to. They were too eerily the same.

Wonderful, he thought sarcastically, as the fan blew hot air against the back of his neck, *just what this city needs: a serial killer.*

6

'Have you met the new neighbor?' Mrs. Killingsworth asked as her dog, a tiny pug with a pushed-in snout and bulging eyes snorted and dug in one of her flower beds. 'Hannibal, you stop that!' The pug ignored her and tore into a freshly turned mound of earth. 'He never listens!'

A matronly woman forever working in the yard in her husband's overalls, Mrs. Killingsworth had been pushing a load of peat moss in her wheelbarrow. She'd been headed toward the back of the house but had stopped when she'd noticed Samantha struggling to get her trash can to the curb for the next day's pickup.

'What new neighbor?' Sam asked.

'A man around thirty-five or forty, I'd say. He moved in about a quarter of a mile down from you in the old Swanson place.' Edie Killingsworth motioned a gloved hand, indicating a spot farther down the oak-lined street. 'I heard he's leased the house for the next six months.'

'You've met him?'

'Oh, yes, and he's quite something, if you get my drift.' Gray eyebrows rose over the tops of wire-rimmed glasses held in place by a chain.

The sun was intense. Bright. Edie Killingsworth's photo gray lenses were nearly black. Hannibal gave up digging and trotted over to plop down at her feet, where he panted, showing off his long tongue.

'Something? Like what?' Sam asked, realizing what was to come as she wiped her hands on her jeans. Ever since Sam had moved in three months earlier, Edie Killingsworth had taken it as her personal mission to see Sam hooked up with a suitable candidate for marriage.

'I'd say he's something like Harrison Ford, Tom Cruise and Clark Gable all rolled into one.'

'And Hollywood hasn't discovered him yet?' Sam said with a grin, as Charon ducked into the thick privacy hedge that ran on either side of her property.

'Oh, he's not an actor,' Edie was quick to correct. 'He's a writer who just happens to be handsome as the devil. And that east Texas drawl of his, my stars,' she fanned herself emphatically, as if the mere thought of this hunk caused her to melt inside.

'If you say so.'

'I know a good-looking man when I see one. And I'll bet you dollars to doughnuts the new tenant has money, as well. Milo Swanson's tight with a dollar, he wouldn't rent to just anyone. You and I both know he'd charge an arm and a leg.' She nodded, the brim of her floppy hat waggling and shading her face as she reached down for the handles of her wheelbarrow. 'Anyway, the man just moved in last week. You might want to go down and welcome him to the neighborhood.'

'Maybe I could whip up some Jell-O,' Sam suggested.

The older woman chuckled and waved Sam's sarcasm away with one gloved hand. 'A bottle of wine would be better.' She extracted a checkered handkerchief from one frayed pocket. 'There's a wonderful Pinot Noir from Oregon down at Zehlers – Molalla Vineyards makes it, and I guarantee it would be lots better than any flavor of Jell-O.'

'Duly noted,' Sam said, as the dog sniffed at her shoes.

'I hope so.' Edie mopped the sweat from her forehead, then picked up the handgrips of the wheelbarrow again and made her way to the back of her property. Hannibal, tail curled, trotted after her. Sam smiled. Edie Killingsworth was the one person who had welcomed her to the neighborhood only days after she'd moved in. The older woman had brought over a casserole, fruit salad and yes, a bottle of Pinot Noir in a well-used picnic basket and invited Sam to visit anytime.

Now, Sam glanced down the street to the old Swanson place, a quaint cottage in sad need of updating. A beat-up Volvo wagon sat in the drive, and boxes, broken down and flattened, had been left at the curb with a trash basket. Curious, her ankle aching, she walked past the neighboring houses, all on lots shaded by live oaks and shrubs. When she was close enough to the Swanson place, she looked past the rambling cottage to the dock and there, rising on the swells, was a sailboat, a large sloop, its sails down. For a second she thought it looked just like the one she'd imagined she'd seen a couple of nights earlier – the one with the man at the helm in the middle of the storm.

But it had been a dark night.

Her nerves had been stretched thin.

There were lots of sailboats – thousands of them around these parts.

Even if she had seen one that night, there was absolutely no reason to think it was this one. She shaded her eyes with her hand and stared at the sleek craft as it swayed on the water. Its name, *Bright Angel*, had been painted near the stern, but even from a distance she noticed that some of the paint had chipped. There was a box of tools lying open on the dock as if the owner was working on the boat. So the guy drove an aging Volvo and spent his time sailing or working on his boat when he wasn't writing whatever it was he wrote.

Maybe Mrs. Killingsworth was right.

Maybe a bottle of wine . . . and a Jell-O mold were in order.

'I don't care what you say, I don't like it.' Eleanor was reading George Hannah the riot act when Sam limped into the station the next afternoon. Soft jazz emanated from hidden speakers tucked into the neon-lit displays of Louisiana artifacts separating the reception area from the business offices and studios, but the music did nothing to soothe Eleanor. Not today. Sweeping a glance in Sam's direction, she paused long enough in her tirade to comment. 'You got the cast off! Good. Feelin' better?'

'Like I lost ten pounds.' Her ankle was still swollen and hurt like crazy, but at least she was cast free and only used the crutch when she really needed it. She'd had to forgo heels or even flats for running shoes, but anything was an improvement.

Eleanor, despite her foul mood, cracked a smile as the phone lines jangled. 'Well, you got here just in the nick of time. I was telling George that no matter what the ratings are, I'm not interested in any kind of scandal. This guy who keeps calling you – your personal nutcase – has got to stop.'

'You heard about last night,' Sam said.

'Yeah, I heard. Tiny's got it all on tape.' Eleanor, dressed in black, looked like the proverbial avenging angel as she paced in front of Melba's desk. 'The way I see it, we still got us a problem, here, a major one.'

In her usual unruffled manner, Melba was taking call after call while George Hannah, dressed in a natty, expensive suit, was taking his tongue-lashing like a man, hands clasped in front of him, expression respectfully solemn, head nodding slightly as if he agreed with every word spewing from Eleanor's lips.

Melanie breezed in from outside, bringing with her the scents of expensive perfume and coffee steaming from a paper cup she'd grabbed on the way in.

'What's weird about this is that no one else heard the conversation, none of the listeners, as he called after the show was off the air.' Melanie took a tentative sip and licked her lips. 'It didn't affect the ratings.'

'It doesn't matter.' Eleanor took them all in with one sweeping, argue-with-me-and-you'll-die glare. 'There's enough interest from the program the night before.'

'So we should capitalize on it,' George said, glancing at Samantha. He offered her a thousand-watt smile. George Hannah, for all his faults, was charming in his own self-aggrandizing way. And always interested in the bottom line.

Eleanor was having none of it. 'Look, George, we've all been down that road before. You, me and Samantha. Now, I don't want a repeat of what happened in Houston.'

Samantha froze, feeling as if every pair of eyes in the room had turned on her. For the first time the station owner looked uncomfortable.

'That is ancient history,' George said quietly, his smile fading as he, too, remembered the tragedy that had nearly destroyed Samantha's career nine years earlier. 'No reason to dredge it up now.'

Thank God, Sam thought, sensing the color had drained from her face.

'What're y'all talkin' about?' Melba asked as the phone jangled. 'Oh, damn.' With a pissy look, she took the call.

'I mean it, George,' Eleanor said, touching him on the elbow of his pin-striped suit. 'We need to tread lightly. This guy sounds like a major wacko – one right out of *Play Misty for Me*, or *Scream*. It's no joke.'

'I didn't say it was one.' The station owner held up a hand. 'I think it's serious. Very serious.'

Eleanor's expression said it all: she didn't believe George for one minute. Lips pursed, she turned toward Samantha. 'Okay, so what happened with the police? You called them . . . right? What did they say?'

'That they were busy, that I should come in and fill out a report, that after that they'd send someone out to the house tomorrow—'

'Tomorrow?' Eleanor tossed up her hands.

'There's something about a problem with jurisdictions because I live in Cambrai, where I received the threatening letter and a call, but I've also gotten calls, here, within the city limits of New Orleans. Maybe the Sheriff's Department will have to get involved.'

'Well, it doesn't matter which branch handles it, just make damned sure someone does! Jesus H. Christ. *Tomorrow!* Fine. Just . . . fine.' Eleanor forced herself to calm down as she moved her gaze to each and every one standing in the reception area. 'In the interim we're all gonna be real careful, you-all got me?'

'You know it,' Melanie said, smothering a smile.

'And you, don't you get fresh with me, girl. I want you to keep track of all the calls that come in here. Make sure the computer's got their number. Isn't that what damned caller ID is for?'

'Yes, *Mom*,' Melanie said sarcastically, just as she'd done to Sam the other day. 'But the call came up as an anonymous number, probably from some system that couldn't be identified. There wasn't anything I could do.'

'That's the problem, you know,' Eleanor said under her breath. 'I get no respect around here.'

Melba pressed the hold button. 'The advertising director's on line one, for you.' She caught Eleanor's eye. 'A Mr. Seely called, wants you to call him back.' She handed a pink slip of paper to George. 'I would have directed him to your voice mail, *if* we had it, but since we don't . . .' George lifted a dark eyebrow as Melba twisted in her chair. 'And here' – she slapped a couple of notes into Samantha's palm – 'your dad phoned again.'

'We keep missing each other,' Samantha explained, noting that the second caller had been David. So he didn't think it was over. David was like a terrier with a bone; he wouldn't give it up for anything. And Sam was the prize. She should have been flattered, she supposed, but wasn't.

The impromptu meeting broke up, and as Sam headed down the aorta, Melanie fell into step with her.

'What happened in Houston?' she asked in a whisper.

'It was a bad scene and a long story.' Sam didn't want to go into it, didn't want to remember what had happened to the scared teenager who had called in to her show asking for advice – seeking help. Dear God, the girl's voice still haunted her dreams at night. Dark memories skated through her mind, but she wouldn't dwell on them. Couldn't yet face the pain, nor the guilt. 'I'll tell you about it later,' she said, knowing she was lying.

'And I'll hold you to it.'

'Good,' she said, but knew she'd never discuss what had happened in Houston.

She made her way to her computer and read her e-mail. She sifted through the usual stuff until she came to a note from Leanne Jaquillard, reminding Sam that they had 'group' at the Boucher Center the next afternoon and the center was a madhouse getting ready for the benefit. Sam typed a quick reply, saying she'd be there.

She volunteered at the center once a week, but because of her trip to Mexico, she hadn't seen the teenage girls she counseled for the better part of a month. They were an interesting group, all in some kind of trouble, all from highly dysfunctional families, all attempting to get their lives back on track. They were some of the sweetest, most troubled and devious girls she'd ever met. Leanne was no exception. If anything she was probably the most troubled of the lot, a ringleader by nature. Street smart, undereducated, with a hard exterior that belied the frightened girl inside, Leanne Jaquillard had become the unelected leader of the group and the only member who kept in touch with Sam between sessions.

The girl was just plain needy and reminded Sam of herself at that age – the difference being, of course, that Sam had grown up in a loving, well-to-do family in Los Angeles. At any sign of trouble, Samantha's parents had reined her in, talked with her, dealt with her rebellion and anxieties. Leanne wasn't so lucky. Nor were the other girls in the group. Sam considered them 'her girls' as she didn't have any children of her own.

Yet, she reminded herself. Someday she would have a baby. With or without a man. She didn't want to think that time was running out. She was only thirty-six and these days women had babies well into their forties, but the truth of the matter was her biological clock was ticking so loudly that at times she couldn't hear anything else.

Her ex-husband hadn't wanted children, but David Ross had. That had been one of his most attractive attributes, one of the reasons she'd continued to see him, to try and force herself to fall in love with him.

But it hadn't happened.

And it never would.

David Ross wasn't the man for her, and the disheartening thought was she was beginning to feel no man was.

Oh, for God's sake, Sam, quit wallowing and don't give up hope. You should take some of that advice you hand out so readily every night on the airwaves. She gave herself a swift mental kick and told herself she was lucky she hadn't made the mistake of marrying David. Damned lucky.

Ty Wheeler leaned back in his chair, the heel of one boot propped on the expansive desk, ice melting in his short glass. A bottle of Irish whiskey was uncapped nearby and his old dog was lying on the rug, close enough that Ty could reach down and scratch the shepherd behind his ears. A single banker's lamp offered dim illumination through its green shade in the shadowy cottage.

Listening to the radio, Ty sipped his drink and heard Dr. Samantha Leeds's voice as she talked with the lonely people who called her in the middle of the night. His lips twisted. Poor sods. They all hoped she could solve some of their problems, or, failing that, allow them a connection to her.

Such as it was.

He stared through the open French doors to the lake beyond. Insects buzzed through the night, and the water lapped softly. A breeze lifted the curtains and offered some relief from the heat, but Ty didn't much notice. His concentration was centered on the woman's low, sexy voice wafting through the speakers of his radio.

She was talking about commitment and fidelity – favorite topics with the late-night crowd, and he considered calling the number she kept reeling off, asking her a question or two that was on his mind.

'Hello . . . who's this?' she asked, and he glanced down to the desk where a publicity shot of the woman stared up at him. Dark, near-auburn, red hair, bright green eyes, perfect porcelain skin stretched over cheekbones most women would kill for. Her mouth was wide and sensual, her smile fresh, not seeming posed ... but then for all he knew the shot could have been computer enhanced, airbrushed and whatever the hell else professional photographers did to make their subjects appear more good-looking than God had intended.

'Linda,' a voice raspy from years of cigarettes identified the caller.

'Hi, Linda, did you have a comment or a question?' Samantha's voice. Sultry as a hot Delta night.

'An observation.'

'Observe away.'

Ty imagined her smiling, white teeth flashing behind full lips. In his mind's eye he saw her eyes, bright with an intellect and depth that she often hid, preferring to disguise that side of her. But it was there. He could feel it. Hear it in the undertones of her words, sense it in her throaty chuckle, knew that it lurked just beneath the surface. There were incidents where she'd exposed herself, of course. It was her profession to probe deeply and therefore give up a little of herself, but those moments were rare in this medium of radio, and what she offered to her listeners was a kind voice, keen intelligence and startling wit, but only rarely did she bare her soul.

Not that it mattered. Not that he cared, he reminded himself. She was just part of his research; an integral part.

'I'm thinking monogamy is societal and that since we're basically all animals, anyway, monogamy is a fallacy.'

'Is this your personal experience, or your comment on our lifestyle?' Sam inquired egging the caller on subtly.

'Both I guess.' Linda cleared her throat.

'Do you want to expand on that?'

'I'm just saying it as it is.'

'Are you? Does anyone else want to comment on Linda's observation. Linda, would you mind staying on the line?' Dr. Sam asked, obviously searching for some kind of controversy, the kind of thing that caused the audience to react and listen, the true reason George Hannah had hired her and put her on the air. Ty knew enough about Hannah to realize the guy didn't give a good goddamn about the listeners – only about the numbers so that he could sell advertising space. George Hannah had learned about audience reaction to Samantha Leeds in Houston, and he was capitalizing on it. So was Eleanor Cavalier, though she was more subtle.

'Sure, I'll hang on. No problem . . .' Linda was saying.

'Hello, this is Dr. Sam.'

'And this here is Mandy. Linda's got it all wrong. Monogamy is the Lord's will and if she doesn't believe that she should start reading her Bible! She could start with the Ten Commandments!'

'Are you married, Mandy?'

'You bet I am. Fifteen years. Carl and me, we was high school sweethearts. We got ourselves three sons, and we've had our ups and downs, but we stick together. We go to church every Sunday and—'

Absently Ty stroked his dog's broad head as he concentrated on the conversation playing through his speakers.

Dr. Sam spoke to a few more listeners and the argument about fidelity and marriage raged. He glanced at the phone, a shiny rotary relic from another century that had come with the house and sipped his whiskey slowly, letting it roll over his tongue. On the desk in front of him were dozens of notes, scattered pages filled with disjointed thoughts, facts that didn't link together and questions circled over and over again as he'd tried to come up with answers, to write a story that had been on his mind for a long, long time. Ever since he'd been a cop in Houston.

Balanced on a corner of Milo Swanson's desk, Ty's laptop glowed, waiting for him to transcribe more of his notes onto the screen.

But the words hadn't come tonight, and he knew why. He was blocked – that damned writer's disease that assailed without any glimmer of forewarning.

There was only one way to break it.

He had to meet the good doctor face-to-face.

7

'I want you to check out what's happening to Samantha Leeds.' Melinda Jaskiel handed Rick Bentz the report. 'She's a night-time DJ – radio shrink, and she thinks she's being harassed.'

'I've heard of her,' Bentz admitted. 'My kid listens to her sometimes.' He was seated at his desk, chewing an old wad of Nicorette gum and wishing he could have a smoke. And a shot of Jack Daniel's . . . yeah, that would be the ticket. But he wouldn't.

'Dr. Sam, as she calls herself, doesn't live in the city, has one of those nice places up on the lake in Cambrai. When this started a couple of days ago, she called the local PD. They were kind enough to fax over a copy of their report, and the officers in charge seem more than happy to have someone from the city help them out.'

He skimmed the pages, and Melinda, folding her arms across her chest leaned a hip against his desk.

'I'd like to keep a lid on this one,' she said. 'The woman's a quasi celebrity around here. No reason to let the press get wind of it yet. They're already sniffing around, hoping we've got a serial murderer on the streets. Let's not give them anything else to stir up the public.'

Bentz wasn't about to argue. His post was tentative at best in the department, and he was only helping out with homicide, mainly because of Melinda. He wasn't going to blow it. He'd do whatever she asked. His duties included everything from burglary and arson to domestic violence. And he agreed with her one hundred percent about keeping the Dr. Sam story quiet. The last thing they needed was copycats calling up the station.

There would probably be enough of those as there was just from her audience.

'I'll check it out,' he said, and shoved the Rosa Gillette file aside. He'd spent the last few hours going over the autopsy report and evidence on the prostitute's murder. She glanced down at his notes.

'Don't give up on the murders,' she said, 'but do check out Samantha Leeds. It looks like she's got herself a bona fide nutcase. I just want to make sure he's not dangerous.'

'You got it,' he said, ignoring the computer screen where pictures of the two dead women, Rosa Gillette and Cherie Bellechamps, flickered side by side.

'I know you'd rather work on this,' she said, motioning to the autopsy reports. 'And I don't blame you. But we've got other things to worry about as well, and the Homicide team can handle it.'

He lifted a disbelieving eyebrow. He had more experience than the other men, but didn't say it. He couldn't. Because once before he'd given it all up.

'Brinkman will be back soon.' Melinda peered at him through rimless glasses. Smart, savvy, forever dressed in a suit, her makeup and short hair always perfect, she was his direct superior, but never threw her weight around. She didn't mention that without her he wouldn't have gotten the job here in New Orleans; they both knew it. 'Look, Rick, I know you're overworked, overwrought and underpaid, but we're short-staffed with vacations and officers out sick. I understand that you don't like being shuffled from one area to the other, but until your next review, that's just the way it is.' She offered him one of her infrequent smiles. 'Besides, once upon a time you told me you didn't want to work murder investigations any longer.'

'Maybe I changed my mind.'

'I hope so. In the meantime, I'd like you to talk to Samantha Leeds.'

It wasn't a request; it was an order. He understood. But it didn't mean he had to like it. Not when there was more important work to do – a killer on the loose.

'Montoya can help you with the legwork.'

He nodded. 'You owe me one.'

'And you owe me a dozen. Payback time.'

'I thought I was past all that.' But he knew he never would be. The past had a way of hanging on, like a bad smell. You just couldn't wash it off. No matter how hard you scrubbed. He didn't just owe Melinda his job, but also life as he knew it.

'Okay, look,' she said, tilting her head to one side and studying him. 'I'll pass your good intentions and deeds on to the powers that be. It'll make points.'

Bentz leaned back in his chair and offered her a half smile. 'And here I thought *you* were the powers that be. The way people talk I figured you were some kind of goddess around here.'

Behind the fashionable lenses her eyes twinkled. She pointed a finger straight at his chest. 'God. I'm God. All-powerful and without gender. It would behoove you to remember that.'

He gave her the once-over. Beneath her navy suit, she hid a toned, fit body. Nice chest, small waist and long legs. 'The without gender part might be hard to forget.'

'Watch it. That could be construed as sexual harassment these days.'

'My ass. *You're* the boss.'

'Don't forget it.' His phone rang, and she added, 'Fill me in once you talk to Ms. Leeds, okay?'

'As I said before, "you owe me."'

'And hell's about to freeze over.'

She walked away, and Bentz snagged the receiver from its cradle. 'Rick Bentz.'

'Montoya,' his partner replied, and from the buzzy connection Bentz guessed the younger detective was talking on his cell phone while driving his unmarked. Probably pushing the speed limit. 'Guess what? I got a call from Marvin Cooper, you remember him over at the Riverview Apartments where we found the last victim – the Gillette woman?'

'Yep.' Bentz leaned back in his chair until it groaned in protest.

'So he tells me that Denise, the roommate, she's asked about Rosa's ankle bracelet. Says she always wore one, it was a gift or something. So I hightailed it over to the apartment building and Marvin tracks down Denise and she tells me about the gold bracelet.'

Bentz rolled his chair back to his desk and, cradling the phone between his shoulder and ear, searched through the reports on Rosa Gillette. 'She wasn't wearing any jewelry,' he said into the mouthpiece as he pulled up the files on Rosa Gillette and Cherie Bellechamps. 'Neither was the first one.' He double-checked the photos flickering on his computer.

'Maybe it's nothing,' Montoya said. 'But maybe not. Denise thinks maybe the third hooker, Cindy Sweet, might have ripped Rosa off. I don't think so.'

'Our perp wouldn't be the first guy to take home a little souvenir.' Rick zoomed in on the images of the victims, Rosa's ankles, then both women's entire bodies. Nope. No jewelry visible. So the killer was taking trophies. Not a surprise.

'Anything else I oughtta know? Shit!' There was a blast of a car horn over the crackle of the cell phone. 'Some idiot nearly pulled into my lane. Christ, doesn't anyone know how to drive in this town?'

'Only you, Montoya, only you. We'll talk later.' Bentz frowned down at the report Melinda had handed him. 'I've got to go out for a while. Jaskiel asked me personally to look in on a radio DJ who's getting threatening calls.'

'Like you don't have enough to do.'

'Exactly.' He hung up, spit out his tasteless gum, hankered for a cigarette and grabbed his jacket.

Sam ran her fingers over the bindings of the books she'd held on to since college. Though she hadn't looked at the tomes in years, she kept them on the bottom shelf of her bookcase in the den, just in case. She was certain she had a copy of Milton's *Paradise Lost* from some required English literature course she'd had to take during her years at Tulane University. 'I know it's here,' she muttered to Charon as he hopped onto her desk. Then she saw it. 'Aha!' Smiling, she pulled out the hardback and tucked it under her arm. '*Voilà*. Come on, you, let's go down to the dock for a little R&R.'

She stashed the receiver to her cordless phone, the book, a can of Diet Coke and her sunglasses in a canvas bag that was already bulging from her beach towel, then, wincing against the pain in her ankle, walked outside and down a brick path to the dock. The sun was high, sending rays of light glancing over the water. Dozens of boats skimmed the lake's surface and water-skiers and fishermen were out in abundance.

Sam loved it here; the house had already started to feel like home. Though David had argued relentlessly that she could have had as much success in Houston, she loved New Orleans and this spot that she called home. For the first six months she'd lived in an apartment closer to the heart of the city. Then she'd found this cottage and fallen in love with it. Despite its morbid history. David had really blown a gasket over that one – that she'd actually bought a place and put down roots. In a house where a murder had been committed.

A *solved* murder she told herself, a crime of passion.

She settled into a chaise under the table umbrella, popped her can of soda and flipped open the pages of the musty-smelling book. Maybe this was a long shot; maybe 'John's' calls had nothing to do with Milton's epic, but she couldn't ignore the feeling that there was some connection, if only a feeble one.

Pelicans and seagulls flew overhead, and a jet cut across the clear blue sky as Sam skimmed the text wherein Satan and his army have been thrown into hell and the fiery lake.

'It is "Better to reign in Hell than to serve in Heaven,"' she whispered, reading Satan's words from the text. 'Now, there's a line.' She glanced at the cat stalking a butterfly that flitted out of his reach over the water. 'Yeah, I know. I'm probably waaaay off base here.' Quickly scanning the pages, she wondered if she'd misinterpreted the caller's intent when he'd phoned.

She lost herself in the words as she sipped her drink while basking in the warmth of the sun. Bees hummed, a lawn mower chewed blades of grass somewhere down the street and Mrs. Killingsworth's pug started barking wildly, probably at a squirrel or a kid on a bike. A boat engine coughed, echoing across the water, sputtering and gasping. Sam didn't pay any attention. Just kept reading, her mind conjuring up the images Milton had scribed over three hundred years earlier.

The sun had lowered considerably when she looked up and saw the sailboat; not just any sailboat, but the same sloop she'd seen docked at Milo Swanson's house, the very boat she'd thought had been gliding the waters late at night, though the sails were now down and the boat was being propelled by an engine that hesitated and died, only to cough and start up again.

A man was straining at the wheel, guiding the sloop closer to the dock and for once, it seemed, Mrs. Killingsworth was right. Even from a distance, she could tell he was fit, strong, and good-looking. His shirt was open, flapped in the wind and offered a view of a broad, tanned chest gleaming in the sunlight. Cut-off jeans hung from his hips, fraying over athletic thighs that strained as he kept his footing. His body glistened with sweat. Thick, dark hair blew across a high, tanned forehead. Dark glasses covered his eyes, and sitting at his feet, nose to the wind, was a dog, some kind of German shepherd mix, she guessed.

With difficulty he guided the dying craft into Sam's slip, then threw his line over a mooring and tied up. As if he knew her. As if it was his right. The engine gave up a final growl, then died.

Sam straightened in the chair and set her book aside as she studied an angled face with strong cheekbones and a square jaw covered with a couple of days' worth of shadow. Nope. She didn't recognize him as he scrambled over the deck and started working on the engine. He didn't so much as cast a glance her way.

She pushed herself upright and got to her feet. 'Can I help you?'

No response. He was too engrossed in his work.

'Hello?' She walked along the dock. The dog gave off a sharp bark and finally he glanced over his shoulder.

'Sorry,' he said, still working on the engine. 'Got a problem here. Thought I could make it home, but . . . oh, damn.' He slanted her a self-deprecating grin, then turned his attention to the engine. 'This darned thing decided to give up the ghost.'

'Can I help?'

He stared at her from behind dark glasses anchored over a slightly crooked nose. 'You a mechanic?'

'I have been on a boat before.'

He considered, looked her over once again. 'Sure, come aboard. But it's not just the engine. The damned keel's been giving me trouble, and the sails are ripped. I shouldn't have taken her out today.' Frustration lined his forehead where thick, coffee-colored hair caught in the breeze. He straightened and slapped the boom with an open palm. 'I knew better.'

Barefooted, she climbed carefully onto the deck, wincing just a bit when she put all her weight on her bad ankle. 'I'm Samantha,' she said. 'Samantha Leeds.'

'Ty Wheeler. I live right around that point.' He gestured to the small jetty of land, then squatted near the engine and fiddled with a wire or two. Satisfied, he tried the ignition. It ground. The engine sputtered. Wound down pitifully. Ty swore under his breath. 'Look, it's no use. Probably the fuel line. I need to run to the house and grab some more tools.' He swiped the sweat from his forehead and scowled up at the boat. 'She's not mine, not yet. I'm just trying her out.' He shook his head. 'Now I know why she's such a bargain. *Bright Angel*, my ass. More like *Satan's Revenge*. Maybe I'll rename her if I decide to buy.'

Sam didn't move a muscle. She couldn't breathe for a second and told herself she was overreacting. It was a coincidence he'd mentioned Satan, that was all. So she was skimming through the pages of *Paradise Lost*, so what? There was nothing to it. *Nothing*.

He checked his watch, then the lowering sun. 'Do you mind if I leave her here? I'll run down and get my tools. I live just down the street, about half a mile.' He checked his watch and frowned. 'Damn it all.' Glancing up at her again, he said, 'I really thought I could make it back to my dock, but she' – he glared at the engine – 'had other ideas. I'll try to get back today, but, it might be tomorrow. I've got to be somewhere in an hour.'

'I suppose that would be okay,' Sam said, and before she could second-guess herself he was out of the boat, dog at his heels, marching toward the house.

Shading her eyes, she watched as he crossed the broad expanse of lawn, passed under one of the shade trees, rounded the porch and headed for the gate near the front of the house, as if he'd known exactly where it was.

Though that wasn't such a big leap. The gate had to be on one side of the house or the other. He had a 50 percent chance of figuring it out. He'd just gotten lucky.

She settled into her deck chair again and opened the book, but she couldn't concentrate and soon she heard Hannibal barking madly, then thought she heard a car pull into the drive over the rise of the wind. Slamming the book shut, she got up too quickly, felt a pain in her left ankle and muttered to herself at her own stupidity.

By the time she reached the back porch, she heard the soft peal of her doorbell and she flew through the rooms yelling, 'I'm coming.' At the door she looked through the peephole and saw a tall, barrel-chested man wearing a tan jacket. His hands were jammed into his pockets and he was chewing gum as if his life depended on it. Sam opened the door as far as the chain lock would allow.

'What can I do for you?'

'Samantha Leeds?'

'Yes.'

'Rick Bentz, New Orleans Police Department.' He flipped open a black wallet that displayed his badge and ID. Gray eyes drilled into hers. 'You filed a report down at the station. This is a follow-up call.'

Everything looked in order, the picture on his ID matched the face staring sternly at her, so Sam unlocked the chain and opened the door. Bentz walked in, and Sam sensed the man was keyed up. 'Let's go over what happened,' he suggested. 'We can start with' – he glanced down at his notes – 'the call you got at the station and, it says here you got a threatening letter here at the house. You called the local police about it.'

'And the message left on my machine while I was on vacation. This way.' She guided him into the den, handed him a copy of the letter and marred photograph, then changed tapes in her answering machine. 'These are both copies. The originals are with the Cambrai police.'

'Good.'

Sam played the message that had haunted her for nearly a week.

Bentz listened hard as he stared at the publicity photo with her eyes cut out.

'*I know what you did, and you're not going to get away with it. You're going to have to pay for your sins.*' The voice she'd become so familiar with oozed through the room, filling the corners, sliding behind the curtains, scraping her mind.

'What sins?' Bentz asked, and a glimmer of interest sparked in his eyes as he scanned the room, taking stock, she supposed, of her small library and equipment.

'I don't know.' Sam was honest. 'I can't figure it out.'

'And the calls to the radio station, they were about the same topic – sin?' he asked, his gaze moving over the desk and book-case as if he were studying her den to get a better picture of who she was.

'Yes. He, um, he called himself John, told me that he knew me, that he was, and I quote, "my John." When I said I knew lots of them, he insinuated that I'd been with a lot of men and he, um, he called me a slut. I cut him off.'

'Have you ever dated or been involved with a John?'

'I've thought about that,' she said. 'Sure. It's a common enough name. I think I went out with John Petri in high school and a guy named John . . . oh, God, I don't remember his last name in college but that's about it. Neither one of them were more than a couple of dates and nothing happened. I was a kid, and so were they.'

'Okay, so go on. He called again?'

'Yes. The other night . . . it's on tape, but it was after the show. He called in and Tiny, he's the technician that was setting up for the next prerecorded show, took the call. The caller asked for me, said he was my "John" and that he hadn't called in earlier during the show because he'd been busy and that what had happened was my fault.'

'What had happened?'

'I don't know.' She shook her head. 'It was eerie and sounded sinister, but then I was jumpy. I thought I might come home and find my house burned down or ransacked or something, but . . . everything here was as I left it.'

'You're sure it was the same guy who called here?'

'Positive. But my number's unlisted.'

Bentz scowled down at the photo as he leaned against a corner of her desk. 'This is a publicity shot. Right? There were dozens of 'em made. Handed out.'

'Yeah.' She nodded.

'And this is a copy from one of those.'

She swallowed hard. 'I . . . I assume that he must have an original.'

'Why do you think he cut out your eyes?' he asked, his eyes thinning.

'To scare the hell out of me,' she said, 'and, for the record, it's working.'

'Did he ever mention your eyes or something you saw when he called?'

'No . . . not that I remember.'

'I'll need a copy of the tapes from your program.'

'I'll get them to you.'

'I'll get the original letter, picture and message tape from Cambrai.'

'Fine.'

'But you don't mind if I take these until I see the originals?'

'No.'

Carefully he placed the letter, envelope and picture in a plastic bag, then asked if he could look through the house. What he was looking for, she wasn't certain, but she gave him the tour and they ended up in the living room as dusk was beginning to settle outside. She turned on the Tiffany lamp near the window and listened to the sound of crickets and mosquitoes as he sat on the couch and she took a chair on the other side of the coffee table. The paddle fan turned slowly overhead.

'Just tell me what happened, from the beginning,' Bentz said as he placed a pocket recorder on the glass top of the table.

'I already told the officer at the station.'

'I know, but I'd like to hear it firsthand.'

'Fine. Okay. Well.' She rubbed her hands over her knees. 'It all started when I got back from Mexico . . .' She launched into her tale, told him about losing her ID in the boating accident in Mexico, again explained about the letter she received, the threatening call on her answering machine and the phone calls to the station. She mentioned that she'd thought someone had been watching her house, then dismissed it as a case of nerves. All the while Bentz wrote in a small notepad and recorded what she was saying.

'You ever get threats like this before?'

'Nothing so personal,' she said. 'There are always crank calls. It comes with the territory, but most of them are screened. Once in a while somebody gets through.'

'Do you know anyone who would want to hurt you, or just scare you?'

'No,' she said, though David's image flashed through her mind.

'What about your family?'

'I don't have much,' she admitted. 'My father's a retired insurance broker and lives in LA in the house where I grew up. My mother passed away and my brother . . . well, he disappeared a long time ago. About ten years, just around the time Mom died. I . . . I, uh, haven't heard from him in years. For all

I know, he could be dead, too.' She linked her fingers and felt the same deep sadness she always did when she thought of Peter. As children they'd been close, as adolescents, they'd drifted farther and farther apart and as adults they'd had nothing in common.

'Names?'

'What? Oh, Dad's is Bill, er, William Matheson and my brother is Peter, Peter William. My dad doesn't have a middle name.'

'Address?'

She gave it to him from memory and explained that she had friends scattered all over the country, and a couple of cousins in the Bay Area near San Mateo. Other than that, she had no family to speak of.

'You were married?'

Sam nodded. 'Yes. It was a long time ago.'

He lifted his eyebrows, encouraging her to continue. 'I was a freshman at Tulane University when I met Jeremy.'

'Jeremy Leeds?'

'*Dr.* Jeremy Leeds. He was a professor. My professor. He taught, er, teaches philosophy.' And she'd been a fool to fall for him, a naive girl who'd been enamored by an unconventional teacher – handsome, a rogue, one with a brilliant mind and a sexy smile.

'He's still there? At Tulane?' Bentz asked, looking up from his notes.

'As far as I know.' She met the questions in the detective's eyes. 'Jeremy and I don't talk. Haven't for years. We didn't have children, and he remarried soon after our divorce. Other than that, I don't know anything about him.'

'But you live in the same town,' Bentz pointed out.

'City. New Orleans is pretty big, and I left for a while. Lived in Houston.'

'Were you married then?'

'Yes, but the marriage was falling apart. I thought it might just be a separation, but it turned out differently. I stayed. We split up.' She glanced out the window, didn't want to think about those years.

'You haven't married since?'

'No.' She shook her head and leaned back against the cushions. Glancing at the clock near the archway leading to the kitchen, she realized Ty had left over an hour earlier. He'd said he might be back today or tomorrow. She crossed her fingers and hoped he'd be delayed because she didn't really know how she could explain him to the policeman.

'Been involved with anyone lately?' Bentz was asking, and Sam was brought back to the inquisition.

Here we go, she thought, and realized that one of the reasons she hadn't wanted to contact the police was because she didn't want to involve David. 'Not currently, no, but I have had a few boyfriends since I was married.'

'Anyone named John?'

'Just the ones I told you about. Years ago. No one since.'

He scratched another note as Charon wandered into the dining room from the kitchen, a black shadow that hid beneath the table and peered through the legs of the chairs. 'The cat belongs to you?'

'Yes. Three years now.'

'And the boat?' He looked through the open French doors and past the few trees to the dock where Ty's sloop was moored, the masts visible in the gathering darkness.

'No. That's a friend's . . . well, actually a neighbor's.' She explained, and the cop stopped writing, just stared at her as if she'd announced she'd just flown in from Jupiter.

'So he's a stranger?'

'Well, yes, but . . . He said he'd come back for the boat later today or possibly tomorrow. He just lives down the street and had some trouble with the sails and his engine.'

Bentz frowned. Lines creased his forehead. 'Listen, let me give you some advice, okay? Lock your doors, use your alarm system, don't go out alone and don't acquaint yourself with strangers. Even neighbors.' He ran stiff fingers through his hair, pushing brown curls off his forehead. He seemed about to say more, as if he intended to give her a lecture, then thought better of it. 'Okay, you get the picture. Now, do you have anyone who would consider you an enemy?'

'"Enemy" is a pretty harsh term.'

He shrugged.

'The only person I can think of is Trish LaBelle, and I wouldn't call her an enemy, more of a rival. She works over at WNAB, hosts a show similar to mine. There's been talk of some kind of feud between us, but generally we just avoid each other when we're at the same social or charity function. I wouldn't really call her an enemy, and I don't think she's behind anything like this. In fact, it wouldn't make much sense because though the calls scare the hell out of me, they increase ratings. Listeners are intrigued with it. It's the same mentality as a crowd gathering around a building that's on fire, or other motorists rubbernecking at an accident scene.'

'So you're thinking that it would make more sense for someone at the station to be behind it, to try and boost ratings?'

'No way! That's . . . that's sick. Who would terrorize an employee to improve the listenership?'

'You tell me.'

'It's not what I was thinking. It just makes more sense than blaming Trish.'

He didn't comment, but asked, 'Any other people jealous of you? Want your job? Or hold a grudge against you?'

Again, she thought of David. Damn, why did she feel that she had to protect him? 'Not that I know of. Nothing recent.'

'What about the guy on the desk?' Bentz asked, as if he could read her thoughts. 'You said you weren't dating anyone, but you've got some guy's picture near the computer and it's not the same guy in the graduation shot. That one's your brother, right?'

'Yes. Peter. The other one is a man I was dating, David Ross.'

'But you broke it off? Or did he?'

'It was my idea not to see each other anymore.'

'He go along with that?' Clearly Bentz was skeptical.

'He had to,' she said bluntly.

Bentz rubbed his chin. 'But he didn't like it.'

'No. He thinks, er, thought we should get married.'

'You were engaged?'

'No.'

'He give you a ring?'

She felt her cheeks burn. 'He tried. Last Christmas. But . . . I couldn't accept it.'

'So that's when you told him it was over?'

'That's when it started falling apart. I'd dated him for about five or six months, then decided to take the job here, in New Orleans. George Hannah had left the station in Houston and moved to New Orleans a few years ago, then convinced Eleanor, my boss, to work for him at WSLJ. It was George's idea to resurrect the Dr. Sam show here and Eleanor agreed. Eleanor had to do some fast talking for me to join on but I figured it was time.'

'To move from Houston?'

'And to get behind the mike again. I'd given it up nine years ago, there was . . . a difficult incident at the station and I went into private practice for a few years, but Eleanor convinced me that I belonged in radio and the truth was that I missed it, I felt that I helped a lot of people.'

'But you gave it up for a while.'

'Maybe that was a mistake,' she admitted. 'I let one bad incident sway me and I decided to give it another shot. It was time for a change in my life and I knew someone who would take over my practice, that my patients would be in good hands.' That was glossing over her rationale for leaving radio nine years ago, but she saw no reason to go into the details of that horrid time in her life right now.

'Did David Ross agree?' Bentz asked, taking notes. 'That you belonged in radio.'

'Hardly.' She still remembered the pinch of David's lips when she'd told him her decision. His shock. It was almost as if he thought she was betraying him. 'He didn't like the idea at all, but my mind was made up, so I moved here last October and he tried to give me the ring at Christmas and then we just saw less and less of each other. Until Mexico. He bought the trip as a surprise, and I decided to go, just to see if I'd made a mistake by trying to break it off.'

'Had you?'

'No.'

'But you still keep his picture.'

Sam sighed. 'Yeah, I know. It's not that I don't *like* him. I just don't think we're right for each other.' She caught herself and stiffened her shoulders. 'I don't think we need to get into the ins and outs of my love life.'

'Unless he's the caller.'

'I said, it's not him,' she reminded him, bristling. 'I'd recognize his voice.'

Bentz didn't let up. 'When was the last time you saw him?'

'About a week ago,' she admitted, as Charon hopped into her lap. 'In Mexico.'

'On that surprise trip?' Was there just a hint of judgment in his tone?

'Yes. I met him in Mazatlán . . . he thought it was going to be romantic, and as I said I just wanted to be sure I hadn't made a mistake.' She read the questions in his eyes. 'Believe me, I hadn't. If I wasn't sure before, I am now.'

'You didn't mention him before.' It was a statement, not a question.

'I know, but he couldn't have left the message or sent the letter; it was postmarked here, in New Orleans, and he was in Mexico. It wasn't his voice on the tape. I would have recognized it, if it was. He didn't call in, Detective.'

Bentz's jaw slid to the side as if he didn't believe a word she was feeding him. 'I'm out here because you filed a report,' he said slowly, as if to a stubborn child. 'I expect your cooperation.'

'I am cooperating,' she argued, though even she heard her defensive tone. It was true, the man got her back up. She felt as if she had to justify her actions.

'But you're holding back,' he accused, staring at her so intently she wanted to squirm.

'I just don't want a big scandal, okay? I'm a celebrity of sorts around these parts, but because I'm on the radio, the general public doesn't really know what I look like. I have some anonymity, and I'd like to keep it that way.'

He chewed on that for a while, nodded, as if he understood, and finally snapped his notebook shut, clicked off the recorder and pocketed both. 'I think this about covers it, but I'll want copies of his calls to the station and I'll check on the phone records and get back to you.' He pushed up from the couch.

'Thanks.'

'You might want to keep a low profile.'

She nearly laughed out loud. 'That could be tricky, Detective. I am a radio personality and though most people don't recognize me on the street, some do. I'm involved in a lot of charity work. In fact the station's hosting a big event soon for the Boucher Center. I'll be there. I can't exactly hole up and hide.'

'You should consider it.'

She shook her head. 'We both know I can't. Why don't you just catch the guy.'

'We will, but in the meantime' – he glanced at the cat purring contentedly on her lap – 'you might consider trading in kitty for a rottweiler or a Doberman. You know, a mean sumbitch.'

'Charon's pretty tough,' she said, as the cat stretched and started licking himself as if to prove her wrong.

The hint of a smile touched the gruff man's lips. 'That's good to know,' he said as she gently shoved Charon aside and walked Bentz to the door. 'The department could save a lot of money by using alley cats rather than trained dogs. I'll write up a report for the commissioner. I'm sure he'll be in touch with the K-9 Division.'

'Glad to be of help,' she quipped as she walked him to the door.

He paused on the porch, his light mood disappearing as he stepped into the thickening twilight. 'Just remember to lock your door. The caller might only be a prankster, but I doubt it. Phoning into a radio-station talk show is one thing, sending this' – he lifted the plastic bag containing her mutilated publicity picture – 'is another. Whoever did this is a real sicko, and he wants to scare the life out of you.'

'I know,' she said as she shut the door and threw the new dead bolt, grateful that she'd had her locks changed and the alarm system jury-rigged. The system was old and faulty, and the alarm company had promised to install a new one 'in a couple of weeks.' In the meantime she was stuck with this dinosaur.

She thought of everything that happened to her in the past few days and tried to convince herself that the person terrorizing her wasn't out to harm her, but the truth of the matter was she was scared to death.

8

'. . . so I never see my old man,' Anisha said with a frown. She was one of the six girls who had shown up for the session and was slumped in an old easy chair, her ankles crossed, her expression dark. Nervously, she twirled a lock of curly black hair around her finger. 'I guess I shouldn't expect to.'

'Have you tried to contact him?'

'In jail?' Anisha snorted through her nose. 'Why should I?' Her smile was far too cynical for her fifteen years. 'I got me a stepdaddy. My third one.'

And so it went. Six troubled girls, all with problems, all with chips the size of oil tankers on their slim shoulders, all to varying degrees, trying to get their young acts together.

The session was housed in an old camel-backed shotgun house not far from Armstrong Park. It was early evening, the sun was just beginning to set. The small room was hot, the jalousie blinds half-open, allowing in the barest of breezes and the sounds of traffic from Rampart Street. The back of Sam's blouse was sticking to her despite the fan rotating from a table in the corner.

The girls were flopped on old chairs and a couch, talking about getting back into school, or staying in, or taking night classes as some of the teenagers had babies of their own. Some brought up the benefit for the center; they were excited, they'd been asked to attend and were looking forward to it. But Leanne, uncharacteristically quiet, sat next to Samantha and brooded, as if guarding a secret, though Sam suspected it was Leanne's way of punishing Sam for being gone for nearly three weeks.

'Is anything bothering you?' she asked the girl at a lull in the session. 'Something you want to talk about?'

Leanne lifted a shoulder. She was a pretty girl with porcelain white skin, brown hair and green eyes. Right now, she was playing with the fronds of a potted fern, trying to show disinterest.

'She's just mad cuz her and Jay broke up,' Renee, a heavyset black girl accused around a wad of gum.

'That's not it,' Leanne shot back, but quit fiddling with the plant long enough to skewer her friend with a harsh glare. A telltale blush crept up the back of her neck to ears studded with half a dozen pieces of metal.

'She's usin' again,' Renee added, lifting a dark, knowing eyebrow.

'Are you?'

'Just when I split with Jay. And it was my idea.' Leanne inched up her chin insolently. 'He tried to control me.'

'Cuz he didn't want you usin' any of that shit,' Renee said.

'Ain't no one controls me.'

'Yeah, right,' Renee scoffed, rolling her eyes.

Sam held up a hand. 'Let's hear what Leanne has to say.'

'I don't want to say nothin',' the girl insisted, crossing her thin arms under her breasts and looking pointedly away from Sam. She shot Renee another look that was guaranteed to kill. 'And you just shut up. It ain't none of your business.'

'Maybe we should all think about that,' Sam cut in, diffusing the argument before it exploded out of control. 'We'll discuss it next time. Everyone think about boundaries. When do you give a friend space? When do you step in? What are the consequences? Okay?'

Grumbling, the girls shuffled to their collective feet.

'I'll see you all next week, and if anyone runs into Collette, ask her to join.'

'Collette moved,' Renee said. 'Up ta Tampa.'

This was news to Sam. All the girls were supposed to tell her if there was a change in their living arrangements, though few ever did.

Talking among themselves, the girls picked up their books, backpacks and purses, then clambered down the stairs, platform shoes stomping on the bare wood. Leanne hung back, ostracized for the moment by Renee, who, whenever Leanne was in disfavor, became the leader. Renee smiled at Sam, then sent Leanne a smug look.

'I hate that fat bitch,' Leanne grumbled.

'Can you rephrase that.'

'I hate that big, fat fuckin' bitch.'

'That's not what I mean.'

'I know what you mean.' Leanne scowled as she snagged her purse from the couch. 'But I hate her.'

'Are you angry with her or yourself?'

Leanne started for the door. 'I don't need any of this shit.'

'Yeah, I think you do.'

'But Renee's a pig.' The girl whirled and faced Sam again. 'She's always stickin' her nose in where it don't belong. Rootin' around, like my granddaddy's old sow out in the field.' She made snorting noises to accentuate her point.

'Maybe she's trying to be a friend,' Sam suggested.

'A friend? Renee Harp don't know the meanin' of the word. She'd turn on me like that.' Leanne snapped her fingers. 'Besides, it ain't none of her business. What goes on between me and Jay that's our shit.'

'Do you want to talk about it?'

'Time's up, ain't it?'

Sam stuffed her notes into her briefcase. 'We can talk on the way out.'

'It ain't no big deal.' Green eyes studied the edge of the carpet, where fringe covered polished wood. There was a long pause and an even longer sigh. 'I did get high,' she admitted, looking younger than her seventeen years despite her harsh makeup and too-tight clothes. 'I just had a lot of pressure, that's all. Marletta was on my case and . . . then Jay got pissed at me and I thought I'd show them both.'

'By smoking crack.'

'Yeah. So?' She started down the stairs, not wanting to hear a lecture, thought Sam had no intention of giving her one.

'You tell me.' Sam caught up with her on the first floor, where Leanne was walking through the series of rooms to the front door. The girl shouldered it open and stepped down to the sidewalk where the heat of the day had collected.

Twilight had descended, the streetlamps were beginning to glow and the other girls in the group were already walking down the street chattering, two smoking long cigarettes. They split up at the corner, heading in different directions and disappearing along narrow streets.

'Maybe it wasn't such a great idea to get high,' Leanne admitted as they stood beneath a streetlight. She seemed sincere as she cocked her head to look directly at Sam for the first time in over an hour.

'Just think about it. You were trying to punish your mother and your boyfriend, but who did you hurt? What did you accomplish?'

Leanne rolled her expressive eyes. 'Myself, I know.' She smiled and it was a killer smile, perfect white teeth and pretty lips.

'So, how do you feel?'

'I'm okay.'

'You're sure?' Sam asked. There was something about Leanne that touched her. Beneath her armor of filthy language and tough attitude was a softer soul, one who sent her e-cards, a little girl trapped in a tough-looking teenage body.

'Yeah, I'm sure. For a screwup,' she said, and laughed as a pack of teenage boys sauntered by. More than one of the boys eyed Leanne. Out of habit she tossed her short hair out of her face and met the boys' gazes with a challenging, amused grin.

'You're not a screwup,' Sam assured her. 'Remember, no negative names.'

'Right. I'm *not* one, but I did mess up. Big-time.'

'You took a step backward. Now it's time to go forward again.'

'Yeah, I know,' Leanne said, but her gaze was following the boys, who had stopped two streets up to join a group of people listening to the street musicians who were performing in front of the park.

'Then I'll see you next week.'

'Okay. Sure.' With a wave, Leanne dashed across St. Peter, pausing at the next corner to light a cigarette. She was a smart girl, whose mother, Marletta, had been arrested not only for dealing drugs but prostitution as well. Marletta, faced with losing her kids, had been clean for a couple of years, but Leanne had watched and learned from her mother. At seventeen Leanne had her own rap sheet for drugs and soliciting. Attending Sam's young women's group, being a part of a drug-counseling program that included routine testing and doing community service were all a part of her sentence.

Sam headed for her car but felt something, someone watching her. Assuming it was Leanne, she glanced over her shoulder, but the girl was nowhere in sight. The crowd that had paused to watch the band was increasing as the music played, people gathering around the brass ensemble that had set up near the entrance to the park. But one man stood apart from the others – a tall, broad-shouldered man in a black-leather jacket, dark pants and sunglasses despite the shadows crawling across the city. He wasn't looking at the performers. Instead he was staring straight at Samantha. Hard. He was too far away, and it was too dark to get a good look at his features, but Sam had the sensation that she'd seen him before, perhaps even knew him.

Goose bumps rose on her flesh, though she told herself she was being silly, for as she watched, he turned his attention to the band, melded into the group of people surrounding the musicians and seemed to disappear.

As if he'd never been there.

Maybe he hadn't been looking at her, but someone or something behind her. Maybe she was letting the events of the last few nights get to her, but as she walked along the street to her Mustang, she had the very real sensation that things were only going to get worse.

★　　★　　★

The night was hot, just the way he liked it, the air heavy against his skin as he paddled through the cypress to the tiny cabin on stilts hidden here, deep in the bayou. No one knew about this place; no one could ever know. He docked and climbed up a ladder to the bleached white porch surrounding the one-room shanty. The smell of the swamp filled his nostrils, the feeling he was free here, safe, made his tense muscles relax. He loosened his fly and took a piss over the railing, not only relieving himself, but letting the other creatures of the night know this was his place. *His.*

He heard the bats in the trees as he zipped up. Boots ringing hollowly, he made his way inside the cabin, where he lit a kerosene lantern. The ancient wood walls, filled with knotholes and gaps between the boards, glowed warmly. Mosquitoes droned, fireflies flickered through the open doorway and the sluggish water lapped against the old pilings. Alligators and cottonmouths swam in this part of the bayou, and he felt akin to the slippery beasts, a part of this dark night, this water forest.

There was no electricity, and the old chimney had started to crumble, not that he would dare light a fire. Smoke could be seen or smelled ... no, he would keep in the relative darkness, only chancing the lantern. He opened the single cupboard and peered inside. A spider scurried into a crack as he reached into a corner where a worn velvet sack lay hidden. Inside the soft folds were his treasures, items he carefully withdrew. A cross suspended from a necklace. A fine gold chain just big enough to fit around a woman's slim ankle. An old locket from another lifetime. Just the beginning.

Carefully he placed his treasures on the rickety table next to his battery-powered radio. He surrounded the necklace, locket and ankle bracelet with his rosary, creating a perfect circle with his souvenirs squarely in its center. Then, satisfied, he checked his watch, waited forty-five seconds and pressed a button on the radio. Then she was with him. Over the hoot of an owl and crackle of static he heard the sound of the fading intro music and her voice – clear as if she were standing next to him.

'Good evening, New Orleans, this is Dr. Sam ready to take your calls at WSLJ. As you know we've been tackling a series of tough subjects about love, sin and redemptions. Tonight we'll discuss forgiveness . . .'

He smiled inwardly. Forgiveness. She was purposely baiting him, engaging in his game. Expecting him to call. He conjured up her face in his mind, remembered seeing her only a few hours earlier on the street near the park. She must have felt his gaze, been drawn to him, for she'd looked straight at him in the twilight.

Blood pumped furiously through his body, ringing in his ears, bringing an erection.

'. . . let me know what you think, how forgiveness has touched your life or conversely, how it hasn't? Is it always possible?' she asked in that smooth, coaxing, sexy voice, the voice of a Jezebel, a seducer, a whore. Sweat broke out between his shoulder blades, and he stood, walking restlessly, concentrating on the words – her words – touching him, caressing his mind, just as if she was speaking to him. Only to him. 'What is it that constitutes forgiveness and can we always give it?'

The answer was no. Some acts were too vile to be forgiven and for those there was only one answer: retribution. His cock was suddenly rock-hard, straining against his fly. He needed relief. He imagined her hands, her mouth, her tongue as he touched himself.

Dr. Sam's voice was farther away now, muffled by the static on the radio and the buzz in his mind, but soon, oh, so soon, Samantha Leeds would understand.

About forgiveness and retribution.

About atonement and punishment.

About paying.

For her sins.

All of them.

He'd make her.

Just you wait, Doctor. Your time is coming. Then we'll see what you think about forgiveness, he thought, stroking himself.

Then we'll hear you beg.

9

'I don't like it, Sam,' William Matheson was saying from his condo in Santa Monica the next morning. The phone connection was clear and her father sounded as if he was in the next room rather than over a thousand miles away. 'I don't like it at all.'

'Neither do I,' Sam admitted, balancing the receiver against her shoulder as she laced up her Nikes, 'but it's all part and parcel of the business.'

'Then give it up. Open a private practice. All this radio stuff is just fluff. Doesn't do anyone a whole lot of good, and it sounds dangerous.'

'I shouldn't have told you,' she said, straightening and tossing her hair from her eyes.

'I would have found out.'

'I know. That's why I thought I should give you the straight scoop.'

He sighed, and she sensed his frustration. Life hadn't turned out the way her father had planned. Not for him, not for his wife, or children.

'I just don't want to see you go through a replay of that nasty business in Houston.'

'I won't,' she said, but felt a chill deep in her heart.

'I don't have to remind you it all started with a phone call to the station.'

'No, Dad, you don't. I remember it all very well.' *As if it were yesterday*, she added silently as she walked from the living room into the kitchen. Goose bumps rose on her arm when she remembered the plaintive worried call from a desperate girl.

'Well, just keep it in mind, will you? I worry.'

'I know you do. Enough for both of us . . . or maybe enough for a small city. Don't worry about me, Dad, I'm fine. Everyone at the station is alerted, and I've talked with the police. My guess is that whoever called has moved on. He had his twisted fun, and now he's off to torture small animals or scare kids in the park.'

'It's not funny.'

'I know, I know,' Sam said. 'I was just trying to lighten the mood.'

Her father hesitated. 'I don't suppose you've heard from Peter.' Sam closed her eyes. Mentally counted to ten. Always. Dad always asked about her brother.

'Of course I haven't.'

'I didn't expect it.' *But you keep asking. After ten years.* 'It's just that once you're a parent, you're a parent for life. You'll understand when you finally have kids of your own.'

'I imagine I will.' *Now comes the part where he tells me I'm not getting any younger, that Cousin Doreen has two kids in school and another on the way.*

'You know, Samantha, just because you had one marriage already, doesn't mean you have to swear off the institution. Your mother and I were married thirty-four years, and we experienced our ups and downs, but it was worth it, let me tell you.'

'I'm glad, Dad,' she said, though she sometimes didn't believe him. He'd survived his son's disappearance, his wife's death and focused on his only daughter, one who never seemed to listen to any of his advice. 'You know I love you.'

'I love you, too, sweetheart.'

'Are you still dating the widow across the hall?'

'Helen? No . . . well, it's not really dating. We just play golf or bridge together once in a while.'

'Trust me, she considers it a date.'

'Is that your professional opinion?' he asked, and Sam heard the smile in his voice. For the moment, his worries about his daughter were allayed.

'You bet it is. You'll be getting a bill.'

He laughed. 'No freebies for the old man?'

'Especially not for the old man. Look, Dad, I've got to run, but I'll call again. Soon.'

'Do that and, Samantha, be careful, would you?'

'Promise, Dad.'

'Good girl.' He hung up and Sam dropped the receiver into its cradle. She glanced out the window to the dock where the *Bright Angel* rocked against her moorings, sails down against a backdrop of blue sky. Shaking her head, Sam rubbed the tension from the back of her neck. No matter what she did, no matter how successful she became, how she proved herself, her father would always think of her as his little girl. Nor would he give up on Peter, despite the fact that whether it was a biological truth or not, in Sam's mind, her older brother was as good as dead.

Ty showed up sometime after noon. With a heavy toolbox and a bottle of wine. 'For your trouble,' he said as he handed her the bottle on her porch. Again his eyes were shaded, again he wore cutoffs, again the dog trotted after him. 'I got busy and it got dark, so I didn't come back yesterday . . . if I'd had your number, I would have called.'

'No problem,' she assured him, though she didn't quite believe her own words. There was something disturbing about the man, something inertly sensual and, she sensed, dangerous.

Or was she just getting paranoid?

Had the surly detective's warnings convinced her not to trust anyone?

As Ty skirted the house and took the outside path to the lake, Samantha stashed the bottle of Riesling in the refrigerator and caught a glimpse of herself in the cut-glass mirror of her antique sideboard. Her cheeks had colored, and she could use some lipstick but refused to stoop to primping for the guy. He was a neighbor with a boat problem. Nothing more.

Nothing.

She caught up with him on the dock. He was already working with the engine, his fingers wrapped around a wrench, his muscles straining as he twisted an old nut. 'You could have borrowed those from me, you know. I do have a few things – pliers, wrenches, a hammer.'

'I suppose, but I knew these would work. Right size. They came with the boat.' Glancing over his shoulder, he offered her a half smile. 'I took the tools out yesterday when I was checking for a leak. Left 'em on my dock, then took her out for a spin.' As if he anticipated some comment, he added, 'I know, not the brightest thing I've ever done. But I didn't think I'd need the motor.' He winced as he gave a bolt a final twist. 'You don't have to say it. I know I'm an idiot.'

'Simple mistake,' she said.

'Simple man,' he muttered under his breath, but she didn't believe him for a minute. She guessed there was nothing simple about Ty Wheeler; nothing simple at all. From the dock, the dog hopped lithely into the boat, took up a spot near the helm and lay down, head on his paws, brown eyes quietly assessing. Overhead, white clouds rolled slowly across a wide cerulean sky where a hawk circled lazily and the boom on the main sail slipped a little.

'Damn.' Ty glanced at the mast, then back at her. 'Wanna help?'

'Sure. But I'd better warn you, I'm not much of a sailor.'

Ty slanted her a look. 'Neither am I.' His shirtsleeves were bunched over his elbows as he rocked back on his heels. 'Think you can keep the boom steady for a couple of minutes?' he asked. 'It keeps slippin'.'

'I'll give it my best shot.'

'It's heavy.'

'I was a weight lifter in college.'

His gaze swept up and down her body, and he swallowed a smile. 'Yeah, right. I guess you never made it to the WWF, huh?'

'Okay, so I lied,' she admitted, stepping aboard. 'But I did play tennis.'

'A killer shot at the net isn't going to help us much. There, now hold on to this.' He placed her hands on the boom, then they both strained against the weight of it as he locked it into place once again.

'You okay?' Ty asked as he tested the lock. He pulled on the smooth wood. Sweat ran down the sides of his face, and he glared up at the rigging. The boom didn't budge. He glanced her way. 'You can let go now.'

Her arms ached a little. 'Didn't realize how outta shape I was.'

Again a quick glance down her body. 'We got the job done.' He removed his sunglasses long enough to swipe the sweat from his forehead and for the first time since she'd met him she was look-ing into dark hazel eyes – green-brown that shifted in the sunlight. 'Thanks.' He shoved the shades up to the bridge of his nose again.

'You're more than welcome. Anytime you need to, pull in for repairs.'

White teeth flashed. 'Let's hope it's not too often.' His gaze swept the deck of the *Bright Angel*. 'Maybe God is telling me I'm not cut out to be a boat owner. You know the old saying? What's the second happiest day of a boat owner's life?'

'I give. What?'

'The day he buys the boat. And what's the happiest day of his life?'

She waited.

'The day he sells it.'

She threw him a smile and motioned to the sloop. 'And I always thought guys had love affairs with these things.'

'Some do. But a boat is just like a woman. You've got to find the right one. Sometimes you make a mistake. Other times you get lucky.' He was staring at her through the dark lenses. Hard.

'And they say men are like cars – never perfect. Never coming with all the right options.'

'And what are those?' he asked.

'I don't think I know you well enough to say,' she teased as she climbed off the sloop. Pain shot up her bad ankle, and she winced.

'Are you okay?'

'Just an old war wound kicking up.' The pain lessened as she watched him fiddle with the engine. With pliers, wrenches and other tools she didn't recognize, he worked on the motor, tried to start the boat, wasn't satisfied with the sputter that commenced and leaned over the engine again. His old dog waited patiently in the shade of the wheel, brown eyes watching Ty.

Sam tried not to study the way his back curved or the fluidity of his tanned shoulders as he worked. Corded muscles flexed, then relaxed and his cutoffs gaped enough that she saw a slice of white just under his waistband.

Don't go there, she silently warned herself, *you don't even know this guy*. But she couldn't help noticing the way his thin lips flattened over his teeth or the narrowing of his eyes as he worked.

He tried the engine again and it sputtered unsteadily. 'I suppose that's as good as it's gonna get until I take her in for major repairs,' he grumbled as he reached under a seat, withdrew a rag and wiped his hands. His smile was irrepressible as he slapped the boom. 'Yep, one hell of an investment.'

'Could I get you anything? Some of the wine? Or a beer? If I look hard, I think I could even scrounge up a can of Coke.' Detective Bentz's warnings about dealing with strangers and changing her locks echoed through her mind, but she steadfastly shoved the policeman's admonishments out of her head. At least for the time being. Until she learned more about this man.

He climbed off the boat. 'I'd better take a rain check.' He looked about to say something, then glanced toward the lake, where a fish jumped, silver scales catching in the sunlight, and seemed to think better of it.

'What?' she asked, intrigued.

'I probably shouldn't tell you this, but I ran into one of our neighbors the other day, the old lady across the street.'

Sam groaned inwardly. 'Don't tell me. She thought you should knock on my door with a box of chocolates or bottle of . . .' She let her voice fade, remembering the Riesling cooling in the fridge. 'Oh. That's why . . .'

'Yep.' He raised his hands, palms outward. Sucked in his breath. 'Guilty as charged.'

'And the boat?'

'Really did break down.' He shook his head. 'I couldn't fake that.'

'Well, that's something,' she said, a little stung. Not that he'd really lied, but . . .

'For the record Edie told me that you were a cross between Meg Ryan and Nicole Kidman and that I'd be out of my mind if I didn't meet you.' Sam wanted to drop right through the dock as his shaded eyes met hers. 'So that's why I pulled in here, rather than at the dock next door. I had to see for myself.'

'And?'

'Hey, anything I say now is gonna get me into deeper trouble, I think.' He rubbed the back of his neck and glanced away. 'If I tell you you're prettier than either Meg or Nicole, you'll laugh at me and tell me to get lost. It'll sound like a come-on line and if I say "Nah, the old lady needs her glasses readjusted," you'll be offended. Either way I lose.'

She thought of her nosy neighbor likening Ty to Harrison Ford, Tom Cruise and Clark Gable. 'Edie Killingsworth watches too many movies.'

'Nah, she's just one of those women who can't stop themselves from matchmaking. She was probably already working you.'

'Maybe. She told you I was single?'

'Implied as much.' He glanced at her ringless left hand. 'No hardware.'

'Not for a long time. I'm divorced,' she admitted. 'And you?'

His lips tightened just a fraction, as if he didn't want to talk about it, as if he didn't want to give up too much of himself. 'Single.' From the boat, his dog whined. 'Hush, Sasquatch, and no, I didn't name him,' he added, as if reading her mind while thankful to change the subject. 'My sister's prize German shepherd bitch had a litter that was supposed to be purebred. However, when the pups were born, it was obvious that she had managed to jump the fence before they brought in the show dog to do the honors and father the litter. Anyway, my sister ended up with six paperless pups and I got the runt, this guy here.'

He threw a smile at his dog. 'Sarah had already named him. She lives up in Bigfoot country, up around Mt. St. Helens in Washington State. That was twelve years ago.'

Ty gave a sharp whistle, the dog bounded out of the boat and raced the length of the dock to stop right at his heels. His tail swept the dusty planks, his tongue lolled from his head and he panted loudly.

'Trained well,' she said, and scratched the old shepherd behind his ears. He froze. His eyes trained on the cat. His muscles quivered. Charon had been stalking across the lawn. Spying the dog, he stopped dead in his tracks at the base of a live oak tree. His black hair stiffened and he glared at the intruder with wide, unblinking eyes.

'Don't even think about it,' Ty warned. The dog whined a little but stayed put as Charon slunk like a quick black shadow toward the safety of the hedge.

Ty rubbed the shepherd's big head. 'You'd better be on your best behavior, or the lady will throw you out.'

'What makes you think *his* behavior will have any influence on me?' Sam asked, surprised that she was nearly flirting with this stranger. But it felt good to laugh and talk without any restrictions, without worrying about how he would take her comments. If he didn't like them, tough. He could be on his way. 'The dog can do just about anything he wants,' she said. 'You, on the other hand, need to be straight with me.'

'Always,' he said quickly. Almost too quickly. He was standing close enough that she had to crane her neck up to look at his face. Crow's-feet bit into the corners of his eyes, and there was a small scar over one eyebrow. His skin was tanned and tight, and he looked as tough as leather. Like he could take care of himself and anyone else he wanted to.

Stupidly, her heart pounded a bit. Despite his easy drawl and good looks, he was a stranger – someone unknown, a man who appeared outwardly calm, but beneath the veneer seemed restless.

She reminded herself that somewhere lurking in the streets of New Orleans there was a man who had decided to terrorize her, knew her name, her address and where she worked. A man she didn't know. One she wouldn't recognize.

So who was she to say that this man, this *stranger* who lived down the street wasn't the 'John' who had phoned the station during her broadcast or the creep who had sent her the letter and mutilated picture?

'Edie did let it slip that you're Dr. Sam,' he admitted. 'As in Samantha Leeds, beautiful woman, great cook, *and* radio psychologist.'

Her nerves tightened. 'So, are you in the market for a shrink?'

'Depends upon who you talk to.' That damnable smile grew irreverently. 'Just don't call my sister. She'd have me signed up for sessions for the rest of my life.' He folded his arms across his chest, stretching the seams of his shirt. 'You could retire then.'

'I doubt that you need my help.'

'Is that your professional opinion?' He was toying with her. Flirting again.

'I don't know you well enough to make an honest evaluation. But if you want to look at ink blots or talk about how your mother didn't love you, we'd better set up an appointment.'

'I thought you only did the radio stuff.'

'I do. At least for the time being. Maybe you should tune in.'

'I have.' His shadow fell across her crown, and her pulse jumped a little.

'Have you ever called in?'

He shook his head. 'Not yet.'

'So what do you think?' She couldn't keep a nasty little feeling of dread from dripping into her bloodstream.

Ty scratched at the stubble that was beginning to darken his jaw. 'Well, I don't know what to make of it. Seems like a lot of lonely people just calling up to spout off about something. I think they just want to connect with another person or maybe claim their fifteen minutes of fame.'

'Fame or infamy?'

'You tell me.' He was staring at her through those dark lenses, but grabbed a plastic deck chair, twisted it around and straddled it, leaning over the back and pinning her with his hidden gaze. The breeze had died, the sun harsher now, bright beams bouncing off the water. 'You seem to be the real thing.'

'How about you?' she asked 'How real are you?'

'As real as it gets,' he said, as a speedboat dragging a wake board roared past, creating a wide frothy wake. Laughter rolled across the swells as the kid on the board wiped out. Quickly, the driver of the boat did a sharp 360 in order to retrieve the boy bobbing on the surface. 'But then what's real?'

'Touché,' she said, again getting a glimpse of a more complicated man than showed outwardly. The good-ol'-boy with the aw-shucks charm wasn't cutting it. No, Ty Wheeler was more than a long, tall Texan with a sexy smile. What was worse, he was getting to her. Big-time. Though it was ludicrous, a part of her was intrigued with this man, wanted to peel off the layers, find out what was hiding beneath the easy-going veneer. But that was foolish. Playing with fire. This man was trouble. And right now she had enough trouble to last her a lifetime.

He could only be a neighbor. Even a potential friend wasn't worth thinking about, and anything else was out of the question. Period.

If her involvement with David had taught her anything, it was that she wasn't ready for a relationship.

Boy, are you getting ahead of yourself here ... you've barely met the man and already you're thinking in terms of a love interest. Get real, Sam.

'You know, usually I don't socialize with my fans.'

'Who said I was a fan?' He cast a thousand-watt smile her way. 'I just mentioned I'd listened to the show.' He inclined his chin toward the *Bright Angel* as it swayed slightly on the swells. 'Maybe you'd like to take a ride with me sometime.'

'After everything you've told me about the boat? After I've helped you fix her. Call me crazy, but I don't think so.'

'When she's totally seaworthy.'

'And when will that be?'

He lifted a shoulder. 'Probably the next millennium.'

'Call me.' She rattled off her phone number.

'I will,' he said, and stared at her a little longer through his shades. Then, whistling to his dog, he walked back to his sloop. With a final wave, he cast off, leaving Sam barefoot on the dock, arm raised to shade her eyes as she watched him motor off.

The man's trouble, she told herself again. *If you're smart, Sam, you'll forget him. Right now. Before this flirtation goes any further.*

But she had the sinking premonition that it was already too late.

10

'So what do you think he meant, "It's all your fault"?' Montoya asked as he crushed his paper coffee cup and tossed it over Rick Bentz's desk to land in the wastebasket in the corner.

'Two points,' Rick said automatically.

'Three, man. That was a trey if I ever saw one. I parked that sucker from downtown.'

'If you say so.' Rick was flipping through the reports on Rosa Gillette and Cherie Bellechamps.

'So – what did the caller mean?' Montoya asked.

'I don't know.' Rick scratched at his chin as he thought about his interview with the lady psychologist.

'You shouldn't even be thinking about it, you know. We've got enough to handle as it is.'

'I do what Jaskiel tells me to do.' He shoved the reports aside. 'Look, Montoya, you and I both know I'm lucky to have this job. That I ended up with an office is unbelievable.'

'You earned it, man. You put in your years.'

'In LA.'

'And you got into some trouble. Big deal. The bottom line is you know your shit; otherwise, you wouldn't be here, right?'

Montoya was right. Twenty years with the LAPD should have counted for something, but as it was he was lucky to land a job anywhere. To say the recommendations of his superiors in the City of Angels hadn't been stellar would be a gross understatement. Everyone here knew it. Including Montoya. Not everyone understood the reasons. He cringed as he thought of them . . . of an unlucky boy who happened to point what turned out to be a toy gun at his partner. Bentz had reacted and a twelve-year-old was dead because of it. His family had sued, rightfully so, and Bentz had been put on probation. He might have regained his badge if he hadn't poured himself into a bottle for a couple of years. The powers that were at the LAPD decided he was far more trouble than he was worth – a media catastrophe. 'Yeah,' he said now, in answer to the younger cop's question. 'I know my shit.' *All of it. And it stinks.*

'So don't give me any crap about you luckin' out and gettin' the job. Jaskiel hired you to work on the cases she assigns because she trusts you, and she knows you'll work your ass off, round the clock. The way I see it, you don't want any free time anyway. Old man like you, what you got to go home to?' Montoya asked. 'Now that your kid is about off to college, you won't have any reason to go home at night, right?'

'Kristi's still at home,' Bentz argued, thinking of his daughter, the only family he had left in the world. Kristi's mother, Jennifer, was dead. She'd divorced Bentz long ago and everyone thought it was the job, which was a big part of it, but there was more, of course, and Bentz was left with one great kid and a secret he'd never share. He glanced at the double fold frame that sat on his desk. One picture was of Kristi at five, upon entering kindergarten, the other was her senior picture, taken just last September. It seemed impossible that she was eighteen and soon would be moving up to Baton Rouge. 'She's not off to All Saints until next month.'

Montoya parked a hip on Rick's desk, picked up a letter opener and twisted it in his fingers. 'So you think the stalker who's calling the lady shrink, he's dangerous?'

Rick considered the mutilated publicity shot, handed a copy of it to Reuben. 'Looks that way.'

Montoya's jaw tightened. 'Whoever did this is one messed-up mother.'

'Yeah, if this is all on the up-and-up I'd say, "yeah, the guy is dangerous."'

'But,' Reuben encouraged.

'But it could be all for show. Publicity. Ratings of the *Midnight Confessions* have soared since the first incident, and the station's been in financial straits for a couple of years. George Hannah bought WSLJ, thought he could turn it around and didn't. Maybe this is a publicity ploy.' But Rick didn't think so.

Montoya's face screwed up as he glanced down at the photo-copy. 'It's still sick-assed shit.'

'Yep. I'm waiting for a report on the note and the picture – I got the originals from the Cambrai PD, then sent them to the lab.'

He held up the photo. 'You know what this reminds me of?'

Bentz was one step ahead of his younger partner. 'The hundred-dollar bills with the eyes blackened.'

'Could be the same guy.'

'I considered it. Even put it in my report, but wouldn't he have just marked out the eyes with a felt pen – like he did on the bills?'

'You'd think ... but maybe this creep is smarter than we think.'

'It's a long shot.' One Bentz was considering.

'But a possibility, or you wouldn't have thought of it,' Montoya said.

Bentz reached for his coffee cup. The coffee was tepid and weak. 'I'm not ruling anything out.' Truth of the matter was, the photo with the cut-out eyes bothered him more than the calls to the station. He had a bad feeling about this one, real bad. Was the guy a prank or was he going to raise the stakes? And what about the psychologist? Samantha Leeds should be freaking out, not letting strange neighbors moor their damned boats at her place.

Reuben dropped the copy of the mutilated picture onto a stack of files. 'So what have we got on your serial murderer?'

'A little more. Semen was left behind on both women. The lab says it's the same blood type. Same with hair samples.'

'No surprise there.'

'And it's the same MO, from the looks of it. Both working girls, both strangled by some kind of bumpy noose, both posed afterward. He's not afraid to leave fingerprints around, and we can't find a match, so he hasn't been printed – no priors or military or job where it's required.' Bentz tossed Montoya the file. 'Also, in both instances, there were other hairs found. Synthetic. Red.'

'A wig?'

'Yeah, but it's missing, nothing close was found in the apartments and, according to people who knew the victims, neither ever wore a red wig, not even when they turned tricks.'

'So they were wearing one at the time of death and the killer took it, is that where you're going?'

Bentz nodded. 'As if he wanted his victim to look like she had red hair.'

'Jesus. Like Dr. Sam.'

'Maybe.'

Montoya sucked in his breath. 'It's still a pretty big leap.'

'I know.' Bentz wondered if he was grasping at straws, but he couldn't dismiss the eyes being cut out and the red hair. 'We're checking out manufacturers and local outlets who sell wigs and I'm cross-checking cases, to find out if there are any other homicides where there was a red wig involved.'

'It's not much, but somethin',' Montoya said, scraping the letter opener against the side of his goatee as he thought. 'I checked on the ex-husband of Cherie Bellechamps – Henry? Turns out he had a life insurance policy that he'd never let lapse. Ended up with nearly fifty thousand dollars.'

'Where was he when the second victim was killed?'

'In bed. At home.'

'Alone?'

'Nah, he's got a girlfriend who swears he was with her all night, but she's got a record. Nothin' big. Shoplifting, DUI, possession – cocaine. Seems to have been clean in the last couple of years, since she hooked up with Henry Bellechamps. By the way, it's not Henry or Hank, he goes with the French pronunciation. Henri.'

'Bully for him,' Bentz growled.

'Even if he had an alibi, it could have been a hit. He could have found someone to off his ex and pay off the killer.'

'Then why the second victim? To throw us off? A copycat?' Bentz didn't think so.

Montoya's beeper went off. He dropped the letter opener onto the stack of files on Bentz's desk, then pulled his pager from a pocket of his black slacks. With a quick glance, he checked the readout, and added, 'I'm not convinced he didn't off his ex, but I can't connect him with the Gillette woman. I gotta take this call. You got anything else?'

'A bit of a problem,' Bentz said, leaning back in his chair. 'In the first case, the woman was raped before she died, but with Rosa, it looks like she might have been dead first.'

'Might have been?'

'The ME's not certain . . .'

'Why not?'

'My guess is that the guy did it, just as the women died. That's his turn-on, killing them.'

Montoya's dark eyes narrowed. 'Shit.' He shoved his pager back into his pocket. 'About task-force time, isn't it?'

Bentz nodded. 'I've already cleared it with Jaskiel and set the wheels in motion.'

Montoya scowled. 'So we'll be dealing with the Feds.'

'Yep. The local guys.' Bentz forced a smile he didn't feel. 'It's party time.'

Sitting at the scarred table, he listened to the night through the open window. Bullfrogs croaked, fish splashed, insects droned and water lapped around the poles holding up the tiny cabin, his one spot of refuge. His head clamored and he felt the need again. The need to hunt. But he had to be careful. Choose wisely.

He glanced down at his work and smiled as he picked up one of the dark beads and oh so carefully sharpened the facets with his file. It was delicate work and caused him to sweat, but it was worth it. In the end, each bead would cut soft flesh like a razor. His callused fingers wouldn't bleed as he touched the glass, but a soft white throat would easily succumb.

He thought of the lives he'd taken, the rush of watching a woman realize she was dying, the feel of the beads in his hands as her breath left her lungs. God, it made him so hard he couldn't think . . . could only hear the pounding in his brain, the thunder of lust as it ran through his blood. He relived each moment and knew he had to do it again, to keep the memories alive.

As the images faded, his hard-on softened. He turned his attention back to his work, filing, sharpening and polishing the beads until it was time for the program, then he snapped on the radio at just the right moment. The music was fading and Dr. Sam's voice whispered over the crackle of interference.

'Good evening, New Orleans, and welcome . . .' Her voice was so erotic, so sexy.

The bitch.

He stopped working for a minute, listened to the first caller's complaints, then reached into his toolbox. He had two spools. Twenty-pound test fishing line . . . strong, clear, easy to string through the beads, or piano wire . . . even stronger, but not as flexible. The beads wouldn't slide like liquid through his fingers, the sensation wouldn't be so fluid. Which way to go? He'd used them both before. Neither had failed him.

Dr. Sam's voice answered the listener's question. She sounded so calm. Rational. Seductive. He reached down to touch himself, but stopped. He had work to do. He dropped the spool of piano wire back into the box, then tore open the packet of fishing line with his teeth. Removing the line, he pulled hard, watching as it stretched and held.

The muscles in his arms bunched. The line cut into his palm but didn't break.

He grinned. Yes, it would do nicely.

As Dr. Sam continued her program, talking to the idiots who called her, he began stringing his sharpened beads, careful to put them in the correct order, ensuring that his rosary was perfect.

Nothing less would do.

I I

Melanie clicked off her cell phone and fumed as she pulled into a parking space in the lot of the strip mall. It had been a bad week. Bad. And it wasn't getting any better she thought, slapping the dash and wishing that the damned air-conditioning in her hatchback would find a way to turn on. It didn't and the temperature in the car was hovering somewhere near two thousand degrees by her estimation.

Her T-shirt was wrinkled and clinging to her, and she was sweating between her legs. She climbed out of the car and tried not to dwell on the fact that Trish LaBelle seemed to be dodging her calls. Great. Already there was talk at WSLJ that *Midnight Confessions* was being expanded, but not one word about Melanie getting any kind of promotion and she deserved it.

Samantha's job was a piece of cake. Melanie could handle it with her eyes closed. Hadn't she proved that while Sam was in Mexico? So the ratings had dropped an iota. That was to be expected. Given enough time, Melanie was certain she could create a new, hipper audience. She was young and with it. But she needed the chance to prove herself.

She walked into the oven of a dry cleaners and gave her name to a petite blond girl with inch-long black roots, bad teeth and a permanent sneer.

So if WSLJ wouldn't give her a job behind the mike, she'd decided to call the rival station, WNAB, where Trish LaBelle worked. Trish hated Dr. Sam. Melanie figured Trish would jump at the chance of meeting with Sam's assistant and even offer her a job.

So far Trish hadn't returned her calls.

Yet.

Melanie wasn't one to give up. She'd always been a scrapper; never gotten any breaks that she hadn't made for herself, so, if she had to, she'd damned sure make her own.

'Here ya go.' The girl hung her plastic-encased clothes on a hook near the till and Melanie handed over her bank debit-card. 'Sorry. The machine's broken. Ya got cash or a check?'

'I left my checkbook at home . . .' Melanie said, flipping through her wallet and seeing only two crumpled one-dollar bills. Not enough. The day was on a fast downhill slide. She felt bloated and achy; her period was due to start any time, her job was going nowhere, what little family she had didn't give a shit about her and her boyfriend, again, couldn't be reached.

Yep, things were rapidly going from bad to worst.

'There's an ATM on the next block.' The twit in need of a bottle of Clairol snapped a wad of gum and waited with bored patience.

Melanie seethed. 'It's not my fault your stupid machine is messed up.'

The girl shrugged her skinny shoulders and gave Melanie a bored look that said, 'tell it to someone who cares.' She held Melanie's stare and for a second Melanie considered grabbing her clothes and taking off. After all the skirt, blouse and short jacket were *hers*.

As if she'd read Melanie's mind, the clerk swept the hangers from the hook and hung them on another rail behind the counter.

'Fine.' Melanie snapped her wallet shut. 'I'll be back.' But she wasn't going to bother today. She was too frazzled. She stomped into the blinding sun, flipped her sunglasses over her nose and slid into the sunbaked interior of her hatchback. The steering wheel was nearly too hot to handle. Twisting on the ignition, she threw the car into reverse and as the radio blared, stepped on the gas. In the rearview mirror, she caught a glimpse of a huge white Cadillac pulling out at the same time. She stood on the brakes as the boat slowly slid from its spot and an elderly man who never so much as glanced in her direction rolled slowly out of the lot.

'Idiot,' Melanie grumbled. 'Old fart.'

She backed out, rammed her hatchback into first and sped out of the lot. Before the first light, she passed the old guy and resisted the urge to flip him off. It wasn't really his fault he was old.

She hit the freeway and flooring it, opened the sunroof and all the power windows. Wind blew her hair around and she felt better. She couldn't let one minimum-wage clerk with a bad attitude bug her. She'd pick up her clothes later. In the meantime she'd concentrate on plan B.

One way or another, she'd land a promotion and end up behind the mike. She let herself daydream a little, considered just how far she'd go. Maybe eventually television. She had the looks. A slow smile spread across her lips and she reached for the cell phone while cruising along at seventy. She'd try to call her boyfriend and plan to meet him. *If* she could get hold of him.

She just needed to unwind.

And he knew just how to help her.

Sam's palms were sweaty and her heart raced, but she told herself, as she entered the booth, that she was being apprehensive and silly.

Nothing had happened.

For nearly a week.

Though each night she'd experienced the same case of nerves as she'd started her program, 'John' had remained silent. Had he given up? Was he bored with his joke, if that's what it was? Was he out of town?

Or was he waiting?

For just the right moment.

Stop this, Sam, it's getting you nowhere. Be grateful he's gone.

Still, she was tense as was everyone at the station in varying degrees. Gator and Rob kidded about her 'boyfriend,' Eleanor stewed, Melanie thought it exciting, and George Hannah hoped that the ratings would continue to climb.

They hadn't. Without John's calls, the listenership's numbers were falling back to where they'd once been, which, Sam thought angrily, had been good. George, his silent partners and even Eleanor had been satisfied.

But no longer.

Eleanor told her 'Not to worry, honey. At least the pervert's gone. That's good enough for me. As for George, he can think up some legitimate way to attract a bigger audience. Let's just hope John never calls back.'

Right, Sam thought, but a part of her wanted to talk to him again, if only to find out *what* it was that made him tick. *Why* he'd decided to call her. *Who* he was. From a psychologist's viewpoint, he was interesting. From a woman's viewpoint, he was terrifying.

She closed the door to the booth behind her. Slipping on the headset, she settled into her chair, then adjusted the controls, checked the computer screen and glanced through the glass window to the adjoining booth. Melanie was seated at her desk, fiddling with knobs, then gave her a thumbsup gesture, indicating that she was ready to screen the calls for the night. Tiny was with her, taking his seat, saying something to Melanie that Sam couldn't hear. They laughed, seemed relaxed and Tiny cracked open a can of Diet Coke.

Over the past few nights, Sam had steered the subjects of her nightly discussion away from sin, punishment and redemption and back to relationships, which, of course, was the basis for the show. Things were getting back to normal. The way they were before John had first called. So why had the electricity she'd felt every time she sat in this chair not abated, but in fact, heightened?

Melanie signaled through the glass and the intro music filled the booth. John Lennon's voice, singing '*it's been a hard day's night*,' boomed from the speakers, then faded.

Sam leaned into the microphone. 'Good evening, New Orleans, and welcome. This is Dr. Sam with *Midnight Confessions* here at WSLJ and I'm ready to hear what you think . . .' She started talking, relaxing, cozying up to the microphone as she invited her listeners to call in. 'I just spoke to my dad a couple of days ago, and even though I'm over thirty, he thinks he can still tell me what to do,' she said as a way of connecting with her audience, hoping that someone would identify with her and phone in. 'He lives on the West Coast, and I'm starting to feel that I should be closer to him, that he might need me now that he's getting up in years.' She went on for a while talking about the relationship between parents and children when the phone lines started to flash.

The first was a hangup, the second a woman whose mother was suffering the aftereffects of a stroke; she was torn between her job, her kids, her husband and her feeling that her mother needed her. The third was from a hostile teenager who resented her parents trying to tell her anything. They just didn't 'understand' her.

Then there was a backlash, from parents and kids who thought the teenage caller should listen to her folks.

Sam relaxed even more. Felt at ease behind the mike. Sipped from a half-drunk cup of coffee. The debate waged on and finally a woman called in on line three. She was identified as Annie. Sam pressed the button for the call. 'Hi,' she said, 'This is Dr. Sam, who am I talking to?'

'Annie,' a frail, high voice whispered. A voice that was vaguely familiar. But Sam couldn't place the name with a face. She was probably a regular caller.

'Hello, Annie, what is it you want to discuss tonight?'

'Don't you remember me?' the girl asked.

Sam felt the warning hairs on the back of her neck rise. *Annie?*

'I'm sorry. If you could remind—'

'I called you before.'

'Did you? When?' she asked, but the raspy voice hadn't stopped, just paused to draw a breath and kept right on whispering through the studio, on the airwaves.

'Thursday's my birthday. I would be twenty-five—'

'Would be?' Samantha repeated and a chill swept through her blood.

'—you remember. I called you nine years ago, and you told me to get lost. You didn't listen, and—'

'Oh, God,' Sam said, her eyes widening. Her heart stopped for a second in a horrid nightmare of déjà vu. Annie? *Annie Seger?* It couldn't be. Her mind spun wildly, backward to a time she'd tried to forget.

'*You've got to help me. You're a doctor, aren't you? Please, you're my only hope,*' Annie had confided all those years ago. '*Please help me. Please.*' Guilt took a stranglehold on Sam's throat. *Dear God, why was this happening again?* 'Who is this?' Sam forced into the microphone. From the corner of her eye, she glanced at the adjacent booth, where Melanie was listening, shaking her head, her palms turned toward the ceiling, as if the caller had, once again, gotten past her. Tiny was staring hard through the glass, his eyes trained on Sam, the can of soda in his big hand forgotten.

'—and you didn't help me,' the breathy voice accused, hardly missing a beat. 'What happened then, *Dr.* Sam, you remember, don't you?'

Sam's head was pounding, her hands slick with sweat. 'I asked for your name, Annie – your full name.'

Click. The line went dead. Sam sat frozen.

Annie Seger.

No! Her stomach clenched.

It had been so long ago and yet, now, sitting in the booth as she had been then, it all came rushing back, like a tidal wave, crashing through her brain, leaving her numb and cold. The girl had died. Because of her. Because she couldn't help. *Oh, God, please not again.*

'Samantha! Samantha! Snap out of it!' Melanie's voice permeated her brain, but still she could barely move. 'Jesus Christ, pull yourself together!' As if from a distance, Sam felt Melanie's hands on her arms, yanking her out of her chair, thrusting her across the small space, toward Tiny, pushing her away from the desk and the microphone. Still in shock, Sam stumbled, her ankle twisting. She snapped out of it. Realized she was here, in New Orleans and on the air. 'Don't you know there's all this dead airtime going on? For God's sake, pull yourself together.' Melanie was saying as she slipped on the headphones and reached for the mike. 'Get her out of here,' she ordered Tiny.

'Wait a minute. I'm okay.' Sam wasn't about to budge.

'Prove it.' Melanie glared at her and waved her into the hallway. Tiny pulled Sam out of the room as Melanie leaned into the microphone and, as she flipped it on, her voice became smooth as warm silk on a hot Louisiana night. 'Please excuse the interruption, we've experienced some technical difficulties down here at WSLJ. Thank you for your patience. *Midnight Confessions* with Dr. Samantha Leeds will be back in a few minutes, after our local weather update.' Expertly Melanie pressed the buttons for the automated recording that would play the weather forecast and a couple of pretaped advertising spots.

'What went on in there?' Tiny asked, then realizing his fingers surrounded Sam's upper arms, he let go and put a little distance between them. The hallway seemed eerie and darker than usual, the glass case holding old records giving off an odd, ethereal glow. But of course that was crazy. It was just Sam's nerves. The corridor and record case hadn't changed.

Drawing in several deep breaths, Sam pulled herself together. She couldn't allow another prank to rattle her so.

'Who was that girl on the line?'

'I don't know,' Sam admitted, leaning against the wall. She wiped a hand over her forehead and forced some starch into her spine. *Think, Sam, think. Don't let some crank caller get the better of you.* 'I – I don't know who it was. Can't imagine who would do anything so sick, but whoever it was she wanted me to think she was Annie Seger,' *Oh, God, not Annie. What was happening? The girl had been dead nine years.* Dead. Because Sam hadn't read the situation correctly, hadn't heeded the girl's cries for help. Sam's head pounded, and the coffee she'd drunk earlier curdled in her stomach.

Don't let it get to you, Sam. Don't!

'She said she was Annie and then you freaked out,' Tiny accused. 'You acted like you knew her.'

'I know . . . but I don't . . . er, didn't . . . it's all so unbelievable.'

'What is?' He seemed about to touch her again, but, thinking better of it, shoved his hands deep into the pockets of his oversize jeans.

'Annie Seger was a girl who called into my program a long time ago when I was working in Houston.' It seemed like it was just yesterday. Sam remembered pushing the button, answering the call and listening as a teenager hesitantly explained that she was pregnant and scared to death. 'Annie phoned in several nights in a row, asking for advice.' Inside Sam cringed when she remembered the girl's calls. At first Annie had seemed scared, but no matter what Sam offered as advice, she rejected it, claimed she had no one to talk to, no one to confide in, not her parents, not her pastor and not even the father of her baby. 'I tried to help her, but she ended up committing suicide.' Sam pushed the hair off her face and saw the pale shimmer of her reflection in the window of the booth. Beyond the glass Melanie sat at her desk, talking into the microphone, controlling the show. It all seemed surreal, being here late at night in the dim hallway, remembering a time she'd tried so hard to forget.

'You think it was your fault she killed herself?' Tiny asked.

'Annie's family blamed me.'

'Heavy.'

'Very.' Sam rubbed her arms and tried to grab hold of her composure. She had a show to do; a job to finish. She saw Melanie tear off the headset and roll back the chair. Within seconds she flew out of the room. 'You've got sixty seconds before you're back on the air,' she said to Sam. 'Are you okay?'

'No,' Sam admitted. *Dear God, I'll never be okay again.* She started for the booth. 'But I'll wing it.'

'Eleanor's on line two. She wants to talk to you.'

'I don't have time.'

'She's furious,' Melanie said.

'I imagine. Tell her I'll talk to her after the show.' Sam couldn't deal with the program manager now; not until she was off the air.

'What was the deal with that girl who called in?' Melanie asked, as Sam slid into her chair and automatically checked the controls.

'You tell me,' Sam snapped. 'You're supposed to be screening the calls.'

'I have been! And I recorded her request. She didn't talk in that stupid falsetto voice, either, she just said that she had a problem with her ex-mother-in-law and wanted your advice.' Melanie glowered at her boss. 'So are you going to pull yourself together and take charge or what? Otherwise, I'll take over.' Her voice softened slightly and her defensive attitude slipped away. 'I can do it, you know. Easy as pie. Tiny can run the call-in booth. Just like when you were in Mexico.'

'I can handle it, really. But thanks.'

Melanie flashed a smile that seemed to hide some other emotion. 'I'm a shirttail relation to Jefferson Davis, you know.'

'I've heard.'

'I can step up to the plate if I have to. It's in my genes.'

'Well, thank God for your genes, but I'm okay.' Sam wasn't going to let another crank call spook her out of her job. 'I'll handle it. You two' – she motioned to Tiny and Melanie – 'just screen the calls and tape 'em. We've only got another fifteen minutes. Tell Eleanor to sit tight.' She adjusted her headphones and pulled the microphone close to her mouth, adjusting the angle as the advertisement for a local dot com company faded.

'Okay, this is Dr. Sam, I'm back in the saddle. Sorry for the interruption. As you probably already heard, the station's experiencing some technical difficulties tonight.' It was a bald-faced lie, and she probably lost a few credibility points with her listeners, but she couldn't deal with the issue of Annie Seger right now. 'Okay, so let's pick up where we left off a few minutes ago. We were talking about our parents interfering in our lives, or needing us, or telling us what to do. My dad is the greatest, but he can't seem to accept it that I'm a grown woman. I'm sure you've had similar experiences.'

The phones lines were already blinking like mad. If nothing else the crank calls were drawing interest. The first caller, on line one, was identified as Ty.

A lightning quick image of a tall man with a killer smile and flinty, unreadable eyes seared through her brain. Her stomach tightened, though she told herself the caller wasn't necessarily her new neighbor. 'Hello,' she said, 'this is Dr. Sam, who's this?'

'Ty,' he said, and she felt a mixture of relief and wariness as she recognized his voice. She wondered why he'd been listening to her program, how he'd managed to be the first caller after the woman who had claimed she had been Annie had been on the line.

'What can I do for you, Ty?' she asked, and tried not to notice that her palms were suddenly damp. 'Are you having trouble with your parents? Your kids?'

'Well, now, this is a little off tonight's subject. I was hopin' you could help me out with a relationship problem.'

'I'll try,' she said, silently questioning where this was leading. Was he telling her that he wasn't available, that there was already a woman in his life? Then why the flirting just the other afternoon? 'What's the problem, Ty?'

'Well, I just moved into a neighborhood and I've met this woman that I'm interested in,' he said in his soft drawl, and some of her apprehension fled.

'Is the feeling mutual?' Sam couldn't help but smile.

'Oh, yeah, I think so, but she's playing it pretty cool.'

'Then how do you know she wants to get to know you better? Maybe her being cool isn't an act.'

'That's what she wants me to believe, but I can see it in her eyes. She's interested, all right. More than interested. Just too proud to admit it.'

Samantha's grin widened, and heat washed up the back of her neck. 'She's that transparent, is she?'

'Sure is, only she doesn't know it.'

Great. 'Maybe you should tell her.'

'I'm givin' it some serious thought,' he said slowly, and Sam's heartbeat accelerated into overdrive. She wondered how much of the undercurrents in the conversation Melanie and Tiny were hearing . . . or for that matter, if everyone tuned into WSLJ caught the subtleties.

'But prepare yourself, Ty, this woman might not be as captivated with you as you'd like to think.'

'I guess I'll just have to find out now, won't I? I'll have to make a move.'

Oh, God. Her lungs tightened. 'That would be the logical next step.'

'But you and I both know that sometimes logic doesn't have a whole lot to do with what happens between a man and a woman.'

Touché. 'So what are you going to do, Ty?'

There was just a half a beat of hesitation.

'I'm going to find out just what the lady likes,' he drawled, and Sam's mouth went dry.

'And how're you going to do that?' Rapid, sensual images of Ty Wheeler with his broad shoulders, dark hair and intense eyes flitted through her mind. She wondered what it would be like to kiss him, to touch him, to make love to him.

His laugh was deep. 'I think I can figure it out.'

'So you're going to try and take your relationship to the next level?' she asked, her throat tight.

'Definitely.'

'When?'

'When it's least expected.'

'Then you'd better not tip your hand.' She was having trouble breathing.

'I won't.'

'Good luck, Ty,' she said.

'Same to you, Dr. Sam. Same to you.'

Her heart was pounding so hard she could barely hear herself think and as she saw other phone lines blink to life she wondered if any of her listeners had caught the undercurrents of the conversation.

'Thanks for calling in, Ty.' She forced herself to check the display board and saw that the calls were stacking up like jets over O'Hare.

'Anytime, and, oh, Dr. Sam?'

'Yes?'

'Sweet dreams.'

12

Ty's voice had been as low and sexy as a Delta night.

Samantha's mouth was suddenly desert-dry and she was tongue-tied for the first time in all her years of radio. Heat rushed up her neck, and she tried to get her bearings. 'The same to you, Ty,' she finally managed, her voice sounding throatier than usual. 'Sweet dreams.' Quickly, before she lost her train of thought completely, she pressed a button, read the computer screen and said, 'Hello, this is Dr. Sam, you're on the air.'

'Hi, this is Terry . . . hey, who was that guy you were talking to? Do you know him?'

Sam sent a scalding glance toward Melanie. Wasn't she screening the calls, for God's sake. 'Did you have a question about a relationship?'

'And that Annie, earlier. What was that all about?'

Melanie was shaking her head.

'I don't know. Now, did you have a reason to call?'

'Well I was gonna ask about how to handle my teenage son.'

'What about him?'

Terry turned her attention back to her boy, but as soon as the next call came in, it was back to questions about Annie. The phone lines never quit blinking. The questions about the breathy girl on the phone kept coming. Finally, the show was over. As the first strains of 'Midnight Confession' played, Sam finished the show with her signature sign off, '. . . there is always tomorrow. Sweet dreams.' As soon as the words were out of her mouth, she clicked off her microphone, ripped off her headset, and stormed out of the studio to the glassed-in room where

Tiny and Melanie were gathering up the paperwork and resetting the equipment for the *Lights Out* program.

'I thought you were screening the calls,' she charged.

'I was. You should have heard what came in here.' Melanie threw her headset onto the desk. 'It was a nightmare.' The tech room was dark except for a desk lamp, the colored lights of the equipment and recessed bulbs over a bank of computers and recorders.

'She's right,' Tiny said, rushing to Melanie's defense. 'No one wanted to discuss anything but Annie.'

'Or Ty. There were a couple callers who asked about him.' Melanie tossed her blond curls from her face. Sweat sheened on her face. 'I tried, Sam. It's not easy sometimes.'

Sam cooled off. It wasn't Melanie's fault that the woman pretending to be Annie called in. 'Did you keep track of all the calls?' Sam demanded.

'Every last one of 'em,' Tiny assured her as he tapped two fingers on a lined sheet of paper on the desk he was sharing with Melanie. 'Right here on the log. I wrote down the telephone number *and* the name, if it was available. Some of the calls came in anonymously, of course. If they're initiated from a company with a private phone system, then caller ID can't identify them.'

'Then what good is caller ID?' Disgusted, Sam leaned over the desk, her eyes scanning Tiny's log.

'It's a start. And we've got most of 'em. Here.' Tiny spun the lined paper around, then rolled his chair over to the bank of recording equipment and computers to finish arranging the presets for the next three hours. Sam's gaze raked over the sheet covered with Tiny's cryptic scrawl. As he'd said, every telephone call was listed. Beside the names were numbers and in some cases notations. Samantha ran her finger down the list, came to the name Annie, where there was a number and an identification name of a pay phone.

Of course. Whoever had phoned in was too clever to call from a private residence. 'I'll need a copy of this ledger.'

'For the police?' Melanie zipped her briefcase.

'And myself.'

'What was that all about in there?' Melanie asked, hitching a thumb at the darkened studio. Through the window, faint light shimmered from the streetlamps three floors below, throwing in relief the equipment in the booth, microphones on long, skeletal arms bent at odd angles, and the desk surrounded by banks of levers and dials. It seemed sinister somehow. Evil. But that was ludicrous.

Melanie broke into her thoughts. 'Come on, Sam, who was that Annie girl who called? She acted like she knew you, and you freaked out.'

'Play back her request. When she called in. Before you connected her to me. You said you taped it.'

'Yes, but—'

'I've got it,' Tiny interjected. 'Just give me a minute . . . Here we go—'

A woman's voice came on after Melanie answered. 'This is Annie. I would like to talk to Dr. Sam about my mother-in-law. She's interfering in my marriage.'

'Hold on. It'll just be a minute,' Melanie had assured her, and then the breathy, accusatory call.

Sam's skin crawled.

Tiny stopped the playback, but cast a look over his shoulder, checking Sam's reaction. 'Who is she?'

'I don't know who the caller really was, but she wasn't Annie Seger.' *Who would call in and pretend to be Annie Seger and why would anyone dredge that entire tragedy up again?* 'But – I know this sounds weird, but I think I've heard her voice, but it's not quite right . . . I can't place it.' She closed her eyes. *Who, Sam, who would do this to you? What kind of cruel joke is it?* Aware that Melanie and Tiny were staring at her, she shrugged and shook her head. 'I can't place it. Not now. But I will.' Her skin felt cold as death, and she rubbed her arms. 'It was a prank.'

'Another one. Like the calls from that John guy,' Tiny surmised.

'Oh, this is different,' she said, thinking back to those horrid, lonely nights when Annie Seger had called in to the station in

Houston, when the show's ratings had skyrocketed, when Dr. Sam's name had become a household word, when a young, pregnant girl had taken her life. Had it been neglect on her part? Had she read the situation wrong? Had there been any clues that Annie had been suicidal? How many times had she asked herself those same questions? How many nights had she lain awake, replaying the desperate phone calls in her mind, feeling guilt settle over her like a shroud, wondering if there was anything she could have done to help the girl.

'Of course it's different. The caller was a woman this time.' Melanie looked from Sam to Tiny, who was frowning as he adjusted the volume of a prerecorded track. Then Sam realized Melanie didn't know the story, had been in the booth when she'd told Tiny about Annie Seger.

'Samantha said the woman was pretending to be a girl who had called in while she was in Houston and the kid ended up dead,' Tiny said, as if making sure he'd gotten all the details straight.

'What?' Melanie drew back, appalled. 'Dead? But . . . oh God, that's sick.'

'Beyond sick.' Tiny folded his arms over his chest.

'My speciality,' Sam pointed out, finally recovering a bit of her composure. 'Remember, I'm a shrink.'

The phone jangled, and they all jumped. Line two flashed impatiently. 'I'll get it. It's probably Eleanor.' Sam punched the button for the speaker phone. 'Hi, this is Samantha.'

'Glad I caught you in.'

She froze. Her heart missed a beat. 'Who is this?' she said, but recognized the smooth, sexy voice immediately. *John.* Out there lurking somewhere. He hadn't given up. He was just biding his time. Waiting for her to feel relaxed.

'Don't play games, Samantha. You know who I am.'

'You're the one who's playing games.'

'Am I? I suppose I am. Are we having fun yet?'

Sam wanted to slam down the receiver, but couldn't sever the connection, not if she ever wanted to nail this creep. Motioning frantically to Tiny and the recorder, she kept talking. 'I wouldn't call it fun, John,' she said, hoping that Melanie and Tiny would catch on. 'Not fun at all.'

'I caught your program tonight.'

Spurred into action, Tiny pressed the right buttons and gave her a quick nod as the recorder began taping. Melanie stared at the speaker phone as if mesmerized.

'But you didn't phone in.'

'I'm calling now,' he pointed out in his well-modulated voice.

Had she heard it before? Had he called her without claiming to be John? Was it someone she knew? *Think, Sam, think! This creep acts like he* knows *you. As if you've met.*

'I wanted to talk to you alone. What we need to discuss is personal.'

'I don't even know who you are.'

His chuckle was deep and rumbled through the room.

Melanie bit her lip.

Tiny's eyes bulged behind his glasses.

The booth seemed close and dark and dangerous, the sound emanating from the speaker pure sin. Sweat prickled on Sam's scalp.

'Sure you do, *Doctor*, you just don't remember. Aren't you putting two and two together yet? You with your degree and all . . .'

'What is it you want?' she asked, taking a seat and staring at the speaker as if she could will a vision of his face to appear. 'Why are you calling me?' She could barely think, but she knew she had to keep him on the line. She grabbed a pen from a cup on the desk, flipped over the log and scratched out a quick note – CALL POLICE – that she shoved under Melanie's nose.

'Because I know you for what you are, Samantha. I know that you're a hot-blooded cunt. A phony. That degree you're so proud of isn't worth the paper it's printed on.' He was getting angry now, his well-modulated voice becoming agitated. 'Women like you need to be punished.' His words reverberated through the speaker more rapidly, as Melanie hurried out of the room and into the studio next door. Through the glass window, Sam saw her hit the lights and pick up the headset. She glanced over her shoulder and nodded as she punched a free line, quickly dialed and nodded back to Sam and Tiny. The corresponding light for line three flashed to life.

Keep him on the line, Sam, just keep him talking. Maybe he'll slip up. Maybe the police will arrive, maybe there's a way to trace the call.

'You're a whore, *Dr.* Sam,' John charged. 'A fifty-dollar-an-hour hooker!'

'I don't know what you're talking about.' *Try to remain calm. Keep him on the damned line. Find out more about him, record it for the police.* Her palms were sweaty, her heart thundering.

'It's all in your past, Dr. Sam, that past you hide from the world. But I know. I was there. I remember when you were out selling it on the streets. You're a hooker – a fake – and you'll pay. The wages of sin are death,' he reminded her coldly. 'And you're gonna die. You're gonna die soon.'

She swallowed back her fear, her fingers clamping around the pen in her hand. *Who is he? Why is he so angry? What does he mean he 'was there.' Where, damn it?* 'Why are you threatening me, John? What did I ever do to you?'

'Don't you know? Don't you remember?' he nearly yelled.

Annie's words earlier – Don't you remember me?

'No. Why don't you tell me? Where did we meet?' she said, her voice somehow steady though she could barely breathe. Her skin was hot, her insides cold as death.

John didn't say a word. That was creepier still. Knowing he was there, listening, not speaking. Through the glass window, Sam caught Melanie's gaze. She was talking and nodding, gesturing with her hands as if the police could see through the phone lines.

'John, are you still there?'

'Are you on a speaker phone?' he asked suddenly. 'It's echoing.'

'Listen, John, why are you calling me—' The phone rang loudly and line four flashed impatiently. Sam ignored it. 'What is it that you want from me?'

'You are, you lying cunt. You're on a speaker. I thought I told you I wanted this to be personal!'

'It is, believe me. Now, tell me, John, what is it you want from me?'

'Retribution,' he said. 'I want you on your knees. I want you to beg for forgiveness.'

'For what?'

But the line went dead. As if he'd heard the incoming call and gotten scared. 'Damn,' Sam swore, trembling inside. Feeling weak. Vulnerable. Violated. *Don't let him do this to you. Don't let him get to you.* But the hatred she'd felt, the rage he had against her was horrifying.

'I got it all,' Tiny assured her, as she hit the button for line four. 'WSLJ.'

'Dammit, Sam, is that you? What the hell's going on over there? You were supposed to call me back.' Eleanor's voice bellowed from the speaker phone. 'Are you all okay?'

'We're fine.'

'That was some weird stuff on the phone tonight,' Eleanor said. 'I couldn't believe it when that girl saying she was Annie Seger called.' There was pause as Eleanor drew in a breath. 'Sam, tell me you're okay.'

'I think I already did.'

'Yeah, but I remember what happened. I was there, y'know. In Houston.'

Suddenly self-conscious that Tiny was hearing every bit of this conversation, probably was recording it, Sam cut Eleanor off. 'Look, we're all tired. Let's not go into it now. I'll come into the station early tomorrow and we'll talk. There are other things we're going to have to go over.'

'Other things?' Eleanor's voice was instantly wary.

'The other prank caller, the guy who calls himself John, phoned in after the program again. I just hung up.'

'*After* the show? What's that all about?'

'I don't know, but it's the second time he called once the program's gone off the air. As if that somehow makes it more personal, I guess. The first time he said he was busy, and I was to blame. This time he didn't offer up any excuses for not calling during the show, got really upset when he realized I was using a speaker phone and became threatening. Tiny's got everything on tape. We'll listen to it tomorrow.'

'I don't like it, Sam. Not at all.'

'Neither do I.'

'We'll have to call the police again.'

'Melanie just did.' She glanced through the window and saw Melanie nodding, still gesturing as she talked into the microphone. 'It's handled.'

'My ass! This has gone way too far, you hear me. *Way* too far. Now, I don't want any of you walking outside alone tonight, okay? Go in a group to the parking garage. Be sure Tiny's with you or take a cab. Y'all hear me?'

'Loud and clear,' Sam said, as Melanie hung up in the other room.

'I'm serious, Sam. I don't like this garbage.'

'Me, neither.'

'You tell the police they'd better figure out how to catch this bastard, or they'll have to deal with me.'

'That'll get them shivering in their boots.'

'Hey, I have no time for jokes. This is serious.'

'I know, Eleanor.'

'Good.'

'And tomorrow, we are gonna get to the bottom of it. All of us. Tiny, Melanie and you are to meet me in my office at one in the afternoon.' She let out a breath. 'Mother of God. Be careful. I'll see ya tomorrow.'

'We'll be there,' Sam said, and hung up as Melanie charged into the room.

'The police are on their way.' She glanced at the speaker phone. 'Did he say anything else?'

'The guy's a maniac,' Tiny said. 'It was weird. Beyond weird.'

'You've got that right.'

Rubbing the back of his neck anxiously, Tiny added, 'I'd better go down and wait for the cops.' He grabbed his jacket and backpack, was searching for his pack of Camels as he walked out the door.

'What now?' Melanie asked.

'We wait. For the police.'

'I know, but I don't think they can do anything.'

Sam wasn't going there, wasn't going to give in to her own thoughts that John would somehow escape being found out and apprehended by the police. 'Let's just hope they catch this guy and soon.'

'And if they don't?' Melanie asked.

Sam didn't answer. Didn't want to think about it, but the caller's threats echoed through her mind as surely as if he was whispering in her ear.

The wages of sin are death, and you're gonna die. You're gonna die soon.

He was sweating.

His blood pounding, the heat of the night heavy and damp.

The conversation burning through his brain as he walked briskly from the phone booth along St. Charles Avenue. Through parked cars he jaywalked, crossing the streetcar rails and hurrying past the universities – Tulane and Loyola, side by side, brick-and-stone structures that appeared in the dim light of the security lamps as fortresses, castles built in honor of almighty academia. His skin prickled as he glanced at the buildings. He could smell the sweet seductive scent of young minds. Just as his had once been.

College.

Philosophy.

Religion.

Where he had learned the truth; where he had understood his mission. Where it had all begun.

Oh, his mentor would be proud.

A few students wandered the great expanse of lawn talking, laughing, smoking, probably getting high. Warm light glowed from some of the windows, but he barely noticed as he ducked through the shadows, half-running, his heart pounding, her words ricocheting like hot bullets through his brain.

Why are you threatening me, John? What did I ever do to you?

She didn't remember.

Didn't recall the horror that had changed his life – ruined it.

Rage screamed through his blood, and he broke into a jog, running faster toward the heart of the city, toward the siren song of Bourbon Street, where he could blend into the crowd that forever walked the city streets, where he could hide in the throng and yet be nearer to her.

What did I ever do to you?

Soon she'd know.

Soon she'd understand.

It would be her last thought before she died.

13

'. . . if you think of anything else, let us know,' one of the two officers who took Sam's statement said, as he and his partner left the kitchen of WSLJ, where Sam, Melanie and Tiny had given their statements. Tiny had been in and out of the reception area, checking the prerecorded program, making sure that everything was running smoothly.

'God, I'm glad *that's* over.' Melanie grabbed her purse and briefcase. 'What a marathon.'

'They're just being thorough.'

'Think they'll catch anyone?' Tiny asked as he rummaged in the cupboards, found a bag of popcorn and set it inside the microwave.

'I can only hope,' Sam said around a yawn. Bone-tired, she didn't want to think about either of the callers for the rest of the night. It was nearly three in the morning. All she wanted to do was drive home, fall into bed and close out the world. Her head was beginning to ache, her ankle starting to throb.

'I think that popcorn belongs to Gator,' Melanie said, as Tiny pushed the timer.

'He'll never miss it. Are you guys all right to walk out of here alone?'

'We'll manage,' Sam said dryly. She couldn't imagine Tiny as any kind of a protector. 'Come on, let's go, Melanie.' She gathered her things and the popcorn kernels started exploding over the hum of the microwave. The smell of butter filled the kitchen as she and Melanie made their way downstairs and outside the building.

Ty was waiting for her. Parked illegally in front of the station at three in the morning, he leaned one jean-clad hip against the fender of his Volvo and stared at the door of the building as Sam and Melanie stepped into the warm summer night. His arms were folded over his chest, and even in the watery light from the streetlamp she noticed his jaw was dark, with a couple days' worth of beard. He was dressed in a T-shirt, jeans and leather jacket. Reminiscent of an older, more jaded James Dean. *Great*, she thought sarcastically. *Just what I need.* And yet a tiny thrill of anticipation swept through her.

The smell of the river was close, the air heavy, the sound of a lonesome saxophone echoing over the quiet hum of what little traffic there was, and a man who had been a stranger little more than a week before was waiting for her.

Ty pushed himself off the car. 'I thought I'd come down and see that you were okay.'

'I'm fine. Just dead on my feet,' she said, but couldn't help feeling a little glow of warmth for him.

To Melanie, he said, 'Ty Wheeler. I'm Sam's neighbor.'

Sam belatedly found her manners as a car cruised past. Through the open window the sound of heavy bass thrummed from huge speakers. 'Oh, right, Ty, this is Melanie Davis, my assistant, Melanie, Ty. He's a writer who owns an old dog and buys broken-down sailboats.'

Melanie gave him a quick once-over and offered a curious, friendly smile. 'A writer? Like a journalist?'

'Nothing so noble, I'm afraid,' he drawled. 'Novels. Fiction.'

'Really?' Melanie was impressed. 'You're published?'

Ty's smile flashed white in the darkness. 'Hopin' to be.'

'What's your book about?'

'Kind of a *Horse Whisperer* meets *The Silence of the Lambs*. It's got a farm theme running through it.'

'Give me a break,' Sam said, and Melanie chuckled.

'Actually, I thought I'd come down and see that you' – he touched Sam on the elbow – 'were all right.'

'Right as rain,' she lied.

His fingers tightened before he dropped his hand and again she felt that ridiculous little glow. 'So where's the car?'

'About two blocks over.' Despite all her talk about feminism and being a strong single woman, she was more at ease having Ty with them and rationalized that it wasn't necessarily because he was a man, but that there was greater safety in numbers.

'You're the Ty who called in earlier tonight,' Melanie guessed, and Sam could almost see the wheels turning in her assistant's mind as she remembered Ty's questions about pushing a relationship to another level. 'Oh . . . I get it.' Her eyes twinkled in the weak light.

'Yep. I did call in,' he admitted. 'Didn't like what I was hearing on the airwaves, so I phoned the station to change the tone of things. After I hung up, I decided maybe Samantha would like a ride home. When I got here I saw the police car.'

Melanie didn't comment, just lifted a curious eyebrow as if trying to get a bead on Ty's connection to Sam.

'I think I'd better drive,' Sam said. 'I don't want to leave my car here and then not have a way into the city tomorrow.'

'I'd drive you,' he offered, but Sam didn't want to bother him, nor be dependent.

'And I'd feel better having my own wheels.'

'Whatever you want.' He shrugged. 'But I'll walk you to your car and you can drive me back to mine.'

'You really don't have to,' Sam said, but Melanie had different ideas.

'Hey, he came all the way down here in the middle of the night to see that you were safe. Give the guy a break. Let him walk you – us.' She sounded almost envious, and Sam wondered where her boyfriend was, the one she never talked about. Maybe they'd broken up. It certainly wouldn't be the first time Melanie had fallen head over heels in love only to change her mind a few weeks later.

'I'd feel better about it,' Ty said, as he fell into step with them. 'As I said, I was listening to the program and caught that weird call. From Annie – whoever she was. It freaked you out.'

'That wasn't the half of it.' Though Sam would have preferred to tell Ty about 'John's' call later, at another time, Melanie was fairly bursting at the news and couldn't hold her tongue. As they passed the wrought-iron fence encircling the thick shrubs of Jackson Square, Melanie eagerly explained that 'John' had phoned the station once Sam had signed off.

'So he'd rather talk to you alone,' Ty said solemnly as they crossed in front of St. Louis Cathedral. Lamplight splashed against the white facade. Three sharp spires knifed into the blackness of the night sky, reaching upward to heaven, the cross atop the highest steeple barely visible as it pierced the inky heavens. 'What does he want?'

'Retribution,' Melanie said.

'For what?' Ty's jaw tightened.

Sam shook her head. 'I don't know.'

'Your sins.' Melanie was reaching into her purse, jingling coins as she searched for her keys. 'He's always talking about your sins. It's like he's some . . . priest or something.' They reached the parking structure just as Melanie extracted her key ring. A dozen keys jangled. 'I'm here on the first floor.' Unerringly she zeroed in on her little hatchback and unlocked the door. 'Want a ride up?' she asked.

'I'm just on two.' Sam didn't need her assistant acting as if she were a wimp, and said sarcastically, 'I think I can make it.'

'I'll walk her,' Ty added, and though a part of Samantha still wasn't sure about her new neighbor, she really didn't think he would do her any harm. He'd had plenty of opportunities when they were alone and no one had known they were together; it seemed unlikely, even if he was the caller, which she doubted, that he would risk attacking or kidnapping her when Melanie had seen them together. Besides, truth to tell, she felt safe with him . . . comfortable.

'Fine.'

Melanie was in her car in seconds. She switched on her head-lights and engine, then backed out of her spot. Waving with one hand, she honked her horn, and it echoed loudly as she tromped on the gas. The little car zoomed to the exit in a cloud of exhaust.

'Flamboyant, isn't she?' Ty observed, as they took the stairs.

'And melodramatic and extremely efficient.'

Sam's red Mustang was the only car parked on the second floor of the gloomy lot. Half of the security lamps were burned out, the few remaining concentrated around the elevator and stairs.

'Right out of a Hitchcock movie,' Ty said, his bootheels ringing on the dirty concrete.

'That's a little overly dramatic, don't you think?'

'I just hope you never walk here alone,' Ty said, scowling.

'Sometimes. But I'm careful.'

His gaze swept the empty spaces. 'I don't like it.'

She bristled a bit. She hardly knew the guy. He didn't have to automatically step into the role of protector, or big brother or whatever. 'I can handle myself.' *Oh, yeah, Sam, like you handled yourself when the woman claiming to be Annie phoned in. You lost it, Doctor. Big-time.*

'If you say so.'

'I've made it this far.' She already had her handbag open and had found her keys – the duplicate set she'd had made since her trip to Mexico. 'Look, I appreciate your concern. Really. It's . . . it's nice, but I'm a big girl. An adult.'

'Is that a nice way of saying "get lost." '

'No!' she said quickly. 'I mean . . . I just don't want you to feel obligated somehow, or that you need to take care of me because I'm one of those pathetic, weak, porcelain-doll kinds of women.'

One side of his mouth lifted. 'Believe me, that's the farthest thing from my mind.'

'Good. Just so we understand each other.'

'I think we do.' He stepped closer, and she smelled the scent of his aftershave, saw the way his eyes had darkened with the night, noticed that he was staring at her lips. Oh, God, was he going to kiss her? Her skin tingled at the thought of it, her silly pulse kicked up a notch, and as he leaned closer she braced herself, only to feel his lips brush chastely against the side of her cheek. 'Take care,' he said, then stepped away as she unlocked the car door and swung it open.

Her heart was pounding. Her mind leaping ahead to vibrant images of deeper kisses, of bodies touching, of skin rubbing against naked skin. She started to slide behind the wheel seat when she noticed the piece of paper . . . an envelope on the bucket seat. 'What the devil—?' She picked it up, saw her name scrawled across the envelope and without thinking, slid out the card. 'No,' she whispered as she read the words.

The inscription, *Happy 25th Birthday* had been circled in red, then slashed through the middle at an angle.

Sam dropped the card as if it burned her fingers. She felt the blood drain from her face.

'What is it?' Ty reached down and picked up the folded sheet. 'Jesus, what—?' He opened it and saw a single word spelled out in red letters: *MURDERER*. 'How did this get into the car?'

'I – I don't know.' Sam closed her eyes for a second. Remembered the horror that had happened in Houston, the girl who had killed herself. Her head pounded, and she sagged against the back fender.

'Are you okay?' Ty's arm was around her shoulders. 'This has something to do with the woman who claimed she was Annie. She said something about it being her birthday Thursday.'

'Yes. Annie Seger.' *Who* would do such a thing? *Why?* It had been nine years. *Nine* years. She shivered inside. 'I don't get it. Why is someone trying to terrorize me?'

'And how did they get into your car. It was locked, right?'

'Yes.' She nodded.

He looked over the window and door, pointed out the scratches on the paint. 'Was this here before?'

'No.'

'Looks like it was forced. Does anyone have a spare key?'

'My extra key is at the bottom of the Pacific Ocean,' she said shaking her head. 'I lost the entire set when I was in Mexico.'

'So you only have the one key.'

'I had a duplicate made. It's in my drawer at home.' Some of her fear was seeping away as she stared at the scratches on the door and realized Ty's arm was around her. 'David had one, but he gave it back while we were in Mexico – it was in my purse when it went overboard.' There were questions in Ty's eyes, and she added, 'It's a long story.'

'You don't think this David had a copy made?'

'He wouldn't do that,' she said, but heard the doubt in her words. 'Besides, he's in Houston.'

'You think.'

'He's not a part of this,' she said, shaking her head emphatically, as if to convince herself. Clearing her throat, she stepped out of Ty's embrace. She didn't need to be falling apart and into his arms. Her knees were no longer weak, and the horror she felt was slowly being replaced by anger. She couldn't, *wouldn't* let some anonymous creep threaten her or ruin her life. 'It's . . . it's over between David and me. Has been for quite a while.'

'Does he know it?'

'Yeah.'

Ty's jaw slid to one side as if he didn't quite believe her, but he didn't argue the point. His gaze swept the deserted parking structure before returning to Sam. 'Who's Annie Seger?'

'A girl who called in to my radio program in Houston. Nine years ago.'

'She's the same one who phoned you tonight?'

'She claims to be.'

'But Annie's dead,' he deduced. 'And this pervert, whoever he is, blames you? Is that what you think?'

'Yes.' She nodded. 'It must be the guy who calls in . . . John or whatever his real name is. He's always talking about sin and retribution, that I'm guilty of some crime, although lately he's acted like I was a prostitute or something. It . . . it doesn't make any sense, doesn't hang together. Tonight when he phoned in after the show, he told me I was going to die.'

Ty's eyes narrowed. 'So he's escalating. His threats are more specific.'

'Yes.'

'Damn.' He raked stiff fingers through his hair. 'So you think he called in, pretended he was a woman ... is that it ... or that ... or that he has an accomplice and ... that this is what? Some kind of conspiracy to scare the hell out of you?'

'I – I don't know,' she admitted and again felt weak, an emotion she detested.

'We have to go to the police.'

'I know,' she said, hating the thought. She was bone-tired and wanted nothing more than to fall into a long, hot bath, towel off and fall into bed to sleep for about a billion hours.

'Let me call.' He reached into his pocket and pulled out a cell phone. Sam braced herself for another ordeal. How many times had she already been questioned? Four times? Five? She was beginning to lose count.

And the stalker was still at large. She rotated the kinks from her neck as Ty talked to the dispatcher, who promised that the officers who had been at the station less than half an hour earlier would meet them at the garage.

The two uniformed cops made it in fifteen minutes, driving to the parking garage with their siren wailing and lights flashing. They asked questions, checked out Sam's car, put the card in a plastic bag and called for other officers to dust the Mustang for fingerprints as well as check the interior for other evidence, then looked over the structure of the vehicle to ensure that it was safe to drive.

By the time all the officers had finished and driven away, it was after three.

Ty's mouth was a thin, hard line. 'I think I should drive you home.'

She was touched, but shook her head. 'Don't be ridiculous. I can drive.'

Ty wasn't having any of it. 'Listen, Samantha, whoever did this is sick. We both know that. He broke into your car tonight, right? What's to say that he didn't tamper with it? Drain the brake fluid, or plant a bomb or—'

'The police checked it.'

'They can miss things.'

'I don't think so, and I'm not going to start jumping at my own shadow. I can't live my life scared. If I do, I lose, Ty. He wins. That's what he wants. To scare me to death. Make me nervous and edgy. He's playing a psychological game with me, and if he killed me, it would be over. And tampering with the car is too . . . impersonal. This guy calls me up, he sends me letters, he lets me know he's around. He didn't like it when I was on the speaker phone. He wants to be intimate with me. To be personal. To get into my head. I know it. I feel it.'

'And do you "know" or "feel" that he could be a killer? For God's sake, Samantha, he's threatened to kill you.'

Sam was thinking hard now, rubbing her arms despite the heat, biting her lip and starting to understand the man who called himself John. 'I know,' she admitted. 'But it won't be until I've repented, not until I understand the sins I've committed. He's into some kind of religious thing – sin, retribution.'

'You can't take the chance. Isn't this enough proof that the guy's unhinged, that he's going to do you major harm?' Ty asked. 'He's accused you of murder. He's spouted a lot of biblical mumbo jumbo, maybe he believes in the old "An eye for an eye," type of retribution.'

'But not yet.' As weary as she was, she was certain that she wasn't in immediate danger. John wanted to terrorize her. He got his thrills by trying to scare her out of her wits and then communicating with her. He wanted her to beg for forgiveness. She glanced at her car. 'Don't worry, I – I'm going to be fine. I'm starting to understand him.'

'Believe me, *no* one understands this creep. Come on, let me drive you home.'

'It's nice of you, really, to be so concerned, but I'm okay. A big girl, you know,' she said, though she wasn't certain she meant it any more than she thought it was a good idea to let Ty take on the role of bodyguard. She barely knew the guy. He seemed sincere enough, and she had a sense of safety around him, but his timing, showing up when she'd started getting the prank calls made her second-guess his motives. God, she hated this . . . this newfound fear. John had stripped her of her independence, but she intended to fight back.

'Okay, then I'm going to check out the car again, and I'll follow you. All you have to do is drive me to my car, and I'll make sure you get into your house all right.'

'Promise?' She was too tired to argue any longer. What would it hurt for him to see her to her house? It wasn't as if it was out of his way. 'Fine. If that's what you want.'

'It is. Now, I don't suppose you have a flashlight.'

'Ask and ye shall receive,' she said, and opened the trunk.

'Not funny, Sam.'

'Oh, ye of little faith and humor.' She pulled out an emergency roadside kit – flares, matches, reflective signs and a flashlight. For the next few minutes Ty checked under the hood and the body of the car, lying on the grimy cement, shining the flashlight's small beam across the wheel axles and exhaust system. He tested the lug nuts on her wheels and looked over the ignition and steering column. By the time he'd finished his forehead was damp, sweat running down the sides of his face.

'I guess there's only one way to find out for sure,' he said and snagged the keys from her hand. 'Stand back.'

'No way. I'm not going to let you—'

'Too late.' He slid into the bucket seat. 'Back off in case I get blown to smithereens.'

'This is ridiculous.'

'Humor me – the one of little faith and humor – okay?'

'You're impossible.'

'So I've been told.'

Seeing that he wasn't about to budge, she backed up a few steps, her stomach tightening. He jabbed her key into the ignition, twisted and the Mustang's engine caught on the first try, firing to life. Ty stepped on the throttle, gunning the engine. Exhaust spewed out of the tailpipe, the roar of six cylinders deafening. But there was no explosion. No flying glass. No twisting of metal.

'I think it's okay,' Ty said through the open window. 'Hop in.' Leaning over he opened the passenger door. Since there was no changing his mind, she crossed the short span of grease-dappled concrete and climbed into the passenger side of her car.

'You don't have to baby-sit me,' she said, as he drove down the ramp to the first floor and out into the street, where street-lights glowed watery blue and there was little traffic.

'Is that what I'm doing?' He slanted her a glance as he slowed for a traffic light and her heart nearly stopped. There was something about him, something she didn't quite understand that warned her to be wary, yet she couldn't resist him, couldn't help but trust him. As the interior of the car glowed red in the reflection of the stoplight, she caught his eyes, saw promises in his gaze she didn't want to understand. 'I'm baby-sitting?' he asked again.

'Seems like.' Forcing her accelerating heartbeat to slow, she held up one finger. 'You called the station after I got the weird call from Annie.' Another finger jutted upward as the light changed and she watched his profile – strong jaw, deep-set eyes, high forehead, bladed cheeks, razor-thin lips. In an instant she wondered what it would feel like to kiss him . . . to touch him . . . The car shot forward, and she realized she hadn't finished her thought. 'You waited for me at the station door.' A third finger joined the first two as Ty rounded a final corner and pulled into a spot behind his Volvo. 'You walked Melanie and me to the parking garage.' Her pinky straightened. 'You checked out the car and drove me here. And' – her thumb raised and she splayed her fingers in front of his face as her car idled – 'and you're going to follow me home.'

He grabbed her hand. Hard warm fingers wrapping around hers. 'And,' he vowed solemnly, 'when we get back to your place, I'm gonna walk you inside.'

'You don't have to—'

'I *want* to, okay?' His eyes, dark with the night, held hers and his fingers tightened. 'I would never forgive myself, Samantha, if something happened to you. Now, we can sit here and argue semantics all night, but I think we should go. It's late.'

She swallowed hard. Retrieved her hand. 'Fine.'

One side of his mouth lifted. 'I'm holding you to it.' Then he was out of the car, jogging to the Volvo, and sliding inside. His brake lights flashed as Sam crawled over the gearshift and landed behind the steering wheel. After she adjusted the position of her seat, she punched the accelerator, watching in her rearview mirror as the Volvo pulled away from the curb and followed her.

Ty Wheeler seemed to have appointed himself her bodyguard.

Whether she wanted him to or not.

14

On the way home Sam punched the first button on her radio, caught the end of the *Lights Out* program and drove through the deserted streets toward the lake and the small community of Cambrai. She met a few cars, the oncoming headlights bright, but, for the most part, her attention was focused in the rearview mirror and the twin beams from Ty's Volvo. What was he thinking? Why was he making her problems his? What did he want from her? She turned onto her street, and she couldn't help but second-guess him. Did his boat really break down?

'Stop it,' she growled as she pulled into her driveway and pushed the button on her automatic garage-door opener. She was tired, her nerves shot, paranoia taking hold. As the garage door cranked upward she pulled inside. It had once been a carriage house but had been converted to house a horseless carriage sometime in the nineteen twenties. Later a breezeway had been added, attaching the garage to the kitchen. As she climbed out of the car, Ty's car wheeled into the drive. He was out of his car in seconds and following her into the house.

'No arguments,' he advised when he noticed she was about to protest. 'Let me check the place out.'

'It's been locked.'

'So was the car.'

He walked ahead of her through the door and strode along the glassed-in breezeway as if he'd done it all his life. Inside the house, Sam shut off the alarm that she'd activated for once. She'd forgotten it time and time again, just wasn't used to setting it. Thankfully, tonight, the troublesome thing seemed to be working, but Ty wasn't satisfied. He walked slowly through the kitchen and dining area where, perched on one of the chairs, Charon watched with wide, suspicious eyes.

'It's all right,' she mouthed to the cat.

With Samantha on his heels, Ty did a room-by-room search of the house. He didn't bother to ask her permission as he opened doors to cupboards and closets, even tested the locked trapdoor of the crawl space tucked under the stairs. Then he took the steps two at a time to the second floor. Without a word he walked into the guest room, with its lacy curtains, daybed and antique dresser, through the shared bath and finally ended up in her bedroom.

Following after him, she felt uneasy and exposed. Naked. All the private corners of her living space bared. He slid one glance at the oversize canopy bed, then proceeded into the walk-in wardrobe where her clothes, shoes and handbags were strewn haphazardly.

Within seconds he emerged. Sam was leaning against her armoire. 'Satisfied?' she asked. 'No bogeymen?'

'Not so far.' He tested the lock on the French doors leading to her balcony, gave the lever a shake, then grunted as if he finally was convinced that the house was safe. 'Okay . . . so I guess I can give you the all clear.'

'Good.' She stretched and started for the door, but Ty didn't follow.

'Why don't you tell me about Annie Seger?' he asked, leaning against one of the bedposts. 'I know you're tired, but it would help me to know why someone is blaming you for her death.'

'That's a good question.' Sam shoved her fingers through her hair and thought for a second. 'I can't really tell you the answer as I don't understand it myself.' She lowered herself into the rocker by the French doors and wrapped the faded afghan her great-grandmother had knitted decades ago around her shoulders. Ty had been kind to her, interested. The least she could do was try and explain. 'I was hosting a show like the one I'm doing now, only at a smaller station. I'd only been out of college a while and was separated from my husband, so I was on my own for the first time in my life, and the show was enjoying quite a bit of success. Jeremy, that's my ex, thought it was going to my head, and tried to make it an issue, like the catalyst for the divorce, but it was more than that. A lot more.

'Anyway, things were going relatively well.' She remembered how each day she would push thoughts of Jeremy and the divorce from her mind, tell herself she hadn't failed, that the marriage had been destined to fall apart, then drive to the station and bury herself in her work, listen to the callers, try to sort things out for others as she hadn't been able to for herself.

'One night, this girl calls, says her name is Annie, and that she wants some advice.' Samantha remembered the girl's hesitancy at first, how embarrassed she'd seemed, how frightened. Pulling the afghan closer around her neck, Sam said, 'The girl, Annie, was scared. She'd just found out she was pregnant and couldn't tell her parents because they would flip – maybe turn her out, that sort of thing. I got the impression that they were very strict and religious, that their daughter being unwed and in a family way would be socially unacceptable.

'I suggested she talk to a counselor at school or her pastor, someone who might be able to help her and guide her in her decision, someone she trusted.'

'But she didn't?' he asked, still leaning against the bed-post.

'She couldn't, I guess. A few nights later she called back. More scared than ever. Her boyfriend wanted her to get an abortion, but she didn't want one, was adamantly against it for personal as well as religious reasons. I told her not to do anything she wasn't comfortable with, that it was her body and her baby. Of course, as the audience is hearing this, the phone lines are lighting up like fireworks on the Fourth of July. Everyone had an opinion. Or advice. I asked her to call back when I wasn't on the air, that I would give her the names of some counselors and women's services where she could get one-on-one help.'

Sam let out her breath slowly as she remembered those painful days. 'Maybe I wasn't the best one to be giving out advice at the time,' she admitted, thinking back to that black period in her life. 'I'd only been in Houston a few months, and the reason I got the job is that the woman who was hosting the program had quit. I was only supposed to be a temporary fill-in, but audience response was great, even if the pay wasn't, so they offered me a raise, and I stayed on.'

She rolled her eyes at her own naïveté, pushed back with her toe and began slowly rocking. 'Even though we were on the road to divorce anyway, my husband didn't like it. I was in the lime-light for once, not him, and it eroded the marriage all the faster I think. I wasn't going to give up the job and within weeks – possibly days – he found someone else . . . or, more likely, he'd been seeing her all along, but that's another story,' she added, surprised at herself for confiding so much. 'We were talking about Annie Seger. The upshot was that Annie ignored my advice, never called after hours, but phoned in every other night or so. And the audience went crazy. People started phoning in like mad. Everyone from the president of the local chapter of Right to Life and several youth ministers to someone from the local paper. The thing just kept getting bigger and bigger. Mushrooming. I had lawyers calling me with offers of money, couples wanted to adopt Annie's baby. Young mothers called, women who'd suffered abortions or miscarriages or marrying the wrong guy because they were pregnant and had been forced to get married by their folks. It was a circus. And in the middle of it was a lonely, scared sixteen-year-old.'

Sam shivered, remembered being seated at a windowless booth in the heart of the station, taking the calls, wondering if Annie would phone in again. George Hannah, the owner, had been beside himself with glee at the ratings, and Eleanor, too, had reveled in the increased listenership. 'Everyone at the station was thrilled. We were beating out the rival station, and that was what mattered. Ratings were through the roof, by God! And the bottom line looked good.' Sam couldn't hide the sarcasm in her voice.

But, aside from all the hoopla, Annie had been desperate. And Samantha had failed her. Even after all of these years, Sam still felt the girl's despair, her fear. Her shame.

'I tried to get through to her, but she couldn't find the strength to confide in anyone close to her. She had family but seemed terrified of them. Couldn't or wouldn't talk to a school counselor or anyone from her parish. She became angry with me, for some reason. As if I were to blame. It was awful. Just . . . awful.' Sam drew in a long breath and said, 'Then, after the seventh or eighth time she'd called in, about three weeks after the initial time she'd contacted me, she was found dead. Overdose and her wrists slit. Her mother's prescription for sleeping pills and about half a fifth of vodka along with a pair of bloody gardening shears were nearby. There was a suicide note on her computer. It said something about Annie being ashamed, feeling alone, not having anyone to confide in, not her parents, boyfriend or me.'

Sam remembered seeing the front page of the paper the next day with Annie Seger's face in black and white. A pretty, privileged girl, captain of the cheerleading squad, an honor student, dead by her own hand.

A girl who had been pregnant.

And alone. Someone who had reached out for help and gotten nothing.

The girl's high-school picture had made Annie seem more real, more helpless, more tragic to Sam. Annie had been so damned young. Sam had been devastated and the images of the smiling girl in the black-and-white photo of the paper still haunted her. 'I quit the job after that. Took some time off and spent it with my dad. Went into private practice in Santa Monica. It was all Eleanor could do to persuade me to get behind the mike again and host another program.' She plucked at the afghan with her fingers. 'And now it's all happening again.'

'So Thursday would have been Annie's twenty-fifth birthday?'

'I guess.' Sam lifted a shoulder. Felt cold to her bones. Tightened the blanket around her though the temperature in the room was probably over eighty degrees. 'I just don't know why anyone would bring it all up again.'

'Neither do I,' he said, and held her gaze for a second longer than necessary. 'Listen, if you hear or see anything that bothers you – anything at all – give me a call.' Pulling a pen from his pocket, he crossed to the nightstand and wrote on the notepad by her phone. 'Here're my numbers – home and cell. Don't lose 'em.' He tore off the top page, walked to her chair and handed her the information.

'Wouldn't dream of it,' she said, and had to stifle a yawn.

Ty glanced again at the bed with its fluffy duvet, decorative pillows and slatted canopy. 'Go to bed, Champ. You've had a long day.'

'Very long,' she agreed, thinking it had lasted forever.

To her surprise, Ty reached forward, pulled her, afghan and all, out of the chair and drew her into the circle of his arms.

'You will call me,' he said, leaning down so that his forehead touched hers.

All thoughts of sleep vanished. The cozy room with its sloped ceiling seemed to shrink. Become warmer. 'If it comes down to that.'

'Even if you just get scared.' With one strong finger he lifted her chin. 'Promise.'

'Oh, sure. Scout's honor,' she agreed, her heart drumming wildly. The scent of old leather mingled with a lingering trace of some aftershave and that pure male scent she hadn't smelled in a long, long time.

'I'll hold you to it.' He glanced down at her mouth and in a second she realized he was going to kiss her.

Oh, God. Her throat went dry, her skin tingled in anticipation. As if he knew exactly what she was feeling, what kind of response he'd already evoked from her, he had the audacity to smile, that irrepressible, cocky, half grin that made her breath stop.

'Good night, Sam,' he said, and he brushed a kiss across her forehead before releasing her. 'You keep your doors locked and give me a call if anything bothers you.'

You bother me, she thought, as he released her and walked out the door. *Damn it, Ty Wheeler, you bother the hell out of me.*

*   *   *

Two hours later Ty flipped through his notes as he sat at the keyboard, the dog at his feet, the windows open to let in the breeze. Ice cubes melting, a drink sat on his desk, nearly forgotten as he flipped through his notes on Annie Seger. He knew the info by heart, yet studied it as if he'd never heard Annie's name before.

Which was ridiculous, as he was related to her in a roundabout way.

His third cousin. Which was the reason he'd been thrown off the case.

He perused the yellowed newspaper clippings, reading over the facts that he'd memorized long ago:

Too frightened to tell her parents that she was in a family way, she'd sought solace in a local radio psychiatrist, Dr. Samantha Leeds, and couldn't heed the doctor's advice. She'd felt she had nowhere to turn, and when the father of her child had told her that he didn't want to raise a family, she'd gone into her bedroom, turned on her computer, written a note and when sleeping pills and vodka hadn't done the trick, slit her wrists.

It had been a scandal that had rocked a wealthy section of Houston. Soon, the Dr. Sam show had gone off the air but not because of poor ratings. Contrarily, the popularity of her program had soared to new heights and her fame, or infamy, had skyrocketed.

But Samatha Leeds hadn't been able to live with herself, or so it seemed. She'd quit the show and the radio station and gone into private practice until the past six months, when the same people who had worked with her in Houston had lured her to New Orleans.

Ty took a sip of his drink. Crushed the ice between his teeth.

He remembered the entire scenario with Annie Seger. He'd been one of the first to arrive at her house and had witnessed the devastation of not only her, but her entire family.

Annie had been a pretty girl with a few freckles dusting her nose, short reddish hair and blue-green eyes that had sparkled in life.

A waste.

A shame.

Carrying his drink, Ty walked outside to listen to the lapping of the lake against the dock. Sasquatch followed him outside and, nose to the wind, trotted off the verandah to the yard, where he lifted his leg on a stately old live oak.

Crickets chirped and a solitary frog croaked as his dog wandered between the trees and sniffed the ground. Ty glanced at the *Bright Angel*, sails down, gently rocking against her moorings. Somewhere far off a siren wailed plaintively, muted by distance. Far into the horizon the first gray light of dawn was breaking.

Ty thought of Samantha Leeds, only a quarter of a mile away.

A beautiful woman.

An intelligent woman.

A damned fascinating woman.

A woman he imagined he could make love to over and over again. Telling himself he was a fool, he fantasized about what it would be like to take her to bed, to feel her ragged breath as she lay beneath him, or the feel of her skin, soft as silk, against his body.

No doubt about it, she was getting to him.

And he was letting her.

Which was a colossal mistake.

He tossed back his drink and whistled to the old shepherd as he walked into the house.

The last thing, the very last thing he could do was lose his sense of purpose; his objectivity. He'd made a promise to himself and no one, especially not Annie's radio-psychologist was going to stop him.

'*Why didn't you help me, Dr. Sam. Why?*' The voice was young and frail and seemed far away, through the patchy fog and dense trees. Samantha followed the sound, her heart pounding, her breath tight as she tried to peer through branches dripping with Spanish moss and blocking her view.

'Annie? Where are you?' she called, and her voice echoed through the woods, reverberating loudly.

'*Over here . . .*'

Sam ran, tripping over roots and vines, squinting in the darkness, hearing the sounds of the freeway in the distance over the lonely hoot of an owl. Why had Annie lured her out here, what did she want?

'I can't find you.'

'Because you're not looking hard enough.'

'But where . . . ?' She broke through the trees and saw the girl, a beautiful girl with short red hair, big eyes and fear cast in her every feature. She was standing in the middle of a cemetery with headstones and raised coffins, a filigreed iron fence separating her from Samantha. In her arms she held a baby wrapped in tattered swaddling clothes. The baby was crying, wailing horridly, as if in pain.

'I'm sorry,' Sam said, walking along the fence, searching for a gate, trying to get closer. 'I didn't know.'

'I called you. I asked for your help. You turned me away.'

'No, I wanted to help you, I did.'

'Liar!'

Sam dragged her fingers along the posts, hurrying faster, trying to gain entrance, but no matter how many corners she turned, how far she ran through the rising mist and shadows, she couldn't find the gate, couldn't get close, could never reach the girl and the baby whose muffled cries tore at Sam's heart.

'Too late,' Annie said. 'You're too late.'

'No, I can help.'

She saw the girl move then and shake out the blanket. Sam screamed as the folds opened and she expected the baby to be tossed onto the ground, but as the worn blanket unfolded, it was empty, the baby having disappeared.

'Too late,' Annie said again.

'No. I'll help you, I promise,' she said, breathing hard, feeling as if her feet were cast in concrete.

'Don't . . .' a male voice warned.

Ty's?

John's?

She whirled but couldn't see anything in the black woods. 'Who are you?' she cried, but no one answered.

Somewhere far off someone was singing 'American Pie.'

The fog grew denser. Sam ran faster. Her legs felt like lead, but she had to reach Annie, talk to her, before . . . before *what?*

Sam's eyes flew open.

The clock radio was still playing the last chords of the song that had followed her through the dream.

Sunlight streamed through the French doors and overhead the paddle fan stirred the morning air in her bedroom.

She was home. In her bed. Safe.

The dream faded into the dark recesses of her mind where it belonged, but she was in a sweat, her head pounding, her heart racing. It had been so real. Too real. And she knew it would be back.

15

'We need to talk,' Eleanor said. Seated at her desk, she waved Sam into her office. 'Sit down, oh, just a minute.' As Sam took a chair on the opposite side of the desk, Eleanor reached for the phone, punched a number, and said, 'Melba, hold all my calls, would you? Sam and I don't want to be interrupted except for Tiny and Melanie. They're supposed to be here in' – she glanced at her watch – 'about fifteen minutes. Send them back right at one, okay? Fine.' Dropping the receiver into its cradle, she turned her attention toward Sam. 'There's some weird stuff happening around here.' Folding her arms across the ink blotter covering her desk, she leaned forward. 'I listened to the tape of last night's show this morning. And I had Tiny add in the last call from your friendly stalker. Okay? Then I talked to George and eventually the police, one of those officers who came by last night. But now, I want to hear it straight from the horse's mouth. What do you think's going on?'

'Other than that someone's trying to terrorize me.'

'One person?'

'Or two,' Sam said, 'though I doubt there's some big conspiracy out to get Dr. Sam.'

'Okay, so why would anyone bring up Annie now?'

'I don't know.' Sam glanced out the window to see blue sky and rooftops. 'It's been so long. I was hoping it was all behind me.'

'You and me both.' Eleanor sighed, then took off the back of her earring. 'So let me get this straight. The woman who calls herself Annie calls while you were on the air, then once you've signed off, about half an hour later, this creep 'John' phones again. They've got to be related.'

'I agree – he seems to think I've sinned, that I need to repent and now I know why. He's blaming me for Annie's death. But they didn't come from the same phone. The call from the woman was labeled by caller ID as a pay phone downtown in a bar, and John's call was again from a different phone booth, in the Garden District. The police are checking into it.'

'So you think this John-person conned some woman into calling you or that he disguised his voice, right? I think the police can check that sort of thing. I've told George that we need to tape all incoming calls, not just those on your program. There's no problem there,' she added, wincing as she adjusted the diamond stud in her earlobe. 'Except that George is thrilled with the ratings. Just like in Houston. More listeners have tuned in on the nights John calls and the nights thereafter.'

'Wonderful,' Sam said sarcastically. 'Maybe we should find a couple more psychos to call in.'

'I don't think that's in George's plan. But he does have a point. The e-mail we've been getting backs up his theory. The result is,' she said, lines furrowing across her smooth brow, 'that George is seriously considering expanding your program. Not just Sunday through Thursday, but including Friday and Saturday nights as well.'

'So much for my social life, right?'

'We'd work it out – initially it would be your baby, of course, but then we could incorporate guest hosts or pretaped segments, or figure out which nights were the most popular.'

'You're for this?' Samantha asked.

'I'm for anything that keeps the ratings up as long as it doesn't prove dangerous. Now, so far, I don't like what the caller's saying. Not one bit. And this business about Annie Seger, I don't get it.' Her dark eyes flashed. 'For the record, I don't like it either. I want security beefed up and you to be doubly careful and we'll play this by ear. Let's just give it a little time.'

'Okay, but there's something else you should know.'

'Oh great.' The lines over her eyebrows deepened. 'Now what?'

'I received a greeting card last night.' Sam described the birthday card. 'It was in my car.'

'*Inside* your car? But didn't you lock the doors . . . ?' she asked, then waved off her own question. 'Of course you did, you're not an idiot. As I said I already talked to the police last night, but I want to know what you think. What the hell is this all about?'

'I don't know, but I intend to find out,' Sam said. 'I've already talked to the police.'

'You had a busy night last night,' Eleanor observed. 'I'll tell George I want a guard not only at the front door of the building, but here, on the premises, at all times. No two ways about it. Until this all dies down. It's one thing for the nutcase to make calls to the station, another one to threaten you personally.'

The intercom line beeped and Eleanor took the call. 'Send 'em back, and thanks, Melba,' she said. 'Tiny and Melanie are gonna join us. Maybe they have a different spin on this.'

Within minutes, there was a sharp rap on the door. Melanie breezed in, with Tiny dragging at her heels.

They dropped into a short couch wedged between a file cabinet and a bookcase.

'Okay, Sam's filled me in on what happened last night, but I'd like your impressions.'

'Sam's got a maniac stalking her,' Tiny offered, rubbing his hands together nervously and avoiding Sam's eyes. 'I think he's dangerous.'

'He's probably just getting his rocks off by scaring her,' Melanie disagreed. She tossed her blond curls off her shoulder, and added, 'He's probably some tightly wound religious nut.'

'Even so, he could be dangerous. I listened to the tapes three times, and I think Tiny's right. This guy is definitely off-balance. I want everyone to be extra careful. Don't go out alone at night.'

'It seems he's just targeting Sam.'

'So far,' Eleanor said. 'Because it's her show, but it's personal with him.'

'And a game,' Samantha added. 'Tiny's right, the guy could be dangerous, but Melanie's got a good point. The creep is getting his jollies by scaring me.'

'So be careful. Get a watchdog, carry Mace, don't go out at night alone, check your car before you get in. Whatever it takes until we find who the son of a bitch is.' Eleanor's dark eyes focused on each of them. 'I already talked to George about adding security and upgrading our equipment so that we can trace our calls – so far I haven't heard back. I don't even know if it's possible. But, if we have to call in the police or hire a private detective or whatever, I'm willing to do it. This has *got* to be monitored.'

'You mean stopped,' Sam corrected.

'Of course. Stopped.' Eleanor pointed a polished nail at each of them. 'And I want to hear about it the second something out of the ordinary happens. Don't wait until the next day, you call me directly. You all have my cell number. You can catch me anytime.'

The phone rang, and she glanced at her watch. 'Damn. Well, I guess we were finished here anyway. I just hope we don't have any more trouble. We've got that charity gig coming up – for the Boucher House and we've invited all the media. I wouldn't want them to get wind of this.'

'We *are* the media,' Sam reminded her.

'You know what I mean.'

The phone jangled again and Eleanor reached for the receiver. The meeting was over. Tiny and Melanie had already made good their escape. Sam was halfway to the door when she heard her name. 'Wait – Sam—' Eleanor called after her.

Samantha looked over her shoulder as Eleanor ignored the third ring.

'You get in touch with the police again and you put the fear of God into them, y'hear? Tell the officer in charge he'd better nail this sucker's butt or else there's gonna be hell to pay!'

'Oh, that'll make things move along faster,' Sam mocked.

'It damned well better.'

★   ★   ★

'Isn't this your radio shrink?' Montoya asked, flipping a copy of a report across Rick's desk. The air conditioner was on the blink, the office an oven. Bentz had propped a fan on the credenza behind him. It droned and swiveled, pushing hot air around the room.

'My what?' he asked, then caught sight of Samantha Leeds's name. 'Shit.' Bentz glanced up at Montoya who smelled of cigarette smoke and some cologne he couldn't name. Even in the sweltering heat Montoya looked cool in his black shirt, matching jeans and leather jacket while Bentz was sweating like a pig. 'More trouble?'

'Looks like.' Montoya paused to straighten a picture of the skyline that Bentz had mounted over a cabinet as Bentz scanned the report.

'Seems like her personal pervert hasn't disappeared. Not only called the station, but left a threatening note in her car?'

'Mmm.'

'Was the car impounded?'

'Nope.'

'Why the hell not?' Bentz growled.

'It was dusted there.'

'And?'

'Nothing yet.'

'Why doesn't that surprise me?' Bentz wondered, opening his drawer for a piece of gum and thinking it was time to give up on trying to quit.

'Because you're used to the way things work around here.' Montoya reached into his jacket pocket and withdrew a cassette. He dropped a cassette onto the desk, right in front of Bentz's half-drunk can of Pepsi and the photos of Kristi. 'Here's the tape of last night's show. The upshot is that last night, she got a couple more calls.'

'From the guy calling himself John.'

'And a woman – a dead woman.'

'I heard that one myself,' Bentz admitted, leaning back in his chair and still hankering for a smoke. 'Annie.'

'You tuned in?' Montoya's grin stretched from one side of his mouth to the other. He was obviously amused at the thought of Bentz sitting by the radio, phone in hand, ready to call dial-a-shrink.

'Yeah, I've listened every night, ever since I interviewed her. No one named John called last night.'

'Wrong. The pervert did call in. But it was after the show went off the air. It's on the tape. The technician, Albert AKA Tiny Pagano, caught it on that tape.' He motioned to the cassette on Bentz's desk.

'Just what we need.' Bentz had hoped Dr. Sam's personal nutcase had given up his threatening calls. From the looks of the report, he'd been overly optimistic. 'How'd you get a copy of this?' He found the gum and popped a piece into his mouth.

'From O'Keefe. He was one of the officers on duty last night and knew you were assigned the case. He and another guy interviewed Dr. Sam at the station, then were called to meet her at the parking garage because of the note in her car. According to O'Keefe the doc was pretty shook up.

'Do you blame her?'

'Hell, no.' Scratching thoughtfully at his goatee, Montoya asked, 'So what do you make of it?'

'Nothin' good.' Bentz chewed on the flavorless piece of gum. 'Annie Seger. Who the hell is she?' he asked.

'Don't know. I suppose we should leave it to the harassment boys. It's really not your case. No one's dead.'

'Yet.'

'I figured you'd have that attitude.'

'Thanks.' He had more work to do than time to do it; not only was there a possible serial killer on the loose and now the FBI was involved, but there were the usual number of homicides to investigate as well – domestic disputes turned bad, drive-bys, gang-related, sour drug deals, or people just pissed off at each other and ready to pull out a gun or knife.

Montoya produced a pocket recorder and played the tape where it was marked, the first call being the one from the girl claiming Dr. Sam had killed her, the second from the stalker. Rick heard Annie's breathy voice again, then John's smooth, suggestive tone, his icy calm that slowly eroded as the conversation with Dr. Sam progressed.

Montoya snapped off the recorder as a wasp slipped through the window screen and buzzed angrily at the glass. 'I'd say John's not giving up.'

'And the threats are more pointed.' Both recordings left Bentz with a bad feeling – a real bad feeling. The wasp made the mistake of coming close and he swiped at it angrily. He missed and the angry insect danced against the filmy glass of the window in a desperate attempt at freedom.

'Definitely more pointed.' Montoya found a rubber band on Bentz's desk, drew back and let it fly. Snap! The wasp dropped dead to the floor. 'Do you think they're related – the call from Annie, then the one from John?'

'Could be.' Almost had to be. Bentz didn't believe in coincidence. 'Unless one triggered the other – the girl heard John's call and thought she'd come up with something of her own.'

'So she just *knows* about Annie Seger.'

'Someone does.'

'Okay, so what was that crap about Dr. Sam being a hooker? A working girl? Does that make any sense?'

Bentz chewed his gum thoughtfully. 'We'll check it out. I want to know every day of Dr. Sam's history, who she is, what makes her tick, why she decided to become a radio shrink. I want to know about her family, her boyfriends, this' – he pulled a file and checked his notes – 'David Ross, a guy she went to Mexico with and every John, Jack, Johnson, Jackson, Jonathon, Jay, any man she's ever dated that could be the caller.' The phone rang loudly. Bentz made a grab for it, but as his fingers grazed the receiver, he stopped short.

The woman they'd been discussing, the radio-shrink herself, appeared in the outer office. From the look in her eye he was willing to bet that a bad day was just about to get worse.

16

Bentz braced himself.

Samantha Leeds was marching through the desks sprinkled outside his door and heading toward his office.

Dressed in a skirt that buttoned up the front and a sleeveless white blouse, she was a good-looking woman, and the set of her jaw suggested she wanted answers and wasn't going to leave until she got them.

'Detective Bentz,' she said as she swept through the door. Layered reddish hair bounced around a heart-shaped face with cheekbones most models would kill for. Green eyes zeroed in on Bentz and didn't let go.

Montoya gave her a quick once-over, and apparently, liked what he saw. He'd been about to leave, but now resumed his spot near the file cabinet as she gave him a cursory glance, then leaned across Bentz's desk.

'Can I talk to you?' Sam demanded. 'Now?'

Bentz's phone rang again.

'Yeah. Just hold on a sec.' He held up one finger and took the call. It was a short conversation from someone in the lab about the type of fibers found on the bodies of the two prostitutes – what manufacturer used the synthetic material for the wigs, specifically the red wigs that were missing from the murder scenes. The report was being faxed to Bentz, and the technician confirmed that the hairs were identical. As every piece of evidence had confirmed they were dealing with one killer and two victims. So far. The Feds would go nuts. He hung up and focused his attention on the woman standing in front of his desk. She was trying to look cool and composed, but she was nervous as a cat. Her fingers fiddled with the strap of her purse, and she shifted from one foot to the other.

'Have a seat,' he offered, then motioned to Montoya. 'My partner. Detective Montoya. Reuben – Dr. Leeds, A.K.A. Dr. Sam.'

Samantha eased into one of the worn chairs on the far side of the desk.

'Pleased to meet you,' Montoya oozed, slathering on his Latin charm.

'Thanks.' She nodded. 'I assume you were told about what happened last night.'

'Just got the report.'

'What do you think?'

'That this guy isn't going to give up. That he's got a real vendetta against you.' Rolling his sleeves over his elbows, he asked, 'What do *you* think?'

'I think whoever sent the card thinks I killed Annie Seger and that the caller who identifies himself as John is somehow linked to Annie – though I don't know how. She is dead, you know.'

'Tell me about her.'

Samantha took a minute, leaned back in the chair and cradled her purse in her lap. 'I hosted a similar program in Houston nearly ten years ago. A girl who said she was Annie phoned in. She was sixteen, pregnant and scared out of her mind. I tried to help, to steer her in the right direction, but . . .' Samantha paled and looked out the window. One of her hands fisted, then slowly opened. 'I wish . . . I mean I had no idea how desperate she was and . . .' Sam's voice trailed off for a second. She took a deep breath and cleared her throat before she controlled herself. '. . . Annie swore she couldn't confide in anyone and . . . she killed herself. Obviously someone blames me.'

'And last night someone impersonating Annie called your program,' Montoya said.

'Yes.' Sam fiddled with the gold chain surrounding her neck, avoided Bentz's eyes for a second. 'It wasn't Annie, of course. I . . . I went to her funeral, I mean . . . I was asked to leave, but

Annie Seger, the Annie Seger who called me in Houston nine years ago is definitely dead.' She blinked hard, but didn't break down.

'You were kicked out of the funeral?' Bentz asked.

'The family blamed me.'

He reached for his pen. 'The family?'

'Her parents, Estelle and Jason Faraday.'

'I thought her name was Seger.'

'It is – was. Her mother and biological father were divorced.'

Bentz made a note and caught a glimpse from Montoya as the sound of a truck on the street below rumbled through the small room. 'What about her father?'

'I – I don't know. I mean, I did some research after the fact . . . oh, God, I think he lived in the Northwest somewhere.' Her eyebrows drew together, and her smooth brow furrowed.

'His name?'

'Wally . . . Oswald Seger, I think. Something like that.' She managed a tight, humorless smile. 'I knew all this stuff nine years ago. In fact I fed on it. Tried to make some sense of it, but then . . . well, I decided to let it go.'

Bentz didn't blame her, but it all had to be dragged up again; whoever was terrorizing her had made sure of that. 'You have notes? Names, addresses, anything?'

She hesitated, her eyes thinning. 'I think so. I saw the box of notes and tapes and all when I moved. I almost threw it out, but packed it away in the attic with the Christmas ornaments and old tax records. I can get it for you.'

'That would help. Call me when you find it, and I'll have someone pick it up. I'd like to see anything you've got.' He made a note and asked, 'What else do you remember about Annie? Did she have other relatives and friends?'

'A brother. Ken, no . . . Kent.'

'And the boyfriend? The father of her baby.'

'Ryan Zimmerman, I think. He was a couple of years older. A big athlete, I think, but I really can't remember.' She shook her head. 'I've spent a long time trying to forget.' Lines of strain were evident around her eyes and mouth. The doc was putting on a pretty good show, but the harassment and threats were getting to her. She was sweating, and the dark smudges beneath her eyes indicated she hadn't slept much in the last couple of days.

'I heard the tape,' Bentz said. 'John referred to you being a prostitute again. What's that all about?'

'He's sick.'

'So there's no truth to it?'

In an instant, she was out of her chair and leaning over the desk, her hands flat on a stack of letters and files. The defeat he'd witnessed seconds ago had disappeared. Two spots of color tinged her cheeks. 'I thought I'd already made this clear!' she said, her green eyes snapping fire. 'I have never, not one second in my life been a prostitute of any kind . . .' Her words faltered, and she closed her eyes as if to pull herself together. Bentz's gut tightened. He saw Montoya tense as well. They'd hit pay dirt. He felt it. 'Listen,' she said quietly, her face now draining of all color. 'I have never sold myself for any amount of money, but there was a time when I was in college where, for a research paper, I got to know a couple of streetwalkers . . . here, in New Orleans. I went out with them, saw how they made their money, the kind of men who tried to pick them up, how they discerned a good trick from a bad, the whole psychology of the street life. It wasn't just about prostitution but the subculture of the city at night.' She slowly sat down and looked straight at him. 'But I don't see what that would have to do with anything . . .'

'You did this for a class?' Montoya cut in, obviously doubting her.

'Yes!' She whipped her head around. 'I got an A.'

'Any way we can verify that you were enrolled?'

'Look, I didn't come down here to be humiliated. If you doubt me you could check with my professor . . . oh, God.' She bit down hard on her back teeth and looked up at the ceiling as if searching for cobwebs.

'What?'

'He's my ex-husband,' she admitted and gave her head a little shake. 'I, uh, was his student. But you can call him. Dr. Jeremy Leeds at Tulane.'

'We'll look into it.' She seemed suddenly tired, nearly wilted in the chair. As if her outburst had taken all the fire out of her. But she'd get it back. Bentz knew people, and this woman, he was certain, was a fighter.

'Who knows where you park your car?'

'Everyone at the station. We all use that garage. And . . . some of my friends, I guess. It wouldn't be hard to figure out as it's the closest garage to the building where I work, and my car is pretty distinctive, a 1966 Mustang.' Her fists curled in her lap. 'Look, Detective, last night I was scared out of my wits,' she admitted. 'And I don't like the feeling.'

'I don't blame you. If I were you, I wouldn't go out alone, and I wasn't kidding about changing the locks and getting a rottweiler. Maybe even a bodyguard.'

She was standing now, her backbone stiff again, her temper snapping. 'A bodyguard?' she repeated. 'That's rich. You know, it really ticks me off that this guy is winning, that he knows where I live, where I work and what I drive. I shouldn't have to change my lifestyle because of some creep.'

'You're right, you shouldn't have to, but you do,' Rick said evenly, holding her gaze, hoping to get through to her. 'In my opinion, Ms. Leeds, this guy is dangerous. He's escalating his threats, becoming bolder and since we don't know who he is and what makes him tick, you have to be extremely careful and take extra precautions whether you like it or not. I'll call the PD in Cambrai and make sure your street is patrolled frequently and we'll take care of the neighborhood of your offices when you're at work. We'll try to nail this guy's ass, but we can't do it without your help, okay?'

'That's why I'm here,' she said.

'And we'll do the best we can.'

'Thanks.' She stood, offered both him and Montoya her hand, then, swinging the strap of her purse over her shoulder, she walked out the door, unaware that Reuben was watching her hips sway beneath her skirt or the fact that she slightly favored one leg.

He gave off a soft whistle. 'If she decides she needs a body-guard, you let me know cuz I would loooove to guard that sweet lady's ass.'

'I'll keep it in mind,' Bentz said dryly, and wondered at the connection of the caller to a dead girl in Houston. 'Let's find out everything we can on Annie Seger. Who she hung out with, where she lived, her family, boyfriend, the whole nine yards. Check out everyone associated with Dr. Sam.' He tapped a pencil eraser on the edge of the desk. 'This case is getting weirder by the minute.'

'Maybe it's supposed to,' Reuben offered, scratching at his goatee as he stared thoughtfully at the path through the desks Samantha Leeds had taken.

'What do you mean?'

'You've tuned in, haven't you? Aren't you interested?'

'It's part of the case.'

'I know, I know,' Reuben said, his eyes narrowing thought-fully, 'but I'm just willing to bet that ratings are up on Dr. Sam's show, and that's got to be good for business. So bring on the weird. In fact the weirder the better.'

'You think it's a setup?'

'I think it could be.' He flashed his sly smile. 'It's just like those tell-all television programs where the host introduces a normal-looking couple, then brings out the chick the guy is cheating with and the two women get into it . . . it's all set up ahead of time. It has to be, and the audience and viewers get into it. The next thing you know, another guy comes out – the husband's brother or sister and it turns out the wife has been banging him . . . or her. Now the audience is in a frenzy.'

Bentz leaned back in his chair, holding the pencil in two hands, rolling it in his fingers. 'You figure Dr. Sam is in on it?'

'Maybe, maybe not. She seems genuinely scared, but then she might be a trained actress; she's on the radio for Christ's sake. But this happened before and the same team worked with her, right? George Hannah and Eleanor Cavalier for starters? Maybe there are others. I'll bet next week's paycheck that *some*one at the station knows what's going on and that there's money involved.'

'You always think money's involved,' Bentz grumbled, though he'd had similar thoughts himself. He'd met George Hannah, thought the guy was a pompous ass at best, a downright cheat at worst. The station manager, a sharp black lady, was known as a ball-breaker, and Montoya was right, they'd both worked with Dr. Sam in Houston – that much Bentz did know. He cracked his knuckles and thought. What bothered him most was that he had a gut feeling that somehow the guy who called in to Dr. Sam in the middle of the night was connected to the murders of the prostitutes. There wasn't much to go on – just the hair from red wigs, so like Samantha Leeds's, the photograph with the cut out eyes, like the blackened eyes on the hundred-dollar bills. Not much at all.

'And I'm right,' Montoya was saying, '99 percent of the time in these types of crimes, money changes hands.'

'Why then would John call after hours? What good would that do? No one heard him.'

'It could be all part of the scam, let that leak out to the press that the stalker has been calling not only during the program but after, and if the doctor isn't in on it, she'd be even more freaked out. The nutcase is making it personal.'

That stuck in Bentz's craw, but he couldn't argue the logic. 'Then prove it,' he said to Montoya, and the cocky young buck threw him a self-assured I'm-a-bad-ass smile.

'I will.'

Morons.
    The police were morons.
    Didn't they get it? Didn't they see a connection?
    Couldn't they put two and fucking-two together?
    Outside the cabin bullfrogs croaked. The steamy bayou night floated in through the open windows and the cracks in the walls.

He slapped at a mosquito as he read the article on his most recent killing, buried deep in the paper, about as far from front-page news as it could get.

No word had leaked to the press about the murders being linked, yet he'd been careful to leave all the clues . . . *fuck it*, he thought, clipping out the pathetic article with his knife, making sure he cut straight, leaving some margins, as moonlight sliced through the rising mist, filtering into the tiny room to add an opalescence to the light of his single lantern. He was hot. Uncomfortable. Restless. He'd have to do something more to get their attention. And it was time. He glanced through the window, saw the shadow of a bat as it flew by, and felt his heart rate accelerate.

His breathing was shallow as he switched on his radio and heard the familiar strains of 'Hard Day's Night' playing over the static, and then her voice. Low. Sultry. Sexy as hell.

'Hello, New Orleans, and welcome. This is Doctor Sam at WSLJ, and it's time again for *Midnight Confessions,* a program that's as good for the heart as it is for the soul. Tonight we'll be talking about high school. Remember? For some of you it's going on right now, for others it's been a while, maybe longer than you want to admit.

'Nonetheless, we've all experienced going to high school either private or public, run by the church or the state. And we all felt peer pressure and the urge to rebel, experienced the sweet pangs of first love and the sting of rejection.

'Remember your first day of school? How nervous you felt? How about the first time you saw your high-school sweetheart? Your first crush? Your first kiss . . . and maybe a whole lot more. Tell me about it, New Orleans . . . Confess . . .'

Blood thundered through his brain. High school? The cunt wanted to talk about *high* school? And first love?

Sweat broke out over his forehead and slithered down his spine. He walked to the cupboard and as he pinned his trophy – the minuscule scrap of newsprint – inside the door, he conjured up Dr. Sam's face.

Perfect white skin, hair a deep, dark red, full lips that covered a razor-sharp tongue and eyes the color of jade. And just as cold. God, she was a turn-on. And a bitch. He listened to her voice, luring the innocent to call in, to confess, to ask her for advice.

'Who's on the line?'

'This here's Randy.'

You and me both, he thought, his erection pressing hard against the fly of his jeans.

'What's going on, Randy?'

'Well, uh, high school was a big deal for me. I was a football player, down in Tallahassee and, um, I met my wife there. She was the homecomin' queen and man, she was purty. I never seen a woman so purty as Vera Jean.'

Oh, yeah, yeah, so who *cares?*

'And what did you do about it?'

'I married her, that's what I did. Thirty-five years now. We got us four children and two grandchildren with another on the way.'

'So high school was a good experience for you?'

'Yes'm. It sure was. But fer my kids, it was a differnt story. The oldest he got involved with drugs, the second, well, she did all right I guess, but the third. She got herself in a family way as a junior and the boy was a no'count. Wouldn't marry her.'

'How's your daughter today?' Dr. Sam asked, as if she cared, as if she could offer some advice.

His lip curled. He had two hours, then he'd call. Give a warning . . . yeah, tell her it was about to come down. And then he'd hunt.

Another woman would do tonight, he thought as he listened to her voice and wanted to jerk off. If only he could be with her. He touched himself briefly, the tips of his fingers brushing against his fly, but no . . . not this way . . . not until the time was right. There were things he had to do. Wrongs he had to right. Women . . . all those women who reminded him of Annie, lying, whoring cunts and the one man he had to deal with, a man who had betrayed Annie. Judas! You, too, will pay. Rage seared through his blood and screamed through his head as he heard Dr. Sam's voice.

Blood pounded in his ears as the low, dulcet tones of her voice reached out to him, from the city, across the swamp.

And he couldn't have Dr. Sam – not tonight. The timing wasn't right. And he had something else planned for her, a surprise. For Annie's birthday. If all went according to plan, Dr. Sam would find his special present tomorrow night. He only wished he could see her face when she got his gift, but he couldn't risk it. He'd have to wait. Until just the right moment.

But soon . . . Oh, God, it had to be soon . . . Lust, anger, revenge and need, his need was so great. His cock throbbed. He'd have to substitute again . . . find another whore to quiet the rage that tore through his soul, to sate the need coursing through his veins, to sacrifice.

He knew he was a sinner, but he couldn't help himself . . . . His blood was on fire.

He reached into his pocket and drew out his special rosary. The sharp beads glittered in the light from the lantern, winking at him, promising him they would do his bidding.

Then he fell on his knees and began to pray.

As Dr. Sam spoke to him through the little radio, he fingered the sharp beads and whispered, 'Glory be to the Father and to the Son and to the Holy Spirit . . .'

17

Sam nearly jumped out of her skin when she saw the man on her porch. Then she realized it was Ty. She hadn't expected to see anyone, but smiled to herself. There was something right about him reclining on the front-porch swing, jean-clad legs outstretched, a bottle of beer cradled between his hands, his face cast in shadow where the weak light of the single bulb on the porch didn't quite reach. He seemed at home there. Calm. Rocking gently to the music of the wind chimes and cicadas. And yet there was a restless quality to him, a darkness she didn't understand, a danger that lured her as much as it frightened her.

'Don't make more of it than it is,' she muttered to herself, but her heartbeat kicked up a notch as she pressed the electronic opener and nosed the Mustang into the garage.

So what does he want, she wondered as she switched off the ignition and tossed her keys into her purse. *Why is he here? What does he expect?*

No, Sam, what do you expect?

Her throat went dry and for the briefest of seconds she wondered what it would be like to kiss him. To touch him. To . . . *Don't go there. You don't know him well enough. There's something he's not telling you, something he's hiding, something dark. It's the middle of the night, for crying out loud. Why is he waiting for you alone? This is no good.* No good! But a drip of anticipation ran through her blood.

Silently arguing with herself, she slid out of the car, walked through the breezeway and into the house, where Charon greeted her by crying and rubbing against her legs. 'I missed you, too,' she said to the black cat as she tossed her purse onto the counter and quickly disengaged the security alarm. Carrying the cat, she walked to the front door and slid the bolt.

Ty was still on the swing, eyes in shadow. He glanced up at her, and she felt a tingle – like the cold breath of winter – against the back of her neck. 'You're beginning to make a habit of this,' she said, as Charon, sensing freedom, scrambled from her arms and dashed across the porch.

'Is that bad?' he drawled.

'Could be.'

The swing creaked as he pushed himself to his feet. Intense hazel eyes caught in the pale light. 'Maybe I find you irresistible.'

'And maybe that's a line out of a bad movie.'

'Is it?' One dark, nearly sinful eyebrow raised. He finished his beer in one swallow as the wind chimes tinkled softly.

'I think you can do better,' she said.

'Maybe you give me too much credit.'

'I'm sure I do.'

'That could be a mistake.'

'Probably.'

Leaving his empty bottle on the rail he walked to the door where Sam stood, arms folded over her chest, one shoulder propped against the jamb. The faint odor of musk tickled her nostrils. Night-darkened eyes regarded her slowly and she felt a nervous sheen of perspiration on her skin. He leaned closer, placed his bent arm over the top of hers on the doorframe. His nose was nearly touching hers, his breath warm against her face. 'You know, I just thought I'd make sure you got home safely. Most women would want to thank me.'

'I'm not most women,' she reminded him, but her heartbeat skyrocketed.

'No, Sam, you're not.' He was close enough that she could feel his heat. Her heart pounded wildly, and she read the dangerous promises in his eyes. His gaze fell to the open collar of her blouse, as if he could see her pulse jumping in the hollow of her throat. 'That's probably why I'm here.'

'A knight in shining armor – is that what you'd have me believe.'

His chuckle was low and sexy. 'Never.'

'So your intentions aren't chivalrous?'

He snorted. 'Who says I have intentions?'

It was her turn to cock a disbelieving eyebrow. 'Peddle that to someone who believes it. What would you have done if I hadn't shown up here?'

'I would have checked with someone.'

'Who?' she asked, and noticed his smile grow slowly from one side of his beard-shadowed jaw to the other.

'Whoever I had to.'

Was it the night with its full moon and hot breeze, or was it something else, something more primal, something within, that made her wonder how it would feel to have his skin rub against hers, how she would respond to the feel of his hands on her body? Or was it because she needed to escape the craziness that had become her life, the fear and tension that had become her companions in the last few weeks. Or . . . was it more basic? Was it simply that she'd been without a man for a long time, and she craved a man's touch? Or that something deep within her, something she didn't want to examine too closely, was attracted to secretive men with an edge?

'The least you could do is invite me in,' he suggested, his voice low.

'I'm considering it.' She was aware that he was the barest of inches from her, too damned close. 'If you behave.'

'Sorry, darlin', but that's a promise I just can't make,' he drawled, and deep inside she quivered. What would it be like to make love to this man, to lie in his arms, to wake up with morning dancing in his eyes and desire running through his veins? Her throat caught.

'I think I owe you a glass of wine. It only seems fair to open the bottle and share it with you since you brought it over.'

'I'm all for fairness.'

She stepped out of the doorway, and he followed her to the

kitchen, where she found the unopened bottle of Riesling in the refrigerator.

'Need help?' he asked, as she kicked off her shoes and snagged the corkscrew from a drawer.

'Not me, I was a Girl Scout.'

'Where they taught you to uncork a bottle of wine.'

'And I've got the merit badge to prove it.'

'I think you're mixed up. Boy Scouts get merit badges. Girls get brownie points.'

'A lot you know,' she grumbled. She pulled hard. The cork and corkscrew released from the bottle with a soft pop. She twirled the corkscrew in her hand, blew across the end and tucked it into her belt as if it were a six-gun.

'Very funny.'

'I thought so,' she said over her shoulder as she stretched to reach the wineglasses in a tall cupboard. *One glass, just have one glass*, she told herself as she poured, all the while aware of Ty standing behind her, one shoulder propped against the door to the breezeway. 'Here.' She handed him one of the stemmed glasses and took the other for herself.

'What should we toast to?' he asked, one dark brow lifting.

'Better days,' she suggested.

'And nights.'

Her breath caught in her throat. 'And nights.' She touched the rim of her glass to his. She sipped her wine and watched as he took a swallow from his glass, noticed the way his Adam's apple worked over the open collar of his shirt, remembered all too vividly the sinewy muscles of his arms and chest.

What was she thinking? Why was her mind running to thoughts of hot kisses and hotter caresses? She didn't know this man. Couldn't trust him. Shouldn't be thinking about making love to him, for God's sake. And yet as she finished her wine, she knew that he cared enough to wait up for her, he cared enough to show up at the station and drive her home safely, he cared enough to risk his own life.

If he'd wanted to harm her, he'd already had plenty of opportunities.

'This is all getting to you,' he said as if reading her mind.

'I suppose.'

'It would get to anyone.' Hazel eyes held hers, and she noticed the striations of green and brown in their depths. 'Come on,' he said, removing the corkscrew from her belt. 'Let's forget this for a while.' Linking his fingers through hers, he grabbed the neck of the bottle with the hand holding his glass and propelled her through the living room.

'Hey, wait . . . where are we going?' she asked.

'You'll see. Hold this.' He handed her the bottle and glasses, unlocked the French doors and led her outside to the back-yard.

Moonlight spangled the dark water of the lake and cast a silver glow on the grass, shrubs, trees and the masts of Ty's sail-boat. Of course. His car hadn't been parked in the driveway and Sam had thought he'd walked to the house. Instead, he'd used the boat.

'Wait a minute, what have you got in mind?' she asked, as he took hold of her hand again and pulled her toward the dock.

'You took a rain check, remember?' he said, jogging. Barefoot, she had to run to keep up with him. 'I think it's time I collected.'

The *Bright Angel* loomed before them. 'And I think you're nuts.'

'Your professional opinion, no doubt,' he said, as they reached the dock, and he helped her onto the sloop.

'No doubt.' This was just plain crazy. And wonderful. As she clutched the glasses and bottle to her chest, he untied the moor-ings, started the engine, switched on the running lights and pulled away from the dock. In deeper water he unfurled the sails.

'Isn't this illegal?' she asked, as the sails snapped and billowed in the wind. The sloop cut through the water, and the shore slipped away, blending into the darkness, a few sparse house-lights glowing warm and bright.

'What? Isn't what illegal?' He was squinting into the darkness, hands on the wheel, legs braced on the deck.

'Sailing at night.'

'Don't know. But if it is, it shouldn't be.'

She inched forward and was standing next to him at the helm, the breeze fingering through her hair as the prow of the boat cut through the dark water. It was exhilarating and freeing after all the nights alone, the hours she'd spent worrying and tense. Stars winked bright in the blackened heavens, and the water stretched endlessly as Ty worked the wheel, making sure the sails caught the wind, the boom moving as he constantly loosened and tightened the lines.

'Is this how you live your life?' she asked, as he turned into the wind.

'What do you mean?'

'Not playing by the rules.'

'Maybe I play by my own.'

'That's ducking the question.'

'Maybe.'

He swung the wheel around, and the boat shifted, spray flying in the air, Sam nearly losing her balance. His shirt flapped in the breeze, and she was reminded of the night she'd been certain he'd sailed near her house, that he'd been peering through her windows.

He found a spot in a dark cove where he dropped anchor and lowered the sails. Stars twinkled brightly, the moon shone a watery blue. Sam reminded herself that they were completely alone. One man, one woman. Practically strangers.

No one knows you're here. No one knows you're with Ty.

Somewhere from the shore an owl hooted over the breeze.

'Maybe you should tell me about yourself,' she suggested.

'And bore you to tears?'

'I won't yawn.'

'Promise?'

'Scout's honor,' she said, holding up two fingers as the breeze tugged at her hair.

'Right. The Girl Scouts.' He chuckled. 'As I said, it's a long and boring story.'

'Something tells me that nothing you'd say would bore me.'

He laughed and the sound was low and sexy as it echoed across the water. 'You just want me to spill my guts so you can psychoanalyze me.'

'No way. I've had enough for the night.' She leaned against the mast. 'It's your turn. You know a lot about me. Probably more than you should. Let's even the score.'

'And I would do that by spilling my guts,' he said, sipping from his glass and gazing at her with those intense eyes.

'That's right. Tell me all,' she said boldly, grabbing hold of the boom with one hand and leaning closer to him. 'Including your deepest, darkest secret.'

He slid her a glance. 'Is this like Truth or Dare?'

'The kids' game,' she said, remembering back to when she was fourteen with Peter and a couple of his friends sleeping outside on the trampoline, a flashlight spinning between them, the unlucky victim having to either tell the truth about a very deep secret or accept a dare from the other players and do something awful the other kids came up with. 'Yeah, it's kind of like that,' she said, 'so shoot.' She twirled her half-empty glass in the moonlight.

'I choose "dare."'

'You can't.'

'Sure I can.' His gaze held hers. 'I chose "dare."'

She felt a wicked little shiver of anticipation as water lapped at the sides of the sloop.

'Dare me to do something rather than tell the truth.'

Even in the darkness she saw the challenge in his eyes and despite the rational side of her mind telling her she was making a mistake of monstrous proportions, she took a gulp of her wine, and said, 'Okay, I dare you to tell the truth.'

'Uh-uh-uh. That's cheating. You lose your turn.' He finished his wine and closed the distance between them, the toes of his shoes nudging against her bare feet.

'Wait a minute, that's not how we played,' she objected, but felt his arm slide around her waist. 'I can't lose a turn.'

'My boat,' he said. 'My rules.' Through the cotton of her blouse she felt his hand splay over the small of her back. Heat seeped through the fabric, and she was suddenly having trouble drawing a breath. He was too close, his touch far too sensual. She was out in the middle of a vast lake, and no one knew where she was. Yet she couldn't resist him. 'It's how I used to play the game,' he whispered, his lips close to her ear. 'So tell me, Samantha. Truth or dare?'

'I – I don't know . . .' Her heart was racing, her blood on fire.

'Sure you do.'

She swallowed hard, knew the wine was affecting her. 'Okay . . . dare.'

'I dare you to kiss me.'

Oh, God. The arm around her tightened, pulling her close as the boat rocked gently on the water and the masts creaked overhead.

'That's right, kiss me,' he commanded, his breath hot against her neck. 'And don't stop.'

'Ever?' Sweat collected on her forehead.

'Until I say.'

'I don't know, that could be dangerous.'

'Definitely,' he promised. 'I'm counting on it.' His mouth was so close it touched her hair. Her knees turned liquid.

'But—'

'Shh. No questions. I said "dare," and dare it is.' The hand at her back yanked her hard against him, forced her hips to his and she felt his erection hard and straining against his fly, pressed firmly against her mound.

She licked her lips and he caught the motion. Though their mouths had not yet touched, she knew that she was going to do just as he asked. 'Come on, Sam,' he said, and her skin tingled. 'I dare you. Kiss me.'

Water lapped. The wind sighed. Dark desire stole through her veins. She leaned forward. Closing her eyes, she wrapped her fingers around his neck, drew his head down to hers and molded her mouth to his. She parted her lips and he groaned, moved against her, pushing his legs between hers, stretching the seams of her skirt as his tongue plunged past her teeth.

He was hard, and hot, his muscles straining as he kissed her. *Don't do this, Sam, don't go this far . . . you don't know him . . .* He found the curve of her neck and nipped.

Inside she pulsed, wanting, feeling the buttons of her blouse slipping open, the air against her bare skin, the feel of his lips and teeth against her breast as his hands slipped beneath the waistband of her skirt, probing, touching, hot fingertips against her bare skin.

She throbbed for him, her fingers scraping off his shirt, her hand on the fly of his jeans as he pulled her onto the deck. He was breathing hard, his hands and lips everywhere, and she couldn't stop.

A dim thought that he could be the person terrorizing her sizzled through her mind, but was quickly gone, lost in his musky scent and the taste of salt upon his skin. His hands were everywhere, stripping, touching, caressing, finding erotic spots on her body she hadn't known existed.

'You want me,' he said, as her fingers slid down the tense hard muscles of his arms.

'No . . .' she could barely get the words out as he unhooked her bra and slid it off her shoulders. 'You . . . you want me.'

'Mmmm.' He kissed her breast, his teeth scraping her nipple. She writhed. Perspiration covered her skin. 'You want me.'

'No—'

'Yes.' He lowered his lips, kissed the other nipple. Harder. Nipping. She arched again, felt the warm moistness between her legs.

Squirming beneath him, hot and wanting, she closed her eyes. Her blood thundered, her body ached for him.

'That's my girl,' he whispered, one hand sliding beneath her skirt to her calf.

'Oh, God,' she cried, as he kissed her abdomen and his fingers caressed her calf, climbing higher, past her knee, bunching her skirt as his tongue rimmed her navel. She couldn't breathe, could only arch, anticipating, wanting, pulsing for him.

'Let go, Samantha,' he breathed against her skin and tugged at the waistband of her skirt with his teeth.

She was so hot . . . so hot . . . and his hand crept ever upward, blunt fingertips skimming her inner thigh, hot breath warming her abdomen. The back of her throat was dry as a desert and she moved restlessly beneath him.

'Let go, I'm here,' he promised, his words pressed against her skin, her fingers holding his head fast as he reached the elastic of her panties and pushed them to the side, giving him just enough room to probe with his fingers.

'Oooh,' she whispered, clawing his hair. 'Ohhhhh, Ty.'

'That's it, Samantha.'

She moved with him, lifting her hips, gasping for air.

Still touching he lifted his head and found her lips, kissing her hard as his fingers worked their magic. Faster. Deeper. Harder.

'I don't think . . . I . . . I . . .'

She couldn't breathe, she couldn't think, and she ached for more . . . so much more. 'Ty . . . Oh, God . . . Ty . . .' She moved with him, kissing him, clinging to him, her fingers digging into his bare back as the first explosion came in a blinding rush. She convulsed, but he didn't stop, kept kneading her, didn't allow her to relax. The heat built again. Hotter.

'You want me,' he whispered into her ear.

'Yes. Damn it, yes.' She scrabbled at the fly of his jeans, yanked hard. With a series of pops the denim parted. He groaned as her fingers surrounded him. He kicked off his shoes and Levi's in a swift motion, then pushed her legs apart with his knees.

'You . . . you want me . . .' she said, looking up in the darkness, barely able to make out his face in the starlight.

'More than you'll ever know, darlin'.' His mouth cut off any other thoughts as he thrust hard into her and held her fast, pinning her to the deck with his body, pushing against her, holding her as if he'd never let go. Heat seared through her again and again.

More, she thought wildly, *I want more* as the tempo increased. His breathing was as shallow as hers, his body straining, muscled thighs pressing hard. She heard a wild moan echoing through the night, not realizing it was her own voice. She collapsed, drained, and he reached beneath her, rotating until she was atop him, her flushed skin cooling as the wind touched it.

Strong hips moved beneath her. Big hands covered her breasts, kneading and moving. She caught his rhythm, pushing down on his shoulders with her palms, breathing in the fresh moist air of the lake, the heat in her building again.

The wind tore at her hair and she looked down into the dark, secretive eyes of this man who had become her lover, this man she barely knew, and her fingers clenched in his shoulder muscles.

He drew in a quick sharp breath and then stiffened within her, the cords of his neck straining, his mouth drawn back as he released. Samantha spasmed, her entire body convulsing as she fell against him, lost to the night, lost to the world, lost to this man she knew better than to trust.

God help me.

18

What have I done?

As the first rays of light streamed through the tiny porthole over the bed, Ty Wheeler called himself every kind of fool.

Samantha was lying tangled in the sheets, her dark red hair mussed, her eyes closed, her breathing regular. Sometime last night, he'd carried her to the berth. They'd made love long into the morning hours and he had short, lightning-swift images of her body, supple and lean, lying beneath him or straddling him. She'd been playful and sexy and coy as hell, a lover like no other. His skin sheened with perspiration at the thought of her, the taste of her, the pure, raw, animal she was.

And after it all, they'd both fallen asleep exhausted.

Ty had sworn to himself he wouldn't get involved, that he had to remain objective, and yet he'd thrown caution to the winds last night and ended up in bed with her. Now, as he heated water on a hot plate, he called himself the worst kind of idiot.

She stirred, moving her lips and sighing in her sleep, and he craved her all over again.

One green eye slitted open. 'What're you staring at?' she asked, stretching lazily, pushing one fist over her head until she touched the wall.

'You.'

'And I must look like hell.' She propped up on one elbow, careful to keep the coverlet over her breasts. 'What time is it?'

'Seven.'

Groaning, she said, 'And we're awake . . . why?'

'Because we're in the middle of the lake and people on the shore, people who might see us are getting up. I'm making coffee.'

'Strong coffee, I hope.' she qualified.

'Guaranteed to put hair on your chest.'

'Just what I need,' she muttered.

He winked at her. 'Believe me, your chest is just fine.'

'Yeah, well, about that . . . about last night . . . I think we should talk about it.'

'Women always do.'

'We have our reasons.' She shook her head. 'I mean we need to discuss the fact that we didn't exactly engage in safe sex, and I don't know much about you. For all I know you could have a wife and a dozen kids tucked away somewhere.'

'There are no children, no wife, and not even a fiancée in my life. I haven't been involved with a woman for over a year, and I'm clean. Believe it or not, I am usually a lot more careful myself.'

'Me too.'

'What about you?' he asked, and was surprised that it mattered, that he cared if she was in a relationship of any kind.

'I did have a boyfriend until about half a year ago, but when I moved to New Orleans, things fell apart.' She sighed and stared up at him with those incredible green eyes. 'We went to Mexico together last month, but nothing came of it. He wanted to get back together, but it didn't happen.'

'You're sure?'

'Very.' She tilted her head to the side. 'Now, was I dreaming, or did you say you made me coffee?'

'That I did. It's instant. I can make it as strong as you want.'

'Good enough.'

'Then I think we'd better head back.' The 'galley' was little more than a hot plate in this single room. He pulled out a jar of Folgers crystals and added steaming water to two cups.

'Ty—?'

'Yeah?' Pausing, he looked over his shoulder. She was still holding the blankets around herself, her shoulders bare, looking sexy as hell.

'I just want you to know that I don't usually . . .' She glanced around the tiny cabin before meeting his eyes again. '. . . I'm not a woman who sleeps with men I don't really know.' She shoved her hair from her face with one hand. 'I don't know what got into me last night.'

'You found me irresistible,' he said, and flashed her that devastating, irreverent smile before measuring coffee into two paper cups.

'Yeah, that's it,' she said sarcastically but couldn't deny the truth therein. She'd acted completely out of character – or had she? There had always been a part of her that had wanted to walk close to the edge, take a step on the wild side, be more like her brother. Peter had never played by the rules. Never.

And it had cost him.

Once their mother had died and he no longer had a source of income, he'd disappeared, only surfacing occasionally, usually broke and full of wild tales about his life that Sam didn't believe. No one could con a person better than her brother.

She found her skirt. Wrinkled beyond repair. Too bad. Mentally chastising herself, she scrambled into her clothes. She couldn't even blame her actions on the wine. Yes, she'd been tired, and strung tight, relieved to find him on her porch, but to just throw all her good judgment, brains and morals out the window wasn't like her. They'd never discussed past lovers, safe sex, the emotional ties that being sexually involved with some-one brings. If one of her listeners were to call in and admit that they'd fallen into bed with a near stranger on a *dare*, by playing some silly kids' game not unlike spin the bottle, Dr. Sam would have read that caller the riot act.

She'd just stood and zipped her skirt when Ty turned, two cups of steaming coffee in his hands. 'Here you go, Sunshine,' he said, handing her a cup. 'Now, I think I'd better go topside and we'd better shove off. Oh – one more thing.' He touched the rim of his cup to hers, as if toasting. 'Here's to Truth or Dare.' Laughter danced in his eyes, and she felt a tug on her heart.

He took a sip and started for the stairs. 'Maybe next time we can play Post Office.'

'Or Spin the Bottle.'

'Or Doctor.'

'You know them all,' she accused as she followed him to the deck, where the wind had kicked up and only a few rays of sunlight had pierced the thick cover of clouds. Ty worked quickly, pulling up anchor, unfurling the sails and guiding the sloop across the gray water. The ride was rougher this morning, coffee sloshed as Sam tried to drink it and maintain balance. She recognized the shoreline of Cambrai as they approached, smiled as she picked out her house with its sun-bleached dock, stately live oaks and vibrant bougainvillea trailing across the roofline over the verandah. 'So tell me about your book,' she said, as he slowed and lowered the sails. 'What did you tell Melanie it was? *The Horse Whisperer* meets—'

'—*Silence Of The Lambs*. It was a joke. Actually I'm writing about some cases I dealt with as a cop.'

'You were a police officer?' she asked, surprised.

'In one of my former lifetimes.'

'So your book is actually true crime?'

He hesitated. 'More like fiction based on fact.' Easing the craft into shallower water, he frowned, and she sensed there was something he wasn't telling her, something secret.

'So, how's it coming?'

'Okay, I guess. I've come across a couple of obstacles, but I'm working through them.'

Vague. 'Where were you a cop?' she asked.

'Texas.'

'A Ranger?'

'Detective. Grab that line, would you?' He motioned to a coil of rope, and he set out the bumpers so that the sloop wouldn't scrape against the wood of the dock, then tied up. 'I'll walk you inside.'

'You don't have to. I'm fine. This is my house, and it's broad daylight.'

'I'd just feel better about it,' he said, and was already striding toward the back porch, not listening to any arguments she could come up with. The French doors were unlocked, just as they'd left them, the alarm system not activated. Samantha hadn't thought about it the night before, had been too caught up in Ty and hadn't really expected to be gone for any length of time.

She'd been wrong, she realized too late.

Charon was hiding beneath a dining-room chair, and there was something odd about the house . . . something that didn't feel right.

Samantha's scalp prickled. 'Maybe I'm just tired, but I think . . . I mean I feel that someone's been in here.' She caught a glimpse of herself in the beveled glass mirror over the sideboard, saw her disheveled image, realized she'd only had a few hours' sleep. 'Maybe I'm imagining things.'

Ty caught her glance in the glass. His eyes were dark; his beard-shadowed jaw suddenly rock-hard. 'Let's check.'

Telling herself she was overreacting, she checked the first floor and found nothing wrong, not one thing out of place, and yet the house had a different smell, the atmosphere seemed off. They climbed the stairs together, the floorboards creaking, the fans whirring as she stepped into her bedroom.

She sensed something wasn't quite right . . . that there was something amiss, but no one was in the bedroom, nor her bath. They checked every room and closet, but the house was empty. Still.

'I guess I'm imagining things,' she said, unconvinced as they walked downstairs again and Charon slid from beneath the dining-room table.

'You'll be okay?' Ty asked.

'Yes. Of course.' This was her house, damn it, and she wasn't going to feel unsafe in her own home.

'Keep your doors locked, your alarm on.'

'Okay, I will,' she promised as they walked outside. The day was clearer, the clouds beginning to thin, heat intensifying and shimmering across the water.

'I'll call you later,' he promised.

'I'll be fine.'

'Yeah, but maybe I won't.'

She laughed, and he pulled her into his arms. Nose to nose, he said, 'Just be smart, Sam.' Then he kissed her. Hard enough that she felt the scrape of his whiskers along with the warmth of his lips. Memories of the night before kaleidoscoped through her mind, and as his tongue traced her lips she sighed, then felt him shift away. 'Call me anytime.'

Then he was gone, lithely hopping off the verandah and jogging across the sun-dappled backyard to the dock where the *Bright Angel* was tugging at her moorings. He pushed off, set sail, and, as she stood beneath the overhang of the roof, she watched the sailboat disappear around the point.

Charon followed her up the stairs and waited as she showered, then followed her into the closet as she pulled on shorts and a T-shirt. She was buckling her belt and about to step into an old pair of tennis shoes when she looked through the door to her antique dresser and saw that the second drawer wasn't quite pushed in all the way, was just slightly open, barely enough to notice.

Telling herself she was imagining things, that she'd probably just not slammed it all the way shut, she crossed the room and straightened it, then, thinking twice opened the drawer that held her slips, bras, camisoles and . . . teddies, except that her red teddy was missing. She only had two, hadn't worn either in months . . . but the red one was definitely missing.

She knew she hadn't taken it to Mexico and hadn't worn it since . . . no, the last time she'd put it on was Valentine's Day, as a joke, as she'd been all alone, just because it was red. So where was it? She searched all the drawers and scanned her closet again, but the teddy was definitely missing.

She bit her lip, told herself not to panic, and tried to convince herself that she'd just misplaced it.

But deep inside she knew that someone had taken it.

Heart thudding, she checked the rest of the house. Her jewelry hadn't been touched. Her television, stereo, computer, silver and liquor were undisturbed. The only thing missing was the lacy scrap of red underwear and her blood ran cold as she considered who would want such a personal item.

No doubt it had been 'John.'

19

Jeremy Leeds, Ph.D. was a prick. Bentz was sure of it as he sat in the tiny alcove that was the professor's office at Tulane. But Leeds wasn't just a normal in-your-face kind of prick, but a self-righteous, sanctimonious, self-serving egomaniac, the sort that smiled condescendingly as he firmly but complacently put you in your place.

Bentz shouldn't have been surprised. Weren't all shrinks certifiable in one way or another?

It was just damned hard to imagine Samantha Leeds being married to the guy. That thought soured Bentz's stomach. It was something the detective didn't want to think about too much as he eyed the crowded niche Jeremy Leeds claimed as office space. Filled floor to ceiling with shelves of books on relationships, sexuality, complexes and the like, the stuffy little room boasted one dusty window and a withering Christmas cactus that should have been thrown out a decade or so ago. Basically the office was what Bentz had expected. But the man wasn't.

Tall and lanky, with longish hair and hawk-sharp eyes, Dr. Leeds didn't look the part of the rumpled, eccentric college professor that Hollywood always conjured up. His steely gray hair curled a bit, but was obviously cut and styled professionally, his beard neat and fashionable, his jacket smooth black leather, his wire-rimmed glasses trendy, as they sat on the end of a straight, aquiline nose. No ratty herringbone jacket with suede patches on the elbows for this professor, and there wasn't the hint of a pipe rack nor the lingering scent of pipe tobacco, though a glass humidor showcased hand-rolled cigars that were certainly Professor Leeds's only visible vice.

'Like one?' Leeds asked as he noticed the detective's gaze upon the glass.

'No thanks.'

'They're Cuban, but don't tell anyone. Hand-rolled. This part of the conversation is off the record, right?'

'Only this part.'

Leeds extracted a long cigar from the humidor and inhaled deeply as he slid it under his nostrils. All for effect. But the scent of aged tobacco wafted through the warm room.

Bentz wasn't interested in the professor's theatrics. He just wanted to get through this interview, for that's what it was, though the spark in Jeremy Leeds's eyes led him to believe that the doctor was enjoying the meeting, happy for the chance to match wits with a slob from the police force, playing a game.

Earlier Bentz had phoned the university, asked about Dr. Leeds's office hours, then upon receiving the information had shown up here, unannounced. The professor had been on the phone, deep in some kind of heated conversation, but had glanced up when Bentz had filled the open doorway. Leeds, startled a bit, had ended the call quickly with '. . . yes, yes, I know. I said I'd get back to you, and I will.' He'd hung up, hadn't bothered to hide his irritation, then with a dismissive wave at the telephone, had asked, 'Is there something I can do for you?'

'Only if you're Jeremy Leeds.'

Bushy eyebrows had shot up.

'Professor Jeremy Leeds,' Bentz had qualified.

'I prefer Doctor.'

I'll just bet you do, Bentz had thought as he'd introduced himself and flipped his ID under the man's prominent nose.

Leeds had reached for his glasses, eyed the badge and sighed through his nose. The corners of his mouth had pinched. 'Officer Bentz.'

'I prefer Detective.'

The professor's eyes had sparked. 'Fine. Detective.' He'd leaned back in his padded chair. 'I suppose this is about my ex-wife. I heard that she was having trouble again.'

'Again?' Bentz asked as Jeremy Leeds indicated a small love seat wedged between a corner and the desk. Bentz had clicked on his pocket recorder and was taking notes.

'Surely you know about Houston.' Leeds didn't elaborate, except to say, 'That was a helluva fiasco, but then Samantha asks for it.' Glancing out the half-opened window, he'd knotted his mouth in irritation. 'That sounds harsh, I know, but I don't put much stock in radio psychology. It's glitz, you know. Nothing serious. Just a medium for a lot of people to sound off. Gives the profession a bad name. Words like 'psychobabble' and 'airwave shrinks' and all. It's degrading and . . . oh, well.' He threw up his hands as if in exasperation. 'Excuse me for ranting. A personal pet peeve, I suppose.' He turned his attention to Bentz and managed to smooth the lines from his brow with an easy, if false, smile. 'What is it you wanted? Specifically.'

'Specifically, you're right. I'm here about Samantha Leeds. You were married to her about ten years ago?'

'Briefly. She was one of my students and we . . . well, we got involved.' His smile faded and his eyebrows drew together pensively. Tenting his hands beneath his chin, he admitted, 'It wasn't one of my stellar moments, you know. I was married to my first wife, separated, of course, and . . . well, you've met Samantha. She's beautiful. Quick-witted and, when she wants to be, charming. As things were falling apart with Louise, my wife, I turned my attention to Sam, and then, even though my first marriage was dead and I was talking to an attorney about filing for divorce, word got out, it was something of a scandal and we eloped.'

'After the divorce was final I take it?'

'Of course.' He looked peeved. 'I'm not a bigamist, just . . . well, I have two weaknesses. One is tobacco from La Havana – Havana.' He was still holding one of his cigars as he motioned toward the humidor. 'The other is beautiful women.'

'Was Louise one of your students, too?'

Leeds's jaw tightened. 'No . . . we'd met in grad school.'

'And you've married again, after the divorce from Samantha.'

Splaying his hands, Leeds said, 'What can I say? I'm an incurable romantic. I believe in the institution.'

Enough with this crap. Bentz needed to get down to business. 'When Samantha was your student did she ever do a paper dealing with prostitution?'

'Not specifically prostitution,' Leeds corrected. 'It was about the psychology of the streets – what makes people turn to selling their bodies or drugs, that kind of thing.' His eyebrows elevated. 'And it was an excellent paper. As I said, Samantha's incredibly bright.' He rubbed his chin, then folded his glasses and set them on the desk. 'It's too bad it didn't work out.'

'What?' Bentz had a guess but he wanted it clarified.

'The marriage.'

'Why didn't it?'

Again the catty smile. 'I could say we grew in different directions.'

'But I wouldn't buy it.'

'She followed her career.'

'And you found someone else?'

A trace of irritation marred Jeremy Leeds's otherwise complacent expression. 'Man is not by nature a solitary creature, Detective. I'm sure you know that.'

'So you're sorry that you aren't still married to Samantha.'

The eyes narrowed, as if he expected a trap. 'I just said I was sorry things didn't work out for us.'

Bentz didn't believe it. Not for a second. This guy was too phony. Too into himself. The man's fingernails looked as if they'd been professionally manicured, his thick hair neat and recently trimmed, not an ounce of fat on his frame. The narrow, full-length mirror hanging near the coatrack said it all.

Bentz asked a few more questions, didn't get a good hit off the guy, then got Leeds's back up when he pried into the professor's personal life, asking where he'd been on the nights that 'John' had called the radio station.

'Come on, Detective. Don't tell me you think I'm involved.' His eyebrows lifted. 'If you presume to think that I had anything to do with what's happening with Samantha, guess again, Detective. I wish her no harm. Don't even care that she's back here in New Orleans.'

He leaned over the desk, all personal, as if they were buddies. 'Look, I admired her as a student, fell in love with her. She has charm. Charisma, for lack of a better word. And she was certainly one of my brightest students.'

'Because she got involved with you?'

A muscle ticked near Leeds's eye. 'Because of her innate intelligence and inquisitive mind. That's what attracted me to her, but, okay, shoot me for being a red-blooded male as I'd be a liar if I didn't admit I thought she was gorgeous and that had a lot to do with my attraction.' His smile was nearly wistful. And phony as a whore's whisper of sweet nothings. An act. 'It was over between Samantha and me a long time ago. I'm sure she's told you as much. It's basically by coincidence that we're in the same city again.'

'If you say so.'

'I do.' His eyes were razor-sharp again. 'I've never moved,' he pointed out. 'I'm still with the same university. Samantha and I had separated when she took that job in Houston. I didn't want her to leave and when she did, well, the marriage was doomed.'

'So you got involved with another one of your students.'

Leeds's grin was unabashed. 'Guilty as charged.'

They talked a few more minutes. Bentz learned nothing more but had the distinct feeling that though Dr. Leeds seemed irritated to have his phone call interrupted and his office hours filled up with the questioning, the professor enjoyed being a part of the investigation, that he found it amusing to be interviewed by the police. His answers were clear, but there was an edge of condescension in his voice; he, of the high IQ, disdained others not as naturally intelligent as he.

Which was pure, unadulterated bullshit.

As Leeds walked him out of the office and into the revered halls of the university, he said, 'Drop in any time, Officer. If I can be of help, any help at all, just let me know.'

More bullshit. The guy was playing games.

Bentz walked outside to the oppressive heat. Storm clouds had rolled in, blocking the sun, threatening rain. The air was thick as Bentz strode through the parking lot and wondered how the hell a classy woman like the radio-doc could have ever been married to a bastard like Jeremy Leeds Ph.D. or no Ph.D. It seemed impossible.

But then he'd never been one to figure out the male/female attraction game. His own ill-fated marriage was proof enough of that.

Sliding into the driver's seat, he flipped down the visor where his emergency pack of Camels was tucked. He punched in the lighter and jabbed a cigarette between his teeth as he nosed his cruiser toward the St. Charles exit of the parking lot. Kids were playing in the park across the avenue, a streetcar, windows open, ferried the curious sightseers and bored locals through the Garden District. The lighter popped. Bentz, waiting for the streetcar to pass and the traffic to thin, fired up his cigarette and drew in a deep lungful of smoke. Nicotine slipped easily into his bloodstream as passengers got off the trolley – a couple of black kids with backpacks and CD players, an elderly man in a plaid cap and a tall, dark-haired guy with wraparound sunglasses. From behind his shades he glanced in Bentz's direction, then dashed through traffic to Audubon Park and past the group of kids kicking a ball around.

There was something about the guy that bothered Rick, though he couldn't put his finger on it. So the commuter didn't like cops. That wasn't a big deal. It wasn't even uncommon. Bentz followed the guy with his eyes, smoke fogging the inside of the windshield. He watched as the man jogged across the clipped grass to the trees and lagoon beyond. The streetcar started up again, gaining speed. Bentz turned on his siren, cut across traffic and the double tracks in the median, turning toward the business district. At the sound of the siren, the jogger glanced over his shoulder, but didn't increase his pace, just disappeared into the trees.

Probably a paranoid druggie with an ounce of weed on him. Nothing more.

Flipping off his siren, Bentz pushed the jogger from his mind as he maneuvered through heavy traffic, all the while considering the fragments of the Samantha Leeds case. Nothing seemed to fit.

Who the hell was John?

How was he involved with Annie Seger?

Why was a woman pretending to be a girl nine years dead?

Was there a connection between what was happening at the radio station and the murders being committed in the French Quarter – or was it just coincidence? Bentz had already talked to the Feds, even phoned Norm Stowell, a man he'd worked with in LA who'd once been a profiler at Quantico when he'd worked for the FBI. Stowell's instincts had proven to be right-on more than once. Bentz trusted Stowell's opinion, more than he did that of the kid who'd been assigned to the case. Stowell had promised to look over the information Bentz had faxed and get back to him.

Bentz took another long drag as he braked for a traffic light near Lafayette Square. Smoking helped him concentrate, and God knew he needed all the concentration he could dredge up.

He thought of Samantha. Any man could fall for her, that much was certain. But why would she hook up and marry a snake like Leeds? And what about that ex-boyfriend of hers, David Ross, in Houston. How did he figure in? The light changed and he stepped on the accelerator. Then there was Ty Wheeler, a man Bentz felt intuitively wasn't on the up-and-up. Something about that guy bothered him. Samantha Leeds's taste in men left a lot to be desired. Who could explain it?

He knew from his own experience that rational thought didn't play much of a role when lust or love was involved. Unfortunately most people, himself included, had a way of mixing up the two emotions.

And that usually spelled disaster.

Samantha Leeds's love life was a prime example.

20

Sam tossed her copy of *Paradise Lost* to one side of her desk. She'd spent the past two hours in the den and had managed to skim most of the text, but decided that she'd been wrong. Her belief that 'John,' whoever he was, had made reference to the work hadn't panned out. At least she couldn't find any link. A headache was beginning to form behind her eyes as she snapped on the desk lamp. Outside, evening was stretching across the lake and her yard, shadows deepening, the twinkle of the first star visible.

So who was John? She picked up a pen and twirled it between two fingers. What did he want? To scare her? Was it all just a game to him? Or was it something deeper, did he actually mean her bodily harm? She was reaching for a text on the psychology of stalkers when the phone rang so loudly she jumped.

She caught the receiver on the second ring. 'Hello?' she said, but didn't expect an answer. Twice earlier she'd answered, and no one had responded. She'd been jumpy ever since, especially since today was Thursday, Annie Seger's birthday.

'Hi, Sam,' a cheery voice called.

'Corky!' It was so good to hear her friend's voice. Leaning back in her chair, Samantha smiled as she stared out the window and watched a squirrel leap from one thick branch of an oak tree to another. 'What's up?'

'I thought I'd check in on you. My mom called yesterday from LA. She'd run into your dad at the country club and he said you'd been having some trouble, that you'd hurt your leg in Mexico and now there was some kind of creep stalking you or something.'

'Good news travels fast.'

'Like the speed of lightning when my mom hears it. What's going on?'

Sam sighed, imagining her friend's face and wishing Corky lived closer. 'It's a long story.'

'I've got some time to kill, so talk.'

'Remember, you asked.' Sam brought Corky up to date, telling her about John, Annie, the phone calls, the mutilated picture.

'Mother of God, Sam, and the girl's birthday is today?' Corky asked, and Sam imagined the concern in her friend's eyes.

'She would have been twenty-five.'

'Maybe you should hire a bodyguard.'

'It's been suggested,' Sam said dryly. 'As well as upgrading my cat for a pit bull.'

'How about moving in with David?'

Sam sighed through her nose and glanced at the framed photograph of David still sitting on her desk near the answering machine. Handsome, yes. Husband material – no. 'Even *if* David lived in New Orleans, it wouldn't happen.' To prove her point to herself, she grabbed the damned picture of David from the surface of her desk and shoved it into the bottom drawer. 'It's over.'

'But you went to Mexico with him.'

'I *met* him there and it turned out to be a nightmare. After everything, I'll be lucky if David and I end up friends. The odd thing about it is that the police even think he might have something to do with the calls I've been getting.'

'David Ross?' Corky laughed. 'No way. Obviously they don't know the guy.'

'And he's in Houston.'

'Okay, so not David. How about someone else? Come on, Sam. Don't you have some big, strong friend who could move in for a while?'

Ty Wheeler's image came quickly to mind. 'No. Besides, I don't need a man to—'

'What about Pete?'

Sam glanced at the photograph of her graduation, her parents and her brother. 'You're kidding, right? No one's seen Pete in years.'

'I have. I ran into him the other day.'

'What?' She couldn't believe her ears. 'You're talking about my brother?'

'Yes.'

'But . . . but . . .' A dozen emotions ripped through her and tears sprang to her eyes. Until that moment she didn't realize that she'd thought it a very real possibility that he'd been dead. 'I'm sorry, Corky, but this is huge. He doesn't even bother to call on Christmas or Dad's birthday . . . is he okay?'

'Looked fit as the proverbial fiddle.'

'So why hasn't he called, where has he been, what's he doing?'

'Hey, whoa. Slow down. One question at a time,' Corky said, and Sam forced herself to rein in her galloping emotions.

'Okay, you're right,' she said. 'Let's start over. Where did you see Pete?'

'Here in Atlanta at a bar. Last weekend. I couldn't believe it.'

Me, neither. Sam's chest tightened. 'How was he?'

'Good, he looked good. But then he always looked good. Even when he was using.' There was a pause, and Sam picked up the snapshot of her family. Peter, taller than the rest of the family, seeming aloof and disinterested in his black leather and dark glasses. *You insensitive bastard,* she thought unkindly. How many times had her father called and asked about him. A hundred? Two?

'He seemed to have cleaned up his act,' Corky offered. 'But he didn't leave me with a number or even tell me how to reach him. I told him he should call you, and he said he'd think of it.'

'Kind of him,' Sam said.

'Hey . . . give him a break. I don't think his life has been all that wonderful.'

'You always had a crush on him,' Sam accused.

'Yeah, I did. Past tense. But who wouldn't? He's still drop-dead gorgeous.'

'If you say so.'

'I do, but okay, I'll admit it. I'm an incurable romantic.'

'And always getting yourself into trouble.'

Corky laughed. 'Yeah, I suppose. Especially with good-looking men.' She sighed loudly. 'If it wasn't long-distance, I'd be calling in to your show all the time, begging you for advice with my love life.'

'Sure you would,' Sam said, but laughed. God, she missed Corky. And in some ways, she missed her brother.

'Unlike you, I haven't given up on love.'

'Unlike me you're not a realist,' Sam countered, as Charon hopped up on her lap and began to purr.

'Pete asked about you, Sam.'

'Did he?' A dozen emotions rifled through her, none of them particularly good. Samantha still had issues with her brother. Big ones. 'What about Dad? Did Pete ask about him? You know, Dad hasn't heard from him in years.'

'Well, no, he didn't bring up your father.'

'It figures.' Sam felt a stab of disappointment which was totally uncalled-for. Why in the world was she ever-hopeful that her brother would develop some conscience about family ties? 'So what's Pete doing?' Sam asked. 'To support himself, I mean.'

'I'm not sure. He said something about working for a cellphone company, putting up towers all around the South-east, but I had the feeling that the job was over. He was living here, in Atlanta, but acted as if he was going to be moving . . . Uh-oh, I've got another call coming in, I've got to take it as I do work on commission, you know, but I wanted to tell you that I'm going to be in New Orleans in a couple of weeks. I'll call with the details as they come in. Gotta go.'

'Bye—' Before the word was out, Corky had clicked off and Sam was left with a dead line. Staring at the picture of her small family, she hung up and tried to shake off the shroud of depression that always clung to her when she thought about her brother. Or her mother.

Deep down, though she knew it was time to let go of the old feelings, Sam still blamed Peter for taking her mother away. Picking up the snapshot, she traced the contours of her mother's face with the tip of her finger and felt the old sadness well up as it always did when she thought of her mother. It hadn't been long after the picture had been taken that Beth Matheson had been killed senselessly, in an automobile accident that could have been avoided.

'Oh, Mom,' Sam swallowed hard. It had been so long ago on that rainy night in LA when, frantic to find her son, Beth had climbed into her sedan and driven off. Not two miles down the road, she'd hydroplaned, hadn't been able to stop for a red light and been killed instantly by another driver turning in the intersection.

All because of Pete's love affair with cocaine.

Addiction, Sam reminded herself, trying to diffuse some of the rage that sometimes overcame her when she thought of her mother's premature death. Peter was an addict. It was a disease. Beth Matheson had been careless and had not only died herself that night, but the driver of the van that had hit her was in the hospital for six weeks.

Water under the bridge.

Sam replaced the photograph. She should call Corky back and try to track down Pete. For her father. *For you, too, Sam.* He's your only brother. You have to get over faulting him.

But he never calls Dad. Nor me. Acts as if his family doesn't exist.

Rather than dwell on a brother who didn't care if she thought he might be dead, Sam reached for the phone again. From memory, she dialed David's work number and was informed that he was 'out for a few days.'

Wonderful. It wasn't that she wanted to talk to him, she just wanted to assure herself that he wasn't involved in any of the calls to the station or the calls here at the house. *Not David*, she told herself. The first call came in when you were in Mexico. He was there.

It's not David. The police are barking up the wrong tree.

Still, she dialed his home number, waited until the answering machine clicked on and hung up. So he wasn't in Houston. So what?

She couldn't sit around and wonder what he was doing. He was out of her life, and she didn't have to remind herself that she wanted it that way. Things were better without him. She'd never really loved him, but when she'd first met him, he'd seemed the right choice for a husband and father of the children she'd wanted.

Thank God she'd woken up before she'd given up on love and married him because of his suitability. 'You're as bad as Corky,' she muttered at herself. She turned to her computer and accessed her e-mail. Most of it didn't interest her, but she saw another electronic missive from the Boucher Center and found a note from Leanne.

DS—

Things aren't going great here. Mom's mad all the time and Jay won't call me back. I think I need to talk to you about something. When you have the time, call or e-mail me.

'Oh, honey.' Sam fired off a quick note, suggesting they meet for coffee, then tried Leanne's home number. It rang busy, so she couldn't leave a message. Leanne had e-mailed her before with similar missives, but Sam had the feeling the girl was in some kind of trouble. Maybe she'd call into the show tonight.

Just like Annie Seger did?

'Stop it,' she muttered out loud. She was just anxious because it was Annie's birthday, and she'd gotten the threatening calls and notes. It had nothing to do with Leanne's plight.

Telling herself she'd call Leanne later, Sam nudged Charon off her lap and climbed the stairs to the second floor. Inside her closet, she parted her long dresses, then bent down and opened the door to the attic hidden under the eaves. Flipping on the light switch she heard an angry hum, then saw the hornet's nest tucked into one corner of the sloped ceiling. Shiny black bodies reflected the light of the single dusty bulb as they crept over the thin paper of their home. Besides the hornets, she spied spiders skulking in cobwebs that draped from the ancient, exposed rafters. She wondered about bats, saw some droppings but no furry little winged bodies hanging upside down. The attic smelled of must and mildew – this was no place for her important papers. She'd have to build cabinets in the den or second bedroom. Gritting her teeth she crawled carefully across the rough plank flooring and glanced down at the dust . . . was it disturbed? The top of the boxes . . . it seemed to be cleaner than it should, as if someone had wiped them to look at the tags . . . but . . . She shook her head. What was wrong with her? No one had been in her attic and the boxes were relatively clean because she'd sorted through them six months ago, when she'd hauled them to the attic. She'd been in here six months ago – no one else had.

And yet she couldn't ignore the niggle of doubt that crept through her mind. Had someone been in her house? She bit her lip and silently told herself to be rational.

Carefully, she read each label, sorting through boxes of old tax records, school papers, reports and patient files until she found the box with Annie Seger's information in it. Dragging the crate into the closet, she heard the hornets buzzing. One mad insect followed her through the long skirts of her dresses, landed on her head and as she swatted at him, stung her on the side of the neck.

'Damn.' She shut the door to the attic, latched it firmly and carried the box into the bedroom, where she dropped it unceremoniously on the floor. Her neck throbbed. She'd have to do something about the nest and soon before the hornets found their way into her closet, bedroom and the rest of the house.

In the bathroom, she doused a washcloth in cold water, then using a mirror inspected and washed the sting. A red welt had already risen on her skin and the only medication she had in the cupboard was years-old calamine lotion which she dabbed on the side of her neck. 'Stupid thing,' she muttered and heard Mrs. Killingsworth's dog start to bark. She walked toward the front of the house to investigate and heard footsteps on the front porch. Expecting to hear the doorbell chime, or a rap of knuckles on the door, she started downstairs.

The telephone rang and she yelled, 'Just a minute,' in the direction of the door as she dashed into the den.

She swept up the receiver before the third ring. 'Hello?' she called into the mouthpiece. No answer. 'Hello?'

Again no response. And yet someone was on the other end of the line. She was certain of it. Could sense that someone was there.

'Who is this?' she said, irritation and a drip of fear in her voice. 'Hello?' She waited thirty seconds, then said, 'Look, I can't hear you.'

Was there someone breathing on the other end or was it a bad connection? It didn't matter. Without saying goodbye, she hung up and tried to convince herself it was nothing.

Or was it?

She checked caller ID.

Unavailable.

Just like the calls to the station.

Don't even think that way. It was a bad connection. Whoever it was will call back.

She walked into the foyer to the front door and realized that the bell had never rung, nor had anyone knocked. Odd.

She looked through the peephole, and through the fish-eye lens saw no one.

Leaving the chain in place, she opened the door a crack and snapped on the exterior light.

The porch was empty. Her wind chimes jingled in the breeze. Across the street Hannibal was staring at her house and putting up a ruckus, barking his fool head off.

Unhooking the chain, she stepped outside. She was alone. But the porch swing was swaying. As if someone or something had pushed it.

Her heart froze. She scanned the front yard and drive. 'Hello?' she called into the coming night. 'Hello?'

From around the corner there was a noise – the scrape of leather on aging planks. Or her imagination?

Heart hammering, she walked to the corner of the porch and looked along the side of the house where the porch fell in shadow. Aside from the patches of light thrown from the dining-room window, the night had closed in.

Squinting, she was certain she saw a movement in the hedge separating her house from the neighbors, but it could have been the breeze filtering through the leaves or a squirrel scrambling over the branches, or even a cat slinking through the shadows.

You're losing it, Sam, she thought, turning back to the front of the house. *You're imagining things.*

But the old porch swing was still rocking slightly, mocking her as it swayed, and the sense that she wasn't alone, that hidden eyes were watching her made her skin prickle. *Who?* she wondered as she walked inside and locked the door firmly behind her. The phone shrilled and she started.

Get a grip!

She let it ring again. And again. Heart hammering, she picked up the receiver. 'Hello?'

'Hello, Dr. Sam,' John's voice intoned and she leaned against the desk for the support. 'You know what day this is, don't you?'

'It's the twenty-second.'

'Annie's birthday.'

'So you say. Who was the girl who called in the other night?'

'Have you thought about your sins? That you should repent?'

'Repent for what?' she asked, sweat dripping down her back. She glanced out the window, wondered if he was outside, if it was his footsteps she'd heard on the porch, if he was calling from a cell phone. She stepped to the window and drew down the shade.

'You tell me.'

'I'm not responsible for Annie's death.'

'Not the right attitude, Sam.'

'Who are you?' she demanded, her muscles tense, her head pounding. 'Have we met? Do I know you?'

'All you need to know is that what happens tonight is because of you. Because of your sins. You need to repent, Sam. Beg forgiveness.'

'What are you going to do?' she asked, suddenly cold as death.

'You'll see.'

'No – Don't—'

Click. The phone went dead.

'Oh, God, no!' Sam wilted into her chair. Dropped her head into her hands. She'd felt the evil in his voice, the cruelty. Something was going to happen. Something horrid. And she was to blame.

Pull yourself together. Don't let him beat you down. You have to stop him. YOU! Think, Sam, think. Call the police. Alert Bentz. And then do whatever you can.

She dialed the police in New Orleans and nearly went out of her mind when she was told Rick Bentz would be paged and he'd have to call her back. 'Tell him it's an emergency,' she insisted before hanging up. What could she do? How could she stop whatever evil John had planned? She jumped when the phone rang again, picked up the receiver, expecting another threat.

'Hello?' she said, her knees nearly giving way.

'This is Bentz. I got a message you called about some emergency.'

'John just called me,' she said. 'Here, at the house.'

'What did he say?'

'He wanted me to repent, that if I didn't, I would pay for my sins, the same old thing, but then he added that if I didn't something bad was going to happen. Tonight. And it would be my fault.'

'Son of a – wait a minute. Let's start over. Slowly. I don't suppose you taped the conversation.'

'No . . . I didn't think of it. It was over too quickly.'

'Tell me everything that's gone on,' he suggested and she obliged. She didn't leave out a thing, mentioning that she'd gotten several hangups, that she'd thought her red teddy was missing, that she felt the house was being watched. Bentz listened and gave her the same advice as he did before, to be careful, lock her doors, get a watchdog, keep the alarm system on. '. . . and you might want to consider staying with a friend. Just until this is over.'

She hung up, feeling a little better. But she knew she couldn't sit around and wait for John to make good his threat. No way. She had to figure out who he was.

Before it was too late.

'. . .You want me to wear those?' the girl asked, staring at the man she'd picked up near the river and motioning to a wig of long red hair and a lacy scarlet teddy, both of which were dangling from his fingers.

'That's right.' He was calm. And weird. And the sunglasses covering his eyes only made it worse.

She'd turned a few tricks before, when she'd been desperate and she'd been asked to do some sicko stuff, but this seemed more bizarre than usual.

But then what did she know? She just wanted to get through it and get the cash.

He walked to the window and made sure the shades were drawn in this crummy little hotel room, a room he wasn't happy about paying for.

He'd been hyped up, and the scratch on his face bothered him. He kept looking in the mirror tacked to the back of the door and tracing the welts with his fingers, welts *she'd* made.

She'd been sitting on a bench in the park, near the wharf, watching the boats chugging along the lazy river. Deep in thought, wondering what she was going to do, she hadn't heard him approach. He'd appeared out of nowhere. The park had been nearly deserted when he'd propositioned her. She'd explained that she didn't have anywhere they could go and he'd gotten pissed off. She'd thought it was finished. But he'd been persistent.

He'd offered a hundred bucks.

She would have taken fifty.

So he'd brought her to this smelly little room just outside of the Quarter. She'd been second-guessing herself ever since his

requests. But it was good money. What did it matter if she had
to put on a red teddy and cover her own short carrot red locks
with this longer, red/auburn wig? The sooner she did as he
asked, the sooner she'd be on her way to score some crack. So
okay. It was no big deal. She'd done worse things than wear
some other woman's things. She wondered if the teddy belonged
to his wife or his girlfriend. Just what kind of freak was he in his
dark glasses?

So now he was looking at her again with those dark, hidden
eyes. Worse yet he rubbed a rosary between his fingers, and that
really creeped her out. She wasn't particularly religious, but
she'd been brought up in the church, and it seemed morally
wrong, just plain spooky, that he'd brought the rosary along.
Sacrilegious.

But . . . whatever. She needed a hit. And she'd get it. If she
could just get through the next half hour or so. She glanced at
the bedside table. Saw the hundred-dollar bill. It was weird, too.
Blacked-out eyes on Ben Franklin.

The John was fiddling with the radio on the bedside table,
pushing buttons and glowering at the electronic display until he
found a talk station, one she recognized. She swallowed hard as
she heard Dr. Sam's voice.

'Can't . . . can't we listen to music?' she suggested, feeling a
new stab of guilt. It was as if Sam was in the room with them.

'No.'

'But—'

'Just get dressed,' he ordered, his lips compressing, his thumb
and finger rubbing the rosary as if his life depended upon it. The
dark glasses and scratch on his cheek convinced her to shut up.

Sliding out of her platform sandals, she stood barefoot on the
worn carpet near the bed, then wiggled out of her tube top. In a
few minutes this would be over and then she could leave.

Dr. Sam's voice floated through the speakers, 'So let's hear
about it, New Orleans, tell me about the love letters or the Dear
John letters you've received.'

The guy froze. Muttered something under his breath, then

whipped around glaring at her. He didn't say a word as she kicked off her shorts and struggled into the lacy teddy. Adjusting the straps, she thought fleetingly that the guy was handsome in an eerie way. She'd concentrate on that, his good looks, and wouldn't listen to Dr. Sam. She'd pretend. Just like she always did and she'd just get down to business, get him off and then be on her way. Stuffing her hair under the wig, she angled up her chin and looked at him defiantly.

'How's that?'

For a moment he just looked at her, studying her like one of those fruit flies under a microscope in that stupid biology class she'd flunked. She tossed her head and the long hair of the wig swished against her shoulder blades.

'Perfect,' he finally said with the hint of a smile, 'Just perfect.'

He approached her and touched her ear, playing with the series of earrings running up from her lobe. Good. He was finally going to get down to it.

He nuzzled her neck and she forced out a moan she didn't feel, just to get it over with. Lolling her head back and closing her eyes as if she was really getting hot, she sensed something odd, something cold slide over her head to circle her neck.

What was this shit? She leaned back away from him and realized that the rosary was around her throat, the sharp beads tight against her skin.

'Hey, wait a minute,' she said, and saw him smile for the first time. It was cold. Deadly. Razor-thin lips drawn back over straight white teeth. She tried to pull away, but he yanked hard and with a flip of his wrist, twined the strands together. The beads cut into her neck, bit into her flesh, cut off her breath.

Panic spurted through her. This wasn't right. She tried to scream. Couldn't. Couldn't drag in a breath of air. Flailing her arms, kicking at his knees and crotch, she fought him, but he sidestepped her bare feet and her hands did little damage against a rock-hard chest. She tried to scratch his face, but he only pulled tighter. Sweat dotted his brow. His teeth clenched with the effort, his lips curling.

No, oh, God, no. Please, somebody help me!

Her lungs were on fire. She thought she would burst.

Please, please. Help me. Please someone, hear what's going on in here and help me!

She flung a fist at the glasses and he jerked back his head. She saw her own terror twice in the dark lenses as the distorted reflection of her face came into view. She was going to die, she knew it. And the baby within her, the one she hadn't wanted, it was going to die, too.

He twisted around to her backside, and she felt a second's relief. Her knees buckled. She gasped. Tried to run.

She dragged in one final breath. Tasted blood, stumbled forward, half-believing she could escape.

Then he wrenched the unholy noose again.

21

'That's a wrap,' Melanie said as the strains of 'Midnight Confession' faded and an advertisement for an e-company started rolling.

Shoving her chair away from the desk, Sam let out her breath. She'd been nervous during the show. Edgy. Certain 'John' would call again, that he'd only phoned her at the house to prove that he could. To scare her. But he hadn't called in.

But he'd been listening. Waiting. Knowing he was stretching her nerves to the breaking point. After the phone call at her house, she'd decided to bait him. Her program tonight had been about communications, specifically love letters, Dear John letters and even threatening notes though she hadn't mentioned the card she'd received in her car.

Listener response had been hot, but 'John' hadn't phoned in . . . yet . . . There was still time. He'd proven that before when he'd called in after her program had aired.

Though it was after midnight now. Technically Friday – the day after Annie Seger's birthday.

She turned off her equipment, studied the unlit phoneline buttons for a second, then met Melanie and Tiny in the hallway.

'No weirdos tonight,' Tiny observed.

'So far,' Sam agreed.

Tiny shoved his glasses onto the bridge of his nose. 'You're disappointed, aren't you? You kind of get off when he calls.'

'Get off?' Sam repeated, her temper sparking. 'No . . . but we can't find him if he hides.' She didn't add that she wanted to lure him out, hook him, reel him in and then see that he never terrorized anyone again. Yes, in a perverse way, she wanted to know what made him tick, but more than that, she wanted him off the streets, away from the phones and out of her life.

'Do you think he'd really call in again after hours?' Melanie asked as she searched in her purse and came up with a tiny box of Tic-Tacs. 'Wouldn't that be pushing his luck? I mean, he's got to have figured that you've been to the police by now. He doesn't know that they aren't tracing the calls – or that we aren't.' She plopped half a dozen tiny mints into her palm and tossed them into her mouth.

'Maybe the guy knows what a cheap-ass George Hannah is,' Tiny grumbled, then waved his hands in the air. 'I didn't say that, okay? I don't want to hear about it in the next staff meeting.'

'It's what we were all thinking anyway,' Melanie said, yawning, as she held up the near-empty plastic box of mints in offering. 'Anyone?'

'I'm good,' Tiny said, declining.

'If you say so.'

Sam shook her head. 'No, thanks.'

Melanie yawned again. 'God, I'm dead tonight. Anyone want to split a Diet Coke?' She was already heading down the hallway toward the kitchen.

'I've still got some.' Tiny turned back to the booth to set up *Lights Out*.

Sam was right behind but had one ear open, listening for the phones. 'No caffeine for me,' she said to Melanie. It was one o'clock on Friday morning; Sam's shift was over for the week, and she couldn't imagine working on the weekends as well.

'Would you mind loaning me a buck for the machine?' Melanie asked as they rounded a corner and passed by a wall lined with pictures of local celebrities who had been interviewed at WSLJ.

'After you took care of Charon and the house while I was gone? I think I can manage.'

'Good.'

Sam found her wallet and handed Melanie a bill as they neared the kitchen. The first strains of soft instrumental music wafted through the hallways. *Lights Out* had begun and the phone hadn't rung. 'Has Eleanor mentioned anything about running *Midnight Confessions* seven nights instead of five?' Sam asked, trailing after Melanie.

'I heard it through the grapevine around her. Gator's not too happy . . .' Melanie's voice faded. 'What in the world . . . Maybe you shouldn't come in here.' Melanie stopped dead center in the doorway and was staring to her left, toward the French doors. The dollar bill that Sam had given her had fallen to the floor.

'Why not?' Sam craned her neck to look over Melanie's shoulder.

Her blood ran cold at the sight of the cake – iced in white frosting and supporting about two dozen red candles. 'Jesus.'

'This has something to do with that Annie girl,' Melanie said, swallowing hard.

Sam pushed past her and strode to the table. Her head was pounding, her heart pumping wildly. 'Who did this?' she asked. 'Who got in here and planted this thing?'

'I . . . I . . . don't know.'

HAPPY BIRTHDAY, ANNIE blazed across the white icing in red letters while the candles were burning, red wax dripping down the sides of the cake like rivulets of blood, smoke twisting upward from the tiny flames.

'Is this someone's idea of a joke?' Sam asked, glaring down at the concoction. She counted. Twenty-five candles. One for every year of Annie Seger's life and death. 'Did you do this, Melanie?'

'Me? Why? Are you nuts?' Melanie shook her head. 'I – I've been in the booth all night. You know it. You were there . . .' Her face crumpled in on itself, and she blinked as if she might cry. ' . . . How could you even think—'

Sam wasn't listening. 'Tiny!' Sam yelled, storming to the corridor, her blood pumping hard, anger, disgust and shame spurring her to the booth where Tiny was adjusting the volume and the pretaped program. He looked up, saw her and held up a finger to keep her quiet and at bay. Her fists clenched and it was all she could do not to burst into the glassed-in room and rip him up one side and down the other. By the time he lumbered into the hallway, her fingernails had dug into her palms and she was livid.

'You look like you could spit nails.'

'I can,' she bit out furiously. 'I found the cake.'

'The cake,' he repeated dully. 'What cake?'

'Annie Seger's birthday cake.'

'Her what? The girl who called in the other night? What the hell are you talking about?' He seemed genuinely perplexed.

'Don't you know?'

'For God's sake, Sam, you're talking like a lunatic.' His face was red now. Anger? Shame? Regret?

Melanie had followed Sam halfway down the hall. 'I think you'd better see for yourself.'

'Jesus Christ, now what?' Lips compressed, beads of sweat appearing on his pockmarked skin, Tiny strode through the maze of hallways and into the kitchen. Sam was right on his heels, following him step for step. Around the corner, into the kitchen, to stop dead in his tracks. 'What the – Shit.'

'My sentiments exactly,' Sam said.

'But who would do this? How could they?' he asked, turning. His skin had paled, leaving the red blotches of his acne even more pronounced.

'My guess is it's either you or Melanie. No one else is here.'

'Except the security guard,' Melanie put in.

'He doesn't even know me.' Sam wasn't buying it, though, for the life of her, she couldn't figure out why either Melanie or Tiny would want to sabotage her this way. Melanie was her assistant and friend, a person she'd trusted to look after her job, house and cat while she was away and Tiny was half in love with her from the minute she'd walked into WSLJ. He was too smart to be reduced to schoolboy antics to garner her attention.

But then *who?*

Melanie said, 'The guard could've been put up to it.'

Tiny seemed genuinely disgusted. 'Are you accusing me, Sam? You really think I'd do something like this to . . . to . . . you?' he asked, a wounded look crossing his eyes behind his thick glasses.

'I don't know.' It did seem far-fetched. Irrational. If whoever was behind it had wanted to rattle her . . . mission accomplished.

'And Gator was here not an hour ago, and so was Ramblin' Rob. I saw him at the record case looking for some moldy-oldy to play tomorrow,' Tiny said.

'The boss was here earlier, too. I saw George in his office, on the phone,' Melanie added.

'Great.' So half the staff could've done the job.

'Don't you trust me?' Tiny asked. His lips folded in on themselves, and he glared at Sam as if she was named Judas.

'Of course.'

'Then knock it off.' He looked like a wounded bear.

'And *don't* look at me,' Melanie said, backing up, palms outward. 'I've been with both of you all night.'

Tiny shook his head and held up a finger. 'You took a break.'

'To go to the bathroom, for God's sake!' she said. 'For the first time in my life I wish George was perverted enough to have some surveillance cameras installed.'

'You and me both,' Sam said, then felt the tickle of a breeze against the back of her neck and noticed the muted sounds of the city filtering into the room – traffic, a solitary trombone, the wind sighing through the palms in Jackson Square. Heart in her throat, she walked to the French doors that opened onto the unused balcony. They were unlocked, just slightly cracked. 'Someone was in here,' she whispered, goose bumps rising on her skin. 'They came through here.' She pushed the doors open and the sound of traffic and voices drifted in with the warm breath of the wind. Laughter and the moan of the trombone.

'They? You think it was more than one guy?' Tiny asked, following her onto the balcony.

'I wish I knew,' she whispered harshly, crooking her neck to see around the corner of the building and searching the night-dark streets of New Orleans. Who had broken into the office and how had he done it? Wrapping her fingers around the decorative railing, she stared across the square to the cathedral, splashed with light, the clock face glowing as bright as a full moon, the tall spires black and jutting toward the dark sky. In front of the cathedral was the park, where palm trees blocked her view of the statue of Andrew Jackson and his rearing horse. The park was supposed to be empty now, pedestrians were locked away from the circular sidewalks at night. Had her tormentor scaled the fence, and was he lurking there, hiding in the shadows, watching her now with hidden eyes?

Despite the humidity, she felt cold from the inside out. 'You bastard,' she whispered, her eyes scouring the depths of Jackson Square before she swung her gaze south, past the stately old buildings, along the narrow streets to the levee and the dark river beyond. Was he skulking in a doorway, secreting himself on a small terrace such as this, taunting her silently with his presence.

'I'm calling the security guard,' Melanie said from inside the building.

'Good.' Sam's gaze swept the railing and floor of the never-used balcony. In the weak light she saw nothing other than pigeon droppings and dirt. 'I'll phone Eleanor on another line. If I don't, she'll be ticked. You' – she turned and pointed a finger at Tiny's chest – 'phone the police and make sure that *Lights Out* is on track – and that no one else calls in.'

'You really think "John's" gonna call again, don't you?' he accused hotly. Was there just a hint of jealousy in his voice?

She glanced at the table where the cake was still displayed. 'No, Tiny,' she admitted, walking inside and staring down at the rapidly burning candles. 'I think he already did.' Bending down, she blew out every one of the twenty-five damning flames just as the phone jangled.

Sam jumped.

'I'll get it,' Melanie said, but Sam was already halfway to the nearest phone available, at the front desk. Line one was blinking wildly.

Bracing herself, Sam leaned over Melba's desk and grabbed the receiver. She punched the button. 'WSLJ.'

'Samantha?'

She nearly wilted at the sound of Ty's voice. 'Hi,' she said, rounding the computer extension and falling into Melba's chair. It was so good to hear from him. 'What's up?'

'I wanted to see that you were okay,' he said. 'I listened to the show and wondered if you'd like me to pick you up.'

At that moment the security guard, a beefy man of about thirty-five, with a shaved head and beginning of a pot belly, walked through the door. 'I'll be fine,' she said into the phone. 'We did get a little surprise down here, and I was about to call the police.' Quickly she told him about the birthday cake.

'I'll be there in twenty minutes.'

'I'm fine.' She nodded toward the guard. 'I'm sure Wes will walk me to my car.'

'Wes, my ass. What good was he when someone broke in? Why didn't he hear it? Why the hell didn't the alarms go off? You wait for me and yeah, call the cops. Pronto. I'm on my way.'

'You don't have to—'

He clicked off, and the light for line one died. 'You'd better check out the kitchen,' she said to Wes as she hung up, and then it hit her. Ty had called on line one. Because that was the number listed in the book or available from Directory Assistance. If line one was in use, the calls automatically switched to line two, then three and four depending upon how busy the lines were. Calls could stack up while waiting for a response.

But John had phoned in on line two, even when none of the other lines were busy. Somehow he knew the number. Either he'd been in the building, worked for the phone company, had access to the phone records or he worked at WSLJ.

A cold drip of fear slid through her blood. Was it possible? Was someone at the station responsible for the terror? How else would the cake be left in the kitchen? Either John or an accomplice knew the ins and outs of this old building, understood how WSLJ ran, and had a personal vendetta against her.

Who?

George Hannah?

Tiny?

Melanie?

Eleanor?

She trusted every one of them. And those she knew less well, Gator and Ramblin' Rob, some of the technicians and salespeople, even Melba. They were all part of her family here in New Orleans.

But one of them hates you, Sam. Enough to scare the liver out of you. She stared at the phone, quiet now, no lights blinking in the semidarkness. The pictures of celebrities, the framed awards, the voodoo dolls and baby alligators all backlit in glowing neon seemed macabre tonight.

Whoever it was who meant to terrorize her had done a damned good job.

Until she found out who was behind the bizarre events of her life in the last few weeks, she'd never feel safe here again.

22

This is your fault.

Ty ignored his conscience, but guilt settled deep in his gut as he opened the door to his wagon and whistled to his dog. He couldn't help think that somehow he trip-hammered someone's interest in Annie Seger. He'd done some research, knew the story inside and out, but he couldn't figure out how his writing a book about the case could ignite anyone's interest.

No one knew about his project aside from his editor, agent and himself. He hadn't even been honest with Sam, and when she found out she was gonna be angry as hell.

Sasquatch barked loudly from inside the house, causing a ruckus.

'Be good,' Ty warned as he slid behind the wheel and rammed his keys into the ignition. He hadn't intended to touch off a new crime spree, nor had he intended to get involved with Sam, though he'd planned on meeting her from the start.

Throwing the car into drive, he gunned the engine and flipped on the headlights. The street was deserted, Sam's house dark, a light glowing on Mrs. Killingsworth's porch.

His idea of getting to know Samatha Leeds and in the process learning what she knew about the case had backfired big-time. Before he'd even started, whoever the hell John was had started calling into *Midnight Confessions*. And then this latest bit – with the breathy-voiced girl claiming to be Annie. What the hell was that all about? Who was she?

He slowed for a stop sign, then took the corner, heading through the outskirts of the tiny lakeside community of Cambrai and rimming the lake, heading toward the bright lights of the city, visible in the distance.

The names of people connected with Annie Seger swirled through his head – her mother, Estelle, a cold, religious bitch if ever there was one and Wally, her natural father, a man who drifted from job to job. Then there was her brother, Kent, a year and a half older and not as popular as his sister. She'd been raised by Jason Faraday, her stepfather, an ambitious, driven, A-type doctor, and her boyfriend had been Ryan Zimmerman, a boy who'd fallen from being an A student and captain of the lacrosse team into partying and drugs. Annie's purported best friend had been Priscilla 'Prissy' McQueen, a backstabbing self-indulgent teenager who'd had a crush on Annie's boyfriend.

He wheeled around a corner and saw the city limits of New Orleans loom in front of him. He reached for his cell phone and punched out a number he knew from memory. It was time to call in the cavalry, much as he hated it.

Otherwise, someone was going to get hurt.

Brrring.

No, Bentz thought, his eyes opening to his dark apartment. *Not now.*

The phone jangled sharply again.

Rolling over, he glanced at the clock and groaned. Two-thirty in the damned morning. He'd been asleep less than two hours. No doubt it was bad news. No one called in the middle of the night just to chat. Snapping on the bedside lamp, he snagged the receiver before the damned telephone could ring again. 'Bentz,' he said, wiping a hand over his face, trying to wake up.

'Looks like we got ourselves another one.' Montoya sounded much too alert for this gawd-awful time of day.

'Hell.' Bentz swung his legs over the side of the bed. His mind instantly cleared, and he thought about the warning Samantha Leeds had received. 'Where?'

'Near the Garden District,' Montoya said, giving off the address. 'Second floor.'

'Same MO?'

'Similar. But not identical. You'd better get over here.' Montoya rattled off the address.

'Give me twenty minutes. Don't let anyone disturb anything.'

'Would I?' Montoya asked before clicking off, and Bentz wondered why he hadn't been called first. He hung up, grabbed a pair of jeans he'd thrown over the end of his bed and kicked his shoes from beside the dresser. He didn't bother with socks and yanked on a T-shirt. In one swoop he gathered his keys and ID, then grabbed his shoulder holster and Glock from the bedside table. Stuffing his arms through a jacket and shoving a Saints cap on his head, he took the stairs to the front door of the apartment building.

Jesus, it was hot. At two-thirty in the morning. Not the dry heat of the desert but that moist, cloying warmth that brought a sweat to his skin at seventy degrees. He jogged to his car, unlocked it and had fired the engine before he strapped on his seat belt.

Another woman dead.

Silently he berated himself. He shouldn't have paid so much attention to Dr. Sam and the damned threatening notes. Not when there were murders being committed. Murders he needed to solve.

But killings that just might be connected to the radio shrink.

His tires squealed as he took a corner too fast and he clicked on the police band, only to hear that there had been trouble down in the French Quarter. He heard the address and recognized the building. Realized it housed WSLJ. Was certain the trouble involved the lady shrink. His gut tightened. John had warned her, then struck again.

This was turning into one helluva night.

He drove like a madman, found the address Montoya had given him and parked between two cruisers. The night was sticky, not much wind. Sweat ran down his back as he wove through the crowd that had already gathered around the grand old house cut into individual apartments.

On the second floor, he found the apartment and stepped inside.

The place was already crawling with the crime-scene team. A police photographer was taking pictures of the dead woman as she lay facedown on the carpet. She was naked, and her head had been shaved, nicks visible beneath the dark stubble covering her skull. A thick braid of shiny black hair was twined in one of her hands and an odd, sweet smell accompanied the usual stench of death. Her skin was smooth, a soft mocha color.

With one quick look, he knew they had another killer on their hands. 'This is all wrong,' he muttered to himself, his gut tight, his jaw clenched as he viewed the latest victim stretched out on the area rug.

'You're telling me.' Montoya slid past the photographer and had heard Bentz's observation.

Bentz squatted down, balanced on the balls of his feet. He touched the skein of hair wound through her fingers. It was oily. Smelled faintly of patchouli. As in Kama Sutra. What the hell was that all about?

'Who's the victim?' Rocking back on his heels, Bentz glanced up at Montoya.

'Cathy Adams, according to her driver's license, but she was sometimes known as Cassie Alexa or Princess Alexandra.'

'Working girl?'

'Part-time prostitute, part-time student at Tulane, part-time exotic dancer down at Playland.'

He knew the place. An all-nude 'dance club' on Bourbon Street.

Straightening, Bentz surveyed the room. Neat. Tidy. Furniture worn, but clean. A few pictures on the wall. Martin Luther King Junior was positioned above a tattered recliner and directly above her head, a colored portrait of Christ gazed down on her. 'This her place?'

'Yeah. According to the landlord she had been sharing this place with a boyfriend, who the landlord thinks might have doubled as her pimp, but the guy – Marc Duvall – moved out about three weeks ago after they had one of their usual knock-down-drag-outs. Same old, same old, she calls 911 but by the time the officers show up, she's calmed down and even though she's got one helluva shiner, won't press charges, claims it was all a mistake. He gets hauled in, but he makes bail. Anyway she gave Marc his walking papers, he skips out, and no one's seen him since. The landlord has had it and served Cathy an eviction notice. I've got an APB out for Marc, but my guess is he's not only out of town, but probably the country.'

Bentz was still surveying the crime scene. 'Whoever did this isn't our boy,' Bentz said, sensing he'd just stepped into an unfamiliar evil. Again he bent down for a better view of the victim. She'd been strangled, from the looks of the bruises on her neck, but the ligature was different from the other victims.

'I know. More upscale neighborhood. No mutilated C-note, no radio playing, garrotted by something different.'

'All the other victims were white,' Bentz muttered.

'But she was a prostitute, and she was killed in her apartment, and she was posed,' Montoya pointed out. That much was true. No one would have fallen on the floor completely facedown, arms outstretched over her head, legs together, toes pointed, a thick braid of her own hair twined in her fingers.

'Differently. She was posed differently.' Bentz thought hard as he stared at the smooth mocha-colored skin of Cathy Adams. He wondered about the woman – did she have children? A husband tucked away somewhere? Parents still alive? His jaw hardened. 'Check on the next of kin, friends, family, boyfriends other than Marc. Find out what else she was into. Talk to the other girls and the owner of the club.'

Montoya nodded, frowned down at the victim. 'Maybe our boy's escalating or mutating. Maybe that's why the signature's changed.'

'It's too different, Reuben.' Bentz didn't like the turn of his thoughts. 'I'll bet we've got ourselves another bad guy. If nothing else, a copycat.'

'Two?' Montoya reached into his jacket pocket and pulled out a pack of Marlboros. Shook one out. Didn't bother to light it. 'No way. They're not that common – what? Maybe 10 percent of the serial-killer population.'

'Somethin' like that.'

'What are the odds of that happening?'

'Not good, thank God.' And yet . . . Bentz's gut told him differently as he walked through the rest of the small apartment, away from the cloying smell of patchouli.

The bedroom was as tidy as the living room, the bedclothes not even mussed. The bathroom filled with women things – hose hanging from the showerhead behind a clear curtain, shampoo and conditioner on the edge of the tub. Using a handkerchief he opened the medicine cabinet behind the mirror and found tubs and jars of makeup, some over-the-counter meds, Band-Aids and tampons. The only nod to her profession was an open box of condoms next to the Alka-Seltzer. No prescription medications. No evidence of illegal drugs.

Clean towels were in a small cupboard, and her cleaning supplies were under the sink.

Bentz, satisfied that he'd seen enough, walked to the front door, where a small crowd had gathered around the uniformed cops keeping the curious at bay. 'I want this place swept clean,' Bentz said to the woman in charge of the crime-scene team.

She shot him a put-upon look. 'Like we usually leave evidence for the cleaning people. Give me a break.'

Bentz held up a hand. 'Sorry.'

'Just give us some room here, okay? The sooner we're done here, the sooner you'll have your report.'

'You got it.' He and Montoya eased out of the room and through the small crowd that had collected in the hallway. 'Have everyone here questioned.'

'I'm already working on it.' Montoya was nothing if not efficient. 'So far no one claims to have seen anything out of the ordinary.'

'I want to see the statements ASAP. And call the lab. Have them put a rush on this. Double-check that they look for hairs from a wig, and cross-check any semen, blood or hair samples with what we have on file on the pending cases, and even the solved ones – not just murder but any rapes or assaults in the past five years.'

'A pretty tall order,' Montoya griped. One cop was questioning the residents, the other keeping them outside of the crime scene.

'Not so tall. We've got computers and the FBI.' He rubbed the back of his neck and glanced back toward Cathy Adams's apartment. 'Where are the Feds?'

Montoya's grin was wicked. 'Guess I neglected to call them.'

'There'll be hell to pay.'

'As you said, this isn't our boy.' He clenched the cigarette between his teeth and searched his pockets for his lighter.

'Yeah, but they'll want to know about it.'

'I'll give 'em a personal report in the morning.'

'You do that,' Bentz grumbled, as they walked down the stairs. He didn't like dealing with the Feds any more than Montoya, but he wasn't going to buck the system. And there were some good agents, guys he could work with. Like Norm Stowell when Stowell had been with the bureau.

'How come you were called first?' Bentz asked.

'I wasn't.' Montoya found his lighter and clicked it to the end of his cigarette as they reached the first floor. 'I was at the station writing up a report for you on the associates of Annie Seger.' He sucked hard on his filter tip then exhaled a cloud. 'I left a hard copy of the report on your desk and was about to go home when the call came in. I took it, drove over here, then phoned you.'

That explained it.

Montoya added, 'When you get a chance, you might want to take a look at the report. Annie Seger wasn't your typical prom queen.'

'I don't imagine.'

'And there's a couple of other things. Samantha Leeds's old man – the guy she was married to?'

'Doctor Leeds.'

'Yeah. He's still around; still teaches over at Tulane. On wife number three, and that seems to be falling apart.'

'I've already had the honor of meeting him,' Bentz muttered, remembering the jerk. 'Helluva guy.'

'I figured. But there was a couple of things I hadn't counted on. Check out the good doctor's patient list – it's only a partial, of course because of the doctor-patient confidentiality code, but the Houston PD were able to piece together some info.'

'I'll look at it.'

'I'm sure you will.' Montoya took a drag and then shot a plume of smoke from the side of his mouth. 'Then check out to see who was first officer on the scene the night Annie Seger died.'

'Someone we know?'

Montoya's eyes glinted as they always did when he'd uncovered a particularly unusual piece of information. 'You could say that.' He shouldered open the door.

Outside, a crowd had gathered – the night people who wandered the streets, interested neighbors, people who listened to the police band and got their kicks out of being a part of the action. *And maybe one of them is the murderer.*

Serial killers were known to watch the results of their havoc. It gave them a rush to watch the police try to find clues they'd endeavored not to leave behind. Some even had the balls or were nuts enough to try and keep up with the investigation, to come forward and offer 'help.'

Wackos.

A news van was parked on the other side of the yellow crime-scene tape, and a sharply dressed woman reporter was talking with her cameraman. She looked up as Bentz ducked under the barrier. Without missing a beat, she kept her conversation running and made a beeline for Bentz. The guy holding the shoulder camera was right on her tail.

'Here comes trouble,' Montoya stage-whispered, 'all gussied up in designer labels.'

'Detective,' the newswoman called, not bothering to smile.

'I'm Barbara Linwood with WBOK. What's going on here?
Another murder?'

He didn't respond.

'I mean, I've heard some of the people here talking. The
victim is rumored to be a prostitute and there's been several
women killed lately – all prostitutes. I'm starting to think we
have a serial killer running rampant in New Orleans.' Her
expression was expectant, eager. She *wanted* a serial killer to be
stalking the streets of the Crescent City. She *wanted* the story.

Again he held his tongue and his pager went off.

'Come on, Detective. Give me a break here. Was another
woman killed? A prostitute?' A breath of wind teased at her hair,
but she didn't notice as she stared at Bentz intently.

'We have a woman dead,' he said, 'and we're in the first stages
of the investigation. I have no statement to make at this time.'

'Enough with the company line.' She was a quick woman,
about five-three, with sharp features, heavy makeup, and a
persistent streak. She wasn't just zeroing in on Bentz but
included Montoya in the conversation. 'If there's a serial
murderer in our midst, lurking in the streets of New Orleans,
the public has the right to know. For safety's sake. Can't you
give me a quick interview?'

Bentz glanced at the camera hoisted on the cameraman's
shoulder. He hadn't said a word, but the red indicator light was
glowing brightly. 'I think I just did.'

'Who was the victim?'

'I'm sure the department will issue a statement in the
morning.'

'But—'

'There are rules to follow, Ms. Linwood. Next of kin need to
be notified, that sort of thing. That's all I can say right now.' He
turned his back on her, but silently admitted she had a point. A
monster was stalking the streets of the city, maybe more than
one, and the public needed to be aware.

'What about you?' she asked Montoya, but got nowhere.
Reuben might want to talk to the TV people and grab a little

glory, hell the guy loved that part of the job. But he wouldn't risk that kind of trouble from Melinda Jaskiel or the DA. Montoya was too savvy and ambitious to blow it.

From the corner of his eye, Bentz saw Montoya disentangle himself from the newswoman and jettison his cigarette onto the street.

Bentz walked past a couple of cruisers with their lights flashing to his own car, where he checked his pager and called in to the station. The message was simple. There had been more trouble over at WSLJ. Dr. Sam had received another threatening message – this time in the form of a birthday cake for Annie Seger planted in the kitchen at WSLJ. Someone was really trying to rattle the radio shrink's cage.

'Hell.' Bentz threw his car into drive and tore off. He rolled the windows down, let the warm Louisiana breeze flow through the interior as he headed toward the business district, leaving the stately old homes behind. Whoever the hell this John was who was harassing Samantha Leeds, he had one perverted sense of humor. All in all, it was a damned nightmare. Was it a coincidence that the prostitute was killed on Annie Seger's birthday? Was there a connection between the murders and the threats being aimed at Samantha Leeds? Or was he grasping at straws?

He blew through a yellow light near Canal Street and slowed down. Just because a murder was committed the same night Dr. Sam received an ugly prank didn't mean squat. And there was no hundred-dollar bill with the eyes blackened, which seemed a very frail link to the mutilated publicity shot Samantha had received. All the references to sin and forgiveness didn't have anything to do with the murders . . . there was no radio tuned into the *Lights Out* program . . . no, he was just tired . . .

And yet his mind wouldn't let go of the possible link. He was missing something, he was sure of it. Something obvious. He wheeled around a corner when it hit him like a fist in the gut.

Not *Lights Out*. The program before it. His hands gripped the wheel. That was it. The time of deaths were earlier, before the bodies were discovered and he'd bet a month's salary that

the program that had been on when the women were killed was
Midnight Confessions.

Why hadn't he seen it before?

The perp offed the women while listening to Dr. Sam.

'Son of a bitch,' he growled, but felt that surge of adrenaline
that always sped through his bloodstream when he was close to
cracking a case. This was it. The link. And the red wig. Because
Dr. Sam was a redhead. Holy shit, how had he missed that. He
drove to the station, nosed his car into a parking spot and headed
upstairs. He wasn't officially on duty until later this afternoon,
but he knew he wouldn't be able to sleep. The questions and
half-baked theories spinning through his brain would keep him
awake for hours.

There was just enough sludge in the bottom of the coffeepot
for one cup, so he poured himself a mug and carried it to his
desk. He didn't bother with the harsh fluorescent tubes overhead, but switched on his desk lamp, then settled into his old
chair and flipped on his computer screen. With a few clicks of
the mouse, the crime-scene photos of Rosa Gillette and Cherie
Bellechamps were displayed side by side.

They had to have been killed by the same guy. Both women
had been strangled with a strange noose, the cuts on their necks,
identical. Both corpses had been left with the radio playing, the
bodies posed as if they were praying, both sexually violated,
both left with a mutilated hundred-dollar bill.

None of which had occurred tonight with Cathy Adams.

And Cathy had been killed on Annie Seger's birthday. Big
deal. Lots of people were born on July 22. It meant nothing.
Nothing. There was no link.

And yet . . .

He'd wait for the report on the latest victim. In the meantime,
he flipped through his in-box. Lying on top were several neatly
typed pages compliments of Reuben Montoya. Bentz scanned
the notes on Annie Seger quickly, then read it over a second
time. Montoya was right. Annie Seger wasn't what he'd expected.
Her parents Estelle and Oswald Seger had divorced when Annie

was four and her older brother, Kent, was six. Estelle had remarried practically before the ink on the divorce papers had dried. Her new husband and Annie's stepdaddy was Jason Faraday, a prominent Houston physician. Oswald, 'Wally,' had all but disappeared from his children's lives when he'd moved to the Northwest, somewhere outside of Seattle. According to the court records, Wally had forever been delinquent in his child-support payments, only coughing up when Estelle had sicced her lawyers after him.

So much for the *Ozzie and Harriet* type of family. Bentz took a swallow of his coffee and scowled at the burnt, bitter flavor.

Leaning back in his chair he propped his heel on a corner of the desk and flipped over the pages. Montoya had been thorough, piecing together info from the high school Annie had attended. If her report cards and the school yearbook were to be believed, Annie Seger had been an excellent student, a popular girl, a cheerleader and member of the debate team. According to a file the Houston police had composed from interviews of family and friends, Annie had gone through several boyfriends before linking up with Ryan Zimmerman, who had been captain of the lacrosse team before he'd run into trouble with drugs and the law and had dropped out of school.

A stellar choice for the father of her child. Bentz frowned as he read on.

Suddenly the popular teen was alone and pregnant. In apparent desperation she'd called Dr. Sam a few times and soon thereafter had ended her life in her plush bedroom over nine years ago. There were pictures of Annie – one in her cheerleading uniform in mid-jump, pom-poms clenched in her hands, another of her vacationing with her family, her, her mother, stepfather, and brother in hiking shorts and T-shirts, posed along the ridge of a forested hill, and of course, the crime scene, where she was slumped over her computer, wrists slashed, blood running down her bare arms and onto her keyboard, a tragic mess that was in stark contrast to what he saw of the rest of the room – the neatly made bed covered with stuffed animals, the plush white carpet, the bookcase where a stereo system was stacked between the paperbacks and CDs.

Bentz glanced up at his desk and stared at the bifold frame of the pictures of his own daughter. He couldn't imagine losing Kristi. She was the single most important thing in his life; his reason for staying off the bottle and making something of himself.

Frowning, he turned the page and found a partial list of Dr. Sam's patients. Only five were listed. The one that jumped out at him was Jason Faraday, the physician who just happened to be Annie Seger's stepfather.

'Son of a bitch,' Bentz muttered, his mind racing. Samantha Leeds had never mentioned that Faraday had been her patient, but then she wouldn't. Couldn't. There were laws about that sort of thing. He swilled the end of the coffee and flipped to the final page.

Montoya's notes said that Estelle and Jason Faraday had divorced sixteen months after Annie's death. Estelle still resided in Houston, in the very house where her only daughter had taken her life. Jason, however, had left Texas and moved to Cleveland, where he'd remarried and had two young children. Phone numbers and addresses were listed.

Montoya had done a helluva job. True to his word Montoya had listed all of the officers of the Houston PD who'd been involved in the case. The first officer to arrive at the scene had been Detective Tyler Wheeler.

'Well, I'll be goddamned.'

Bentz read Montoya's final note.

Detective Wheeler's involvement in the Annie Seger suicide hadn't lasted long. He'd been removed from the case immediately as he'd admitted that he was related to the victim. Annie Seger had been Tyler Wheeler's third cousin on her father's side.

Bentz's gut tightened.

Detective Wheeler had resigned his post.

His current address was Cambrai, Louisiana.

Just down the road from Dr. Samantha Leeds.

The neighbor who was always hanging around.

Coincidence?

No way in hell.

How did a cop with over ten years' experience under his belt give it all up and end up here with a pansy-assed job of being a writer? And why the hell had he ended up down here, in Louisiana, cozying up to Samantha Leeds?

Bentz figured it was time for a stakeout.

23

'I'm taking you to my place,' Ty said, as they drove out of the city, leaving WSLJ, the police, the damned cake and all the craziness behind. It was late, and Sam was bone-weary. She hadn't gotten much sleep the night before as she'd been with Ty on the boat and after the shock of the birthday cake and the interrogations by the police, her nerves were strung tight as bowstrings.

'I'll be fine,' she said, too tired to really get into an argument. 'I've got an alarm system and a watch cat.'

'Seriously, Sam. Just for tonight, since it's Annie Seger's birthday.'

'Yesterday was,' she corrected, rolling down the window and letting in the night air. They were driving around the black expanse of Lake Pontchartrain, and the breeze was gratefully cool, the night finally calm.

'Humor me. For one night. Stay with me.'

He touched the back of her hand and her stupid skin tingled.

'Fine, fine,' she agreed, rubbing her neck where the hornet had left his mark. It was beginning to itch like crazy. 'I don't suppose you've got anything for a headache?'

'At the house.' He glanced in her direction. 'I'll take care of you,' he promised, and she was too damned sleepy to remind him she could take care of herself. What was the point? Besides, she was certain whoever was terrorizing her was connected to the station. Someone had unlocked the door to the kitchen to leave the cake and whoever was calling in, trying to freak her out, knew the number for line two. A number not listed in any phone book nor available through directory assistance.

No, it had to be an inside job, and that thought chilled her to the marrow of her bones.

Shivering inwardly she wondered which one of her coworkers would go to such lengths and for what purpose? Certainly not Gator; he was worried enough about losing some airtime if her show was expanded. Though he might want to scare her out of a job, he wouldn't want her program to become too popular. Nor would any of the other DJs, though Ramblin' Rob was devious enough to do this just for the hell of it. For a few laughs at everyone's expense. The crusty DJ could have learned about Annie Seger easily enough, the story was common-enough knowledge because George and Eleanor had been in Houston. Maybe that was what had triggered it, someone like Rob finding out about the problems in Houston and exploiting them.

To what end? To drive you crazy? To get you to quit? To make you look like a lunatic? Or to lure in a bigger audience.

Then why the mutilated picture and calls to her house? Why the note left in her car? Or John's calls after the program was over. How would those actions promote more listeners?

They wouldn't, Sam. You're running down a blind alley. There's something more, a link you're missing. So what was it? What?

Her headache growing worse by the second, Sam closed her eyes and leaned back against the headrest. She couldn't think about John, the calls or Annie Seger any longer. Not tonight. But tomorrow, when her head was clear and she'd caught up on her sleep . . . then she'd figure it out. She had to.

Ty flipped on the radio and they listened to the end of the prerecorded *Lights Out* program, instrumental renditions of familiar songs, guaranteed to put you to sleep, all engineered by Tiny, the nerd who knew the station inside and out. He'd worked at WSLJ longer than anyone else, part-time from the time he was in high school. While Tiny attended Tulane, Eleanor had offered him a full-time position.

So what about him, she wondered as the Volvo's tires sang against the pavement and the engine hummed. Maybe Tiny wasn't as innocent as he appeared. Or what about Melanie?

Lord knew she was ambitious enough and sometimes she seemed secretive, then there was Melba, over-educated and underpaid . . . or someone in league with Trish LaBelle over at WNAB? It was no secret that Trish wanted Sam's job . . . *Stop it, Sam, you're not getting anywhere*, she thought, *turn off the noise.* As an instrumental version of 'Bridge Over Troubled Water,' played, Sam was vaguely aware that they were entering the Cambrai city limits. It was good to be with Ty, to relax, to be able to trust someone. She opened her eyes just a crack, enough to see his strong profile, bladed cheekbones, dark expression as they passed beneath streetlamps or the headlights of a few oncoming cars illuminated the Volvo's interior.

It was odd to think that she'd known him only a few weeks and she smiled to herself to think how pleased Mrs. Killingsworth would be that her matchmaking had come to fruition. He slowed and cranked the wheel as they turned down the street rimming the lake.

They passed her house, the windows dark, no sign of life within. She nearly changed her mind, and invited him to stay with her and Charon and the hornets, then smiled to herself. Soon enough it would be dawn, but tonight she'd stay with Ty and exhausted as she was, she felt a little tingle of anticipation at being alone with him. She'd thought about their lovemaking often during the day, too often. It seemed so natural to be with Ty. So right. And yet she warned herself that she had made bad decisions in the past, poor choices when it came to men. And he was a virtual stranger to her – what did she really know about him except that he'd shown up at about the same time someone had started terrifying her? And her emotions for him were way out of line.

She couldn't, *wouldn't* fall in love again. Not with Ty. Not with any man. She'd learned her lesson. Or so she told herself as he parked the car and walked her into his cottage – a little house with few furnishings other than a desk, sectional and television. Sasquatch stretched and sauntered up, tail wagging and Ty let the shepherd out through the back door.

'Hungry?' Ty asked Sam.

'Dead would be a better description.'

He whistled to the dog, then helped Sam up a short flight of stairs to the loft, where a king-size bed was pushed beneath windows overlooking the back of the house. Moonlight glinted on the lake and the smell of water drifted in on a warm, Louisiana breeze.

'You know, I don't really think my being here is a great idea,' she said.

'Why not?' He'd already kicked off his shoes.

'I might do something I shouldn't.'

His grin was wicked as he lifted her chin and stared into her eyes. 'A guy can only hope.'

'You're impossible.'

'I try,' he admitted, drawing her into his arms and kissing her until she couldn't think of anything but making love to him.

Don't do this again, Sam! Think. Use your head. How do you know you can trust him?

She couldn't. She knew that much, but she couldn't fight the need to lose herself, to close out all the fear and pain, to trust someone – if only for a night. What could it hurt? She closed her eyes and they tumbled onto his bed, into his world, not knowing what that world was made of. Truth? Lies? Deceit?

What does he want from you?

She didn't know, didn't want to question anything as she closed her eyes and wrapped her arms around his neck. His lips were hot, his tongue insistent and she eagerly parted her lips and kissed him open mouthed as his arms lifted her up, pulling her so close that her breasts were crushed. One hand pulled, pressing her rump ever closer, so that beneath her skirt her mound was pushed against the hard length of his erection.

She ached deep inside and had trouble catching her breath. Her heart pounded and her blood raced as his fingers bunched the fabric, strong fingertips molding around a buttock and probing in her cleft, forcing her closer still, creating a heat and electricity that sparked through her.

She wanted him; God knew she wanted him and the moan that escaped her was just the beginning. One of her legs curled around his and he lifted his head to stare deep into her eyes.

'As I said before, you want me,' he said as the breeze, sifting through an open window tickled the back of her neck. 'And I want you.'

'Do you?' she breathed, perspiration dotting her skin, heat building deep within. The fingers over her buttocks clamped tight.

'What do you think?'

'I – I think I'm in trouble.'

'We both are,' he whispered against the shell of her ear and her skin rippled with goose bumps. 'Oh, darlin' we both are.'

He tumbled backward onto the bed and his lips claimed hers again. Fierce, hungry, hard, he kissed while his hands worked at the fastenings of her skirt and blouse. Knowing she was giving in to a passion she should deny, she pulled his shirt over his head and skimmed the ropey muscles of his arms. In the half light she saw his face, intense, wicked, downright sexy as he removed her blouse then kissed the tops of her breasts as they spilled over the lacy cups of her bra.

Beneath the flimsy fabric her nipples hardened and the need within her throbbed. 'I knew it would be like this with you,' he said as he shoved the strap of her bra off her shoulder and warm air brushed against her suddenly bare nipple.

'Like – like what?' she whispered as he bent his head. She felt the gentle scrape of his teeth on her tender flesh, the tickle of the tip of his tongue.

'Like this,' he said, breathing hard and suckling as his other hand delved beneath the waistband of her skirt, grazing her navel in its quest.

Her legs parted as if of their own accord and she writhed anxiously, wanting, needing, consumed by an ache that seemed to pulse.

He unhooked the clasp at the waistband and the zipper hissed downward as, with both hands, he scraped her skirt and panties over her hips and down her thighs and off her feet. Then she was lying beneath him, her blouse crumpled beneath her, her bra half off, her skin bare.

He lowered himself further, lips touching and tasting, tongue exploring the contours of her skin, his breath moving the curls at the apex of her legs. She closed her eyes, lost herself in pure sensation. He parted her legs, touched her, played with her, tasted her and she writhed, fingers curling in the bedspread, hot images flashing through her mind, desire running rampant.

Don't let him do this to you ... don't let him make you vulnerable, but she couldn't stop. The wanting was too intense, the fire in her blood too hot. She felt the pressure building, the ache, and all thoughts converged on that one spot, the center of the world seemed to pulse where his skin touched hers, hotter, higher, faster . . . her mind spinning until the universe cracked. She bucked, cried out and he held her fast, two strong hands on her legs until she fell back against the bed, panting, her body enveloped in sweat.

'Ooohh,' she sighed, breathing hard as the warm glow of satisfaction wound over her. 'Ty . . . What about . . . you?'

Lifting his head, he winked at her. 'We'll get to that.'

'Now?' she asked, her voice soft.

'Oh, yeah, now.' He stood on his knees. 'Trust me, I'm not letting you off the hook. I'm not that noble.'

'Noble?' she repeated, then laughed as the wind sighed through the open window. 'I didn't think so.'

'What did you think?' He swung a leg over her and straddled her. 'Tell me.'

Sam stared up at him, this man she'd taken so readily for her lover, this stranger who could make her ignore all her doubts, make her cast aside her worries about him. And yet what did she know of this man? His smile was pure sin, his beard-shadow dark, his hair mussed as he held her gaze. Bare-chested, muscles gleaming with sweat, his jeans slung low on his waist, he placed his hands upon her breasts and squeezed. 'What?'

'Oh, that you were . . .' He was kneading her breasts, scraping his thumb over her nipples, turning her on again, so soon. She had trouble collecting her thoughts. 'That you were . . . dark and dangerous.'

'I like that.'

'That maybe I shouldn't trust you.'

'You shouldn't.'

'But that . . . that I found you . . .'

'Irresistible?'

'Damningly so.'

'Then I guess we're even,' he said and reached for the top button of his jeans. He slowly slid the top button out of its hole. Samantha stared, her throat tightening as he flipped his wrists and a series of seductive pops echoed through the loft. She bit her lower lip as he slid his jeans downward and kicked them off.

'See . . . not noble at all,' he insisted, lowering himself onto her and kissing her on her belly before inching up to her breasts.

Again the heat. The damned, moist, all-consuming heat between her legs. Again his tongue tasting and exploring, sliding ever upward, leaving a moist, hot trail upon her skin. 'No woman has the right to look as good as you do, you know?'

'Is that right?' She had to force the words out.

'Oh, yeah.'

'Maybe I should say the same about you that no man should be allowed to do the things you do to me.'

His laugh was a throaty growl. 'Flattery will only get you into trouble.'

'As if I'm not in enough already.'

'A little more won't hurt,' he said as his lips found hers and his tongue plunged into her mouth. He pushed her knees apart and, as he kissed her, thrust hard into her. Deep. Deeper, pushing against her, then slowly easing back.

Her arms wrapped around his head and she lifted her hips, wanting more of him, aching to be with him, closing her eyes to the night and the threats surrounding her. Tonight, oh, God, tonight she would just let go.

'That's a girl,' he said and plunged deep again, and again and again, breathing hard, sweating, his heart pounding as rapidly as her own. She moved with him, forced her anxious lips to his, arched her back and heard his breathing accelerate, felt each of his sinewy muscles tense as he thrust into her and she let go, her body convulsing, her mind splintering. Ty let out a primal roar as he fell against her, clinging to her, holding her close, his body damp, the moonlight streaming through the open window. Sam sighed, her breath ruffling his hair and knew that she was losing herself in this man, this dark, interesting, stranger, a man she wasn't sure she could trust.

Sam was asleep. Dead to the world. In his bed.

Moonlight streamed through the open window, playing upon her face, and Ty was struck by the unlikely thought that he cared about her far more than he should, maybe was even falling in love with her.

You poor, sick, S.O.B. He'd used her. And in so doing, he'd put her in jeopardy. Plain and simple. There was no reason to sugar-coat it. He'd considered her a means to an end, and now he felt like a heel. Carefully he extracted himself from her arms. She moaned in her sleep and rolled over, never once opening an eye. The bed was rumpled, the pillows mussed, the room smelling faintly of her perfume and sex. He hadn't intended to make love to her, but hadn't been able to stop himself. That was the prob-lem – he, who'd always been careful when it came to women, a man who protected his own best interests as well as his heart, lost it when he was around her. Just plain lost it. He studied the lines of her face, the sweep of her eyelashes, the way her lips were open just enough for shallow breaths.

Tearing his eyes away, he reminded himself that he had things to do, things she was better off not knowing about. His conscience nagged him a bit as he stepped into a pair of shorts and didn't bother with a shirt.

The digital readout on the clock showed it was four-thirty in glowing red letters. With the ready excuse of taking Sasquatch outside should she waken, he hurried stealthily down the stairs, the dog at his heels.

Without making a sound he opened the door to the street and saw no one in the bluish illumination from the streetlamp. The night was still, that time of day before dawn when the entire world was asleep. The morning newspaper hadn't been tossed onto his driveway, nor were there any patches of light glowing from the houses lining the street. No A-types were out jogging for their morning exercise, no cars cruising along the narrow road. In this section of Cambrai, it was still late night.

Sasquatch nosed around the front yard and Ty walked to the end of the drive, stopping near the magnolia tree that guarded his mailbox. Heavy leaves blocked the shimmering light from the streetlamp, creating an even darker shadow around the bole of the tree. Ty waited, his eyes straining in the darkness, his ears tuned for even the softest of sounds.

He heard nothing, but a few seconds later a figure emerged from the dense shrubbery. Dressed in black, shoulders hunched, expression hidden in the night, Andre Navarrone seemed to blend into the shadows. 'Helluva time to be out,' he whispered.

'Couldn't be avoided.' Ty glanced back at the house, then to the man he'd known over half his life, another cop turned private investigator. Navarrone's tenure with the Houston PD had been short and infamous. He'd never quite learned that the tactics he'd learned in the Gulf War as a special agent couldn't be implemented in the city. So he'd gone independent. Which was perfect.

Ty stared straight into his friend's eyes. 'I need your help.'

'I figured that much. Otherwise, you wouldn't have called.' Navarrone's smile was a wicked slash of white. He didn't ask what Ty wanted, but then he never did.

And he'd never failed.

Yet.

Sam rolled over and sensed that something was different. Wrong. She wasn't in her own bed . . . no, now she remembered.

A contented sigh escaped her lips, and she smiled. She was with Ty, though she'd argued against it. Images of their lovemaking flashed behind her eyes. The feel of his warm skin, the taste of him, the way he knew just how to touch her . . . She reached behind her and felt cool sheets against her fingertips, just sheets. No skin or muscle or bone.

Rolling over she blinked and pushed up on an elbow. Sure enough she was alone. There was an impression where his body had so recently been, but it was cool to the touch. Maybe he'd gotten up to use the bathroom, or get a drink or . . . the dog. That was it. He'd taken the dog outside.

In the darkness, she found her slip and wiggled into it. She heard his muffled voice through the open window, a hushed whisper and she imagined Ty was encouraging Sasquatch to hurry and do his business. But as she peered out the window, she saw no sign of dog or man on the stretch of lawn between the house and lake. Curious, she walked downstairs where a banker's lamp, left on as a night-light, gave off a soft green glow over a wide desk and allowed her to move through the rooms without switching on any other lights.

In the kitchen she splashed water from the tap over her face and finger-combed her hair, then looked out the window toward the street. Nothing. But he had to be near. She didn't believe that he would leave her alone now, not after he'd driven into town like the cavalry and made a big point of her not staying in her house alone. On top of all that she'd heard his voice – was certain she had. She scoured the darkness and, from the corner of her eye saw movement. Sasquatch rounded the corner of the house and was trotting to the end of the driveway only to sit at the base of the tree and look up expectantly. Another movement and the shadows came to life. She caught a glimpse of a man beneath the tree . . . no, there were two of them. Two. One of the men had to be Ty – otherwise the dog would react differently.

Samantha bit her lip. Ty and who? A man he'd slipped out of bed to meet. A man he hadn't told her about. Squinting hard, she leaned over the sink and stared into the night where moon-light dappled the ground and two men huddled.

She gripped the edge of the counter. One of the men was Ty. So who was he talking to so quietly at this hour of the morning? What was so important as to prod him from bed and out into the night? Dark suspicions nagged at her brain. Hadn't the police insinuated that no one was to be trusted, especially men she hardly knew.

But Ty had only seemed to have her best interests in mind. He'd shown up at the station, not once but twice, when he suspected she might need him. He'd insisted upon driving her home, on checking out her house, on seeing that she was safe. That was why she was here tonight. Right?

Or had it all been an act?

She considered walking out the door and demanding answers, then told herself to hold tight and have faith. That whatever he was doing, it was on the up-and-up. She shouldn't second-guess him, should wait for him here in the house, and when he deigned to return she could ask him what was going on.

No way. She was too wound up, too on edge. Her mind was racing with all kinds of reasons for him to have left her alone in his bed – none of them good. Suddenly keyed up, she couldn't imagine trying to fall back to sleep; nor was it her nature to docilely wait and let some man determine her fate.

She walked into the living area, intent on flying up the stairs to the loft, throwing on her clothes and storming back to her house where she belonged, but on the way to the stairs she passed his desk and laptop computer with its screen saver of brightly colored pipes. She paused, tempted to sneak a peek at his files. Edging toward the desk, she told herself she was breaking a trust, but decided she had to know the truth. There was a reason he'd slipped out of the bedroom, and she'd bet she wouldn't like it.

She leaned over the keyboard. In a matter of seconds, she'd opened his word processing program. There flickering on the screen were file numbers that corresponded to chapters and research information.

What had he said about it? What was his joke to Melanie? That it was kind of like *The Horse Whisperer* meets *Silence of the Lambs?*

She clicked onto the first chapter.

Her heart dropped.

The title of the book loomed at her:

Death of a Cheerleader: The Murder of Annie Seger.

'Oh, God,' Sam whispered, her gaze raking down the page.

Murder? But Annie Seger committed suicide.

Sam's blood turned to ice. How did Ty know anything about it? Where did he get his information? She skimmed the first few pages, her fingers shaking as she scrolled down.

Her heart twisted when she realized how deeply he'd deceived her.

How was he involved in all of this? Oh, God, could he be behind the person calling in – was he John . . . no, she couldn't, wouldn't believe that. But there had to be a connection. 'You miserable son of a bitch,' she muttered, thinking about their lovemaking. The heat. The intensity. The passion.

The lies.

Why didn't he confide in you?

Why did he have to lie?

You slept with the man, Sam. Made love to him.

Her stomach clenched. Bile crawled up her throat.

What the hell was his game?

If he'd wanted to do her harm, he'd had dozens of opportunities.

God in heaven, was it possible? Had she nearly given her heart to a man who had been tormenting her from a distance?

She didn't have time to print out the chapters, she had to leave. Now. Before he realized that she was on to him. She had to grab her purse and . . . the disk! The one in the computer. Proof that Ty wasn't who he said he was. Information on Annie.

With fumbling fingers she pushed a button, extracted the disk and scrambled out of his chair. She tripped on the way back to the loft, dropped the damned disk, and slid her hands over the carpet until she located it again. In the half-light, she dashed up the remaining stairs. She had to hurry. She didn't know how long his meeting with the man in the street would take, but she assumed it would be over soon.

In the loft she didn't risk turning on a lamp, but searched the darkness for her clothes and purse. She didn't bother dressing, couldn't find her belt, didn't care. But her purse . . . with her keys . . . where was it? *Where?* Heart thundering, throat dry, she combed the loft using only the moonlight filtering through the window to aid her vision and running her fingers over the edge of the bed and the floor. She found her bra . . . Ty's wallet . . . but no handbag.

Think, Sam, think.Where did you put it?

Her mind turned backward. She rememberedTy showing up at the radio station and how relieved she'd been to see him. Then there was the ride in his car here. She'd argued against not stay-ing at her own house, but he'd been adamant and she'd been too damned tired to argue. He'd insisted she'd be safer with him and she'd reluctantly agreed.

What a joke!

Then there had been the lovemaking.

Her heart nearly stopped when she remembered how he'd touched her, kissed her, brought her to the edge over and over again. Dear Lord, she'd been such an idiot for the man.

How eagerly she'd tumbled into bed with him. How close she'd come to handing him her heart . . . but she couldn't think of that now. She nearly tripped over one of her shoes, then felt around on the carpet unable to locate its mate. Where the hell was her purse with her keys and ID? She'd carried it into the house and once inside, Ty had kissed her and helped her up the stairs . . . without the damned handbag.

Through the open window she heard the sound of footsteps crunching on gravel.

Damn. He's on his way back inside. She had to escape. Couldn't feign sleep and pretend nothing was wrong. Leaving the shoe, her heart pounding triple time, she crept down the stairs, nearly stumbling on the bottom step. She was sweating, moving through the unfamiliar house. In the dim light from the banker's lamp, she saw her purse on the kitchen table. She grabbed the bag but didn't dare take a chance on looking outside again.

Bare feet skimming across the carpet, she hurried to the back of the house and flipped the bolt on the French doors. Quickly she slipped outside where a verandah and small patch of lawn separated her from the lake. If worse came to worst, she could climb the fence to the neighbor's yard or swim around the point or . . .

She sprinted across the cool flagstones and scurried down three steps. Moonlight played upon the dark water and the sloop tied to the dock. If she knew anything about sailing and had his keys, she could take off in the boat. She ducked along the edge of the lawn, near the shrubs, toward the dock. There was a muffled 'woof' from the edge of the house.

Please, God, no.

'Sam?'

His voice came out of nowhere.

Sam froze.

'What're you doing up?'

Biting her lip, she slipped the computer disk into her purse and turned to the house. Wearing only a pair of dark shorts, Ty was leaning over the railing and staring straight at her.

Busted.

'Sam?'

She let out a long breath. 'To tell you the truth,' she said, 'I'm escaping.'

'From—?'

'You tell me,' she said, not closing the distance. 'What are you doing up at this hour and don't give me some ridiculous excuse about walking the dog, because it won't wash with me. I know better.'

'I was meeting with a friend.'

'Who just happens to be walking down the street at 4 A.M.? Right.' She couldn't hide her cynicism. 'Come on, Wheeler. You can do better than that.' Still clutching her clothes, she added, 'Look, I don't know what's going on here, but I think I'd better leave. This is . . . this is getting too crazy.'

He straightened and the moonlight hit him full in the face. God, he was handsome. 'I suppose it is,' he agreed, and plowed a hand through his hair, pushing it off his forehead. 'I have a confession.'

She didn't move. His words seemed to echo across the yard and ricochet through her brain. 'You know, those aren't exactly the words I want to hear right now. I've heard way too much about confession, sin and repenting in the last few weeks to last me a lifetime.'

Ty's jaw slid to one side. 'Then how about an explanation?'

'That would be a real good idea,' she said. 'Real good.' She waited for a few seconds before he finally started to speak.

'The truth is that I knew about Annie Seger a long time before I met you.'

'No kidding,' she remarked. She would have appreciated his admission more if she didn't think he already knew she'd poked through his computer files. 'You know, Ty, you could have told me.'

'I was going to.'

'When?' she said in absolute disbelief. How stupid did he think she was? 'Were you going to confide in me before or after hell freezes over.'

'Soon.'

'Not soon enough,' she said, her temper flaring. 'Don't you know what's going on here? Haven't you been paying attention? The calls I've been getting from 'John' and the message from 'Annie' and the damned birthday cake and card – for God's sake, Ty, just when were you going to break the news to me? After it was too late and this nutcase made good his threats? Or maybe you're involved in a more personal level. Maybe you know John.'

'No,' he cut in angrily, but something else darted through his eyes, an emotion akin to guilt. Sam felt dead inside. Cold. How could she have trusted him? What was it about her that she always chose so poorly when it came to men. For a bright woman, she was a disaster in the love department. She'd thought Ty Wheeler was different, but he, like her ex-husband and last boyfriend was little more than a user, another great manipulator.

'Or maybe you are John.'

He was taking the stairs from the porch and starting across the lawn. 'You don't believe that.'

'I don't know what to believe,' she said in absolute despair.

'I'm sorry, Sam. I should have told you sooner.' He was close to her now, too close.

'Now there's an astute observation.' She managed to stiffen her spine. 'Look, this is all very ... edifying, but I'm going home.'

'Not yet.' Reaching forward, he wrapped strong fingers over her arm.

'Ex*cuse* me?' She flung off his arm. 'What do you think you have to say about it?' She tried to pass him, but he grabbed her again and this time her attempts to rip her arm from his grasp failed. 'Let go, Ty.'

'Just listen to me.'

'Why? So I can hear more lies? Forget it!' She started toward the house, and he, still holding her arm, walked with her.

'You need to know what's going on.'

'Like you're going to tell me? Give me a break. The only reason you're confiding in me now is that you know I saw you with the midnight stalker or whoever he is out in the street and that I peeked into your computer records and found out you weren't leveling with me. Now, let go of me, or you and I are going to have this conversation at the police department. Got it?'

'Just wait.' Rather than release her, his fingers gripped all the harder. 'I think you owe me the chance to explain.'

'I *owe* you *nothing*.' She couldn't believe the man's gall. They were up the stairs and on the verandah. 'The way I see it everything you said to me from the first time I saw you is a lie. As a matter of fact, I'm pretty damned sure that the disabled boat' – she cocked her head toward the *Bright Angel* creaking against its moorings – 'was a setup.'

'I like to think of it as an excuse.'

'Semantics, Wheeler.'

'There are things you should know.'

'No kidding. Let's start with how you're involved with Annie Seger.'

'I'm her third cousin,' he said, without batting an eye. Or releasing his grasp. 'And I was the first police officer on the scene the night she was found. I got thrown off the case because I was related to her. I've always thought the investigation was botched, and Annie's father wants me to prove it.'

'Her biological father,' Sam clarified, trying not to be intrigued. For all she knew he was peddling her a new cartful of lies.

'Yeah. Wally. He never bought the fact that she committed suicide.'

'So he thinks she was murdered? Why?'

'That's what I'm trying to find out.'

'So what about all this other stuff?' Sam demanded as she threw open the French doors and walked into his living room. 'What about the calls to the station and the damned cake and the threats?'

'I can't explain them, nor can I explain who's behind all this, but I'm afraid that I somehow triggered all this, that I'm to blame. I'm afraid that somehow someone found out I was working on the book, maybe through my research, or a leak. Someone in the agent's office or the editorial staff . . . I don't know. At least not yet.' His lips flattened over his teeth in silent rage. 'But it seems more than coincidental that when I start working on this book about Annie's death, which happened nine years ago, you start being stalked.'

'So that's why you're hanging out with me, the reason you've been around? Out of guilt? My God, Ty, you didn't have to sleep with me to keep me safe or to ease your guilt, for crying out loud!' She yanked her arm away from him. She had to get away. Now.

'I didn't hang out with you because of guilt.'

'Like hell.' Angry tears burning the back of her eyes, she stomped through the house. *Don't break down*, she told herself. *Whatever you do, Sam do* not *break down.*

He was right on her heels. 'Just slow down and listen for a minute.'

'I think I've heard enough.' She was up the stairs and inside the house. His house. She started for the front door.

'I didn't mean for us to get involved.'

Whirling, still holding her purse and her clothes, she nailed him in an uncompromising glare. 'But we did, didn't we?'

'That's the problem.'

'The *problem?* For crying out loud, Ty, the problem isn't that we got involved, the problem is that it was all based on a lie! I'm outta here—'

'You can't.'

'Of course I can. What are you going to do about it? Keep me here. Hold me prisoner? Kidnap me, for God's sake?'

'You need my help.'

'What? No way. You've got it all wrong. I think you meant to say that you need my help. The other way around.'

'Sam, listen to me. There's a nutcase out there, a very serious nutcase. For some reason he's targeted you. It could be because I started poking around and somehow, inadvertently gave him ideas. It could be he was involved in Annie's death, or in her life, or he could just be some wacko off the street who read about the story and is trying to make some kind of name for himself. It could even be all a fraud.'

'A fraud?' she repeated.

'To boost ratings. I wouldn't put it past George Hannah or Eleanor Cavalier.'

'I don't see where you're in any position to call anyone else a fraud. Face it, one minute you're upstairs in bed with me and then the second I fall asleep, you're out in the street talking to some man in the middle of the night. Who was that guy?'

'A friend.'

'I didn't think he was an enemy.'

'A friend who's going to help us.'

'Believe me, Ty, there is no "us." ' She walked out the door in a huff. It was only a quarter of a mile and the eastern sky was lightening and a few birds were chirping. If she had to walk barefoot and in slip, so be it. She had to get away.

Before she did something foolish like trust him again.

'The problem is, Sam, I'm afraid I'm falling in love with you,' he said, and his words grabbed hold of her heart and wouldn't let go. She forced herself to turn and face him again.

'Well, you should be afraid, Ty. It would be a horrendous mistake,' she said, anger pushing out the words as she stared hard at him. 'Don't fall in love with me, because I damned well will *never* return the favor!'

24

The problem is, Sam, I'm afraid I'm in love with you.

'Yeah, right.' *Another* lie.

Sam's head thundered from lack of sleep, her bad ankle had begun to throb again and her feet were dirty and sore as she stormed toward her house. Fired by her fury at Ty's deception and thankful no one was up, that none of her neighbors witnessed her dishabille, she strode down the street. The stars were fading, the sky turning a soft lavender as dawn broke.

Ty's final words wouldn't stop reverberating through her aching head, but she wasn't going to allow herself to believe them. Not for a minute. Words of love had been her downfall in the past, and Ty's admission that he thought he was falling for her was another lie, a last-ditch effort to control her, nothing more. The way Sam figured it, Ty Wheeler was willing to stoop so low his nose would scrape the ground, all for the sake of his book on Annie, hence his career and fame. His interest in Sam was all predicated on his book. Nothing more.

'Bastard,' she ground out.

All she wanted to do was push thoughts of him out of her head, strip out of her damned slip, and shower away all memories of the man and his lovemaking. *That* she would miss, blast it all to hell. Ty Wheeler was the best lover she'd ever had, hands down, so to speak. Not that she'd had that much experience, but in her limited scope, Ty was the best. The way he found that special spot on the nape of her neck and kissed her there while feathering his fingers over her nipples.

'Stop it,' she muttered. So he knew how to take a woman to bed. Big deal. That certainly wasn't the most important quality in a man, though it was right up there. Ty Wheeler and his acumen in the lovemaking department certainly kept her longing for more. 'So forget it. It's over.'

There will be someone else.

She wasn't convinced that there would be, but she couldn't let her mind wander down that dangerous road. She had too much to do. She had to clear her head and start figuring out who was trying to terrorize her. Ty Wheeler and his sexy body be damned.

As she reached the edge of Mrs. Killingsworth's property she resisted the urge to look over her shoulder to see if he was still standing at the edge of his drive watching her march self-righteously down the street. While wearing only her slip. Thankfully she hadn't run into anyone, not even the paper carrier.

Until she reached her property.

A white mid-sized car was parked in the middle of her circular drive, and David Ross sat on her porch swing, leaning forward on his elbows, his hands clasped between his knees as he watched her approach. His face was covered with a day's worth of beard, his eyes red-rimmed from lack of sleep or alcohol or a combination thereof, his tie loosened around his throat, his once-pressed shirt wrinkled, his slacks looking as if he'd slept in them. Dark hair was unruly, as if it had endured hours of being pushed away from his face.

'Where the hell have you been?' He pushed himself to his feet. 'What the devil happened? You look like . . .' He took in her state of undress and the wad of clothes she was carrying. '. . . like . . . like you've had a bad night.'

That's putting it mildly. 'I did.'

'Where were you?'

Sam groaned inwardly at the prospect of dealing with him. She wasn't in the mood for this. *Why now?* she thought as her toe caught on the edge of a flagstone. Gritting her teeth, she climbed the steps to the front porch. 'I was at a friend's. Let's just leave it at that, okay?'

'A friend's?' David repeated before his eyes narrowed in understanding. His lips tightened, turning white against his dark beard shadow. 'Why don't my keys work?'

She slid him a glance that warned him not to mess with her. 'I changed the locks because the police suggested it, because of the threats I've been getting.'

'You've gotten more?' he asked, and some of his hostility turned to concern. Deep furrows lined his brow. 'You didn't tell me.'

'I can handle it.'

'Are you sure?' He waited as she scrounged in her purse and found her keys. 'This sounds serious, Sam.'

About as serious as it gets, she thought but wasn't about to confide in him. She didn't need his overly dramatic concern, nor an inquisition. 'What are you doing here?'

'Waiting for you.'

'I figured that much. The question is "Why?"' She twisted the key in the lock, pushed the door open with her shoulder, then walked quickly inside to shut off the alarm before it started blasting and waking up the entire neighborhood.

'We need to talk, Sam. Face-to-face.'

'You should have called.' She dumped her clothes on a chair in the living room as Charon trotted from behind a potted palm to look up and cry at her as he rubbed her bare legs. 'In a minute,' she said to the cat, then skewered David with her gaze. 'Look, I don't know what you expected showing up here, but this isn't a great time for me.'

'I just wanted to see you.' He'd followed her into the living room and was standing next to her, close enough that she smelled the lingering scents of last night's cigars and alcohol. 'Is that such a sin?'

Every muscle in her body froze. 'What did you say?' she asked, and when he tried to touch her shoulder she drew away.

'I was trying to explain that I missed you and hoped that we could talk things over, see if we could find a way back to us again.'

You're overreacting, Sam. This is David. You trust him. You nearly married him, for God's sake, and here you are thinking he's somehow related to 'John' and Annie Seger and all the crap that's gone on around here. You're losing it, Sam, losing it. David's just here being David.

'It's too late to get back together,' she said, and bent over to scoop up her cat and hold him close. Stroking Charon's black fur, she shook her head. 'I think you should leave, David. Whatever you hoped would happen isn't going to. We've been through this before. It's over.'

'Because you wanted it to be,' he pointed out, and there was more than a trace of anger in his words.

'That's right.'

She was too exhausted to discuss this now. Her feet were dirty, her hair a mess, only half-dressed. As if he was following the train of her thoughts, he waggled a finger at her state of undress. 'Why are you only wearing that?'

'I left in a hurry.'

'From your *friend's* house.'

She bristled. 'I'm not in the mood for a lecture.'

'This *friend* sent you home without your shoes . . . ?' he asked, and she saw from the change in his eyes that he was beginning to put two and two together. 'But what about your car? I looked in the window of the garage. It's not here.'

'I left it downtown.'

'Then spent the night with your friend.'

'What was left of it, yes.'

'I don't think I like this.'

'You probably don't. But it's not your business.' She shoved a lock of hair from her eyes. 'You're not my keeper, David. That was part of the problem with us, remember? Your control issues?'

'I've been working on them.'

'Good.' She didn't think she needed to explain anything else, but David wasn't taking the hint to leave and before she could be more pointed and tell him to take a hike she heard the familiar rumble of an engine. Stupidly, her pulse jumped. Through the open door, she watched as Ty's Volvo appeared.

Great. Just what I need. Another male who thinks he knows what's best for me.

But she wasn't surprised. She'd figured that the minute she was out of his sight, he'd climb into his car and track her down. He'd only let her leave because he was giving her time to cool off. In one respect she was flattered, in another ticked off. After all, the truth of the matter was that he was a liar and a user and all things bad that were male.

'Who's he . . . ?' David asked as Ty cut the engine. Before Sam could respond, he said, 'Oh, I get it.'

'Yes. My friend.'

David's expression turned hard as nails. 'It sure didn't take you long, did it?' he accused.

'Don't even say it.'

Ty climbed out of the car and strode up the walk. He'd taken the time to throw on a T-shirt and damn it all, he looked good. And intense. Sam bristled, ready for another confrontation, one she didn't need. She met Ty at the door and Charon, quick to sense his escape, scrambled out of her arms. The cat leaped onto the porch before rocketing into the bushes.

'You don't know how to take "no" for an answer do you?'

'No.' His hazel eyes sparked and a cocksure smile spread from one side of his beard-shadowed jaw to the other. *Bastard* she thought again, but held her tongue. His eyes lingered on her lips for just a second, then he glanced over her shoulder and something changed in his expression; the playful look was replaced by challenge. Obviously he'd seen David.

Here we go, she thought and made quick introductions and both men were tense, sizing each other up. 'David, this is Ty Wheeler.' Sam wished they'd both just evaporate. There was way too much testosterone floating around for this hour of the morning. 'Ty – David Ross.'

Ty extended his hand. David pretended it didn't exist. Great.

'I've known David for years,' she added, stepping out of the doorway and waving Ty in. 'And Ty is the friend I was telling you about,' she said to David. She saw no reason to hide where she'd been. Besides, David needed a dose of reality. A big one.

Opening the hall closet, she found a raincoat and threw it on. 'I'm going to make coffee. If either of you want a cup, great, but I'm going to warn you both that I've about had it with anyone telling me how to run my life.'

David was right on her heels as she made her way to the kitchen and opened her pantry door. 'I want to talk to you alone,' he whispered.

'There's no reason.'

'I flew all the way here to talk to you. The least you could do—'

'Don't go there, David,' she warned, holding up a finger to cut him off. Pulling out a bag of ground coffee, she nudged the pantry closed with her hip, and added, 'I already told you that if you'd planned to see me, you should have called. End of story.' She poured the coffee into the basket of the coffeemaker and filled the glass pot with water out of the tap.

Ty was leaning against the counter, legs outstretched, watching the interplay between David and her with intense eyes.

'This is nuts,' David said. 'What do you know about this guy?'

Good question. 'Enough,' she lied, and she saw Ty's lips twitch.

'But with all the trouble you're having down at the station, don't you think you should . . . cool it . . . or check him out?'

'I think I'll handle it my way.'

The skin over David's cheekbones tightened, and every muscle in his body seemed tense. Rigid. 'That's the problem, Sam. You always do things your way.'

'Because it's my life.'

'Fine. If that's the way you want it, then—'

'It is. It works for me.'

She snapped on the coffeemaker as David, his face flushing, turned on his heel and stormed out of the kitchen. Italian shoes pounding on the floorboards he stomped through the foyer. The front door banged shut behind him.

'Don't say a word,' Sam warned as the coffeemaker started to gurgle and sputter. 'Not a word. I'm *not* in the mood.'

'Far be it for me to comment on your taste in men.' His hazel eyes sparked in amusement.

'Exactly. Now, I'm going upstairs to clean up and when I come down, if you're still here, you can tell me all you know about Annie Seger.' She leveled him a stare guaranteed to melt steel. 'No more lies, Ty,' she said. 'I'm tired of being played for a fool.' With those final words hanging in the air, she flew up the stairs to her bedroom. The box she'd hauled out of the attic was still where she'd left it on the foot of her bed. All her notes on Annie Seger were inside.

Could she trust Ty? she asked herself, and the answer was a resounding 'no.' Then again, she'd slept with him, spent hours with him, didn't believe for a second that he'd do her physical harm.

But he's a liar. Out for his own gain. He didn't tell you about Annie. He used you.

All for his book.

That was his motive. He wasn't out to scare her or harm her . . . he was out for personal gain.

'Aren't we all?' she asked, yanking off her slip and reaching past the curtain to turn on the spray of her small shower. Within half a minute she'd stepped inside and felt hot rivulets massage her muscles and run through her hair. She wanted to live in that tiny tiled cubicle, but couldn't waste the time, not with Ty downstairs. She shampooed, rinsed and was toweling off five minutes after turning on the hot water. There were still drips on her skin as she pulled on a pair of clean shorts and pulled a T-shirt over her head. Sliding into thongs, she ran a comb through her wet hair and ran a tube of lipstick over her lips. *Voilà.* Good enough.

Seconds later she was down the stairs and found Ty in the kitchen toasting bagels and scrambling eggs. 'You didn't have much to work with,' he apologized.

She hadn't eaten since yesterday.

'Hey, anytime someone cooks for me, I don't complain. No matter what it is.'

'Good, cuz although I am a master chef, I do need utensils and just the right ingredients.' He placed a bowl of grated cheese, onions and milk in the microwave.

'Oh, cram it, Wheeler,' she said, smiling despite herself. She grabbed a butter knife and leveled it at him as she found a carton of cream cheese in the refrigerator, 'And just remember you're not off the hook. I'm still mad at you.'

'I figured.'

She waggled the knife in his direction. 'This lying stuff is bad news. Very bad news.'

'I won't do it again.'

'You'd better not, or I might be inclined to use this weapon where it would do the most good.' She flipped the butter knife in the air and caught it on the fly.

He laughed out loud. 'Okay, now I'm scared.'

'I thought so.' Why couldn't she stay angry with him?

The eggs were sizzling in the pan, and he stirred them with a wooden spoon. 'We're about done, here,' he said. 'I thought we could eat outside.' He hitched his chin toward the back verandah.

'And then you'll spill your guts about Annie Seger,' she surmised, leaning a hip against the counter and watching him play the part of the domestic in his shorts and T-shirt that was stretched across his shoulders. She took in his narrow waist and the backs of his legs – well muscled, tanned, covered with downy hair. Whether she liked it or not, Ty Wheeler got to her on a very basic level.

'I'll tell you anything you want to know,' he promised, and she remembered his claim that he'd feared he was falling in love with her.

'Anything?' she teased and he sent her a sizzling look over his shoulder.

'Anything.'

Her throat went dry just as the bagels popped in the toaster and the microwave dinged.

'Why do you think Annie Seger was murdered? The police have claimed that she committed suicide,' Samantha said, pushing her plate aside. She and Ty were seated at the glass-topped table under the porch overhang, and she'd waited until they'd finished eating before bringing up the question that had been pulsing through her mind for hours.

A hummingbird was flitting between the blossoms of the bougainvillea and sailboats skimmed across the lake. Somewhere down the street a lawn mower roared while overhead the wake of a passing jet was dissipating into the cloudless sky.

Ty rested a heel on one of the empty chairs and frowned. 'So you haven't had time to read my computer disk yet?' Before she could protest, he said, 'I know you took it, and if you'd read through the research, you'd understand.' He leaned over the table, closer to her. 'Annie Seger was despondent, yes, and she had been drinking – she'd gone to a party and some kids had witnessed it. She'd had a fight with her boyfriend, Ryan Zimmerman, probably over the baby and what to do about it. There were witnesses who'd said as much. Annie had even had her friend Prissy drive her home that night. When she got there, the house was empty. She'd tried to call you again, but hung up before she'd gotten through, and that's when things get blurry. Did she sneak into her mother's bathroom and steal the sleeping pills? Did she go out to the garage and find the gardening shears and then go all the way upstairs, write the suicide note and slit her wrists at the computer? Could she have, considering how much booze was already in her system?'

'That's how I thought it happened.'

'That's the way it was supposed to look,' Ty said, 'and it's the easiest explanation. But there were other footprints on the carpet. The maid had vacuumed while Annie was out and there were deeper impressions on the plush pile – a bigger foot.'

'Weren't there tons of people at the scene? Police and emergency workers?'

'Of course and Jason, the father, said he'd come into the room to check on her. Since he found the body, no one thought anything of it.'

'A big footprint on the carpet. That's not much to go on. In fact it's nothing,' she said.

'I know. And there was potting soil from the gardening shed on the carpet, but not on any of Annie's shoes.'

'Still thin.'

'How about this then? Her fingerprints were all over the gardening shears, true, but she was right-handed. It would seem that she would have slit her left wrist first, made the deeper cut. Instead it was just the opposite.'

'You think.'

He nodded.

'Ty, this isn't enough to write a book about or argue her suicide,' Sam pointed out as she watched Charon slink through the shrubs. Absently she rubbed her neck, scratching at the bump left by the hornet's sting. 'Why would anyone want her dead? What's the motive?'

'I think it has to do with her baby.'

Samantha's stomach clenched. As horrid as it was to think that Annie ended her life, the thought of her baby dying as well was even more painful.

'I don't think she would have killed the baby. Her boyfriend wanted her to get an abortion; she refused. It was against her morals. Against her faith. She was raised Catholic, remember. Killing herself and killing the baby were both mortal sins.'

'But she was despondent. You said so yourself.'

'But not suicidal. That's a big leap. There's more. The baby's blood type. No one paid attention, but Annie Seger's baby couldn't have been fathered by Ryan Zimmerman. The blood type proves it.'

Sam felt the hairs on the back of her arms lift. 'You think someone killed Annie because she could point the finger at them?'

'Possibly. Maybe a married man. She was underage. The law would charge him with statutory rape if the guy was older. Or it could have been someone in her own family. Incest. Or her boyfriend could have come unglued and killed her in a fit of jealousy. That's the part I haven't figured out yet.' He leaned back in his chair, his gaze holding hers. 'But I will,' he promised, 'And while I'm doing it, I'm gonna figure out how this all ties in with the calls you been getting at the station. Somehow "John" is connected to this thing. 'We've just got to find out how, and then nail his ass.'

25

'. . . it's definitely not the same guy unless you've got a split personality,' Norm Stowell said from his cell phone somewhere in Arizona. Bentz wasn't surprised. He'd already decided he had two killers on his hands. He glanced at the pictures on the computer screen in his office and could split the two cases right down the middle. Norm was still talking. 'MO will evolve, we know that. As the killer learns what will work for him, he makes subtle changes in his approach or access route, but his signature remains constant. You've got two guys out there. One's pretty messy – is careless with his clues, doesn't seem to worry that you'll nail him with his hair or fingerprints or semen, but the other guy – he's clean. Neat. Careful. Definitely two perps.'

'That's what I was afraid of,' Bentz said as he shoved a report on the wig fibers to one side of his desk.

'I'll fax you my profile of your killers when I get home, and for the record, I'm sending a copy to the field agent. Seems your partner hasn't been forthright with the Federal boys, and they're none too happy.'

'I'll talk to him. Montoya's a little green, but he's good.'

'If you say so.' Norm wasn't impressed, but then little did impress him. He was jaded far beyond his years – a short, stocky man who had never given up his allegiance to the crew cut he'd gotten at boot camp at Fort Lewis over thirty years earlier.

'So here's what you've got to look for in the guy who's killed Bellechamps and Gillette. He's a white man, probably in his late twenties or early thirties. He must not have a prior as you said he's careless with his fingerprints, body fluids and hair. If that's the case, something triggered him to start killing, some emotional trauma. He's got a job, but it's not very grand, and he's smart enough, but is from a highly dysfunctional and probably abusive family. He's got a feeling of abandonment or deep-seated hatred of some woman in the family, probably a mother or stepmother or older sister or grandmother. He could have been sexually molested, and in his history he has arson and cruelty to animals or smaller children. He was probably a bed-wetter in grade school and something's happened to him recently, something major that triggered him killing. Maybe he lost a job, or a girl-friend, or has been cut off from his family, which could likely be the major source of his income.'

'A gem of a guy,' Bentz muttered into the phone.

'And dangerous as hell. He could live alone, or he could be married, or have a girlfriend, but whoever he's living with, she's in danger. This guy's escalating, Rick. You might have to let the public know what's going on for safety's sake and because some-one out there might know a guy who's been acting weird lately – unusually anxious. He could be pouring himself into a bottle or abusing drugs. Besides that, if he's involved with a woman, she should know about the danger to her. If she knows what he's doing, and we both know that a lot of women who are emotion-ally trapped in bad relationships will even be a part of their man's crimes. Anyway this woman has probably seen his violence or suffered from it herself. Potentially she could be his next target – unless we get her to turn him in.'

Bentz thought the odds of that were somewhere between slim and none, and closer to none.

'As I said, this is just the high points. I'll fax you what I've come up with, then get to work on your second guy.'

'I'd appreciate it, Norm. Thanks,' Bentz said, and hung up, his worst suspicions confirmed. Two monsters were on the loose in New Orleans, killers with no conscience, murderers who hated women. He flipped through the computer files again, checking open cases that hadn't been solved, ones that had bizarre elements. There were several that stood out, the most grotesque being the case of a woman who had been burned to death, her body then dumped at the feet of the statue of Joan d'Arc near the French Market last May 30. It had been macabre and surreal, that horridly charred body lying facedown on the grass, and reminded the press and police that St. Joan herself had met a similar fate.

Sometimes he wondered why he kept at this damned job.

Because someone has to nail these guys, and, for the most part, you're good at it, you sick son of a bitch.

He found a half-full pack of Doublemint gum in his top drawer and jammed a stick into his mouth, then walked to the window and looked outside to the street below. Cars spewed exhaust as they crawled down the narrow streets, and people crowded the sidewalks, but Bentz hardly took any notice. He yanked at his collar. Sweat plastered his shirt to his back. He didn't hear the hum of computers or conversations of the outer offices though his door was ajar. No, he'd blocked out the noise of the station and the scene below as he considered the prospect of two serial killers in the city, at least one of which was connected to the terrorization of Dr. Samantha Leeds. Some way. Somehow. He didn't have any concrete evidence, no tangible link, but the knot in his gut told him whoever was calling was somehow involved with the murders. The mutilated C-notes so like the ruined publicity shot of Samantha Leeds, the radios tuned to her program at the time of death, the fact that the women who'd been killed were hookers and John had accused her of prostitution, but why sin? What redemption? What the hell did it have to do with Annie Seger, for crying out loud?

He walked to the tape recorder on his credenza and pushed the play button so that he could hear for the hundredth time some of the calls, particularly the one from the woman who called herself Annie . . . he'd played it over and over, as had the lab, and he'd come to the conclusion that the call from Annie had been prerecorded. There hadn't been a live person on the phone. The woman proclaiming herself to be Annie hadn't answered Sam's questions directly, but only paused between her own statements . . . As if someone had anticipated what Dr. Sam would ask on the show that night. As if a woman was involved in this mess.

But who?

Someone who knew Annie Seger?

Someone connected to Dr. Sam?

Someone working with 'John'?

And how had the call gotten through the screen at the radio station before being played on the air?

He snapped his gum, reached in his back pocket and found his handkerchief, then ran it over his forehead and mopped his face. How the hell did Montoya wear leather jackets in this weather and manage to keep his cool? The day was sweltering. Unforgiving. Intense. Bentz needed a beer. A sixteen-ouncer – ice-cold in one of those frosty mugs, yeah that would do the trick. And a pack of Camel straights. That old ache for booze and nicotine haunted his blood and he chewed his gum furiously as he walked back to his desk, where copies of telephone records were strewn.

The billing that interested him was from Houston, a cell phone registered in the name of David Ross. Not only had he called Sam's home number, but the station as well, on a few of the nights that 'John' had phoned, but his cell number had a block on it and his name had never shown on caller ID. Just his number. But those calls hadn't even gotten through, not according to the station records. He must've called, then chickened out . . . or decided to use a pay phone. Ross had also been in New Orleans a couple of times in the past few weeks . . . but Samantha had insisted her love affair with the guy was over.

Maybe he didn't like it.

Maybe he was getting back a little retribution.

The phone jangled. He grabbed the receiver. 'Bentz.'

'Looks like we got another one,' Montoya said, his voice serious. 'I'm driving over to a hotel on Royal, the St. Pierre. The story is that we've got another Jane Doe, strangled with a series of weird cuts on her neck. The maid let herself in with her key, ignoring the Do Not Disturb sign as it was after checkout time.

The guy who rented the room is gone, but we might have gotten lucky because the clerk working the desk last night remembers him. I'm on my way to the St. Pierre now. I'll be there in about ten minutes.'

'I'll meet you there,' Bentz said, and slammed the phone down. Maybe they were finally catching a break.

Sam was nervous as she walked into the den. The edge that she'd felt after taking 'John's' last call had never quite left her. She was missing something, something important, a clue as to his identity.

Earlier, Ty had taken her into New Orleans to retrieve her car, followed her here, then made a quick trip home to pick up Sasquatch and his laptop computer. Now, he was seated on the couch, computer glowing on his knees, his notes splayed upon the coffee table. While the television flickered with images of the noon news, and his dog lay near the French doors, he started sorting through the box of Sam's old, musty folders that he'd brought down from upstairs.

TGIF went through her head as it was Friday, her weekend, and she didn't have to work at the station again until Sunday night. Nonetheless she was burdened with the feeling that something bad was going to happen or had happened. 'John's' warning replayed through her head: *All you need to know is that what happens tonight is because of you, because of your sins. You need to repent, Sam, beg forgiveness.*

So familiar, so direct. He'd called her Sam.

At first she'd thought he'd meant the damned cake, that he was just trying to freak her out, but as she'd remembered the tone of his voice, the cold warning, the pure evil of his threat, she was convinced that there was more.

But nothing had happened.

Yet. Nothing's happened yet.

This is just the calm before the storm.

She tried and failed to take heart in the fact that Annie's birthday had come and gone. If the cake was the worst that had happened, she should be relieved. But she couldn't shake the eerie feeling that the cake was just the tip of the iceberg.

In the den, she sat at her desk and noticed Charon cowering on the top of the bookcase, eyes round.

'Sasquatch is okay,' Sam assured the cat. 'You'll get used to him.'

Just like you'll get used to having Ty around? Remember, he lied to you from the git-go, and now he's pursuing this half-baked theory of his.

She crumpled a wad of paper and tossed it at the cat, who couldn't help himself and swiped at the 'toy.'

Ty was convinced that Annie Seger had been murdered and the killer had gotten away with it. Sam wasn't so certain.

Could the Houston police have been so wrong? So negligent? Or had they covered up? It seemed unlikely, and even if Annie's murder had 'slipped through the cracks' nine years ago, how did 'John' and the call from the woman posing as Annie link to the past? Why was this all happening now?

Could it have been someone in the station trying to rekindle interest in a nearly forgotten case, all for publicity? Was someone at the station involved, or had one of the employees inadvertently passed along information about the phone lines into WSLJ?

Stop this. It could be anyone. A phone company employee, or someone who had worked at the station in the past, or any guest or repairman or visitor who just looked the system over when Melba's back was turned. Someone else might have stumbled across the number. With all the computer links and technoknowledge available, any nutcase could have figured out the phone-line numbers. It's not that big of a deal.

Scraping back the chair from her desk, she reached for the phone. She needed to call her father and tell him that Corky had seen Peter, that her brother was alive, and seemingly clean and sober. *This is Peter's responsibility,* her voice nagged, but she didn't care. She wasn't bailing Peter out, as she might have been accused in one of the upper-division psychology courses she'd taken. This was real life, and her father deserved to have his mind put at ease about her brother. After talking to her dad she'd call Leanne Jaquillard.

She'd picked up the receiver and had started to dial before noticing that the answering machine light was flashing. Her stomach knotted. She hadn't picked up her messages in nearly two days. Had she somehow missed another call from John? Another threat? She pushed the play button and heard a hangup. 'Damn.' Then another click. Her skin crawled. It was 'John,' she was certain.

A second later Leanne's voice came through the small speaker. 'Hey, Doctor Sam, I was wonderin' if we could get together? I need to talk to you about somethin' and it really can't wait until group. I mean . . . I want to talk to you about it alone, if that would be okay? Call or e-mail me if you get this.'

Click.

The machine stopped.

Sam breathed a sigh of relief. There were no other messages, no contact from 'John.' She switched on her computer, checked her e-mail, and found yet another note from Leanne asking her to call.

Charon hopped onto Sam's lap and she stroked the cat out of habit. Something was weighing heavily on Leanne, she thought. The girl had never before called her at home. Quickly, she looked up Leanne's phone number on her computer screen, then picked up the phone and punched out the numbers. 'Be home,' she said, picking up a pencil and tapping the eraser end on the desk as the phone rang.

On the fourth ring a woman answered, 'Hello?' Sam recognized Leanne's mother's irritated voice, and she braced herself.

'Hi, this is Samantha Leeds, Leanne's counselor at the Boucher Center. Is she in?'

'No, as a matter of fact, she isn't. That little fart didn't bother comin' home last night. I was just about to call the police and report her missin', but I imagine she'll come draggin' in later this afternoon.'

Sam bristled and tapped the pencil again. The cat jumped off her lap and slunk cautiously out of the den. 'Leanne left me a couple of messages, and I'd like to get in touch with her.'

'You and me both, I shoulda been ta work two hours ago, and I ain't got no one to watch Billy. That's Leanne's job when she ain't in school. I'm tellin' you this is the last time she pulls this kind of stunt on me. I was up half the night worried about her.' There was an edge to Marletta's voice, a fear that she couldn't quite mask. 'She's usin' again, I swear. God, don't you discuss this with her in that stupid group she goes to?'

'What we discuss doesn't leave the room,' Sam said, trying to remain patient and worrying about the girl.

'Well it ain't doin' any good, now, is it? Otherwise, she'd be home.'

'Does she do this often?'

'Much as she can.'

'But you might call the police.'

'What for? Ennytime I do, they jest give me the runaround. I've called too many times already and then Leanne she strolls in here like it ain't no big deal. I'm sick and tired of chasin' after her.'

'Still—'

'It's not yer problem.'

Sam wasn't sure about that. She dropped her pencil onto the desk. 'Just tell her I called.'

'Yeah, yeah, if she ever shows up.'

'Thanks,' Samantha said, and hung up. Her heart twisted for Leanne. The kid had just never had a chance, with no father and Marletta for a mother. Sam decided that she'd call back tomorrow, just in case the message didn't get through, then typed a quick e-mail to ensure the girl knew Sam was trying to reach her. She then dialed her own father, who, she decided for about the thousandth time, was no less than a saint. When he didn't answer she felt a second's disappointment but left a message.

'Hi, Dad, it's Sam. You're out, probably with the cute widow, right? Well, don't do anything I wouldn't do and call me when you get the chance. I just want you to know that Corky ran into Peter, and he's doing great. I haven't talked to him, of course, but I thought I'd pass on the word about brother dear. Call when you've got a chance, okay? Love ya!' She hung up in frustration, then heard Ty's voice from the living room.

'Samantha – I think your cop's on television.'

'My cop?' she said, walking into the living room, where Ty was standing, the remote in his hand, watching the television. Detective Rick Bentz filled the screen. A reporter was interviewing him as he and his partner were exiting a huge house in the Garden District. While the reporter tried to ask questions, Bentz kept muttering 'no comment.'

'What is it?'

'A murder, apparently,' Ty said as the reporter stared into the camera.

'. . . so that's it. Another woman murdered. Another one linked to prostitution. The question that has to be asked is are the killings linked? Do we have a serial killer, here, in New Orleans? It's starting to look that way.'

26

'Bentz has been busy lately,' Ty observed as he clicked the remote and the image on the television faded.

'Criminals don't have weekends off,' she said, bothered by the report. The possibility of a serial killer was sobering and reminded her that there were other problems beside hers in the city. 'So what have you found out?' she asked, motioning toward the notes, pictures and files spread over the coffee table.

'Not much more than I knew before.' He rubbed the back of his neck as if his muscles were strained. 'I've got a partial list of people who were acquainted with Annie, what they've been doing for the past nine years and where they are now.'

'That's a start. Tell me about them.'

'Okay.' He walked back to the couch, sat down and leaned over the coffee table to his computer. Squinting, he clicked the mouse and said, 'Oswald – Wally, Annie's father, is still up in the Northwest ... in ... Kelso, Washington – that's Washington State.'

'I know where it is. He's the guy that asked you to look into this.'

'Yep, good old Uncle Wally. As mismatched with Estelle as he could be. She was white-collar society, he, strictly blue-collar. One job to the other. I never could figure them out, but they were young when they hooked up and she got pregnant with Kent, so, they got married. Then, of course, divorced when the kids were young and Estelle found someone more suitable in Dr. Faraday. Wally never remarried, lives alone in some kind of modular home park and works for a logging company.' Ty glanced up at Samantha. 'Since he wanted me to investigate what happened to his daughter, I don't think he's a viable suspect, but I haven't ruled him out completely. Stranger things have happened.'

'I guess.' Samantha rounded the couch and leaned over the back, reading the computer screen over Ty's shoulder, her head next to his.

'Estelle is still living in the house in Houston where Annie died. She's never moved, never remarried, doesn't even date, spends a lot of time volunteering at the church and lives off of what she got from the divorce and her investments. A shrewd lady, Aunt Estelle. She's parlayed a sizable inheritance into a small fortune. In our one phone conversation, she agreed to be interviewed for the book as long as I see her in person. I'm not exactly at the top of her favorites list but not persona non grata either. She doesn't want Annie's story told, but since it will be, she'd like to tell her side of it.' One side of his mouth lifted. 'She's a controlling woman, and my guess is that she thinks that if she talks to me, I'll take her version of what happened as gospel and print it verbatim.'

'Which you won't.'

'Of course not. The truth is the truth. You can color it any way you want, even try to whitewash it, but it's still the truth. Estelle is a great manipulator, but I'll be hell to control.' He slanted a look over his shoulder. 'It will be interesting to see what she has to say.'

Sam remembered the cold, dry-eyed woman who wouldn't allow Sam to attend the graveside service for her daughter. Tall and graceful, with upswept blond hair and pale blue eyes, she'd looked down her straight nose at Samantha at the gates to the cemetery. 'Please,' she'd said, 'this is a private ceremony. Just family.'

'I just came to pay my respects,' Sam had replied, her heart wrenching with guilt, as if she somehow could have counseled the girl, somehow gotten through to her, somehow prevented this unthinkable tragedy.

'Don't you think you've done enough? My family has been devastated by this, and it's your fault. If you had helped her—'

Estelle's cool facade had shattered and her lips had begun to tremble. Tears had filled her ghostly eyes, and she'd blinked rapidly. 'You just don't understand . . . Please . . . It would be best for everyone if you left.' Beneath her foundation makeup, Estelle had paled. She lifted a trembling hand and swiped beneath her eyelids, careful not to muss her mascara. 'I – I can't deal with this right now.' She turned to a lanky man with thinning brown hair, tanned skin and grief-stricken expression. Sam had recognized him as Estelle's husband, Annie's stepfather, Jason Faraday. 'This is so awful,' Estelle said as the man leveled Sam a look that begged her to back off. 'I . . . I don't want that woman here.'

'Shh. Don't worry,' he'd whispered, wrapping a protective arm over her thin shoulders. 'Come on.' He'd shepherded Estelle toward the freshly turned mound of earth in a green expanse of lawn dotted with headstones, family plots and vaults.

Sam had gotten the message. A few weeks later, the sympathy card she'd sent to the family had been returned unopened.

'Good luck talking to her,' she said now, shaking her head to dislodge the painful memory. 'I don't think Estelle had anything to do with Annie's death. In fact I'm not sure it wasn't suicide. The police did check it out.'

'I was there, remember? On the force. Kicked off of the case because I was related to the deceased and because I was pretty vocal that I didn't like the way the investigation was being handled.'

'You still haven't convinced me that Annie was murdered. I mean the Houston police force is pretty good.' She crossed her arms over the back of the couch as he scrolled down.

'Bear with me.'

'Fine.'

'This is where things get interesting,' he said. 'Jason and Estelle divorced less than a year after Annie's death. As soon as it was legal, Jason remarries a nurse from his office staff, sells his part of the partnership in the group where he worked as a surgeon and he and the new missus pull up stakes and move to

Cleveland. Just like that.' He snapped his fingers. 'But get this, he's been in New Orleans more than once in the last few months. His new wife's sister lives in Mandeville, just across the lake, and he's had a couple of conferences here.'

'Wait a minute. This doesn't make sense. You think a killer got away with murder, and now, nine years later, he's calling me, wanting to dredge it all up again? Why? There is no statute of limitations. Remember, whoever 'John' is, he blames *me* for Annie's death. If he killed her, why blame me, why not let well enough alone and allow everyone to think that Annie killed herself. If what you're saying is true, he went to great pains to make it look like she committed suicide. Why stir things up now? It doesn't make sense.'

Ty looked up at her. 'We're not dealing with a sane man, though, are we? The guy who's been calling you, he's got all sorts of hangups about sin and repentance and atonement. My guess is that something triggered his need to call you and bring the Annie tragedy back into the limelight. Maybe he heard you on the radio show or maybe something happened in his personal life. We already know he's screwed up about God and punishment and sin. He snapped, Samantha.'

She still wasn't buying it, but played along. 'Okay, just for argument's sake, let's say you think the killer could be Jason Faraday.'

'One possibility. He split from Estelle fast and practically gave her everything in the divorce, then pulled up stakes and got the hell out of Dodge so to speak. He started a new life for himself with ties down here.'

'Who else?' She picked at the dying fronds of a Boston fern.

'Annie's brother. Kent and she were pretty close. They'd lived through their parents' divorce and their mother's remarriage. Kent was pretty messed up after Annie died. He didn't work, didn't go to school and suffered from some kind of depression. All this time his mother's second marriage was breaking up. He was the man of the house and during that time he was committed to a private mental hospital for a while, one in Southern California, Our Lady of Mercy.'

'Catholic? For rich kids, right?' she asked, noticing how his dark hair curled at the nape of his neck.

'Troubled kids.'

'But it was run by the Catholic Church.'

'Estelle's a devoted member of the church, so her kids were raised that way.' He slanted her a look. 'It's not a sin you know.'

'I do know. Guess how I was raised?' she asked, walking into the kitchen and dropping the brittle fronds into the trash.

'I don't have to guess. It's all in my notes.'

'Oh, right. You know, Ty, I should be ticked off about this. It's called invasion of privacy, I think.' She was dusting her hands as she padded back into the living room and resumed her position leaning over the back of the couch.

His smile wasn't the least bit abashed. 'So I'm a bastard, what can I say?'

'Add in insufferable, bullheaded and inflexible.'

'Your kind of man.'

'In your dreams.'

'There, too,' he admitted, sending her a hot glance that caused a catch in the back of her throat. Things were moving quickly, probably too quickly. Right now her life was turned inside out, she needed room to breathe, to think, to figure out why some twisted man was tormenting her. It wasn't the time to get seriously involved with anyone and yet . . . and yet . . .

She cleared her throat and picked at a piece of lint on the back of the cushions. 'You were telling me about the members of Annie's family,' she reminded him.

'And I had a thought.' Rotating his head to look her square in the face, he said, 'You know, since you're a hotshot celebrity-psychologist, maybe you could make inquiries to the hospital about Kent, find out about his depression and illness.'

'I'm a psychologist, not psychiatrist . . . big difference in the medical world. They like that MD tagged onto the end of your name.'

'This is a mental hospital, they'll take you seriously.'

'I think I'm known in the medical community as an "entertainment shrink." That doesn't sound too serious to me.'

'You lived in the area?'

'Yes,' she admitted. 'The last I heard one of my college friends is practicing there.'

'So, you've got an in.'

'Patient files are still confidential.'

'I'm not asking you to do anything illegal,' he said, but the undertones in his voice suggested otherwise. 'Just see what you can find out about Kent.'

'So you can print it in a book. I think that's more than illegal. Unethical and morally corrupt might be thrown in.'

'Anything you find out, I won't use.'

'Oh, yeah, right. Look, I'll call my friend, but that's all. This is strictly, strictly off the record.'

'Absolutely.'

'So tell me more about Annie's family. The brother, Kent, where is he . . . no wait, he's here, isn't he?' she guessed. 'Otherwise, you wouldn't be so interested. He's in New Orleans.'

'Close enough. Baton Rouge. He's finally gotten his act together and finished school at All Saints College. He graduated in general studies, worked at the college part-time, though his mother supported him all the way through school.'

'Is he married?'

'Not Kent. He goes through girlfriends like water. Broke up with the last one at the end of May, though he's probably dating again. He always seems to have a woman.'

'And a job?'

'He works part-time through a temp agency. I think Estelle is still paying most of the bills.'

'You've done your homework,' she said, feeling edgy.

He snorted a laugh. 'It's called research when you're an adult.'

Could Ty possibly be right? For years Samantha had believed that Annie Seger had taken her own life and now, if his theory was right, everything she'd believed had changed and the horror of the past, the secret guilt for Annie's death that she'd tried so hard to bury, was back again, stronger than ever.

'John's' calls are proof enough of that. She rounded the couch, and straddled an overstuffed arm. 'So you really think a member of her family is responsible for her death? Her father or step-father or brother?'

'I'm not limiting the suspects to her family. But I'm sure it's someone she knew. It could have been her boyfriend. Ryan Zimmerman lives in White Castle, just up the Mississippi a few miles. His schooling was interrupted, just as Kent's was, and he went through a period where he was drugged-out all the time. Eventually, through drug treatment, he went back to school and finished Loyola, no less. Transferred in from a smaller school in Texas.'

'You've talked to him?'

'Not yet. I'd originally thought I'd start with the smaller play-ers in all of this, get their interpretations of the people closest to Annie, so that I didn't tip my hand. Maybe had a little deeper insight, but now, I'm not so sure.'

'Because of the calls I've been getting.'

'Yeah.' He plowed his fingers through his hair and scowled, obviously angry with himself. 'I worry that somehow I started this ugly ball rolling, and you got in its path.'

'But then, again, maybe you didn't. There's no use in dwell-ing on that. Tell me about Ryan. What about his love life?'

He checked the computer, but Sam guessed he knew all this information like the back of his hand. 'Ryan got married last year . . . but he separated about three months ago. She's a local girl he met while going to school. She wants a divorce, he's against it.' Ty's gaze held hers. 'He doesn't believe in divorce, it's against his faith.'

'Don't tell me.'

'It's not all that surprising,' Ty pointed out. 'Annie and Kent are from the same family. She met Ryan through the church, and, let's face it, Catholics are a distinct minority in Texas unless you happen to be a Mexican-American.'

'So, Ryan got married in the Catholic Church and less than a year later his wife wants a divorce. Why?'

'I'm still working on that. It could be his lack of ambition. He's got a teaching degree but still drives a truck.' Ty moved the mouse around. 'But I spoke to a couple of other girlfriends he had who have insisted that he never got over his first love.'

'Meaning Annie,' Sam guessed, cold inside as she slid onto the cushions from the arm of the couch.

'Right. She stole him from her best friend, Priscilla McQueen, another cheerleader.'

'This sounds like it's out of *Peyton Place*. What happened to her?'

'Prissy still lives in Houston. Married now and has a baby. Her husband works for an oil company.'

'You've got this all on computer?' she asked, motioning toward the laptop.

'And on disk as well.'

'Okay, so I'm trying to make sense of all this. You think that Ryan wasn't the father of Annie's unborn baby, and you know this because of blood types.'

'Right again.'

'So who is?' She nestled into the corner of the couch and twisted so that she was able to place her bare feet against his jean-clad thigh.

'There's the catch. Since there are no DNA tests, it could have been any of several of the men or boys involved in her life. The baby's blood had a RH positive factor, and because Annie's RH factor was negative, the father's had to be positive. Ryan Zimmerman's is negative. But Annie's father, her brother, her stepfather all are positive, like the baby. I checked – have a friend in the Houston PD who somehow got hospital records. So the baby couldn't have been Ryan's.'

'I get it.' Sam curled her toes into the fabric covering Ty's thigh. 'Both my brother and I are positive, because Dad is. But Mom was negative and she had to get an injection after Peter was born and again after me so as to prevent problems with any future pregnancies.'

'This doesn't narrow the field a lot,' Ty said, wrapping his fingers over her toes. 'Most of the population is positive.'

Sasquatch wandered up and Sam reached down to scratch him at the base of his ears, but her thoughts were on Ty's theory and how it all connected. 'I wonder if 'John's' positive or negative – or what his type is. Don't the police have that information?'

Ty sent her a smile that was nearly sinister. 'I'm already working that angle. I don't think they'd give it to me outright, so I'm doing 'research' through a friend – the man you saw me with last night.'

'He's going to get the information for you?'

'I'm counting on it.' He turned off the computer. 'While I'm in Houston, interviewing Estelle.' He slid her a glance. 'Don't suppose you want to come along?'

'I think it would be better if I didn't.' Sam remembered Annie's cold, grief-stricken mother. 'I don't think my presence would be appreciated. You might get more information from her one on one.'

'I could use the company,' he said, linking his hand with hers and tugging her closer to him. He nuzzled her cheek. 'We could have some fun.'

It was tempting. 'No doubt, but I have things I've got to do here.'

'Like?' He slung his arm around her shoulders.

'Catch up on my sleep for one. Someone's been robbing me of it.'

'Are you complaining?' His lips were warm against her skin, and she felt the rush of heat she always did when he touched her.

'Complain? *Moi?*' She feigned innocence. 'Never. But I do have things I need to do. You work on your end of this case, and I'll try to start figuring out the other.'

'Meaning "John."' His smile fell away, and the arm he'd wrapped around her shoulders tensed.

'To start with. How does he know the number for the second line? He called in after hours, line one – the one listed in the phone book – was free and yet he dialed in on line two.'

Ty's jaw hardened. 'You think he's someone who works at the station?'

'I don't know, but it's definitely a possibility.'

'Have you told the police?'

'Not yet. I didn't want to say anything last night because I didn't want to freak out anyone who was working there.'

'Or tip them off,' he said.

'Neither Tiny nor Melanie could have called in.'

'But they could be working with an accomplice.'

She shook her head. 'It's possible, yes . . . but I don't know why they would. More likely it would be George Hannah or someone who would directly benefit from the increased listenership. Melanie wants my job, whether she admits it or not. She's always hoping I'll retire or move on, so she would prefer it if my audience fell off and she could step in . . . well, that's a little far-fetched. And Tiny . . . the guy's got a major crush on me. I know that sounds vain, but it's true.'

'I believe it,' Ty said.

'Neither of them would want to hurt me. We're too close. I'm thinking that someone at the station inadvertently gave the number to a friend or acquaintance.'

'Or on purpose,' Ty added, his lips compressing. 'There's still the very strong possibility that "John" is someone who works with you.' He gave her shoulder an affectionate squeeze, but the look in his hazel eyes was deadly. 'And if the son of a bitch has any connection to the station, trust me, we'll get him.'

27

'Take a look at her neck,' Montoya was saying as he squatted next to the victim in the seedy hotel room. She was posed, just as the others had been, hands folded in prayer, legs splayed. 'Same markings as the others, but check this out,' he pointed to a spot just above the hollow of her throat. 'There's something different here, another mark, like something was dangling from the chain like it had a tail . . . See here . . . maybe a medallion or a charm or a cross. You know, like she was strangled with her own necklace.'

'Or his,' Bentz said, his gut twisting. 'He brings his own special noose.'

'And he took a trophy. See her left ear – all the metal – the earrings? One of them is missing.'

'Was the radio on?'

'Oh, yeah. Tuned into WSLJ.'

Bentz glanced at the night table . . . saw the hundred-dollar bill with the black eyes. All part of the sicko's signature, but what did it mean? Why was Ben Franklin blinded? So he couldn't see? So he wouldn't be recognized? 'Time of death?'

'We're guessing around midnight. The ME's on his way, and then we'll have a better idea.' Montoya clucked his tongue. 'She's younger than the rest.'

She's younger than Kristi, Bentz thought, his jaw clenching. This dead girl, hooker or not, was someone's kid, someone's friend, probably someone's sister and quite possibly someone's mother. His jaw was suddenly so tight it ached. What kind of bastard would do this?

'She's a local girl, been picked up for a few priors.' He handed Bentz a bag with the victim's ID. 'And check this out . . .'

Through the plastic, Montoya shuffled the girl's driver's license, social security card and a few photographs until he came to a worn business card. 'Isn't this what you've been looking for?'

The card was stock for WSLJ radio station, personalized in one corner for Doctor Samantha Leeds, host of *Midnight Confessions*, AKA Dr. Sam.

'Hell,' Bentz said, glancing back at the body on the bed. The crime-scene team was vacuuming, and the photographer was snapping pictures of the area.

'You were so damned sure there was a link . . . well, it looks like you were right,' Montoya said. 'Somehow this girl knew the radio shrink.'

Which wasn't good news. Bentz was working on a theory, one that he wasn't certain held any water, but an idea that wouldn't go away. What if the killer wasn't choosing victims at random any longer, what if he was escalating, the crimes getting more frequent, what if he was moving to his primary target . . . what if his intent was to kill Samantha Leeds?

That's not the way it usually worked; but this case wasn't usual. The guy wasn't tipping off the police or the newspapers or trying to gain some glory, except to call Dr. Sam . . . He wasn't the usual creep . . . Bentz glanced at the ligature around the victim's neck and felt like there was something important in the spacing of the marks surrounding her throat, something he should understand.

'Didn't you say the hotel clerk got a look at the guy?'

'Yeah.' Montoya was moving out of the way of the photographer. 'She's in the hotel office right now.' He flipped out his small notebook. 'Her name is Lucretia Jones, has worked here about nine months, and already gave a statement to the first officers on the scene. I asked her to stick around cuz I figured you'd want to talk to her.'

Bentz nodded. 'Anything else?'

'We've got the original registration he signed as John Fathers.'

'He gave an address?'

'Houston.'

Bentz glanced at Montoya. 'Anyone check it out?'

'Fake. He had the street right – Annie Seger's street – but there's no such number.' Montoya's gaze met Bentz's as they walked into the outer hallway, where a few curious bystanders were craning their necks. 'I'd say the address is another damned good link.'

For once Bentz wasn't glad to have his gut instincts proved right. 'Didn't John Fathers have to give a driver's license, offer up some kind of ID?'

'Apparently not. Just anted up with cash – a hundred-dollar bill for a forty-nine-dollar room. No luggage. It's really not a big deal in a hotel like this. It's all pretty common – guys pick up a hooker, and they rent a room. No one asks any questions.' They paused in front of the elevator. Montoya pressed the call button.

'You said the clerk's in the office?' Bentz asked. 'Let's see what she has to say.'

The elevator doors opened, and they stepped into a cramped car which deposited them into a once-far-more elegant lobby that was now shabby at best. The chandelier, a glimpse of a more prosperous time, was dusty, with many bulbs dimmed, the potted plants near the doors drooping, the carpet threadbare, with a vacuum cleaner left unattended in one corner. What had been genteel eighty years earlier was now downright shabby, a musty, dark alcove with a desk that hadn't been replaced in the past century or two.

Two women in matching black skirts, jackets and white blouses, were working behind the desk, peering at computer screens that seemed out of place in the ancient building. A heavyset guy who could have been a bellman or a janitor was slurping coffee in the doorway leading to a back room. Bentz flashed his ID, explained what he wanted and the taller of the two women motioned both Bentz and Montoya around the desk. 'Lucretia's back here,' the receptionist said. 'But she's already spoken to one of the officers.'

'This'll just take a minute,' Bentz assured her, as she led them down a short corridor to a brightly lit room, where a computer hummed, a table complete with coffee rings dominated the middle of the room and an old couch was pushed against a wall near the microwave and refrigerator. A rail-thin black girl sat drinking a can of diet cola. Her eyes, large to begin with, were huge today, as if she were scared, and seemed to bulge from a head supporting hundreds of tiny braids that were all pulled together at her nape.

She stood as he entered, and the receptionist explained who they were. Bentz waved her back to the couch and took a seat in a folding chair. Montoya lingered in the doorway.

'You were on duty last night?' Bentz asked, and she nodded quickly.

'Yes.'

'And you took the registration for the guest who rented the room where the murder victim was found?'

'Uh-huh. I, um, I already gave the card he filled out to the other officer.'

From the corner of his eye, Bentz saw Montoya nod slightly, indicating the police had already retrieved the registration form.

'So you got a good look at the guy as he registered last night,' Bentz asked.

'Yes.' Lucretia nodded, her tiny head bobbing beneath all that hair.

'What can you tell me about him?'

'Just what I told the other cop – er, officer. He was about thirty, I'd guess, and tall and big – not fat, but . . . strong-looking, like maybe he lifted weights or something, a white guy with real dark hair – almost black and . . . he was wearing sunglasses, real dark, which was kinda different and strange but then . . .' She shrugged her thin shoulders, indicating that she'd seen it all.

'Anything else?'

'Oh, yeah. I remember noticing that his face was scratched, like someone had raked a set of fingernails down his cheek.'

'You remember anything else, what he was wearing?'

'Black – all over, I mean, a black T-shirt and jeans and a leather coat, I thought that was kinda odd cuz it's so hot, but then he had on the shades as well. But he . . . he gave me a weird feeling.'

'Weird, how?'

She glanced away. 'There was something about him, something . . . oh, this sounds so strange, but he seemed kinda dangerous, but kinda cool in a way. He carried himself all tall and like he knew what he was doin'. I don't know how to explain it. I was nervous, probably because of the glasses, but he smiled and it wasn't cold or weird or anything, it was a good smile. Real bright. Kinda reassuring.' She stared at the half finished bottle of cola in her hands. 'I shoulda trusted my first instincts.'

The poor woman was beating herself up because of the dead girl. 'You can help us now, Lucretia,' Bentz said, leaning forward on his elbow, hands clasped between his legs, gaze holding hers. 'I'd like you to come down to the station and describe the man to a police artist, who will draw your guy and then have a computer enhance it, make it look more real. It would help a lot.'

She blinked her too-big eyes. 'Sure. Anything.'

'Good.' Bentz felt a surge of adrenaline. He was getting closer to the guy, sensed he was closing in on the son of a bitch – hoped to living hell that he could stop the bastard before he struck again.

Estelle Faraday had aged. The past nine years coupled with her grief and hours spent playing tennis under the relentless Houston sun had robbed her of the vitality Ty remembered. She'd invited him to sit outside in a wicker chair, under the overhang shading her private verandah. Fans twirled overhead, two steps down a wide pool stretched to a fence guarded by shrubbery. A statue of the Virgin Mary, her arms spread wide, was flanked by terra-cotta pots filled with petunias, their pink-and-white blossoms offering bright splashes of color. A maid had brought iced tea and lemon cookies, then disappeared through glass doors into the huge, two-storied stucco house in this upscale neighborhood. The cookie plate hadn't been touched, ice was melting in tea glasses sweating in the heat.

'I think you should understand,' Estelle said, the diamonds in her tennis bracelet sparkling on her slim wrist, 'that the only reason I met with you face-to-face was to ask you not to write your book about my daughter.' The lines around her mouth grooved deep. 'All it would do is cause the family more pain and embarrassment, and personally, I think we've all suffered enough.'

'I think it's time to write the truth.'

'Oh, save me, Tyler!' She slapped her hand onto the table. 'This isn't about the truth, and you know it. It's about money – some trashy pulp fiction, no, I stand corrected, trashy true – and I use the term loosely, believe me – true crime novel. You and that sleazy agent of yours are only interested in titillation and innuendo. You're going to take your own family's tragedy and turn it into a profit, so don't go there on that lofty, false high road of yours. You're not here in the interests of serving the truth, you're only trying to pad your wallet. I'm sure that Wally is in on it, too. He never gave his daughter the time of day while she was alive. I had to force him into court to pay his measly child support, so Wally only wants to find a way to make a buck.'

'If you say so.'

'We both know it.'

Ty wasn't going to let her rile him. He'd known this wasn't going to be a walk in the park. 'I would think you'd want to know what really happened to Annie and her baby. Your grandchild.'

A dark shadow crossed those opalescent eyes, and she looked away, training her gaze on the smooth, calming surface of the pool. 'It doesn't matter,' she said in a harsh whisper. 'They're both gone, Tyler.'

'I think Annie was murdered.'

'Oh, God.' She shook her head. 'There's always been talk about it, of course, but that's foolishness. The truth of the matter is that Annie was a very confused and scared girl. Too frightened to come to me.' Her voice cracked and her chin wobbled slightly. 'I have to live with that, you know. That my own daughter turned to someone else, a *radio* psychologist who probably didn't even have a degree . . .' Estelle's fist opened and closed, manicured nails digging into her palm. 'She called that . . . that . . . disk jockey instead of confiding in me.'

'I know this is difficult.'

'Difficult? *Difficult?*' Facing him once again, she skewered him with eyes filled with hate and self-loathing. 'This isn't difficult, Ty. Difficult is going through a divorce and facing the ostracism of church and family. Difficult is watching your parents fail and die, difficult is dealing with a child whose heart has been broken by their negligent father. Annie's suicide wasn't difficult. It was hell.'

'If she was killed, don't you want her murderer found and brought to justice?'

'She wasn't murdered.'

'I have evidence—'

'I've heard the theories before about some grass or dirt on the carpet and the gardening shears and . . . and . . . the way the cuts on her wrists . . . it's nothing, *nothing*! Please, for God's sake, Tyler, don't do this, don't make the family suffer any more.' She looked suddenly very old in her perfect makeup and expensive white-and-gold tennis warmup, and for a second Ty doubted his own mission.

'Who was the father of Annie's baby?'

'I don't know.' Her lips pursed. 'That awful boy she was dating I assume – the druggie.'

'No, Estelle. The blood types don't work.'

Two tiny grooves appeared between her eyebrows. 'Then I don't know.'

'Sure you do.'

'I already told you my daughter didn't confide in me. Maybe she . . . maybe she told that radio person.'

'No – you know. Was it your husband?'

Her face turned ashen as she gasped. 'No . . .'

'Your son?'

'Are you out of your mind? This is my home. You have no right!'

'Was she seeing someone else?'

'I'm warning you. If you think you're going to drag my daughter's name through the mud, sully her reputation and destroy what's left of the dignity of this family, you'll be sorry.'

'I just want the truth.'

'No you don't. You want to twist the facts to sell a book.' Her nostrils flared in haughty disdain. 'So noble of you.'

'Jason divorced you. Moved away. Kent had a breakdown, had to be sent to a private mental hospital. Ryan sank into drugs and depression.'

'All the dirty little details for a trashy novel or a television movie of the week. I should never have talked to you, never allowed you into my house,' she said, emotion causing her voice to falter. 'Don't you understand? Annie's dead . . . my baby is dead,' Estelle said softly. 'Nothing is going to change that. You're not going to bring a killer to justice . . . oh, no, all you're going to do is inflict more pain and suffering on a family you're not a part of, so don't give me altruistic explanations, because I don't believe them for a moment.' She gathered herself and leaned forward, resting her elbows on the glass-topped table. 'If you persist in this . . . this witch-hunt, I will stop you in the courts. Defending yourself will cost you a fortune, one I doubt you have. No publisher will take on your project for fear of a lawsuit. I've already spoken to my lawyer, and he's ready to file a suit blocking publication. He mentioned words like "extreme distress, emotional trauma, punitive damages, civil action and libel" to the point that no publisher in their right minds would ever buy your trash. I think it would be best for you to leave now.'

It was Ty's turn to lean forward. Looking over the two untouched glasses of iced tea, he asked, 'You can threaten me all you want, Estelle. You can use all kinds of legal mumbo jumbo and spend thousands of dollars on the best lawyers in the country, but it's all just thick smoke and mirrors. I'm not backing down, no matter what skeletons come dancing out of your closet. Something's not right about your daughter's death, and we both know it.' He stood and looked down on her, watching as her spine stiffened. 'The difference is that I want to know what happened to Annie, and you don't. Because you're frightened of the truth. Why is that? What is it that scares you so badly?'

'Get out,' she said weakly.

'I'm going to find out, one way or another, you know.'

'Get out, or I'll call the police,' she said.

'I don't think so, Estelle. I'm willing to bet that the police are the last people you want poking around in this. But it's too late, because, whether you like it or not, the truth about Annie's death is going to come out.'

'Go to hell,' she said, standing.

He flashed her a humorless smile. 'Something tells me I'm on my way.'

28

'Does this guy look like the guy who grabbed you in the park last night?' Bentz asked.

He slid the computer-enhanced artist's sketch across his desk to the girl, Sonja Tucker, seated on the other side. She'd filed a report early this morning that she'd been attacked late at night by a 'guy in sunglasses,' and when Bentz had learned about it upon his return from the St. Pierre, he'd called and asked her to come back to the station, so here she was, looking nervous, a nineteen-year-old sophomore at Tulane University who was going to summer school and probably was lucky to be alive today.

'It could be,' she said, picking up the composite and studying it closely. She'd told the officer downstairs that she'd been on her way to a masquerade party last night. Dressed to look like a prostitute, she was waiting for the streetcar when a man had accosted her, propositioned her and hadn't wanted to take 'no' for an answer. He'd gotten pushy, tried to grab her and she'd responded by scratching him down the side of his face, then kicking off her high heels and running like hell through Audubon Park, hiding in some bushes near the zoo and learning the valuable lesson of life in the city.

Right now she looked scared as hell.

'It was dark,' she said, chewing on her lower lip.

'But – you got a look at him?'

'Kinda. There was a streetlamp, but he was wearing dark glasses and needed a shave and ...' She stared long and hard at the composite and her fingers shook enough to cause the paper to tremble in her hands. Her skin was pale as death. 'This looks kinda like him,' Sonja finally said, seeming to draw strength in her convictions as she stared at the computer-generated image.

'And he was a stranger to you?'

'Yes, oh, yes. I, uh, I never saw him before. I think I would have remembered him.'

'Why?'

Again Sonja stared at the picture. 'This sounds funny, I know. But he was handsome, kind of . . . in a dark, well, dangerous way. But then . . . well . . . then he started forcing me to go with him and he didn't look so good.'

'Would you recognize his voice?'

'Uh – maybe. I don't know.' Her confidence escaped her again.

Bentz was undeterred and pushed the play button on the recorder he'd positioned on his in box. Several tapes of 'John' calling into *Midnight Confessions* had been spliced together and his low voice filled the room.

The girl shook her head, her ponytail wagging behind her, her eyebrows pulling downward. 'I – I don't know. It could be . . . Play it again.'

He rewound and pushed the play button.

Sonja worried her lower lip, and her features drew together as she concentrated. 'It sounds a lot like him. I – I'm just not sure.'

The same response he'd gotten from Lucretia, the desk clerk at the St. Pierre. Bentz was more frustrated than ever. The picture that the artist had come up with was too generic, could be just about any white, dark-haired guy who kept himself in shape.

'Is there anything else you could tell me about him?'

'No, it was dark and over quickly. I reached for his glasses and he freaked. Like maybe he has weird eyes or something . . . I don't know.' Sonja lifted a shoulder. 'He tried to pull me down the street and I kicked his shin and scratched him and got away. I, um, guess I was lucky, huh?'

'Very,' Bentz said solemnly.

She cleared her throat. 'He killed some other girl, didn't he?'

'We think so, yes.'

'And he was threatening Dr. Sam, the radio psychologist on that tape.'

'Yes.'

'God, I wish I could help.'

'You already have,' he said, standing. 'Thanks.'

'You're welcome.' She gathered up her backpack, but took one last look at his desk. 'Is that, is that your daughter?' she asked, motioning toward the bifold picture of Kristi.

'Yeah.' Bentz smiled. 'One was taken a long time ago, when she was just going off to school, and the other one is her graduation picture. Taken just last year.'

'She's very pretty,' Sonja offered.

'Takes after her mother.'

'Nah.' Sonja wrinkled her pert, freckled nose. 'She looks a lot like you.' And then she was gone. With one of those coiled plastic key rings wrapped around her wrist and her backpack slung over one shoulder, she clomped out of his office in platform sandals. She was right about being lucky, Bentz thought. Sonja Tucker had been just minutes short of death the night before. One girl's luck had been another girl's doom. Losing Sonja Tucker had forced the monster to hunt someone else. His prey had turned out to be Leanne Jaquillard. Was it a coincidence that Leanne was connected to Samantha Leeds? Sonja Tucker had sworn not to know Dr. Sam, and though she'd listened to the *Midnight Confessions* program a couple of times, had never called in.

Not so the victim.

Leanne and Dr. Sam knew each other well.

He rubbed the kinks from his neck and plotted his next move. First they'd make the public aware there was a killer, second they'd put a trace on any call that came into the station. Now that there was a viable link from the killer to Dr. Sam, they had to protect her. They'd watch her house night and day and go through the damned list of people who knew Dr. Sam and Annie Seger.

He gazed down at the composite picture of John Fathers, whoever he really was. Square jaw, cleft chin, high cheekbones, thick hair with a prominent widow's peak and dark glasses covering his eyes.

And scratches running down his left cheek where Sonja's nails had scraped off his skin. 'Who are you, you bastard?' he asked, glaring at the composite they would distribute to the media. He thought of the men in Samantha's life – David Ross, Ty Wheeler, George Hannah – all tall, in good shape, with dark hair and sharp features. The computer operator had taken off John's three-days' growth of beard, had removed the glasses and substituted potential eyes, had even changed the hairstyle and cut . . . yet it was all just a crap-shoot. 'And who's the woman who called in and pretended to be Annie?' Bentz muttered.

The picture with its hidden eyes seemed to mock him. What was with the dark glasses and the blacked-out eyes on the hundred-dollar bills? And the strange ligature around the victims' necks? What was all this garbage about sin and redemption?

Bentz made a note to go over the whereabouts of any man associated with Samantha Leeds who had been in the area since she'd returned from that trip to Mexico . . . the trip where she'd lost her ID, her purse, her keys. The trip where she'd decided to call it off for good with David Ross.

He was missing something, he knew it. Something obvious. *Think, Bentz, think!* Who was in Houston nine years ago? Who was here now? Why did anyone want the Annie Seger suicide dredged up again?

He considered Ty Wheeler, who had inserted himself into Samantha Leeds's life after the Mexico trip. From all reports, he and Samantha were now lovers. That stuck in Bentz's craw. He didn't like the guy. Didn't trust him. Wheeler had admitted to writing a tell-all book about Annie Seger's death, had even come up with a theory that she'd been murdered rather than committed suicide, but in Bentz's estimation, it was all hype. The

Houston PD had ruled suicide and that was good enough for him. Wheeler was just out to make a quick buck.

He took a couple of calls, received a fax of crime-scene evidence and wasn't surprised the hairs from a red wig had been found in the hotel room. A few minutes later Melinda Jaskiel appeared in his doorway.

'Tell me what you think about the murders,' she suggested, folding her arms over her chest and leaning a shoulder against the doorjamb. From the outer office the sound of voices, phones and clicking of computer keys could be heard.

'I think we've got one sick sumbitch on our hands, possibly two.'

'So I've heard.'

Bentz expanded on his theory and brought up Norm Stowell's report, which Melinda had already perused. They talked in generalities for a while, then came back to the murder of Leanne Jaquillard.

'So the girl's mother has been notified?' Bentz asked as he glanced at pictures of the latest victim strewn upon his desk.

Melinda Jaskiel nodded, picked up one of the shots, and scowled at the death scene. 'I'm talking to the press in an hour. It'll be short and sweet, but I'm going to confirm that we have a serial killer on our hands, warn women to lock their doors and stay inside or only go out at night in large groups. We'll distribute the composite drawing and tell the public that they need to be wary, that the killer is escalating and that anyone close to him, a girlfriend or a wife, could be in danger. You know, the same old drill. We'll hold back key evidence, information that only the killer knows so that any nutcase who comes in and confesses will have to prove that he's legit. Otherwise, we'll get any idiot who wants a chance to claim a little infamy in here spilling his guts. I've talked to the FBI. Everyone on the task force agrees.'

'You're not going to mention the link to Dr. Sam and *Midnight Confessions*?'

'Not yet. Have you spoken to her?'

'I'm on my way out there. Just waiting for Montoya. I thought it would be better if we do it in person, at her place. From what I understand she was pretty close to Leanne Jaquillard. The kid was part of a weekly group session for troubled teens that Samantha Leeds holds at the Boucher Center.' Bentz rolled back in his chair, and it creaked in protest. 'I guess she had some family trouble. No dad and a mom who's a real piece of work.'

'I talked to Marletta Vaughn,' Melinda said flatly. 'Not exactly June Cleaver.'

Bentz smiled grimly at the comparison. 'You know, the last time the creep called Samantha Leeds at the station, he threatened her. He told her . . . wait a minute I want to get this right.' He rolled back to the desk and held up the finger of one hand while he flipped through pages in his notebook. 'Oh, here we go . . . he said, and I quote, "All you need to know is that what happens tonight is because of you. Because of your sins. You need to repent, Sam. Beg forgiveness." '

He pushed the notebook aside. 'Even though we found the other victim – Cathy Adams – on the night of Annie Seger's birthday, it seemed to be coincidence, not related. Another perp altogether, so I was hoping the birthday cake left at the station was all that would happen. But I was wrong. Turns out this girl' – he thumped a finger on the picture of the latest victim – 'Leanne Jaquillard was murdered by the guy who registered as John Fathers, who, I believe is the "John" who calls Dr. Sam at the station. It all fits, Melinda.'

'Okay, so if you're right, and this is all tied together, that "John" and our killer are one and the same,' Melinda said, 'how do you explain the call from the woman who claimed she was "Annie"?'

'I'm still workin' on that,' Bentz admitted.

'Do you think it's someone so devoted to this "John" that she would do his bidding?'

'Or it could be someone who hates Samantha Leeds. Someone who's jealous of her, either personally or professionally, or someone who thinks she was wronged by her, as if she took away an old boyfriend, say the first Mrs. Jeremy Leeds or maybe the current one who doesn't like her husband's ex's getting so

much attention, a coworker she's stepped on while climbing to
the top, or a rival like Trish LaBelle over at WNAB . . . I'm not
sure.'

'Or "John" could have paid someone,' Melinda thought
aloud. 'You think the call from Annie was recorded, right? So he
could have hired a woman off the street to make the tape and
say she was Annie.'

'Now you're sounding like Montoya. With him every crime is
about money.'

Jaskiel curved an eyebrow upward. 'It usually is you know,
Rick. Not all of us are noble idealists.'

'None of us are,' he corrected her. 'Not around here.'

'No?' She laughed and seemed suddenly more feminine, less
imposing. 'Maybe you're right, but it seems to me I've heard the
hoofbeats of Rocinante echoing through the halls, and they
usually stop right about here.'

'What the hell are you talkin' about?' Montoya asked as he
breezed in, looking cool as ever despite the heat.

'Never mind,' Bentz said.

Jaskiel threw Montoya a look. 'Don Quixote's steed.'

'Jesus, how do you know this shit?' Montoya asked.

'I read,' she replied. 'And this is something you should
remember, it's part of your Spanish heritage.'

'Yeah, like I care.'

Bentz explained, 'And she does crossword puzzles and
watches *Jeopardy.*'

'When I have the time. Speaking of which' – she checked her
watch – 'I'd better get ready for the fourth estate.' She flashed
them her most-practiced smile. 'Wouldn't want to keep them
waiting.'

'Better you than me,' Bentz said, as she disappeared.

'You ready to rock'n'roll?' Montoya asked.

'Just about.' He handed Montoya the composite.

'This our man?'

'In theory.'

'Shit, he could be anyone.'

'I'm having the computer tech take some photos of the men in Samantha's life and Annie Seger's life, those with type A blood, which, unfortunately is most of them, then I'm going to have the computer compare them. It should narrow the field.'

'Let's hope,' Montoya said without a lot of enthusiasm.

'Let's go.' Bentz snagged the paper from Montoya's hand, then reached for his sidearm and his jacket. He wasn't looking forward to telling Samantha Leeds about the dead girl, but it was better she hear it from him rather than on the five o'clock news.

Priscilla McQueen Caldwell wasn't happy to see him, not one little bit.

Ty didn't care. He figured that as long as he was in Houston, he should check out everyone associated with Annie Seger. Many of her friends had moved away, but Prissy was still in town, living less than a half hour from the airport, and Ty was standing on her front porch while the late-afternoon sun beat against his back. 'I don't know why I should talk to you,' she told him, blocking the doorway to the interior of the small bungalow littered with toys. Over her shoulder he caught a peek of a play-pen and infant swing, but no baby. Probably napping.

'I'm just trying to find out about Annie. You were her best friend. You knew that she was pregnant, and you probably knew that the baby wasn't Ryan Zimmerman's.'

'What does it matter now?' Prissy asked, the screen door propped on one shoulder.

'I think she was murdered.'

'There have been those old rumors flyin' around for years, but nothin's ever come of 'em,' Prissy said, squinting up at him. Wearing a pink shorts outfit, sandals and a necklace with a gold cross, she was a pretty, petite woman with honey-colored hair scraped back in a ponytail. 'You know it's funny, first Ryan calls out of the blue, and the next thing I know is you're here on my doorstep talkin' 'bout Annie.'

'Ryan called you?'

'Sure he did. Didn't you know? He and I were going together when Annie set her sights on him, and that was that.' The corners of her pert little mouth turned down. 'That's the way it was – whatever Annie wanted, she got.' Prissy folded her arms over her chest and inside a baby began to fuss.

'But you still remained friends.'

'Well, not right off, but eventually. Ryan got into drugs and turned away from the Lord.'

'So you gave him to Annie with your blessing.'

'I didn't give him anything. But it turned out okay. I met Billy Ray in church and we just hit it off. Got married after I graduated.' She checked her watch. 'Now, lookit, I don't want him knowin' I talked to you. He didn't like it much when Ryan called, and he's got hisself a temper.'

'Why did Ryan call?'

Priscilla rolled her expressive eyes. 'Well, that just about took all. He wanted me to meet him somewhere – come down to New Orleans. He and his wife broke up and he lost his job and he was lonely and wonder of wonders, he thought of me.' Her smile was cold. '*Now* he needs me. I told him to forget it.'

From the interior a baby started to cry.

'Uh-oh, Billy Jr. is wakin' up. I really got to go.'

'Did Ryan leave a number?'

'Nah. I think he was rentin' some motel by the month until he could get hisself on his feet . . . but I'm not sure 'bout that.' The baby began to wail. 'Look I gotta see to him.'

Ty grabbed her hand. 'You would be doing Annie a favor if you could help me out with this,' he insisted. 'Who was she involved with besides Ryan.'

'I really don't know. It was some big, dark secret,' Prissy said. 'I thought it probably was some married guy, like a friend of Dr. Faraday's, because she was real worried about it and then she got pregnant and couldn't tell her folks. They would've killed her.' Just as the words left her tongue, Priscilla seemed to realize what she'd said. 'Oh. I didn't mean they would really kill her, but you know, Estelle would have had a fit.'

The baby began to wail loudly, and Ty released Prissy's hand. 'If you ever want to talk about this, give me a call.' He slipped a card from his wallet and tried to hand it to her, but she wouldn't take it.

'I won't,' she insisted. 'Look, Annie was my friend, okay? I liked her a lot, even though she ticked me off about Ryan. But as far as I'm concerned, she got real messed up, couldn't face her parents or Ryan about the baby and committed suicide. I won't call you. Ever. Billy Ray wouldn't like it.'

She slipped inside, and Ty left his business card tucked in the frame of the screen door. There was a chance that she'd change her mind, though he thought it was mighty slim.

'But you haven't actually spoken to Peter or seen him,' Sam's father said.

He'd returned her call, but his voice sounded defeated and tired.

Inwardly she cringed as she cradled the receiver between her head and shoulder, then opened a can of cat food and scooped out the tuna/chicken feast for Charon, who was crying loudly and swarming around her bare feet. 'No, I haven't personally talked to him yet, Dad, but the fact that Pete sat down and had a conversation with Corky is encouraging.'

'I would love to have a word with him,' William Matheson said wistfully.

You and me both, Sam thought, but bit back her anger. 'Let's think of this as kind of a breakthrough,' Sam said, accentuating the positive. 'No one that I know of has seen or heard from him in years, and he actually approached Corky in the bar.' That was stretching the truth a little. Corky hadn't said that Peter initiated the conversation, but her dad needed encouragement. 'Now, listen, if I hear anything else, I'll let you know.' She rinsed the empty can in the sink, then tossed it into the trash.

'I suppose I could check with Information in Atlanta. They might have his number.'

'They might.' She didn't think so.

'But it's probably unlisted. It was when he was living in Houston.'

Sam froze. She'd been pulling the trash from beneath the sink, but now she slowly straightened. 'Wait a minute. When was he in Texas?'

'Years ago. I had that private investigator looking for him and he found him down not far from where you were living at the time.'

'Are you telling me that Pete was in Houston and you knew about it but you never told me?'

'I'm not sure it was him, it could have been another Peter Matheson. I never got through, and you . . . well, you were going through so much with the divorce and that Annie Seger mess.'

Which is happening again.

'I didn't think you needed the added stress of knowing that he was in the same town and never called. Besides, as I said, I'm not even sure it was Pete. The pictures I saw of him weren't that good, and he was always looking away or wearing a hat or sunglasses or something.'

'He was there when I was? And you didn't tell me . . . Jesus, Dad, even if it wasn't the right Peter Matheson, don't you think you should have let me know?' She couldn't believe her father's duplicity. This was just so unlike him. 'In all these years, whenever you and I talked you always asked about Peter and never once mentioned that he could have been in Houston.'

'What would have been the point?' her father asked, his voice bristling defensively. 'Whether he was fifty miles from you or five hundred or five, what difference did it make?'

'Dad,' she said firmly, 'I wasn't even sure he was alive.'

'Neither was I. As I said, I'm not even sure it was our Pete.'

Our Pete. He hasn't been our Pete in years. But there was no reason to argue. Sam quieted her hammering heart and finished the phone call. Her father was right. So what if Pete had been in Houston? He didn't know Annie Seger . . . couldn't have. She was just a high-school kid, and Houston was a huge metropolis that stretched for miles and was filled with hundreds of thousands of people.

But, if Pete had been in town, why hadn't he contacted her? With all the publicity about the Annie Seger suicide and the phone calls to the station, he certainly would have known Sam was not only living there but in the middle of the controversy and tragedy of Annie's death. Where was Peter when the press was hounding her, when the police were questioning her, when Annie's family was accusing her of everything from making a public mockery of their young daughter's problems to greed to malpractice?

It might not have been him, she told herself, as Charon hopped onto the kitchen table and began washing his face. *But there was a chance Peter had been there, just as he's surfaced once again, nine years later, when Annie Seger's name had come up again.*

There was just no point in thinking of what-ifs and what-might-have-beens. She was replacing the handset into the recharger when it jangled in her hands, startling her.

'Probably Dad apologizing,' she told the cat. 'Now, get down!' She pushed a button on the handset and brought it to her ear. 'Hello.'

'Samantha.'

'John's' cold voice caused her blood to congeal.

Stay calm. Find out more about him. 'Yes,' she said, and glanced through the kitchen window. Across the street Edie Killingsworth was digging in her yard and Hannibal was romping through the grass, as if nothing evil, nothing sinister were happening. 'Why are you calling me at home?'

'There's something you should know.'

Oh, God. 'What's that, John?' she asked as she saw a police cruiser roll into her drive. If she could just keep the stalker on the line.

'I just want you to know that I kept my promise.'

'Your promise?' she said and her heart squeezed in fear. *The threat. He kept his threat.*

'You mean the cake. I got it.'

'No, there's something else.'

'What?' she asked, dread filling her heart.

'I made a sacrifice. For you.'

'A sacrifice. What sacrifice?'

Click.

The phone went dead.

'What sacrifice?' she screamed again, fear shooting through her. 'What the hell are you talking about, you bastard?'

But he was gone.

'Damn!' She slammed the receiver into its cradle. Through the window she watched Detective Bentz and his partner Montoya climb out of their cruiser. Their faces were set and hard as they walked toward the front door. She flew into the foyer, threw the bolt, and stared at the two men as they climbed onto her porch.

'What's happened?' she demanded, looking from one sober face to the other.

'I'm afraid we've got some bad news,' Bentz said, and she could barely hear him over the hammering of her heart. 'It's about one of your clients, a girl by the name of Leanne Jaquillard.'

'No,' she whispered, her knees starting to fail her, her lungs squeezing tight. She propped herself against the door frame, and the noises she heard, Bentz's voice, Hannibal's yapping and a mockingbird singing seemed far away, from a distant place, hardly audible over the buzz of denial echoing through her brain.

'She's dead,' Bentz said. 'Murdered last night.'

'No!' she said, destroyed inside. 'Not Leanne. He wouldn't. He couldn't.' Tears flooded her eyes and her fists clenched in impotence.

'We think she was killed by the same man who's killed two other women, the man who phones you at the station and calls himself John. Ms. Leeds? Samantha . . . are you all right.'

'No,' she forced out again. 'He just called. That murdering son of a bitch just called and told me he'd made a sacrifice, that it was my fault for not atoning . . . oh, God, no, no, no!' she said, fighting the urge to break down altogether, sobs building within.

'There's more,' Bentz said kindly, touching her arm, gently guiding her back into the cool foyer.

'No . . . no . . .' Leanne had tried to contact her, had even called. 'It can't be. She called here, she was looking for me . . . I can't believe, I mean, there must be some mistake.'

'No mistake,' Bentz said, as Montoya closed the door behind him, shutting out the blistering sun and sultry heat.

'You said there was more,' Sam said, wrapping her arms around her middle.

'Yes. She was pregnant.'

Just like Annie. 'Oh, God, no . . . not again . . .'

Bentz drew in a deep breath as Sam sank onto the bottom step of the stairs. 'She was wearing a red teddy when she was murdered. You said you were missing one, that it could have been taken, so I'd like you to come down to the station and see if it's the same.'

Sam dropped her head in her hands and let the tears drizzle down her cheeks. Leanne was dead. And she hadn't been able to reach her, hadn't been able to help. 'John' had murdered the girl, as well as others.

Bentz sat on the step next to her. 'Are you all right? I know this is a shock, but I'm sure your life is in danger, and I wanted to warn you. Samantha, do you understand, this man is dangerous. He's killed three women, possibly more, and we think that you might be his ultimate target.'

At that moment the phone began to ring.

29

'Answer it,' Bentz said, and Sam forced herself to her feet. The policemen followed her into the kitchen as she picked up the receiver.

'Hello?

'Sam?'

'Ty.' She nearly dissolved into a puddle on the floor and sank against the kitchen counter.

'Something's wrong, isn't it? Sam?'

'It's Leanne . . . one of the girls I work with. He killed her, Ty, and he called me and told me he'd made a sacrifice and the police are here . . . and I have to go down to the station and . . .' She took a deep breath, tried to pull herself together.

'Stay put,' Ty said. 'I'm still in Houston, but I'm on my way to the airport. I'll be back in a few hours. The police are there? Stay with them, don't go out. Jesus Christ, I should never have left. He killed the girl?'

'And some others, I . . . I haven't talked to the detectives yet, they just got here,' she said, regaining a modicum of her equilibrium. 'But Leanne . . . oh, God . . . and she was pregnant . . . just like Annie.'

'Son of a bitch,' he muttered, and then swore again. 'Hang on, Sam, I'm comin' home. Just hang on.'

'I will,' she said before hanging up and turning to find both police officers looking uncomfortable and out of place in her kitchen. 'Now . . . could you please . . . just tell me what's going on?' She swiped the tears from her eyes, but still felt numb inside. Leanne . . . oh, God, how could he have killed Leanne?

They sat around the small kitchen table and Bentz explained

his theory that John was a serial killer, that somehow he was linked to Annie Seger, that Sam was his ultimate target. 'We're not here to scare you, just tell you what's going on. I'll talk to the Cambrai police about extra patrols, we'll have someone watch the house and the station and we'll put tracers on all the phones, here and at the office.' Guilt crossed his dark eyes. 'We should have done it earlier, but we hadn't connected him to the murders. We have two eyewitnesses, one a hotel clerk, the other a girl we think he tried to assault who got away. They came up with a description.' He reached into his pocket, unfolded a piece of paper, and slid it across the table. 'Do you know this man?'

Staring at the sketch, Sam felt cold as death. The drawing was clear, but the features weren't defined. 'What's that?' she asked, pointing to marks on the drawing of the suspect's left cheek. 'A scar?'

'Scratch marks. The potential victim who got away clawed at him.'

'Good,' Sam said as she stared at the composite. 'I – I don't think I know this man,' she said, slowly shaking her head. 'This guy could be anyone.'

'With Type A positive blood. We're double-checking.'

Charon, eyeing the detectives warily, had hopped onto Sam's lap and she petted him absently as they talked. They questioned her about phone calls, had she seen anyone lurking around? Had she been approached? Was her alarm system working? Did it scare intruders off, or was it connected with a service? All the while the sketch was on the table, staring at her through dark glasses. He seemed familiar and yet not.

Once the preliminary questions were over, the detectives offered to drive her into New Orleans, to the station to view and possibly identify the red teddy, the single garment Leanne was wearing when she was killed. It made Sam sick to think of it, to imagine that she had anything to do with Leanne's death. She imagined the girl's terror, her fear, her pain.

If only she could have interceded, taken Leanne's calls for help, she thought again as she sat in the back of the cruiser. Montoya drove. Bentz, one arm over the backrest, twisted so that he could see Sam. The air conditioner roared, and the police radio crackled.

'We think he dresses them up to look like you,' Bentz said, as Montoya drove around the edge of Lake Pontchartrain. Through the window, Sam glanced at the darkening water. A few sailboats were visible, the first stars were winking high overhead and the calm water seemed somehow foreboding and dark. Sinister. Like the evil that lurked in all the shadows, the evil that was somehow linked to her.

'We're confiding in the media, handing out composites and descriptions, hoping someone will recognize him. We won't mention you or the calls to the station, nor will we bring up anything about Annie Seger or Houston, but we hope to flush him out.'

'Or drive him to kill again.'

Bentz didn't say a word.

'He will anyway,' Montoya offered as he switched lanes.

'We have to stop him before he does,' she said, as the lights of New Orleans glittered ever more closely. Montoya was a lead-foot; the cruiser sped past other vehicles driving into the city. Sam hardly noticed. 'We have to do anything we can to end this.'

'That's the idea,' Bentz said, and stuffed a stick of gum into his mouth. 'The department's doing everything in its power—'

'Screw the "department,"' she bit out. 'How many women are dead? Three, you said, maybe more? Because of me and my show and God only knows what else? The "department" hasn't saved any lives so far, right?' She was thinking hard. 'And I'm the connection to him? Then we should use that. Try to reach him through my program.'

'This is a police matter.'

'Like hell, Detective. This is personal. To me. "John's" made it personal. He's called me, sent me threats, broken into my house and now he's killed someone I care about. It's personal to me.' By the time Montoya had parked on the street and Bentz had shepherded her into the building and up a set of back stairs to his office, she was furious. At the killer, at the police, at herself and at Leanne for going with the creep. Why had she decided to hook again? Turn a trick?

She tried to reach out to you, Sam, but you weren't there for her, were you? Just like you weren't there for Annie, and now she and her baby are dead. Dead! *Because you weren't there.*

She marched into Bentz's airless office and waited while he unlocked a cabinet and retrieved a plastic bag. Inside was her red teddy. There was no doubt. She recognized the pattern of lace that covered the breasts, saw the remainder of the tag that she'd cut off when she'd first purchased the flimsy garment, and felt as if someone had punched her in the stomach.

Leanne had been wearing it when she'd died. Why? Oh, poor confused baby. Leanne had only been a teenager.

But someone had stolen the teddy from Sam's house. Probably on the night she'd been with Ty on the boat. Who had walked in and taken something so personal? Leanne? Or 'John'? Or an accomplice?

She sank into one of the visitor's chairs in the hot little office and felt as if the blood had been drained from her body. 'It's mine,' she whispered, dry-eyed, but screaming inside. *No, no, no! Leanne, please . . . Dear God, let this be a nightmare. Let me wake up!*

'He's getting closer to you,' Bentz said, and she shuddered inside. 'But we're going to get him.'

'I believe you.' She met the detective's determined gaze with her own. 'Let's find that son of a bitch, toss him into jail and throw away the key.'

'That's too good for him.' Bentz walked to the fan behind his desk and switched it to its highest setting. 'In this case I'd like to see him drawn and quartered.'

'But first we have to catch him,' Montoya pointed out. He rested a hip on the edge of Bentz's desk and leaned closer to Sam. 'For that, we're gonna need your help.'

'You've got it,' Sam said, her jaw setting. 'I'll do whatever I have to.'

*　　*　　*

The bitch had scratched him.

He stared at his reflection in the mirror he'd nailed over a basin on a stand. Sure enough, despite two days' growth of beard, the wound was visible, three distinct gouges from the cunt's claws. He shouldn't have let her escape. That had been a mistake, one his instructor would never have made.

Don't think about him. You're in control now. You. Father John.

But he felt desperate. Angry. Restless. He glanced around the cabin, his only real home now, not much by his old standards, and yet a place where he felt he belonged. Only on the bayou did he feel some peace, some respite from the thrumming in his brain.

He'd grown up privileged and somehow ended up here . . . cast out of his own family . . . he thought of his mother . . . his sister . . . his father . . . shit, he didn't have a family anymore. Hadn't for years. He was on his own. Even his mentor had abandoned him, the very man who had helped him deal with the monster within him, the one who had shown him the way . . .

Yes, he was truly alone.

If Annie had lived . . .

Whoring cunt – she deserved to die. She asked for it . . . Betrayer . . . Jezebel . . . How could she have been with another man?

He reached into his shaving kit and found a tube of salve and a small bottle of face makeup. After coating his wounds with the ointment, he carefully dabbed concealer over the discoloration on his skin. Squinting in the light from his lantern, he added mascara to his beard-stubble until the wounds weren't visible.

A low moan from the corner caught his attention. He looked over his shoulder to the corner cot and saw his prisoner. A pathetic specimen, bound and gagged, drugged into oblivion, only roused when it was necessary for the victim to realize the magnitude of their sins.

Haunted eyes opened, blinked, then, as if unable to accept their fate, closed again.

Father John looked into the mirror again, stared into his own gaze and inwardly cringed. His eyes had seen too much, and now accused him of crimes he'd committed, sins that he could never repent. And yet the thought of those sins . . . the hunt . . . the capture . . . the terror of his prey . . . and the ultimate blood-lust . . . the kill . . . brought a rush to his veins, a tingle of anticipation flowing through his blood.

He reached into his pocket and found his special rosary . . . cool, cold beads, sharp against the pads of his fingers and thumb. Such a wicked, lovely weapon, the symbol of good and purity and capable of such a hellish death. That's what he liked about it – the cruel irony of it.

He thought of the women he'd killed . . . Annie, of course, but that was before he'd learned from the master, before he under-stood his mission, before he'd perfected his method and employed his treacherous, beloved noose. He'd watched her blood flow, so slowly it seemed now . . . and then there had been the first whore . . . he'd planned that after he'd been betrayed by the one woman he'd trusted . . . the one woman who should have been there for him forever.

He'd heard Dr. Sam's voice one night . . . here . . . away from Houston . . . away from Annie . . . and he'd known he had to set things right, that Samantha Leeds was the reason Annie was dead. He'd been forced to kill Annie because of Dr. Sam.

The nerve of the bitch to start up again, broadcasting her meaningless, psychological mumbo-jumbo. Messing up people's lives.

But soon she would stop. He would see to it.

He thought of the women who had paid for Samantha Leeds's sins. The first victim had been random, the hooker who had been hanging out on Bourbon Street, luring men, offering up her body . . . and it had been such a rush, such a turn-on to watch the terror in her eyes when she'd realized he was going to strangle her with the rosary.

He grew hard at the thought, and he remembered the second victim, another prostitute who had approached him down by the brewery. She'd been tough, hadn't wanted to wear the wig, but had eventually complied, and he'd slowly killed her just like the first. Seeing her horror, watching her struggle while growing so hard he nearly came in his pants.

But the best, the very best, had been the Jaquillard girl. He hadn't meant to kill her that night – but the other one, the bitch he'd found near the universities, the girl dressed like a hooker who had clawed him had gotten away had left him empty.

Then he'd set his sites on the Jaquillard girl, followed her. It had seemed fitting that the girl closest to Samantha die on Annie's birthday. It was only after the frustration of losing one victim that he'd taken the streetcar to Canal Street, walked to the Jaquillard girl's apartment and waited for her in the dark. She'd left the apartment after nightfall and had walked to the river, looking edgy. He'd followed her, approached her as she'd sat on the bench looking at the dark, slow-moving water of the Mississippi. She'd been lost in thought, but eager to score some quick money when he offered the deal.

The rest had been easy. As easy as stealing Sam's teddy had been.

He wondered how Dr. Sam had taken the news about the girl . . . they'd been close, he'd seen them together, heard from his source that Leanne Jaquillard had been special to Dr. Sam. Oh, he would have loved to have been a fly on the wall when Dr. Sam found out about Leanne's death.

Samantha would have known, deep down, that the girl was dead because of her.

He remembered the kill. How she'd begged.

His blood turned hot.

Molten.

Roared through his veins.

His cock pressed hard against his pants as he thought of Samantha with her red hair and green eyes. Soon he would have the pleasure. He reached down, felt himself, closed his eyes and imagined taking Leanne Jaquillard's life—

His cell phone rang jarring him out of his fantasy, causing the pathetic worm on his cot to jump. Angrily, he crossed the stark living area and picked up. 'Yeah?'

'Hi!' Her voice was perky, expectant. He smiled. She was a pretty thing and ambitious, willing to do just about anything he wanted. 'I'm not working tonight and I thought maybe we could get together.'

'Maybe,' he said, glancing at his rousing victim. Time for another dose. Sleeping pills that he'd stolen in Houston.

'There's a new restaurant on Chartres. I read about it in the paper. Authentic French cuisine, but then that's what they always say. Or we could eat in . . . I'd even cook.'

He thought about the hunt, about snuffing out Leanne's life, and he grew hard again. This woman, too, though she didn't know it, would feel the sweet torture of his glittering wreath surround her long neck.

'Let's go out,' he said, wanting the feel of the night to close in on him, hoping to get lost in the crowd, to blend in to the heated throng pulsing down Bourbon Street. 'I'm in the mood for jazz. I'll meet you.' He glanced at his watch. 'At ten o'clock. Corner of Bienville and Bourbon.'

'Can't wait,' she said, and hung up.

Neither can I. He looked around his cabin, the souvenirs he carried with him from a happier time oh, so long ago. Pictures of Annie, pictures of Samantha, ribbons and athletic trophies – a tennis racquet, set of golf clubs, lacrosse stick, fishing rod and skis. Reminders of what his life was and could have been.

But you're a sinner.

He knew that much. Didn't need to remind himself.

Tonight he'd lose himself in the crowds. Drink. Do some coke if he was lucky enough to score. Blend in with the masses and later . . . later . . . he'd come back here, to this dark place where no one could hear a scream, and make his prisoner beg for the mercy of death.

He had work to do. Tonight he would begin to set his plan into motion. He glanced at his moaning victim and grabbed the syringe from his shaving kit. The prisoner saw him coming, started making little choking, gasping sounds beneath the gag and scooted away. But there was nowhere to turn. His prisoner's hands were tied behind the captive's back and the legs were shackled. Terror rose from bulging eyes and his prisoner's head whipped back and forth, spittle darkening the gag.

'It's either this or the gators,' Father John said as he found his captive's left arm and jabbed the needle deep. 'And the gators are too good for you.'

The prisoner started to weep.

Pathetic. It would be so much easier to kill his victim now . . . but that would ruin everything.

'Shut up,' he said and the prisoner mewled. Dr. John kicked hard, in the shins, landing a steel-toed boot against a bare leg. 'Shut the fuck up.'

His captive became soundless, but the tears still streamed. John grabbed the prisoner's hand, clamped his fingers around the prisoner's finger and stripped off a ring. Unable to conceal his smile, he opened the cupboard where he stored his treasures, the trophies from his kill and added the band with its single winking stone. The prisoner started screaming behind the gag again, but one look ended the screams.

Good.

Father John forced his thoughts to his ultimate victim.

Dr. Sam.

But not through the airwaves.

In the flesh.

Such sweet vengeance . . . he had great plans for her. He'd bring her here, make her see the error of her ways, keep her alive until she begged his forgiveness.

And then, when he was tired of the game, he'd kill her with the rosary.

Deftly he made the sign of the cross, then reached for his Ray-Bans.

30

'You're not staying here.' Ty was adamant as he strode through the open door, and Sam flung herself into his arms. 'Come on, darlin' let's get you somewhere safe.' He kicked the door shut and it was all she could do not to fall into a thousand pieces as she clung to him.

'It's just so awful. The same thing happening all over again,' she said brokenly. 'Leanne . . . oh, God, she was pregnant. Just like Annie.'

'Shh. It's going to be okay.'

'It'll never be okay, Ty. Never.'

His arms tightened. His lips pressed against her forehead, then her eyes. 'Sure it will . . . you just give it time.'

'There is none. That – that monster is out there.'

'We'll get him. I promise.' He kissed her tearstained cheek, then finally her lips. His lips were as strong as his words. 'You just stick with me. Things will work out fine.' She wanted to believe him. Oh, God, she wanted to believe him. But the nightmare wasn't over yet and despite his platitudes, she doubted anything would ever be the same.

'Now, tell me what happened,' he said, pulling her into the den, one arm around her shoulders.

Sam drew in a ragged breath. 'It was awful.' He guided her to her desk chair, and while she sat in front of the flickering computer screen, he rested a hip on the desk and listened.

She explained what she'd done while he was away, what she'd accomplished, how she'd failed. She'd tried to reach her friend who worked at Our Lady of Mercy Hospital, but it was the weekend, so she had to leave a voice mail message. She'd also attempted to get in touch with Leanne, but, of course, that had been fruitless, the poor thing was already dead. Twiddling a pencil and feeling cold to the marrow of her bones, she explained about her call about her brother, then the horrid, mind-numbing phone conversation with 'John' just as the police arrived with the news that Leanne Jaquillard had been murdered by a serial killer.

'Jesus,' Ty said. 'I should have been here.'

'You couldn't have stopped it. No one could have.' She dropped the pencil and slumped in her chair. 'God, I'm exhausted.'

'I've got just the thing.' He walked into the kitchen where she heard him rummaging through the cupboards, then twist on the faucet. Water ran. A few seconds later he reappeared with a glass. 'Here.'

'Thanks.' She took a sip, placed it to her head and she explained about the trip to New Orleans and the police station. 'Ever since Detective Montoya dropped me off, I've been here, going through my textbooks and the paperbacks I've collected over the years on criminal psychology, psychosis, and dysfunctions of serial murderers.

'A lot of good that did.' She took another long swallow from the glass. 'I was so stupid. So naive, no, so arrogant. I thought I was beginning to understand it. I really believed this was all just a sick game to John. Oh, I knew he had a violent streak, that was evident in that first cut-up picture he sent me, but I had no idea, I mean, I didn't think for a minute that . . . that he was a killer.' She closed her eyes for a second, trying to pull herself together, to push out the cacophony of guilt that blared in her brain.

'We'll find him.'

'But who is he? I've been trying to figure it out. The police have semen samples and they're comparing them to anyone associated with the women who were killed, with anyone associated with Annie and with anyone associated with me, but it's going to take time.'

'I have some of that information. Remember? Because of Annie's pregnancy.' Ty reached for the phone. 'What's the name of the detective?'

'Rick Bentz.'

'I'm going to call him and tell him everything I know, offer my files, tell them what I've found out and try and convince them that this all started with Annie Seger. Whoever killed her is the man they're looking for.'

'They might believe that Annie committed suicide.'

'Then I'll just have to convince them otherwise,' he said. 'Do you have a direct line to Bentz's desk?'

'His card's on the refrigerator.'

Ty wasted no time. He walked into the kitchen and punched out the numbers to the New Orleans PD. A few minutes later he'd connected with Bentz and was explaining his theory about Annie's death.

Meanwhile Sam made coffee. She had to keep busy, to keep going, to push back the demons in her mind that told her she was responsible for Leanne's death.

Not just Leanne, but others. At least two more women. 'John,' whoever the hell he was, stalked women, hunted them, killed them.

Because of you, Sam. Because of some great injustice you inflicted upon him when you didn't help Annie Seger.

NO WAY! Don't buy into his sick, convoluted thinking. He's twisted, Samantha, twisted. Now, get a grip on yourself and think. Use your brain, use your knowledge. Figure it out. Who is he?

Stiffening her back, she pulled herself together and, as the coffee perked, she half listened to Ty's conversation, but found a pen in her purse and grabbed a tablet she kept by the phone for messages.

Who had been in Houston at the time of Annie Seger's death?

She started with herself and just wrote the names as they came to her: George Hannah, Eleanor Cavalier, Jason Faraday, Estelle Faraday, Kent Seger, Prissy McQueen, Ryan Zimmerman, David Ross, and Ty Wheeler. And Peter

Matheson ... *Don't forget that your dear, disappearing brother might have been in town.* Inwardly she winced. *Not Pete – please, not Pete.* She put a question mark by Peter's name, then crossed out all the women – they could be accomplices, true, but not the actual murderer. From Ty's notes she knew that Jason Faraday and Kent Seger had O positive blood. So did Pete. She didn't know about Ty, or George Hannah, or David, but she crossed Ty's name off the list. He wasn't the killer. Nor was her brother. Pete had never met Annie Seger.

How do you know, Sam? You haven't seen him in years. You didn't know he was in Houston, did you?

She wasn't even sure he'd been there ... no, not Pete ... memories of the dark-haired brother who had taken delight in besting her, outracing her on bicycles, outswimming her when they went to Lake Shasta, outskiing her when their parents had hauled them to the mountains ... she remembered his easy smile, mischievous green eyes, so like hers, and the way he always enjoyed beating her at every game, until he'd slid into a world dominated by cocaine and crack and any other drugs that offered a quick buzz, a new high.

Just like Ryan Zimmerman.

But Pete would never ...

She left his name on the list just as she heard Ty hanging up. 'What did he say?' she asked, still staring at her notes.

'To keep my nose clean, basically. I don't think he trusts me.'

'I don't think he trusts anyone.'

'Comes with the territory.' Ty stared over her shoulder and read her notes. 'Narrowing the field?'

'Trying.'

'Same thing the cops are doing.' Leaning over her back, so that his chest brushed her shoulders, he stretched his arm toward the table and pointed to his name. 'Why did you strike me off the list?'

'Because you couldn't ... wouldn't do it.' With a final sputter and the ding of a soft bell, the coffee announced it was ready. Sam ignored it.

'That's true, but you're basing your choice on emotion rather than fact,' Ty pointed out.

'You want me to put you back on the list?'

'I just want you to think clearly.' Straightening, he scrounged in her cupboard and eventually pulled out two mismatched mugs.

'What about "gut instinct"? Isn't that what you cops call it?' She tossed down the pen. She didn't have enough information on any of these people to make a stab in the dark, much less an educated guess as to their guilt or innocence.

'I'm not a cop, not anymore, and I consider gut instinct, the way I think about feminine intuition. It has its place,' he said, pouring them each a cup and placing a chipped mug she'd gotten from her mother years ago on the table in front of Sam.

'Thanks.' Staring at the list of possible suspects, she sipped the coffee, but found it didn't start to warm the chill deep inside her. Nothing could. Not until the monster was caught.

She stared at the tablet's lined page. One of the men on her list was the killer. She was sure of it. But who? George Hannah? Nah – killing would be too messy; he wouldn't mess up one of his Armani suits.

Remember – the killer calls on line two; he must be associated with the station. You might not know George as well as you think.

She went to another name. Ryan Zimmerman? What did she know about Annie's boyfriend – only that he was an athlete who had spiraled down into the drug scene and eventually pulled himself together?

Kent Seger? Another mystery, but a boy with a history of depression and mental problems after his sister's death. She made a note to call Our Lady Of Mercy again.

What about Jason Faraday – the stepfather who left the family and remarried quickly? What was his story? She tapped her finger near his name.

'Mark him off,' Ty said, as if reading her mind. 'The killer had to have left fingerprints behind. Jason Faraday was in the army, did a hitch in Vietnam. If he were the guy, the police and the FBI would already have arrested him.'

She crossed out Annie's stepfather.

'I, too, was fingerprinted,' he added, 'which is why you should have struck my name. Not because of any emotional attachment.'

'Details, details,' she said, but the joke fell flat. They were both too tired, too mentally exhausted for levity. She leaned back in her chair and wearily pushed her hair from her eyes, felt the drizzle of sweat on her scalp. How could she be so hot on the outside and cold as death deep in her soul?

'Come on, let's go to my place,' Ty said. 'You need to rest.'

'I can't leave. John might call back again. I have to be here.'

'Or he might show up,' Ty reminded her. 'I'd feel better if you packed a bag and stayed with me. He obviously got in once before. Maybe more often, you don't know, but somehow the Jaquillard girl ended up in your lingerie. Someone took it from the house, Sam. He comes and goes at will.'

'We left the door unlocked,' she reminded him. 'That's when it happened, and it's safe now. I've got the alarm system, the police are outside and the phone lines are tapped. Any calls will be traced. Besides, don't you have your friend, that private investigator lurking around?'

'Andre, yes, but—'

'Don't argue. I think John will call here again, Ty, and I hope he does. This time the police will trace his call, this time I'll be ready.'

Ty's eyebrows pulled together. He obviously wasn't convinced. 'What if John decides to pay you a personal visit?'

'I thought I just said the place was staked out.'

'That's not a guarantee that he can't slip by. You know, he's literally gotten away with murder so far.'

'I know, but . . .' she said turning her head coyly and touching the buttons on his shirt. 'I was hoping you and Sasquatch would stay with me. Bodyguard and alarm dog.'

'So now you're pulling out the feminine wiles arsenal?'

'I'm just trying to convince you,' she said, stung that he'd seen through her ploy. Then again, she'd been foolish to use it. 'I just want to be here, okay?' He frowned darkly and seemed about to argue again, but she placed a finger to his lips, shushing him.

'Please, Ty, we've got to do everything we can to catch this creep. Before he hurts someone else.'

'That's what I'm trying to prevent,' he said, 'because I'm afraid you're the next target.'

'Then stay with me.'

'All right, but if there's the hint of trouble, we're outta here.'

'It's a deal.'

Frowning, he finished his coffee in one gulp. 'Let's go down to my house. We'll pick up the dog and a change of clothes and then, if you're so damned hell-bent on spending the night here, we'll come back.'

'I am,' she said, slipping into a pair of flip-flops and carrying the mugs to the sink. She set the alarm, locked the door and followed Ty to his car.

The night was dark and humid, clouds blocking the moon. Insects hovered near the porch light and crawled on the windows. Along the street a few neighboring houselights burned and through open windows came the muted sounds of televisions, dishwashers, music or conversation. She wondered if she'd ever feel safe here again, would ever open her windows and let in the breath of wind, listen to the sounds of crickets, or would she forever be paralyzed, locked up tight.

Don't let John do this to you, she warned herself, *don't let him win. Find the bastard.*

Several cars were parked along the street, some she recognized, others she didn't.

Ty must've noticed her checking out the vehicles. 'The second one on the left. That's the unmarked,' Ty said. 'Your private bodyguards.'

'You can tell?'

'I was a cop, remember?'

'Yeah,' she said, climbing into the Volvo and slamming the passenger door shut, 'but the truth of the matter is that's about all I do know about you. The rest is pretty vague.'

He flashed her a disarming smile as he eased the car around her circular drive and nosed onto the street. 'Hey, I'm an open book. What do you want to know?'

In for a penny, in for a pound, she thought, fiddling with the strap of her seat belt. 'First off, I assume there is no Mrs. Wheeler?'

'Just my mother. Lives in San Antonio. A widow.'

From the sideview mirror, Sam saw the unmarked pull into the street. Headlights flashed on.

'Not too subtle, are they?' Ty glanced in the rearview mirror. 'I was married a long time ago. High-school sweetheart who didn't like being married to a policeman. We were divorced before we had kids, and I've never seen the need to walk down the aisle again.'

'What about girlfriends?'

'One in every port,' he teased, then sobered, the dash lights reflecting in his eyes. 'I really haven't had the time. Anything else you want to know?'

'Probably, but I'll worry about it later.'

Cranking the wheel, he turned into his driveway, then pulled the keys from the ignition and cut the engine. Sam reached for the door handle, but he grabbed her arm, stalling her. 'Look, Samantha, I know we haven't known each other all that long, and I'll admit that my reasons for meeting you weren't on the level. I lied to you, and we both know it. It was a mistake, believe me. I just never intended to get involved with you. But I'm not hiding anything, all right? There's no deep, dark secret I'm keep-ing from you. If I had this all to do over again, hell, I would have been straight with you from the beginning, but that's not the way it worked out.' He pulled her close and dropped a chaste kiss on her lips. His breath was warm against her face. 'Trust me, darlin', okay? I'll do anything to get you out of this mess. Anything.' He traced the line of her jaw with a finger, then let his hand drop. 'I feel like it's my fault this is all happening to you, to the other women.' Pain crossed his eyes and tugged at the corners of his mouth. Cords stood out in the back of his neck. 'I swear to you . . . I'll do everything in my power to keep you safe. I mean it. Just . . . have a little faith.'

Her throat closed as she stared into his night-darkened eyes. He seemed so sincere, so determined. So guilt-riddled. 'I do,' she said, but stopped herself from admitting more, that she was afraid she was falling in love with him, because it was foolish. The words would have sounded silly and trite, and the truth of the matter was, she couldn't trust her own emotions.

Headlights flashed as the unmarked drove slowly past. 'I think we'd better get going,' Ty said as he released her.

Together they walked into his house and it seemed to Sam like eons since she'd stormed out the other night, angry with him for lying to her. Oh, Lord, so much had happened since then and yet it had only been a few days ago.

A few days ago when Leanne had still been alive.

Heart heavy, she followed him to his loft and dropped onto a corner of his bed as he threw a change of clothes and shaving gear into an athletic bag. Thoughts of Leanne Jaquillard darkened her mind. If only she could have helped. If only she'd returned Leanne's calls earlier. If only . . . oh, Lord, she couldn't keep doing this. Hands clasped between her knees, she stared at the carpeting and felt the weight of the world on her shoulders. 'I feel like that if I would have talked to her, if she and I had met somewhere, this could have been prevented,' she said.

Ty caught her reflection in the mirror over his dresser.

'John . . . He told me that he'd made a sacrifice for me. He killed her . . . because of me . . . and . . . she'd tried to reach me and I wasn't there for her.'

Ty zipped the bag, then dropped to a knee in front of her. With a finger, he lifted her chin, forcing her gaze to his. 'You don't know that. Chances are you both would be dead right now. Come on, Samantha, don't do this to yourself. It's a terrible tragedy, God knows, but don't blame yourself.'

'You're a great one to talk. Didn't you just take a serious guilt trip when we were in the driveway?'

'But I pulled out of it.'

Tears filled Sam's eyes all over again. 'She was killed because she knew me. If she hadn't . . .'

'Don't go there, Samantha, please,' he said softly. 'What we have to do now, you and I, is get the guy. It's what Leanne would want.'

'It's what anyone would want.'

Blinking, she pulled every ounce of gumption she could find deep within. 'You're right,' she said with renewed conviction. 'Let's go get him.'

'Oh, we will,' Ty promised as he reached into a top dresser drawer and pulled out a pistol.

Every muscle in Sam's body went instantly rigid. 'A gun? You've got a gun?'

'I thought we'd established that I was with the Houston police? Don't worry, I've got a license. It's legal.' He found a clip on a shelf in his closet and snapped it in place. Flipping on the safety, he slid the pistol into a shoulder holster, strapped it in place and whipped on a jacket. 'Just in case.'

'I don't like guns, not any kind of guns,' she argued.

'And I don't like men who kill women to get their jollies. If anyone tries to harm you, they're gonna be sorry.' She thought he was teasing, trying to lift her spirits, but she caught the hard glint in his eye and knew he was serious. Dead serious.

So if this guy's 'the one' as you told Sam, then why is he so elusive? Melanie asked herself as she dialed her boyfriend's number and leaned back in her bathtub. It was the middle of the night. So why wouldn't he be home? Maybe he just turned off his cell so that he wouldn't be awakened at hours like this.

Or he might be with another woman.

That thought was like a knife twisting in her chest.

God, Mel, you've got it bad.

As she watched a drop of water hang on the faucet, she waited, knew he wouldn't answer and that she'd leave her third message on his cell phone. What was it about him that she found so darkly irresistible?

'Leave a message,' the recorded message advised her.

'Hi, this is Melanie again. Just wondering what you were up to.' She tried to keep her voice light, but inside she felt like an idiot. She was chasing him, just as she had a dozen other good-looking guys who'd mistreated her in the past. There was something wrong with her – she didn't have to have studied psychology to recognize that she always went for the wrong type – but still, she couldn't seem to break herself of the habit. 'An addict,' she told herself as she set the handheld on the counter and closed her eyes. She'd added bath crystals and drew in the scent of their fragrance as steam rose toward the ceiling. 'You're a love slave. Just like your mother and your sister.' Every woman in her family had endured the thoughtlessness of the men. Her mother had been married half a dozen times and never found happiness, her sister was still married to the jerk who beat her when he got drunk and she, the independent one, always chased the tall, dark and dangerous ones.

Things would get better . . . though. Tomorrow she'd call Trish LaBelle again over at WNAB. She hadn't gotten through yet, but Melanie wasn't giving up. Not on her boyfriend and not at a better job – either at WSLJ or a rival station.

It was time to move up in the world. She smiled. Imagined herself behind the microphone hosting *Midnight Confessions.* The two weeks Samantha had been in Mexico had been the best of Melanie's life . . . as she'd essentially become Dr. Sam, even spending her late nights in Sam's house. She'd met her boyfriend only a week or so before and they'd really clicked . . . she remembered how he'd loved her in Sam's big bed and even now she quivered with anticipation.

Yes, she thought, slowly lathering her body, things were going to change for the better. Melanie would make it happen. One way or another.

Rick Bentz stared out the bug-spattered windshield as Montoya ignored the speed limit and flew down the highway.

'Don't you think it's odd that there are three guys missing?' Bentz asked, drumming his fingers on the armrest. The car was hot and smelled of stale smoke. 'All three of them are connected with Annie Seger or Samantha Leeds and they all lived in Houston when Annie died.'

'Everything about this damned case is strange.' Montoya had been smoking. He flipped his cigarette butt outside and rolled up the window, giving the air conditioner a chance to cool off the sun-baked interior of the unmarked cruiser.

They were driving back from White Castle, where they'd talked to Mrs. Ryan Zimmerman, a sharp-tongued woman who had no kind words for her husband.

'I shoulda listened to my folks and never married him,' she'd said in all her self-righteous fury. 'He's no good. I don't know what I was thinking. And now he's lost his job. Just didn't show up one day. How's that for irresponsible?'

She'd sat in the living room of her condominium surrounded by boxes, evidence that either she was moving out or giving Ryan the heave ho.

'Why are you askin' about him, anyway?'

When Montoya had explained that he was a 'person of interest' in the murder of Leanne Jaquillard, she'd changed her tune and attitude faster than you could blink. 'Ryan would never do anything like that. I mean he's big and physical and has a temper, but he's no killer,' she'd insisted.

Montoya had been patient and explained they just wanted to talk to her husband, but Mrs. Ryan Zimmerman decided to clam up and told them to go away. If they wanted to talk to her again, she'd said, she would insist that a lawyer be present.

'So Zimmerman's gone. Nor forwarding address, no job,' Montoya commented as he soared past an eighteen-wheeler zinging down the highway. Bentz scrabbled in his shirt pocket for a nonexistent pack of cigarettes. He had to settle for a hit of nicotine from the last piece of gum in his pack. Montoya flipped on a pair of wraparound sunglasses. 'And Kent Seger's MIA as well. Just up and left All Saints with no visible sign of income.'

'Yep.' Bentz winced as Montoya began to pass a sedan with an old man huddled over the steering wheel, his gray-haired wife so small she was barely visible in the passenger seat. Something bright flashed from inside the car, something blinding that dangled from the rearview mirror. Bentz flipped down his visor.

'And then there's Samantha Leeds's brother,' Montoya ranted on. 'He's dropped out of sight as far as the family was concerned, but, low and behold, he was working in the very town where his sister was a DJ, right during the thick of things. Seems a little too convenient to me. Maybe there's something to Wheeler's theory that Annie Seger was murdered.'

Bentz had to admit it had some merit, but he lost track of the conversation when Montoya pulled ahead of the sedan and Bentz recognized the object that had been blinding him. A rosary was looped around the sedan's rearview mirror and the clear, glittering beads were refracting the hell out of the intense sunlight.

'I'll be damned,' Bentz said as Montoya whipped across the lane to make his exit. 'Did ya get a look at that?'

'At what? The Taurus?'

'No, I'm talking about what was in it. That old couple had a rosary tied to their rearview mirror.'

'So? They probably had a plastic Jesus, too.' Montoya braked for a stop sign. The unmarked car shuddered to a stop. He wasn't getting it.

'A rosary,' Bentz repeated. 'With beads spaced in a distinct pattern . . .'

'What're you talkin' about? So the beads are spaced for the damned prayers, yeah I know . . .' His voice faded, and he sent Bentz a look of disbelief. 'You don't think our guy used a rosary as a garrotte, do you?'

'I think it's worth checking out.'

'So what does this mean . . . that the guy's some kind of priest?' Montoya let a flatbed pass.

'Probably not. You can get those things anywhere, probably even on the Internet.'

'What at Catholics R Us?'

'I was thinking more along the lines of *www.rosary.com.*' The light changed.

'Holy shit,' Montoya muttered, gunning the engine. The cruiser shot forward. 'This is really sick stuff.'

Amen, Bentz thought, but didn't say it.

31

'You know I can't divulge patient information, Samantha,' Dania Erickson said in that well-modulated I-know-better-than-you voice Sam remembered from her days sitting through psych lectures at Tulane. Sam had finally caught up with her old nemesis. Finally, the 'doctor was in' at Our Lady of Mercy in California and not happy about being disturbed.

Tough, Sam thought as she held the receiver of the phone in the office she shared with the other DJs to her ear and stared at the composite drawing of the killer, a flat image that stared up at her through dark lenses. Music from a prerecorded program, some kind of soft jazz, played through the speakers, and the buzz of conversation drifted in through the open door.

Dania had always had something to say back in those days at Tulane, had always tried to ingratiate herself with the teachers, including Dr. Jeremy Leeds, who had ended up as Sam's husband. Sam suspected that her marriage had always rankled Dania, and now Dania wasn't giving an inch. Sam and Dania had been playing phone tag for nearly a week and had finally connected, not that it was doing any good. 'Anything I have is privileged information.'

'I realize that, but there's a serial killer on the loose here in New Orleans. The police have linked him to Annie Seger, Kent's sister. He could be a murderer, Dania.'

'Doesn't change anything, you know that. I did treat Kent years ago, after his sister's suicide, but other than that, I can't divulge any information. It could cost me my job.'

'We're talking about women's lives.'

'I'm sorry, Samantha. Truly, but I can't help you.' With that she clicked off and Sam was left holding the receiver of the phone.

'Great,' Sam muttered. It was Thursday afternoon and in less than half an hour she was supposed to attend a special staff meeting. Everyone at the station was on pins and needles. The police had installed taps and tracers on the phones, the staff was warned not to say a word about a link between Dr. Sam's *Midnight Confessions* and the serial killer, but somehow the word had leaked out. As if she were Pandora and had set Chaos free, the city blamed her for the monster who was stalking its streets.

WSLJ had been besieged with calls. The press wanted interviews. Listeners demanded information. The phone lines never stopped flashing.

George Hannah was thrilled. The audience for *Midnight Confessions* had grown seemingly exponentially overnight. It was the one show to listen to, part of daily conversation at Café du Monde over beignets and café au lait, or the buzz in the bars on and off Bourbon Street, or part of the evening news or watercooler conversation in the business district. Cab drivers, oil workers, bartenders, accountants, college kids – they all had an interest in *Midnight Confessions*. Samantha Leeds, AKA Dr. Sam was the Big Easy's newfound celebrity, more infamous than famous. Yes, George Hannah was beside himself, and the rumors of his selling the station for an obscene sum ran rampant down the 'aorta' and raced through the crooked hallways of the station.

Eleanor was worried sick. She wanted to cancel the show. Popularity was all well and good, but this insanity was too much.

Melba couldn't keep up with the phone lines.

Gator was sullen as opposed to Ramblin' Rob's amusement at 'the whole darned thing. You've created a damned sideshow, Sam, my girl,' he'd said early in the week as he'd clapped her on the back and laughed so hard he'd ended up in a coughing fit that sounded as if his lungs were about to explode.

Tiny was run ragged and Melanie, looking tired, complained of being overworked, needing a raise and wanting a bigger part of the show – better yet, her own show would be nice.

Sam had been offered a job at another radio station in town and some kind of media agent in Atlanta had phoned her, suggesting that there were bigger markets, that she might want to move to New York or LA.

Which wouldn't be a bad idea, considering. If she moved back to the West Coast she could be near her father. *And thousands of miles from Ty.* That thought made her wince. She'd come to love him, there was just no doubt about it, and in the past couple of weeks he'd become an integral part of her life – him and that big, slow-moving dog of his – had moved in for the most part. She didn't kid herself that he loved her; no, he was protecting his interests and absolving some of the guilt he felt because he was certain he'd stirred up this whole mess.

All in all, Sam's life had become a madhouse.

And a killer was stalking the streets.

A killer who had remained silent for nearly a week.

But he hadn't gone away, Sam was sure of it. He was biding his time, watching, ever-present, ready to strike again. She sensed it every time she picked up the phone, every instant she pressed one of the blinking lights on her console, every night when the sun went down.

It was just a matter of time.

Sam had attended Leanne Jaquillard's funeral, a small event with most of the girls from the Boucher Center in attendance. Leanne's mother, Marletta, had been in the tiny, hot chapel near the river, and when Sam had tried to give her condolences, Marletta had turned a cold shoulder. Marletta hadn't been as openly hostile as Estelle Faraday had been years before at Annie Seger's funeral, but the message was the same: Marletta blamed Samantha for her daughter's death. In this case Sam couldn't argue. If Leanne hadn't known her, chances were she'd be alive today.

The police had thought the murderer might attend the funeral and they'd had undercover cops inside the church and hidden cameras taking pictures of the small group of mourners.

John hadn't made an appearance.

Or no one saw him.

In the meantime Sam spent days poring over her notes, her nights in Ty's arms. They made love as if each night would be their last, and Sam wouldn't let herself think where the relationship would lead, if anywhere. It was doomed, started on lies, based on a mutual need to bring the killer to justice.

In her waking hours, when not preparing for the show and coming up with topics she hoped would entice John from hiding, she'd read through the information Ty had gathered on his family, inhaled everything she could about serial killers and the psychology of murder, then tried to make sense of the clues she had as to 'John's' identity and his motivation. And what was with the dark glasses? Did he always wear them? Was it part of his disguise? Sam had a theory.

She dialed the police station, left a message for Bentz and before she was finished checking her e-mail, received a call back.

'This is Rick Bentz. You called?' he asked.

'Yeah,' Sam said, 'I want to run something by you.'

'Shoot.'

'From the minute I received that publicity picture of me, the one with the eyes cut out, I had this feeling that whoever sent it to me was trying to give me a message, not just terror-ize me, but I thought there might be some sort of subliminal information that even he might not realize he was passing along.'

'Such as?'

'That he didn't want me to see him, or recognize him, that . . . there was some symbolism with the eyes being mutilated.' She picked up the composite picture sitting on the desk. 'And both eyewitnesses said the guy was wearing sunglasses, even though it was night, right?'

'Yep.'

'At first I thought it was just part of his disguise, but maybe there's another message here – that he can't stand to see what he's done, that he doesn't want to witness his own act.'

There was a pause. Bentz was mulling it over.

'And then he calls and there's all these religious references, and one of my first thoughts was that he was making reference to John Milton's *Paradise Lost*. He calls himself John, which could be anything from John Milton to John the Baptist, that part I'm not clear on.' She stared at the computer drawing. 'I had discarded the idea, but now I'm not so sure. Somehow I think he's referring to himself as Lucifer, that he was somehow thrown out of heaven or paradise and even though he's blaming me, I'd guess he's blaming himself.'

'This is your theory?' he said.

'Part of it, yes. I do have a degree in psychology,' she said, bristling. 'A doctorate. I'm not your usual dial-a-shrink.'

'Hey, I didn't say you were wrong. I'll give it some thought. And meanwhile, you keep safe. This guy's not done.'

'George should have canceled this.' Eleanor eyed the crowd packed into the courtyard of the old hotel. Palm trees glittered with thousands of lights, huge pots were filled with fragrant blossoms, and mannequins dressed in differing costumes loitered through the hallways, courtyard and hotel lobby. While waiters served champagne and hors d'oeuvres on large trays, music from a jazz combo positioned on the second of three balconies filtered over the crowd.

Champagne flowed from an ice sculpture of the station's logo and George Hannah, smooth in his tux and practiced smile, was in his element, working the crowd, shaking hands, making small talk, looking, as ever, for investors for WSLJ.

'He couldn't have canceled,' Sam said, 'it was too late. This had been planned for months.'

'Then he could have done it up right. Found a decent place to have it, even rented one of the plantations for the night. This place is falling down.' Eleanor's dark eyes flashed as she gazed up at the stucco walls and terraced rooms with their green shutters and filigreed railings. There were cracks in the plaster, some of the paint peeling.

'It's being renovated,' Sam pointed out, searching the crowd for Ty. 'I've seen work crews coming and going all afternoon while we were setting up.'

'This hotel should have been demolished fifty years ago.'

'It's part of New Orleans history.' Sam knew the reasons they'd chosen this smaller hotel. It had character, was situated in the French Quarter and was cheap. George had worked a deal. Which was good for the Boucher Center, who would reap the benefits. Yes, they'd had some complications from the work crews who were restoring and renovating the old rooms, but the hotel staff had bent over backward trying to accommodate the crowd and the workmen had cordoned off the reconstruction areas.

Conversation buzzed throughout the courtyard as the music played. Samantha managed to keep her cool, though she caught surreptitious glances cast her way from some of the guests. She understood why. Her name had been in the papers and on the local news, tied to the series of killings and the maniac who called her. She thought of Leanne. How the girl had looked forward to this event and now was dead. Sam's heart wrenched. Guilt weighed heavily on her mind. If only she'd called Leanne back sooner, if only she'd read her e-mail, if only . . . John hadn't known about her. Her jaw set.

How had John known how close she'd been to Leanne. Who the hell was he? Someone close to her? *Who?* Someone she considered a friend. Through an arbor, she saw Gator lurking near the bar and tossing back one drink after another. Tiny, looking awkward in a too-small tux standing away from the crowd while nervously smoking a cigarette. Ramblin' Rob was schmoozing with a local television hostess and Melanie, in gold lame and five inch heels, was keeping a close watch on every move George Hannah made.

Renee and Anisha, dressed up in high heels and long dresses, practically beamed as they, along with the directors of the center, explained about the programs to the guests who inquired.

Leanne should be here.

Sam tried to ignore the guilt that had been her constant companion since the girl's death.

She's dead because she knew you. Murdered by a psychotic maniac.

'Don't go there,' Eleanor advised as if reading her mind. She, too, was looking at the knot of people collecting around the table for the Boucher Center. 'I know what you're thinking. You couldn't help it.'

'I don't know. I think that if I would have responded to her, called her back sooner or did *some*thing different, she would be alive today.'

'Don't beat yourself up,' Eleanor advised, though she looked nervous and drawn despite her makeup, jewelry and shimmering black dress. She'd insisted upon plainclothes policemen and Bentz had agreed. Hotel security was supposed to be mingling through the crowd and yet Sam had the sinking sensation that if John wanted to be here, he would be. The composite picture in the paper wouldn't be a deterrent, if anything, she thought, trying to second guess him, the fact that the police had some idea of what he looked like would present a challenge. She spotted Bentz, tugging at the collar of his white shirt, looking uncomfortable standing guard in one doorway. Across the courtyard, Montoya was leaning against a pillar and surveying the crowd.

'Try to enjoy yourself,' Eleanor advised.

'You, too.'

'I'll smile if you will,' Eleanor said and managed to do just that as George Hannah approached and introduced her to some parish officials.

Sam forced a grin even though she noticed two people she would rather avoid. Her ex-husband was parting the crowd and heading in her direction while Trish LaBelle was holding court near the bar.

'Samantha!' Jeremy called and she gritted her teeth as he reached her and brushed a familiar kiss across her cheek.

'Don't,' she warned.

'Why not?'

'Just don't.' She saw a flash of anger in his eyes and something else, something darker. 'It makes me uncomfortable.' Where the devil was Ty?

'A kiss on the cheek? After what's been going on with you? For the love of Christ, Sam, I would have thought you would take any friend you could get.'

'I have to draw the line somewhere.'

'So you start with ex-husbands?'

'I only have one,' she reminded him sharply as he snagged a glass of champagne from a tray.

'So far.'

'Ever.'

'You know, Sam, in my professional opinion, all this bitterness indicates that you're still not over me.'

'Can it, Jeremy. That's a crock. You and I both know it. Now, what is it you want? Didn't you say something about there being something going on with me? What's that?' The combo, joined by a smokey-voiced singer, lit into a slow rendition of 'Fever.'

'You've collected a stalker. One who might be a serial killer. It's been reported on the news and in the papers. Why do you think there's such a big turn-out tonight?'

She felt suddenly sick inside. Maybe because she was too close to her ex-husband, or maybe because she'd thought the same thing herself. The people weren't here to support the charity event so much as gawk at her.

Jeremy sipped from his glass and waved at someone across the sea of guests. 'At least you've got what you always wanted,' he said. 'Fame, or, well infamy and that's good news not only for you, but the station as well.'

'Good news? Women are dead, Jeremy. As in never coming back. I don't know how anyone could construe that as good news.' With that she turned and slid through a group of women who were talking local politics. Samantha wasn't interested but she did want to escape Jeremy.

'Are you okay?' Melanie's voice caught up with her. Turning, she found her assistant staring at her. 'You look like you've seen a ghost.'

'Just the ghost of marriage past and believe me, it was hideous,' Sam replied.

'So where's the new man in your life – Ty?' Melanie asked.

'Hopefully on his way.' From the corner of her eye, Sam caught a glimpse of George Hannah locked in an animated conversation with Trish LaBelle. Melanie was watching the scene as well and her expression hardened just a bit. 'What about you? Where's the new boyfriend?'

'Busy,' Melanie said with a sigh. 'As usual.'

'I'd like to meet him.'

'You will . . . sometime,' she said vaguely just as Ty appeared beneath the arched entrance and Sam felt her pulse jump just a bit. He spied her and made a bee-line in her direction. Gone were the disreputable jeans and T-shirts, in their stead was a black tuxedo.

'Time for me to disappear,' Melanie said with a trace of envy. 'The he-man cometh.' She slipped past a huge pot overflowing with heady blossoms, then edged around a mannequin dressed in antebellum splendor just as Ty reached Samantha.

'Sorry I'm late. I got held up. Navarrone. The guy's timing leaves a lot to be desired, then traffic was a bitch.' He caught the stem of a wineglass balanced upon a tray carried by a slim, bored-looking waiter.

'I managed to survive without you,' she teased.

'Did you? Hmm.' His eyes held hers for just an instant. 'And here I thought you'd be pining away for me.' A slow, sexy smile crawled across his face.

'Dreamer.'

The band struck up another song but it faded quickly, as if the speakers had suddenly given out. Few people noticed as conversation droned, but Ty glanced up at the balcony. 'Technical problems,' he said watching as the bass player fiddled with the amplifier.

'Shouldn't be. Half the people in the station can handle this kind of equipment. Rob, George, Melanie, Tiny, even I know how to work the basic stuff.'

A few more people seemed to notice that the music had stopped and Eleanor headed toward Tiny, gesturing toward the second story. Tiny turned for the stairs but not before a screeching of a microphone, feedback of some sort, caught all the guests' attention.

'What the devil?'

Music began to play, but not from the band, no it was the first chord of 'A Hard Day's Night.'

'Oh, no,' Sam said, her heart thundering.

The music played and faded quickly, then Sam's voice filled the tightly packed arena. '*Good evening, New Orleans and welcome to* Midnight Confessions . . .'

'Did you tape this?' Ty demanded.

'No.' She saw George Hannah stop talking and Eleanor chase after Tiny. The courtyard was instantly quiet. '. . . *tonight we're going to be discussing. . . .*' then Sam's voice faded. She felt two hundred pair of eyes upon her. '*. . . sacrifice and . . . retribution . . .*'

He's taped together some of my shows, she thought, her heart racing wildy, her eyes scanning the crowd. He was here. She knew it. But where? She searched the entrances and balconies . . . where the hell was he?

Tiny was climbing to the balcony and Eleanor had turned her attention toward Sam. Marching through the crowd, she glared at Sam. 'Did you know anything about this?'

'Of course not.'

'Get her out of here,' she ordered Ty.

'*This is* Midnight Confessions *and so I invite you to call in . . . what's on your mind, New Orleans? Let me know . .*'

'What the hell's going on?' George was looking straight at Eleanor. 'Is this someone's idea of a sick joke?'

'You tell me,' Eleanor shot back as Bentz, talking into a walkie talkie, joined them.

'Find out where he's broadcasting from,' he said, snapping off the handset and glaring at Eleanor. 'We'll need to get everyone out of here – I've got backup coming and we'll usher everyone into the parking lot across the street.'

George stepped forward. Got in the detective's face. 'You can't have our guests treated like cattle!'

'Have you ever sacrificed yourself?'

'Watch me.' Bentz snapped his fingers to a uniformed cop. 'I want the names and addresses of everyone who walked into the building in the last week. I'm talking construction crew, hotel staff, guests, delivery men, anyone. Now, let's get going.' Already people were moving toward the doors.

Bentz's radio crackled and he snapped it on. 'Okay, I'll be there.' He snapped the handset off and explained. 'Looks like we found the source.' He started toward a stairwell and Sam was on his heels. Glancing over his shoulder, he said, 'Police business. You stay.'

'No way. This is about me.'

Bentz whirled. Sweat dotted his brow and his face was florid. 'You'll damned well do what I say. Until I find out that the scene is safe and secure and the crime-scene team has had a chance to check it out, you stay here.' He glanced at Ty. 'Make sure she obeys.'

He turned again and left Dr. Sam sputtering. Damned fool woman. Didn't she know how dangerous this was? He took the steps down to a basement room where several cops were standing guard.

'This it?'

'Looks like,' one of the plainclothes cops said. 'An old storage room, had been cleared out for the construction.'

But it wasn't empty tonight. A tape player connected to wires running into the walls was on the floor and seated in a folding chair in the middle of the room was a mannequin, stripped naked, wearing only a Mardi Gras mask, a red wig and a rosary knotted around her throat.

'Jesus,' Bentz whispered as he stepped into the dank room.

Using gloves he removed the red wig, then the mask. 'Holy shit.' The mannequin's eyes had been blackened and gouged to resemble the mutilated bills.

Bentz was certain Samantha Leeds would be next.

32

Nearly a week later, Sam was at her desk in the station, reading her ever-expanding e-mail and trying to survive the aftershocks of the party. The police had no suspects, though most people thought someone posing as a construction worker could have entered the building. One of the mannequins had been taken from the floor and stashed in the basement and someone with a rudimentary knowledge of the PA system had jerry-rigged the tape player into the amps. The police had questioned everyone in attendance and all the hotel and construction workers. Ty had been second guessing the police and holing up with Navarrone while Sam had spent every waking minute poring over texts on serial killers, psychotics, anything that would pertain to John. Rick Bentz had stepped up the security around her, both in the city and at her home.

Yet John had remained silent. Never once calling the station. Never taking credit for his actions.

She shivered as she thought of the mannequin with its blackened, sightless eyes and nude body. It had been left as a personal message to her.

A threat.

Or a promise.

And the ratings for *Midnight Confessions* continued to soar through the roof. George Hannah was beside himself and the police had been hinting that the entire scene had been staged, a ploy by the owner of WSLJ to increase the audience.

Sam didn't think so, though she was nearly certain two forces were at work. The monster whose objective was to kill and some-one else who liked to play head games – or was it one person with a split personality? Someone here at the station who was connected with Annie? For God's sake, *who*?

She heard footsteps in the hallway. A minute later Melanie popped her head into the office. 'Show time,' she said, her long curls catching in the light. 'It's time for' – Melanie wiggled two fingers of each hand and lowered her voice for emphasis – 'the meeting.'

'What're you doing here at this time of day?' Sam asked, pushing her dark thoughts aside. 'I came here because I was called in, but don't you have a social life?'

Melanie grinned widely. Her gold eyes twinkled. 'I've got a *great* social life.'

'The new mystery man?'

'Mmmm.' With a Cheshire cat smile she couldn't contain, Melanie nodded. 'I think he might just be "the one."'

'This sounds serious,' Sam observed.

'I'm keeping my fingers crossed and all my toes!' Melanie was practically beaming, and Sam was reminded that she was barely twenty-five.

'So who is the guy? Anyone I know?' Sam asked.

Melanie shook her head, but a naughty glimmer shone in her gold eyes. 'Nah.'

'So when do I get to meet him?'

'Soon,' Melanie said quickly. 'I'll bring him around. Now, you'd better get to that meeting. Boy George doesn't like to be kept waiting.'

'Don't let him hear you call him that.'

'Never,' Melanie swore.

Sam wasn't looking forward to the meeting. Something was up. She felt a new sense of anticipation crackling in the air. Sam had the sneaking suspicion that the popularity of her show, nefarious as it was, would be the topic.

Since the party, WSLJ had been besieged with phone calls from the press wanting interviews, and, moreover, the calls to Sam's program had doubled and tripled. New Orleans was electrified by the show, hundreds of heretofore disinterested listeners sought Samantha's counsel and wanted to hear their own voices echoing over the airwaves. Others sought their own form of infamy, phoning in, pretending to be 'John' or another nutcase. Copycats were slinking out of the city's narrow, dark alleys in droves.

Melanie was going nuts screening the calls, and Detective Bentz had ordered a double-blind. Any and all calls received from 9 P.M. to 2 A.M. were put through a second screen. Melanie screened the calls before a policewoman assigned by Bentz would answer as if she were Dr. Sam. Every phone call was taped and could be traced.

And so far John had remained silent.

The police were confident he would be caught, but even the press releases and the composite computer sketch of the suspect had yielded no arrests. John seemed to have gone underground and, to be honest, the drawing was a little too much like everyman. Any twenty-five to thirty-five, six-foot man with a decent build and dark hair was a potential suspect.

'So put in a good word for me,' Melanie said with a smile. 'You know, tell George that I'm your overworked, underpaid, highly educated and very loyal assistant who's willing to sell her soul for a shot at her own program.'

'I'll remind him,' Sam said dryly as she walked into one of the larger rooms in the station, the library really, but one Ramblin' Rob referred to as the 'Bored Room,' whenever George, the sales force, and any other execs held a meeting.

'Samantha, come in, come in,' George said, as Melanie closed the door behind her.

Dressed in a gray business suit, white shirt, and splashy tie designed by Jerry Garcia, George sat at one end of the table, Eleanor, a dour expression on her face, sitting at his right arm. A few folders and notebooks were scattered on the table. 'No reason to beat around the bush,' George said as Sam pulled out a chair directly across from him and settled into it. 'I'm looking to expand your show.'

'For the record, I'm not in agreement,' Eleanor countered. 'I think it would be a mistake. George here is looking at ratings, advertising dollars, the bottom line, but I think there's more to it than that.'

'Of course there is.' George slid Sam his most disarming smile. 'I'm not oblivious to the down side of what's going on, but I think we should take advantage of the situation.'

'You mean exploit it,' Eleanor said, her dark eyes flashing. 'This isn't a "situation," it's a damned nightmare. Sam's gotten her house broken into, threatening letters and calls not to mention that damned cake or the mannequin at the party for Christ's sake. And now we know that the guy who's behind it is a murderer, a butcher, a serial killer! This isn't about ratings as much as it is about terrorization. If I were you, I'd be thinking about pulling the plug on the show, at least temporarily, until this all dies down. I wouldn't be considering expansion. This joker out there means business. He calls in on line two – as if he's got a list of our private numbers. He calls in after hours. He goddamned murders women.'

'Prostitutes,' George qualified.

'Women,' she shot back. 'You might have noticed the police crawling all over this place because a serial killer is somehow involved. And you want to profit from this – to *expand* hours?' She skewered him with one of her Eleanor I'm-not-taking-any-of-this-nonsense looks. 'What we need here is increased security and I'm not talking about the rent-a-cop you hired. For the time being we've got the police, and they're tracing calls, but we need to make sure some of the security measures they've employed aren't temporary. I want a permanent system to trace calls and every lock on this building changed. The way I figure it, a few weeks ago someone got in the kitchen through the balcony. The police agree. So we've put a new lock on that door, but what's to say he can't get back in? I mean we're talking about a murderer, for God's sake!'

She took a breath.

George leaned back in his chair and threw down his pen. 'That's what I love about you, Eleanor, always stressing the positive.'

'There isn't anything positive about this.'

'But it's what the audience wants.'

'To hell with the audience. I'm talking about the safety of my – *our* – employees.'

George rolled his lips over his teeth and sucked in his breath. 'Samantha, maybe you could help me out here. I'm talking about increasing your audience, expanding the show to a full week and making it worth your while. I'm talking increasing from here in New Orleans to every major market east of the Rockies.'

Sam lifted a brow.

'Okay, maybe that's an exaggeration, but it could be a goal.'

'Jesus H. Christ, do you know what you're saying?' Eleanor asked.

'You know, Eleanor, I don't pay you to argue with me.'

'Like hell you don't. That's exactly why you pay me. To keep your goddamned feet on the ground. To keep you in touch with reality.'

'Okay, so I've got it. Your point's well taken, duly noted, but I still think we need to take care of this opportunity. We'll double the security, change the locks, have escorts walk Samantha to her car or drive her home, whatever it takes. Of course the safety of the staff comes first.'

Eleanor leaned back in her chair and folded her arms over her ample chest, but she didn't argue, just said, 'Make sure you mean it, George, that this isn't just lip service.'

'It isn't. I swear.'

She didn't comment.

'Look,' Sam said, deciding to nip this in the bud. 'Personally I'm not ready to expand to seven days a week, if that's what you're thinking.' She was run ragged as it was, and the thought of seven nights behind the microphone was too much – even temporarily. 'Not unless you hire someone else to share the load.'

'Melanie could do it. With a little seasoning, I suppose,' Eleanor offered up, though she was obviously lukewarm to the idea.

'Not Melanie.' George shook his head. 'We lost listeners when you were on vacation.'

'Well, *some*one.'

'No one can take your place. The audience identifies with you, Sam. I know it would be longer hours, a big commitment on your part, but I'd make it worth your while – a significant raise and bonus if the expanded hours worked, after that you could share the booth with someone . . . maybe even Melanie or Ramblin' Rob or Gator, until the audience trusted them and they could wing it alone a few nights a week.'

'Rob and Gator aren't psychologists,' Sam argued. 'They're radio personalities. The show would lose credibility.'

'Okay, so what about Trish LaBelle over at WNAB? I've heard rumors that she's not happy with her format. She might be interested.'

'Trish LaBelle,' Sam repeated, stunned. Trish's style was harsh. Judgmental. She called it, 'shooting from the hip' or 'telling it like it is.' But Sam thought she went too far, humiliated the listeners who called in, ridiculed their problems with her snide sense of humor.

Eleanor clucked her tongue. 'No way would Trish LaBelle be second fiddle to anyone. Not in a million years. Besides that the woman's poison. I don't like her style. No siree, that's one can of worms I don't want to open.' She skewered George with a harsh glare. 'And don't give me any of that you've "heard rumors" garbage. I know you've talked to her, that this is already in the works.'

The corners of George's mouth tightened. 'I have to do what I think is best for the station.'

'Then you'd better start by making sure your employees are safe.'

'I already said I'd handle that, and I offered the job to Sam, but she doesn't want a seven-day-a-week job. We just went through our options with people already on staff, but' – he turned his palms toward the recessed lights and spread his fingers – 'Samantha doesn't think they're professional enough, that they don't have the right degrees.'

'They don't,' Sam agreed.

'So I suggested Trish.'

'She doesn't either,' Sam said quickly. 'She's got a sociology degree with a minor in psychology.'

What little was left of George's smile disappeared.

'Okay, but that's good enough for WNAB, and I think it's good enough here. What Trish LaBelle does have is AM listeners who might follow her and switch to FM here with *Midnight Confessions*. I think the two of you could make a powerhouse team. Now, you can go it alone, or take on Trish as your partner.'

'Wait a minute, wait a minute,' Eleanor cut in. 'You make it sound like this is a done deal, that Trish is already on board.'

'Not yet, but I'm negotiating with her. It all depends on Sam, but one way or another, we're going to capitalize on the success of *Midnight Confessions*. You, Samantha, have to decide whether you're dedicated enough to run it alone, or if you can share the limelight with Trish.' He leaned forward and placed his elbows on the table. 'One way or another, we're expanding the format to include weekends.'

'So this meeting wasn't about options,' Eleanor said, her feathers way beyond ruffled. 'It was just a formality.'

'And it's over.' He rapped his knuckles on the polished surface of the table to accentuate his point. 'Let me know what you want.' Standing abruptly, he tugged on his tie, then strode out of the room.

Eleanor sighed and threw up her hands. 'Sometimes I wonder why I stay.'

'Because you love it.'

'Then maybe I should hire you because I must need help, serious, deep, psychological help.'

'I don't believe it,' Sam said as they walked into the outer lobby, where Melba was handling calls. 'You're the sanest person I know.'

'Oh, God, then we're all in trouble.'

'I'll be back tonight,' Sam said, checking her watch. She had hours before the show and a million errands to run. She didn't expect to run into Melanie lurking in the lobby of the building.

'Well?' Melanie asked, as they passed the security guard and walked into the blazing afternoon sun. 'What's up?'

'They're thinking of expanding the show.'

Melanie's grin was instantly wide, lighting up her whole face. 'I knew it! That's great news! So – how are they going to do it? Longer hours, more days a week?'

'More days, but it's still up in the air.'

'But you can't possibly handle it all yourself.'

'I told them as much.' Sam scrounged in her purse, found a pair of sunglasses and shoved them onto the bridge of her nose.

'What about me? Did you put in a good word?'

'That I did, but . . . well, George has some ideas of his own.'

'Ideas?' the girl said, stopping short, suddenly deflated. 'Oh, shit, I knew it. He's going to give the show to someone else isn't he?' She kicked at a pebble lying on the cobblestones of the street and sent the stone hurtling against a trash barrel. 'Son of a bitch. Son of a friggin' bitch!'

'Maybe you should talk to Eleanor,' Sam said, surprised at Melanie's vehemence. Disappointment she understood, but this was out-and-out rage.

'After all I've done, all the hours I've worked, the damned sacrifices I've made!'

Sam's heart nearly stopped at the term. 'Sacrifices?' she repeated, telling herself she was being overly sensitive. 'But it's your job.'

Melanie didn't hear her; she was already striding back to the building in her three-inch platforms and gauzy print dress, muttering under her breath, 'This is the last friggin' straw. I've had it.'

Leaning back in his desk chair, Bentz looked at the pathetic man before him.

David Ross was scared. Nearly shaking. 'I think I need a lawyer,' he said, sweat beading on his brow, his hands clasped so tightly, his knuckles showed white. His hair was unruly, his shirt wrinkled. He looked like he hadn't slept in two weeks.

'You came on your own volition.'

'I know, I know.' Ross swallowed hard. 'I just didn't know it would go this far, I mean . . .' He closed his eyes and gathered himself. 'I'm worried about Samantha Leeds. I am, er, was her fiancé. And . . . well, we had a falling-out, tried to patch things up in Mexico and it didn't work. I was kinda desperate and I did some things I shouldn't have.' He reached into his pocket and withdrew a set of keys and a wallet. 'These were returned to me while we were in Mexico – I don't even know if everything's there, but I didn't return them to Sam and when this trouble started, I kept everything figuring that she would get scared, come running back to me and . . . well, it didn't happen and I guess I didn't know Samantha as well as I thought I did.' His smile trembled. 'She's tough. Anyway . . .' He cleared his throat. '. . . I knew that someone was harassing her, I heard about the calls and, I admit, I thought about it myself, even dialed her show a couple of times, but never had the nerve to go through with it. I figured she'd recognize my voice, y'know.'

'Sure,' Bentz said, trying to figure out just what it was that made David Ross tick. He chewed his gum slowly and waited. He knew the guy wasn't the killer – the blood types didn't match and Ross didn't look a whole lot like the composite, not really. But the guy had some guilt he wanted to heave off his chest, and Bentz was ready to listen.

'Anyway, I was hoping she'd come back to me and it all back-fired and now . . . now there's a killer on the loose and I've heard that he might be the same guy who's calling the show . . . and that someone Samantha knew was murdered. I, um, I'm scared.'

'So you're turning yourself in because you forgot to give an ex-girlfriend back her keys?' Bentz leaned forward, placing his elbows on the desk, on top of reports that would make the likes of David Ross piss his pants.

'I just want to clear my name.'

'Does it need clearing?'

Ross's face flushed. 'I didn't need to come down here. Matter of fact, maybe it was a mistake,' he said, growing some balls. 'But I wanted to set things straight.'

Bentz believed him. The only way David Ross was a part of the murders was if the setup had been murder-for-hire, if he were the guy someone was pulling the strings, a man using the killer as his puppet, but serial killers didn't work that way – no the actual kill was the thrill, and if it was murder-for-hire the other women wouldn't now be dead, and Ross wouldn't have shown up with evidence. He wasn't 'John' the Rosary Killer as Bentz had come to think of him. Not only had one of the mannequins at the Boucher Center party been wearing a rosary but sure enough the ligature around each victim's neck was the same pattern as the beads on a rosary and the strange mark on Leanne's Jaquillard's throat was probably a crucifix. 'Anything else you want to tell us?' he asked Ross.

'Yeah. Get him, okay?' Ross's nostril's flared as if he smelled something bad. 'Arrest the bastard or kill him, but get him off the streets. Before he gets to Samantha.'

'That's it. I quit!' Melanie announced, unable to keep the tremor from her voice. She was so mad, so damned mad, and as she stood in front of Eleanor Cavalier's desk, she could barely keep from shaking.

'I'll call you back,' Eleanor said, then hung up and turned her dark eyes on Melanie.

'Sit down and let's talk about this. You can't just up and quit, you know. You're required to give two weeks' notice and—'

'No way. Not after the way I've been treated. When I took this job I was told that there was room for advancement, that with my degree and background in psychology, I'd be in line for my own program.'

'Someday,' Eleanor said, again waving her into the chair on the opposite side of the desk. Like she was going to try and placate her. 'It could happen.'

'Could,' Melanie repeated with a snort. '*Could!* Jesus, Eleanor, I've got a bachelor's degree and I know all the technical stuff inside and out, as well as Tiny, for God's sake! And didn't I take over for Samantha when she was gone. Was I so bad?'

'No, of course not.'

'And who do you call when she's sick? Huh? Me.' She curved her thumb at her chest and shook it. 'Oh, what's the use? I'm outta here!' she said, and whirled on her heels, nearly careening into Ramblin' Rob in the middle of the aorta. The old coot had, no doubt, been eavesdropping. Well, he made her skin crawl. Come to think of it, everyone did. George Hannah was an old lech and Gator, well, he had his own private agenda. Melanie didn't want to think what kind of pervert he was, what he did behind closed doors, but she could just tell. His eyes . . . they creeped her out. Come to think of it, she didn't know why she hung out here and she'd been talking to Trish LaBelle, maybe she could get a job over at WNAB. Yeah, that was it. Then she wouldn't have to put up with lumbering Tiny. God, he was worthless, nearly drooling every time he was around Samantha.

She walked to the stairs and thundered down the steps, her hair flying, her temper escalating as she thought about how much she'd given to this damned station, how much of her life she'd poured into *Midnight Confessions*. Of course, no one knew just how creative she'd been. Not only had she been the dutiful, Johnny-on-the-spot employee, always wearing a smile, always busting her butt for everyone else, but she'd done a little extra, given herself a little more edge toward Sam's job, or so she'd thought.

Shouldering open the door to the stairs, she flew by that fat slob of a security guard and, for once, didn't bother to wave. If the old fart really knew what she was about, how she'd plotted Dr. Sam's demise, only to have it blow up in her face.

Stepping onto the street she felt a blast of hot air and scrambled in her purse for her shades. Jesus, it was hot, maybe she should move to another city, a cooler one, less muggy . . . but she couldn't. Not yet. She'd gained a reputation around town.

One you might just have crammed down the toilet by not giving your notice.

Harsh sunlight glinted off the pavement as she headed toward the parking garage where her little hatchback was waiting, all the while considering the unfairness of what had happened.

No one at WSLJ could understand how much she'd given, how much she'd sacrificed, how much she'd plotted her career path.

She cringed just a bit remembering just how far she'd gone. But then, she'd been given her opportunity on a silver platter when Sam had asked Melanie to watch her house and her cat in Cambrai.

Melanie had jumped at the chance. Once Sam was on her way to Mexico, Melanie had become ensconced in the cozy house on Lake Pontchartrain. While there she'd snooped through 'the doctor's' things, even found the files on Annie Seger in that creepy, bug-infested attic. When Melanie had been alone, she'd tried on some of Sam's clothes.

Melanie had felt decadent and wild and had invited her new boyfriend over to christen Sam's bed. She'd worn one of Samantha's nightgowns, a lacy white thing with thin straps, then lit candles around the room. What had happened afterward had been an orgy the likes of which she'd never seen since and made her ache inside as she sat in the car. Just being in Samantha's big four-poster had seemed to turn her boyfriend on. Also, the knowledge that Melanie had whispered into his ear, that a jealous lover had been rumored to have killed his girlfriend in that very house had seemed to give her lover a rush.

Later, when Melanie had told him about Annie Seger, he'd hatched a plot that had been daring and dark – just like him. He'd encouraged Melanie to gaslight Sam, to leave the note in her car, to rig up the mannequin at the benefit for the Boucher Center, to disguise her voice and create a tape saying she was Annie – they'd even taped the recording on Sam's machine, with one of her blank audio tapes. Later he'd played that tape when he'd called in. The result had freaked Sam out.

Oh, yes, he'd been good. He'd urged Melanie on, advised her that to get ahead, she would have to sacrifice and use any means possible to attain her ultimate goal. Though she'd been a little unnerved by his calls as 'John,' she'd known he'd done it out of love for her, so that Sam would quit and Melanie would be promoted to hosting *Midnight Confessions.*

Only it hadn't happened. Sam had hung in with the station and the program, largely through Melanie's efforts, had increased its audience. Dr. Sam's star had soared into the stratosphere, to the point that the powers that be at WSLJ wanted Sam to expand the program without promoting Melanie at all.

Shit.

It was not only unfair, it was stupid. Melanie could handle Sam's job with her eyes closed. She was younger, smarter, and willing to do whatever it took to promote herself and the show.

Sweating profusely, she marched over the hot sidewalk, then jaywalked to the parking structure. Bee-lining to her car, she ignored the dirt and oil that had collected on the concrete floor. Inside, the hatchback was an oven. Melanie didn't care. Rolling down the driver's window, she blew out a breath of hot, angry air. She needed advice, solid advice, from someone who cared about her, about her career, about her needs.

There was only one person.

She grabbed her cell phone, and punched out the autodial for her boyfriend's cell phone. She'd talk to him, explain what was going on, and maybe he'd calm her down. They could get together and celebrate her newfound freedom.

Maybe, if she was lucky, she'd even get laid. He'd been a little lax in that department lately. She figured it was from the coke, but tonight she might get lucky.

Waiting for the connection, she fingered her keys and eyed the replica of a Louisiana license plate emblazoned with her name. Her boyfriend had given it to her after borrowing her car when she'd first met him. She fingered the raised letters as he answered.

'Hello?' His voice was a balm.

'Oh, God, I'm glad I caught you.' Fighting tears of frustration, she added, 'I've had a helluva day and I just quit.'

'Why?'

'The station's expanding the show. *Midnight Confessions* will be aired every friggin' night of the week, but they don't want me to host any of it. Oh, no, it's either Dr. Sam or no one.' She leaned back against the seat. 'It sucks.'

'Then you did the right thing.'

'I hope so. I'm calling WNAB right now.'

'Why don't you wait on that? I'll come pick you up and we can go out? What'd'ya say?'

'I might be lousy company.'

'I doubt it.' He laughed. 'You know, I have just the thing to get you out of your bad mood.'

'What's that.'

'A surprise.' His voice was low. Sexy.

She felt a thrill. The dark side of him appealed to her. 'Will I like it?'

'Let's put it this way, it'll be a night you remember for the rest of your life. I promise.'

Standing in front of the statue of Andrew Jackson, Father John clicked off his cell phone. He smiled to himself. Things were progressing perfectly . . . almost as if divine intervention had been involved.

Through his Ray-Bans he watched a mime entertaining passersby just outside the gate to the park. He'd witnessed Melanie marching out of the building housing WSLJ, had expected her to call and had known that she'd want to see him. But then she always did. For all her bristly, independent exterior, she was really weak and needy, a single girl who was estranged from a family in Philadelphia. An easy target.

Absently he stared at St. Louis Cathedral. Its white walls were nearly blinding in the fierce sunlight, its high spires and dark crosses knifing in Christian defiance against a clear cerulean sky. Inside were the devoted. Or the curious.

Yes, he thought as he strolled along the path toward one of the wrought iron gates guarding the small park, Melanie Davis had been more than accommodating and now her purpose had been fulfilled. She'd aided and abetted him in reaching his ultimate goals without realizing exactly who he was. She'd been so willing, so easily manipulated, an oh, so willing pawn. He'd sought her out upon learning that she was working at the radio station as an assistant to Dr. Sam. He'd approached her in a bar on Bourbon Street and charmed her. Within days, he'd uncovered her weakness, brought to light her incredible ambition, and he'd used it against her. To his advantage. For Samantha Leeds's downfall.

It had been so simple.

But then it always was, he thought, as he walked past the mime's open suitcase with its paltry few dollars. A flock of pigeons scurried and fluttered out of his path.

As easily as he'd uncovered Melanie's weakness, it had been far simpler to figure out his prisoner's need. His captive had developed a hunger for any chemical that could be swallowed, snorted, smoked or shot into the body, and Father John had willingly fed that craving, offering up substances that debilitated the body and left it weak. That was the secret, the key to success, to find one's enemies' weaknesses, unearth their appetites and feed their ravenous addictions, all in the guise of being helpful.

He turned from Decatur onto North Peters Street, increasing his pace. Night would soon fall. He welcomed the darkness, looked upon it with anticipation, for tonight Melanie Davis was to pay for her sins.

Walking past the Old French Market, he headed for the river, drinking in its heady, dank smell. He reached into his pocket, touching his sacred weapon, feeling the sharp tensile strength of the holy noose, knowing it wouldn't fail him. His heartbeat quickened as he crossed the streetcar tracks, then made his way up the grassy rise. Atop the levee he viewed the slow-moving Mississippi. God, she was magnificent. Wide. Dark. Ever moving. Seductive.

For a second he closed his eyes and let his thoughts tumble ahead. To the coming night. To Melanie Davis and his plans for her. His fingers tangled in the rosary – sweet, sweet instrument of death to those who sinned.

At this moment Melanie was expecting the surprise of her life.

What she didn't know, was it would be her last.

33

'Somethin's up,' Montoya said, edgy and nervous, his black hair gleaming under the harsh lights of Bentz's kitchen, where three rosaries were lying on the table beside a plastic tub and various dishes, saucers, plates, even old margarine containers held a few glittering beads.

'What's up? What do you mean?' Bentz picked up one of the beads and rolled it in his fingers. Plastic, the facets rounded.

Montoya reached into the fridge and grabbed a bottle of near beer. 'You got anything stronger?'

Bentz shook his head. 'If you want booze, there's a tavern two blocks down.'

'You're off duty.'

'I'm never off duty,' Bentz grumbled.

'Shit.' Montoya eyed his partner's's half-drunk cup of coffee on the counter, the near-empty glass pot pushed against the stove where a stale loaf of bread and a container of lite peanut butter was testament to Bentz's dinner. Montoya twisted off the cap of the bottle. 'This is un-American.'

'No fat, no booze, no nicotine. It's about growing older.'

'You're barely forty, for Christ's sake ... just don't tell me there's "no sex," okay, cuz I don't wanna hear it.' Montoya kicked out one of the kitchen chairs and took a seat. 'And what's this?' He motioned to the table where Bentz was conducting an experiment.

'What's it look like?' Bentz asked.

Montoya swilled half his bottle. 'A damned campfire project.'

'Guess again,' Bentz said.

'Okay, okay, I see the rosaries. This is about the weapon the killer uses. I thought we already established that. We checked the wounds, saw that this sick-assed creep strangles his victims with a rosary. Hell, he left one on the mannequin at the party. So he's a wacked-out Catholic. There are enough of them out there.'

'Watch it.' He pinned Montoya in his glare. 'I'm one.'

'Hey, me too, me too . . . well, I was.'

'You will be again,' Bentz predicted. 'We all go back.'

'Another aging thing?'

'Yeah. Now, take a look. This one's a duplicate of the one we found wrapped around the mannequin's neck.' Bentz wrapped the first rosary with its clear beads around his hands. Then he placed both hands in a big plastic tub and gave a little tug. Beads split off, singletons, those in segments, all flying into the plastic vessel. 'Not too strong,' he observed. 'Not meant to be used as a weapon.'

'We knew this, too.' Montoya reached into the tub and picked up three beads held together by thin wire. 'Okay, so where did he buy the superstrength version?'

'I'm betting he didn't.' Bentz held one of the beads up to the light, stared into the clear facets. 'My guess is that he made his own. Selected really sharp beads, sharp enough to cut skin, strung 'em together with some heavy-duty wire and probably prayed as he counted off the Hail Marys and Our Fathers.'

'Wouldn't it be easier to just use a rope or the wire?'

'Not symbolic enough. Our boy gets off on all of this . . . there's all sorts of undercurrents here . . . you know, I'm starting to think Samantha Leeds knows what she's talking about. She suggested the killer made some kind of reference to *Paradise Lost*. I think I'd better pick up a copy.'

'I might have the *Cliff's Notes*,' Montoya admitted, and when Bentz started to smile, 'Hey, I had a lot of shit to get through in college. So I used the notes and the Internet. It saved me a bundle on books.'

Bentz dusted his hands and reached for his coffee cup. 'You said somethin' was botherin' you.'

'Yeah. I've been tryin' to track down the two guys from Houston – Annie Seger's boyfriend and her brother. They're both supposed to live around here, right – one in White Castle, the other in Baton Rouge? Both have jobs and they're both AWOL. Missing in action. Why?' He took another swallow from the alcohol-free beer and made a face. 'I hate to say it, but I'm startin' to buy into Wheeler's theory that it has something to do with Annie Seger's death. Maybe she didn't commit suicide.'

'You think John killed her?'

'Yeah,' Montoya said, 'and I think he's either Kent Seger or Ryan Zimmerman.'

'Okay, then what about motive?' Bentz flashed him a mirthless smile. 'And don't try to sell me that it's all about money, cuz I'm not buyin'.'

'Me neither. Not this time. But there's something we don't know about Annie Seger,' Montoya said, then drained his bottle and set it on the table near the tub of glittering rosary beads, 'but we damned well better find out.' He climbed to his feet and asked, 'Where the hell are Zimmerman and Seger?'

'Good question.' One Bentz couldn't answer. Yet.

'I've got a bad feelin' about this.'

'Just now?' Bentz snorted. 'I've had a bad feelin' all along.'

Voice mail picked up. Ty didn't even get a chance to talk to Estelle Faraday. He just had to leave a damned message. Again. 'Estelle, this is Ty Wheeler. I've talked to the police here in New Orleans and given them all the information I have. If you haven't put two and two together yet, it looks like the serial killer here is somehow tied to Annie's death. Family secrets be damned, Estelle. People are dying. If you know anything about this and are holding back evidence, you're guilty, and the police will charge you with the appropriate crimes. This is serious. You can either talk to me or the New Orleans Police Department, but if another woman dies, I will personally hold you responsible. You've got my number.' He slammed the receiver down and walked into his living room. He'd dropped Sam off at the station an hour earlier, and her program was due to hit the airwaves in an hour.

He flipped on the radio, listening to the tail end of Gator Brown's program. Hot jazz flowed through the speakers, the kind of music that wound Ty up rather than calmed him down. But, then, tonight he was restless. On edge. Feeling the electricity of the storm rolling in. He checked his watch. Navarrone was supposed to meet him, share information with him.

But he hadn't shown up yet. Not that Ty was worried about him. Navarrone was a creature of darkness, felt more comfortable in the camouflage of the night after years of working with the CIA.

Whistling to his dog, Ty walked outside, felt the wind kicking up and watched the *Bright Angel* bob against her moorings. The moon was blocked by clouds, and the heat was oppressive. Muggy. He felt as if he was wearing a second thick, damp skin.

He thought about John, lurking somewhere in the depths of the city. Waiting. Ready to pounce.

So where are you, you son of a bitch, Ty wondered, as Sasquatch sniffed around the shrubbery. *And what the hell are you doing tonight?*

Estelle Faraday sat by the pool in the darkness. The water glowed a bright aquamarine, compliments of a single, flat submerged bulb. A tall, glass pitcher of cosmopolitans was sweating on the table and her stemmed glass, nearly drained of the pink concoction she'd claimed as her most recent favorite drink, was in one hand. It tasted more bitter than usual, tainted, but she didn't care. What possibly could be wrong with vodka? Sipping her drink, she tried to drive the demons from her head.

But they were still there, relentless, clawing and screaming at her brain.

She'd feared it would come to this, prayed that her worries were ill founded, but she knew now they weren't. Ty Wheeler's urgent messages on her voice mail convinced her. He wasn't going to give up. She'd suspected as much when he'd shown up here in Houston. Even so, she'd threatened him, foolishly hoping that he'd back off.

Instead, he'd called her bluff.

But then, he hadn't been the first.

Oh, she'd been so naive, she thought as the night closed in and she remembered her daughter – bright, beautiful, and attracted to the wrong kind of boys . . . not just the wrong kind, but boys she should never have been with.

And she'd gotten pregnant by one. It seemed a legacy in this family, a damning genetic flaw she'd passed on to her daughter.

Tears of regret and shame filled Estelle's eyes. She sipped her bitter drink, and when the glass was drained, poured another and swiped at her eyes with the back of her hand. No one was home. She was alone. Again. Even the maid had taken the night off to be with her children and grandchildren.

Dear God, how had she ended up alone? she wondered fuzzily. She'd had it all when she was younger. Good looks, money and a future as bright as a newly minted silver dollar. But she'd been headstrong and wanted to show her snobby parents she could make her own decisions.

She'd never loved Wally. She knew that now. She'd probably known it then, but he was a good-looking, witty boy from the wrong side of the tracks. Never mind that he hadn't gone to Yale or Harvard or even Stanford, oh, no, he hadn't even taken night courses at the local junior college. He'd been raw and wild and spent all his time working on motorcycles. But, in the beginning, he'd been kind to her at a time when kindness was as rare as a torrent in the desert.

Estelle had found Wally deliciously different. Her parents had been horrified. She'd never intended to marry him, of course, but circumstances had changed her goals.

'Don't kiss boys, Estelle,' her mother had warned her often enough when Estelle started high school. 'It's the devil's doing. Remember there are only two types of girls – bad and good. You'll never have any self-respect if you do any of those nasty things. Trust me. Be a good girl. You'll never regret it.'

But Estelle kissed plenty of boys and nothing bad had happened. In fact she'd liked kissing, especially when a boy pressed his tongue into her mouth. Oh, how she'd replayed those intimate kisses over and over in her mind. Though she'd felt a little naughty when her dates had progressed and boys had pawed at her, worming their fingers into her bra cups and stroking her breasts, she'd also liked the feel of her blood running hot, of that darkness between her legs aching. And when a boy had reached beneath her skirts and panties and touched her in that private spot, she'd tingled and gotten moist and wanted more. She'd acted like an animal, gasping and grinding her hips and *wanting*. She'd read about passion for years, hiding under the covers with a flashlight and feeling her face heat while between her legs she'd felt that funny, achy feeling that left her yearning for more and finally, as she began making out with boys, she realized there was a way to assuage that need.

So when she began to experiment and allowed a boy – after the fifth or sixth date and promises of love, of course – to touch her, she'd known it was a sin, one she couldn't really confess to the priest, but she couldn't stop herself. She enjoyed it, *craved* it, thought depraved thoughts about it and wanted it all the more. Unlike her mother's dire predictions, the boys were so attentive, so eager to kiss and touch her, so ready to tell her how beautiful she was, how they loved her.

Stupidly she'd believed them.

She'd lost her virginity at sixteen to a boy her mother had thought was the perfect match and afterwards, he'd never taken her out again, never called, and bragged to his friends about his conquest. Her mother had continually asked about Vincent, what had become of him, why she wasn't going out with him and she'd felt the first realization of what her mother had professed.

From then on, every boy wanted to do it with her. When she'd rebuffed them, they'd gotten angry, reminding her that she'd spread her legs for Vincent Miller.

In some respects Estelle had enjoyed scandalizing her mother. Until she'd relented and done it with a boy she really liked and turned up pregnant. Abortion was out of the question, and as she was a minor, she'd let her mother talk her into lying about 'taking a semester abroad at a private school' when in reality she only went as far as Austin, where she gave the baby up for adoption.

'It's the kindest thing,' her mother had insisted, and Estelle had made the single biggest mistake of her life. She'd gone away, had the boy, and watched as the doctor who'd delivered her firstborn had regarded her with cold, judgmental eyes and handed the squalling infant to a nurse who had whisked him away.

Foolishly Estelle had blamed her mother and upon returning to Houston found Oswald Seger. At least Wally had been kind. Considered her feelings. Hadn't pushed her, and when they had finally gone all the way, he'd called the next day and sent her a single red rose that she still remembered.

Wally had exhibited a romantic side, along with his love for all things mechanical, and as soon as she was eighteen, they'd eloped.

Kent had been born ten months later, Annie in the next couple of years. Her horrified parents had cut her off, only to reclaim her at the birth of their grandson. And the rest, as they say, had been history, a history she'd rather forget. She realized when the kids were little that she'd never be happy with an oil worker for a husband, that Wally's fascination with motorcycles and boats was coupled with his inability to balance a checkbook or save a nickel.

Fortunately she'd met Jason Faraday . . . well, she'd thought it was fortunate at the time. Now, as she finished her third cosmo and the alcohol seeped into her system, she wasn't so certain. There were other secrets, ones she'd never looked at too closely, ones that haunted her days as well as her nights. She couldn't survive another scandal . . . there had been far too many.

Head spinning, she gazed at the pool. Into its clear liquid depths. Into the aquamarine seduction of the smooth water.

Nearby stood the statue of the Virgin. Pale in the thickening dusk, her arms spread wide, welcoming, inviting.

Tears slid down Estelle's cheeks as she finished the pitcher, downing the last of the liquor in one long, biting swallow. She stood and her knees buckled slightly. Her head spun, but she knew what she had to do as she approached the edge of the pool. She thought of those people she'd loved, oh, so foolishly; those she'd lost. All her children. They were gone to her. She'd given them all away, in one form or another, and one had become a horrible monster. *What kind of mother are you?*

She kicked off her sandals, then wove her way around the pool to the deep end where the light was the brightest. God the drinks had been strong . . . almost as if they'd been doctored, but that was impossible.

Unless . . . no . . . her last visitor wouldn't have put anything into the bottle of Absolut. Of course not. Not that it mattered. Not now. Her toes curled over the warm tile lip. She teetered, held steady a second, her mind blurry. Her unsteady gaze fastened on the statue of Mary – Holy Mother – Blessed Virgin. 'Forgive me,' Estelle whispered, then closed her eyes and fell forward.

34

'What do you mean, Melanie's not showing up?' Sam demanded as she made her way to the booth later that same night. She'd spent the day going over the minutiae of Annie Seger's life and had found no further clues to figure out who John was. Aside from the police department, Ty's associate, the never-seen Andre Navarrone, was also trying to piece together the puzzle. Before the killer struck again.

'Just what I told ya,' Tiny said, with a shrug. 'Melanie's not coming back. Ever. She got real mad today and stormed into Eleanor's office and quit. Eleanor's fit to be tied because Melanie didn't even give her two weeks' notice.' He offered a sloppy smile. 'Go figure.'

'What about the policewoman?'

'She'll be here, I think, but until then, it's just you and me, babe.'

'Babe?' Sam repeated, her nerves already past the fraying point. She whirled on Tiny, and it was all she could do to keep her voice level. 'Did you call me babe? Listen, Tiny, I want you to do me a favor, okay? Don't ever call me 'babe' or 'chick' or 'broad' or any other of those derogatory male terms again.'

'Geez, I meant it as a compliment.'

'Well, geez, it's not one, okay?' she snapped, then noticed the wounded look in his eyes and felt immediate remorse. 'Oooh, guess I'm a little more stressed-out than I realized. Sorry. You just hit a hot button with me.'

'Yeah, well, I won't do it again,' he said, obviously still smarting as he headed into the booth beside hers. Sam glanced at her watch and figured she had just enough time to call Melanie and point out that she was needed before she was on the air. Rather than disturb the setup in her booth, she found a free phone at Melba's desk, dialed and waited, looking over the various and grotesque objets d'art backlit by wavering neon.

'Come on, come on,' she said, glancing at her watch again. Melanie's answering machine picked up. 'Hi, I'm out . . . you know the drill, leave a message after the tone.'

The machine beeped.

'Melanie? Melanie . . . are you there? It's Sam. Come on and pick up, would ya? We could use some help down here. Please. Melanie? Melanie . . .'

The receiver was picked up.

'Mel—'

Then it was slammed down.

Samantha jumped and decided it was no use. Melanie was ticked, and there was no changing her mind. Not tonight. Obviously she had a point to make. Hurrying back to the booth, Sam nearly collided with the policewoman, Dorothy, carrying a paper cup of coffee as she rounded a corner.

'Oops . . .' She managed not to slosh. 'Years of practice,' she explained, then added, 'I heard we're on our own tonight.'

'So I've been told.' Sam had reached her booth and was opening the door. She glanced into the neighboring area and saw Tiny already at his desk, headphones in place.

'Don't worry about it,' Dorothy said as she held her cup in one hand and opened the door to the booth with the other. 'I know the drill, and between you, me and Tiny, we'll do fine.'

'I hope so,' Sam said, wishing Melanie weren't so mercurial and stubborn. Despite her flaws, Melanie was always interesting, usually upbeat, and forever hatching one ambitious plan after another. That was her problem, Sam thought, the girl was too ambitious for her own good.

As soon as she closed the door of her booth behind her, Sam shoved all lingering thoughts of Melanie aside. She had work to do. And a plan. One she hadn't shared with Ty or Eleanor or the police, one she wouldn't try unless she felt safe. But she was convinced that nothing could happen to her. Ty drove her to and from the station, the house was locked, the alarm in place, and here at work, the security guard and police were everywhere.

But she had to reach John, to help the police catch him before he found his next victim.

Adjusting the mike and headset, she double-checked the sound levels and made sure the computer display was working properly. At a signal from Tiny in the adjoining booth, she heard the intro music and waited until the last words faded. Then she leaned into the microphone. 'Good evening, New Orleans, this is Dr. Sam with *Midnight Confessions,* a talk show as good for the heart as it is for the soul. Tonight we're going to talk about sacrifices,' she said, the topic she thought would most compel John to call. 'We all make them. Every day. Usually for a person we love, or the boss, or for something we want. It's all a part of life. But sometimes we feel that we sacrifice too much, that we give and give and give, and it's not appreciated, never enough.' Already the lights on the console were flashing. One, two, three and four, blinking as she talked. From the corner of her eye she saw Tiny and the policewoman, talking, nodding, screening the calls. The first name appeared on the screen. Arlene.

Sam punched the line. 'This is Dr. Sam,' she said. 'Who's this?'

'Hi. I'm Arlene.'

'Welcome to the show, Arlene. I assume you called in because you have some personal experience with or an observation about sacrifice.'

'Yes, yes. That I do. I'm a mother of three children . . .' Arlene started expounding about giving everything for her kids and unconditional love while Sam read the other names leaping on the screen. Mandy was on two, Alan on three, Jennifer on four. The show was half over. So far John hadn't taken the bait.

Sam hoped it was only a matter of time.

*   *   *

'You want me to pretend to be Dr. Sam?' Melanie asked and rolled her eyes at her boyfriend. Still angry over what had happened at the station, she'd already downed two glasses of wine in rapid succession and now was standing in the kitchen alcove of her studio apartment, slicing limes and mixing drinks. Her boyfriend, dressed in black jeans, matching T-shirt and bulky leather jacket was pacing from one end of the room to the other. He seemed nervous tonight and that same little tingle of excitement that she always experienced around him was heightened tonight. She didn't know a lot about him but considered him the ultimate badboy, an irreverent man who didn't give a damn about what people thought or social convention.

The Chardonnay was having some effect. She was less tense, her muscles melting a bit, the knife a little awkward in her usually deft fingers.

'I think it would be an interesting game,' he said, looking through her window and adjusting the shades for more privacy.

'Oh, I forgot you're into games.'

'Isn't everyone?'

'No . . . not really.' She squeezed some lime juice into a couple of old-fashioned glasses already swimming with gin and tonic water. 'You know, you can ditch the shades. It's night.'

'My eyes are giving me trouble again.'

'Oh.' She kept forgetting that he had some condition that didn't allow his pupils to dilate properly and he was always trying to filter out excessive light. But here, in the apartment, she'd turned down all the lamps and only a few candles burned. 'Whatever you want.' She was in no mood to argue. In fact she was starting to mellow out and she thought what might really help was a long night of lovemaking. Sneaking a surreptitious glance at her daybed, she imagined him naked with her, driving into her in that same furious way he had in Sam's bed weeks ago.

' "Whatever you want," ' he repeated. 'Now those are interesting words.' He grinned that killer smile of his. Her heart raced as he looked at her. Definitely a bad boy. Not the kind to bring home to Mom and Dad. Not suitable marriage material, but she didn't care.

'As far as I'm concerned everyone at WSLJ including their resident radio shrink can go screw themselves. I'm done with them. There are plenty of jobs in this city. I don't have to put up with the shit they shovel down there.'

'Of course you don't.' He crossed to the stereo system where he flipped a switch and Samantha's voice immediately came through the surround-sound theater system she'd installed herself.

'So is sacrifice a good thing? Is it necessary?' Dr. Sam was asking the audience.

Melanie thought she might puke. How had she put up with that self-righteous bitch for as long as she had?

'She's still trying to lure John into calling,' Melanie said.

'I'll bet he bites.' He flipped the blinds shut.

'Serve her right if he did. He freaks her out, you know?'

'I suppose.'

'Oh, yeah.' She carried the drinks across the small room. 'Maybe I should call in – no, no, better yet, *you* call in. You do a wicked impersonation of John. Sometimes I think . . . I mean, I know this sounds crazy, but sometimes I wonder if you are him?'

'Wouldn't you be scared if I was?' He was staring at her intently.

'Spitless. That guy's weird and now . . . now they're linking him to some murders. But it's just kinda coincidental that he started calling about the same time that we started pranking Dr. Sam and dredging up all that stuff on Annie Seger.' She handed him one of the drinks. 'It just makes me think.'

'Not bad thoughts I hope.' Sipping from his glass, he looked at her through those darned glasses, the same kind that were drawn on the composite drawing of the killer. Was it possible? No way.

'Sometimes I think you play head games with me,' she said, taking a big gulp of the gin and tonic. 'You *like* to scare me. It turns you on. You *want* me to think you might be that nutcase that calls in.'

'Didn't I just say we all play games?'

She giggled. Took another long swallow, started to feel a little more tipsy. Free. Unbound. Maybe leaving WSLJ was a good thing. She waggled a finger at his nose. 'You always turn the tables on me.'

'And you like it.'

'Yes,' she said, wrapping one arm around his neck and staring up at him. 'Yes, I do.'

'So do I.' His voice was so low and sexy, a soft Texan drawl she found titillating. 'So, indulge me . . . just sit here and pretend that you're Dr. Sam, doing the show.' He motioned toward her daybed.

'And who will you be?' she asked as she heard some whiny voiced woman through the speakers. The caller was complaining about taking care of her elderly parents. *Oh, can it,* Melanie thought.

'Who will I be? John, of course.'

'Of course,' she said dryly, then muttered under her breath. 'I guess I shoulda seen that one comin'.'

'So – is that what she'd be wearing?' he asked, pointing toward her shorts and halter top.

'This? The snooty-nosed doctor from LA? No way.'

'Then change.'

'What?'

'Complete the fantasy.'

'I don't want—'

'Come on, Melanie. Indulge me. Indulge yourself.'

She liked the thought of that and with only a few niggling doubts, she walked to the closet alcove and pulled out a khaki wrap-around skirt and white sleeveless blouse – it was sooo Dr. Sam. Stepping into the dressing area by the bathroom she tore off her clothes, hesitated at her underwear, then stripped it off. If she wanted to get laid tonight, she figured she'd better grab his attention. Fluffing her hair, she walked around the divider and found him holding both drinks.

'I freshened yours,' he explained handing her the glass, then clinking the rim of his to hers. 'To leaving the past behind,' he said.

'Especially WSLJ.' She took a long swallow and wrinkled her nose. The drink tasted a little off.

'Don't you like it?' he asked and she didn't want to hurt his feelings.

'It's . . . it's a little strong.'

'I thought you were in a party mood.'

'I am,' she said, her head spinning slightly, her lips mushy. She was getting drunk and fast, but then she hadn't eaten much and she'd had two . . . or was it three glasses of wine before her first hard drink and now . . . 'Maybe I should sit down.'

He smiled. 'Whatever you want. Now . . . how about pretending you're Dr. Sam.'

Boy, he just wouldn't give up tonight. But what did she care. Melanie gave him a naughty look, then lifted the receiver of her cordless phone and lowered her voice to a deep, heavy, whisper, 'Good evening, New Orleans, this is *Midnight Confessions*, and I'm your host, Dr. Sam. Tell me whatever you want to, pour your heart out, confess all your sins and—'

'Wait a minute,' he cut in.

'Why?' Boy, her head was spinning. 'Isn't . . . isn't this wha . . . what you wanted?'

'Just about. But it could be better.'

'Better?' she said and her tongue was thick. Too thick. She couldn't talk, couldn't really think straight.

'You need this.'

'Wha—?' she said but saw him reach inside his jacket and pull out a long red wig. 'Oh . . .' she thought of Samantha Leeds's dark red hair. 'Do I really need to . . . ?'

'Yes, Samantha, you do.'

'But my name's Melanie . . .' He was reaching over, pulling her hair up to the top of her head and he was pushing a little too hard. 'Ouch. Wait . . . I'll do it . . .' she said but couldn't get her hands to obey her mind. This was so weird. She was drunk . . . no beyond drunk . . . as if . . . as if she'd taken something . . . as if someone had slipped her a mickey . . . as if . . .

'There,' he said and she saw that his face was flushed, sweat was dripping down beneath the edges of his dark lenses. 'That's more like it.' He looked at her appraisingly with a cold leer that sent a shiver through her heart. 'Now . . . listen . . .'

He'd turned his head toward the speakers as if mesmerized. 'But I thought you wanted me to—'

'Shut up! What I want is for you to shut up!'

'Wait a minute.' Why was he being so mean to her? Unbidden, tears filled her eyes.

'Hey . . . shhh . . .' he said, more kindly and he leaned over her, kissed her. She felt better though her head was whirling. 'Why don't you strip, Sam.'

'I'm not—'

'It's all a game.'

Oh yeah. Now she remembered. She fumbled with the buttons of the blouse and felt his hands take over.

'You have to repent.'

'Wha—?'

'For your sins.'

Her blouse was open, exposing her bare breasts.

'See . . . you're a slut, Samantha.'

'But I'm not—'

She was vaguely aware of something being draped over her head, hard, cool stones – a necklace surrounding her throat. In the background over the buzz in her brain she heard Dr. Sam talking about sins and sacrifice and—

The necklace tightened, cut into her skin. 'Hey!' Her mind was foggy but this seemed wrong. 'You're hurting me.'

He cinched the noose tighter and she couldn't speak, couldn't scream. This . . . this was going too far. *Stop it! I can't breathe!* She tried to scream but no words came and her fingers scrabbled at her throat, trying to pull the horrid necklace away. This was no game, she realized. She caught a glimpse of John's face, his teeth bared, his lips pulled back like a horrid beast, his eyes hidden by black glass.

Don't! Please! Oh, God, all the fears that had been nagging at the back of her mind, all the worries that she'd steadfastly tamped down erupted. *He's John. The caller. The murderer. He's going to kill you! He planned it all along.*

But . . . but . . . her lungs ached, her flesh burned. She tried to gasp, came up with nothing. She kicked and clawed and fought, but he was strong, so damned strong.

'That's it, New Orleans, come on, talk to me, tell me of the sacrifices you've made . . .' Dr. Sam was saying as if from a distance, her voice far away . . .

Father John twisted his nasty weapon, gritting his teeth, staring into gold eyes that had trusted him. Foolish, foolish girl, he thought as her struggling subsided and she lay limp, devoid of life, the sinner's soul purged from her body. His hands ached, the knuckles white from the effort of snuffing out her life.

The blood was rushing through his head, the thrill of the kill making him hard, his ears attuned to the last rattle in her chest and the melodic voice of his next victim, the one woman yet alive he wanted . . . *Your turn's coming, Dr. Sam . . . so very soon and I've got something special planned for you.*

He released the rosary and slowly began stripping the skirt from Melanie's body. He was hard. Hot. Aching. Samantha's voice warmed his blood, stirred his lust. As he mounted the dead woman, he closed his eyes. He was with Samantha. Body and soul. They were in her bed, that fabulous canopied bed, just like with Melanie when she'd gone down on him, placing her lips around him, there, in Samantha's private room with the smell of her everywhere . . . he'd been so close to her then, would be again soon. Even closer. Her message tonight about sacrifice was meant for him.

Only for him.

She was ready, he knew it. She would atone for her sins and then she would sacrifice herself. To him.

★　　★　　★

Ty glanced at his watch. There were only forty-five minutes of Sam's program left, and it was time to leave. But Navarrone hadn't shown up yet. He finished his drink and reached for his shoulder holster.

'And so you think sacrifice is just a part of life?' Sam was saying to a caller, which made Ty all the more anxious. What was she doing, egging the killer on?

'Yeah, that's right. I'm sick of everybody whining about it,' a nasal-voiced man said.

Through the open window Ty heard the distinctive yap of Mrs. Killingsworth's dog putting up a ruckus.

Sasquatch had been lying on the rug near the door. He got to his feet, ears pricked forward. A low rumble came from his throat.

'It's okay,' Ty said, walking to the sliding door and slipping outside, where insects thrummed and the radio was muted. But something wasn't right. He felt it as surely as the hot breath of the wind. Squinting, he stared into the darkness toward the boat. He thought he saw a shadow move, but told himself he was imagining things.

He couldn't wait any longer. Not if he wanted to make sure that Sam got home safely. He heard her voice, still answering questions and giving out advice over the airwaves. 'Come on,' he said to the dog, the hairs prickling on his arms as he reached for his pistol and shoulder holster. 'Let's go.' He was out the door when he saw the dark figure move from out of the shadows.

He reached into his shoulder holster, his fingers wrapping around his pistol. 'Navarrone?'

'Yeah.' Andre met him at the Volvo.

'You bastard, where the hell have you been?'

'Get in the car, and I'll tell you about it,' the other man said as he walked to the passenger side of the Volvo. 'I think I know who the killer is.'

Sam glanced at the clock. The show was nearly over. She'd waded through the calls, one after another, waiting, listening, handing out advice, her muscles tense, her nerves stretched like piano wire.

So John hadn't called while she was on the air. That wasn't really a surprise. He could call later, or when she was at home.

'So you wouldn't sacrifice for anyone,' she was saying to a woman who had identified herself as Millie when, in her peripheral vision, she saw Tiny waving frantically, pointing at her computer. She glanced down. John's name came up on line three.

'I did enough of that while I was married,' Millie was saying. Sam had to keep her on the line, keep her talking, so that if John was listening to the show he'd know that she was tied up. Meanwhile, his call would be traced.

'What about if you remarried?'

'That'll be a cold day in hell,' Millie said with a snort. *Don't stop, Millie. Keep talking*, Sam thought, sweating as she watched line three blink. The trick was to take his call before he gave up in frustration. He had to know that the call would be traced, so he was probably timing the call. 'Thanks for calling in,' Sam said, as the policewoman stood in the window between the booths, using hand signals to remind Sam to take the call and somehow see that John was intrigued enough with the conversation not to hang up. She punched line three. 'Hello, this is Dr. Sam. You're on.'

No one answered.

'Hello? This is Dr. Sam,' she said again, hearing the dead air space. 'You're on the line now.'

She waited again, the buttons for line three continued to flash, the caller hadn't hung up.

'Can you hear me? Did you want to talk about sacrificing?' she asked, trying to fill the dead air. 'Hello? Caller are you there?' She looked through the glass to the policewoman, who held up a finger, punched line three so they didn't lose the call and pointed at Sam to answer another line.

Sam went on to the next call, a girl named Amy, all the while aware that line three was still lit, that John's name was still on the computer screen, that he was out there somewhere, listening to the show and attempting to make contact.

What if he was killing someone right now? That's what he does, Sam. He murders women while listening to your show. That's what he did to Leanne, to the others. Right now he could be taking the life of . . .

She saw Tiny standing in the window, waving frantically, and she realized that she'd missed something, that Amy had hung up. 'Excuse me,' Sam said into the microphone. 'It seems that we're experiencing some technical difficulties here at WSLJ. We have a couple more minutes, so please call in.' Line one began to flash. The name on the computer screen was John.

He'd called back. She punched the button. 'This is Dr. Sam and you're on *Midnight Confessions*. Who's this?'

'You know who I am, Samantha. I'm John, Father John, and I know all about sacrifices. In fact, I've just made another.'

35

'Hello?' Sam's voice sounded frantic on the airwaves.

Ty's heart nearly stopped. He stepped on the accelerator, but then slammed on his brakes as traffic was snarled within the city limits. 'Do you hear that?' He shot a glance at Navarrone.

'It's Kent Seger. He's called in.'

'John? Are you on the line? This is Dr. Sam.'

Ty pounded a fist on the steering wheel, grabbed his cell and punched auto dial.

'Hello?' Sam was saying.

Click.

'He's gone,' Navarrone said, as Ty waited for someone from WSLJ to answer his call. What had Sam been thinking, baiting Seger like that. Ty's guts clenched at the thought of Kent being near her, even talking to her.

'Come on, come on,' Ty growled into the receiver as he maneuvered down a side street. It was late, a Thursday night, traffic usually thin, but not tonight. Testily, he shot Navarrone a glance. 'You're sure the killer is Kent Seger? Not Peter Matheson or Ryan Zimmerman?'

Navarrone met his glance with one of his own, silently asking Ty if he'd ever failed him. 'It's Seger. Has to be. Matheson doesn't live around her. Zimmerman's got a different blood type from the killer. That leaves Annie's brother.'

No one was answering at the station. Ty was beginning to sweat.

He'd never known Navarrone to be wrong, but there was always a first time. 'What the hell's wrong with traffic?' Sirens screamed through the night. Cars pulled over as two police cars and an ambulance, lights strobing, sped past.

The phone clicked in his ear. 'WSLJ.' A woman's voice he didn't recognize. Probably the cop assigned to the station.

'This is Ty Wheeler. I need to speak to Samantha Leeds.'

'Sorry. The show's over,' a woman said.

'She's a personal friend.'

'The show's over.'

'Hell, just tell her I'm on my way.'

The line went dead.

Something was wrong.

Sam stripped off her headset and pushed the button to play 'Midnight Confession' signifying that the show was over. As the first notes were audible, she shoved back her chair and flew out of the booth.

Dorothy Hodges was already in the hallway.

'We've got him!' the officer told her. 'I just got a call from Detective Bentz. The phone booth we have listed on caller ID is only a few blocks from here, on Chartres. That's where John called from. There's already a unit on the scene. Others are on their way. Including Detective Bentz.' Her eyes were bright with victory. 'That bastard's ass is grass.'

'About time.' Tiny was standing in the doorway to the booth, a portable headset around his neck.

'Let's go,' Sam said, starting for the door.

'No way.' The policewoman turned instantly sober. Into cop mode. No more easy smiles. 'Both of you stay here. This is police work.'

'But—'

'I'm serious,' Officer Hodges insisted.

Sam couldn't believe it. 'But I'm the reason he's being apprehended.'

'And you're the reason he started this in the first place.' The cop leveled a finger at Sam's chest. 'Bentz thinks you were the ultimate victim, so you just sit tight until all this goes down. He's not apprehended yet.' Dorothy wasn't budging an inch and acting like she suddenly saw Sam as the enemy. 'And, just so you understand me, I'm telling Wes to make sure no one comes in or out. Got it?'

'No way.'

Officer Hodges's eyes narrowed. 'Listen, Ms. Leeds, your life has been threatened by the very guy we're trying to run to the ground, so you sure as hell will stay here, or I'll cuff you and take you down to the station.'

'But I'd be with you.'

'What you would be is in the way. Now stuff it,' the woman said, and she took off, leaving Sam and Tiny standing by Melba's reception desk.

'She's right,' Tiny offered. 'Besides, I can't go anywhere, I've got to stick around for *Lights Out.*'

'I don't.'

'So you're going to be crazy instead? Come on, Dorothy's right. You'd better stay here, Sam. At least until that boyfriend of yours shows up. He just called, talked to her—' he said, hitching a thumb at the cop's retreating backside. 'He's on his way.'

Sam gritted her teeth and checked her watch. It irritated her to sit around and wait. John had contacted her . . . this was about her, and not only did she want to witness him being unmasked and apprehended, but she was still keyed up. This didn't seem right. It was almost too easy. He was smarter than this, or at least he had been. Why would he risk everything by staying on the line tonight, toying with the police when he had to have known that the lines were tapped and the call was being traced. No, something was wrong about this, definitely wrong.

And Ty was late.

She glanced at her watch.

This wasn't like him.

'So you're telling me that Ryan Zimmerman was adopted,' Ty said to Navarrone as he nosed his Volvo into a parking space half a block from the radio station. 'And that his biological mother is Estelle.'

'That's about the size of it. She got pregnant before she married Wally. The family hushed it up, said she was going to some fancy boarding school, when she was really giving up the baby through a Catholic hospital. It turns out he was adopted by a couple from Houston who end up living in the same school district where Estelle raised her own kids. She wasn't aware that Ryan was her son, of course, not until Annie started dating him and bringing him around, and somehow Annie let it slip that Ryan was adopted.

'He looked enough like the father of the baby she'd given up that Estelle started doing some checking. Hired a PI. That's who I got the info from.' He glanced at the building housing WSLJ. The PI also found out something else.'

'The name of the other guy Annie was involved with,' Ty guessed.

'Yep.'

'Worse news.'

'It seems that Annie was doin' it with both brothers.'

Though he'd almost figured it for himself, Ty felt a moment's shock. He'd been reaching for his keys. Stopped. 'Both?'

'Well, she only thought she was screwing one ... and she wasn't happy about it, but when she went to her mother saying Kent was sexually molesting her, Estelle wouldn't believe her. Refused.'

Ty felt bile rise in the back of his throat. 'Great mom.'

'One of the best,' Navarrone agreed.

'So Kent was Annie's baby's father?'

'Looks that way.'

'No wonder Estelle didn't want to talk about it.'

'Who would?' Navarrone reached for the door handle. 'I've already talked to Bentz about this. Everyone's on the same page.'

'Listen to this,' Montoya said, gunning his car around a corner as the police band crackled. 'There's been an accident ...'

Bentz was way ahead of him. 'On the same block as the phone booth that John called from. What the hell's going on?'

The words had barely gotten out of his mouth when they turned onto Chartres and saw the crowd that had gathered. An ambulance was on the scene, lights flashing red and white, pedestrians clustered on the sidewalks and on the street. Traffic was at a standstill.

Before the cruiser had come to a full stop, Bentz was out of the vehicle, his Glock in one hand, his badge in the other. Uniformed and plainclothes cops were keeping a crowd at bay but the curious couldn't help but stop and stare. The night was hot. Breathless. Bentz slapped at a mosquito as he eyed the accident scene where a minivan with a shattered windshield and a dented bumper was stopped. Crumpled in front of the damaged vehicle a man was sprawled on the street. Two emergency workers were huddled over him, taking vitals, but, to Bentz's way of thinking, it didn't look good.

A few feet away the driver was crying and wringing her hands. A frantic woman with wild eyes was shaking her head, giving an officer her statement. '. . . he just came out of nowhere,' she was saying, obviously in shock, but otherwise seeming unhurt. 'He was stumbling and reeling and I slammed on my brakes but . . . but . . . oh, God, I hit him. First the bumper then he rolled over the hood to the windshield. He flew off when I stopped. Oh, Lord, it was awful. Just awful.' Another woman, probably a passenger in the rig as both doors were open, was trying to console the driver, and the cop was listening intently, but the driver was barely in control, ready to fall into a million pieces. 'He's not dead is he, please . . . don't tell me . . . he can't be dead.'

'I saw the whole thing,' a man standing between two parked cars piped in. Wearing a baseball cap, T-shirt and sloppy shorts, he added, 'It's like what she said. This guy, he just came running into the street all weirded-out, kind of mumbling and half-running, like he didn't know where he was, and she nailed him.' The driver gasped at his choice of words, and the witness said, 'Oh, sorry, but he was really out of it. It was like . . . like he didn't even see her. Maybe he was drunk. Or stoned.'

'You got an ID?' Bentz asked one of the attendants.

'Not yet. We're trying to keep him alive.'

The driver gave a little squeak.

'Let's try to stabilize him and get him out of here,' the same emergency worker said. 'Get the stretcher.'

'I've got the wallet,' his second attendant cut in. 'I was lookin' to see if he had any allergies.' He handed the wallet to Bentz, who flipped it open. A Louisiana driver's license issued to Kent Seger was the first piece of ID. 'Well, hello John Fathers,' Bentz muttered to himself, looking over the rest of the items in the wallet. Nothing out of the ordinary. Seven dollars, a social security card, student ID for All Saints College, a Visa card and a single photograph . . . one of Annie Seger.

'You find anything else?'

'Yeah, look . . .' one of the attendants, said, withdrawing a long chain of beads. 'Looks like this guy was a priest or somethin'. He's got himself a rosary.'

'That he does,' Bentz said. 'Bag it, would ya?'

'Yep.' In a second he was holding the plastic bag and staring down at the barely breathing body of Kent Seger. To Bentz's trained eye, it looked like the guy was a goner. Which wasn't a shame.

Bentz decided the owner of the minivan had done the city a favor. A pair of shattered sunglasses had fallen onto the street, plastic lenses splintered against the curb and the half-dead man lying on the cobblestones, could very well have posed for the artist's sketch of John Fathers. His face was cut and bruised, his eyes closed, but the resemblance was there.

Good riddance, Bentz thought.

'Hey, over here!' Montoya waved Bentz toward a phone booth, where the receiver had been left dangling, the blazing lights of the ambulance casting the glass walls of the booth in eerie light. 'Take a look at this.'

Bentz felt the tightening in his gut – that same premonition that he wasn't going to like whatever it was Montoya had found.

'This is it, you know,' Reuben said as Bentz walked past a few gawkers and smelled the sweet, pungent odor of marijuana. 'This is where John made his last call to the radio station.'

'The guy's ID says he's Kent Seger.'

Montoya's eyes narrowed. He glanced at the accident scene. 'You thought Kent Seger was John, didn't you?'

'He was one of the suspects. Just one. Kent Seger's blood type is the same as John's, and I got a call from a guy named Andre Navarrone less than an hour ago. He has an interesting theory that he says he can back up. He thinks Kent Seger was sexually abusing his sister, Annie, ten years ago in Houston. Navarrone thinks that Annie was pregnant with Kent's kid. It's his contention that Kent killed Annie, but transferred the blame to Sam. He also figures that something triggered this rampage – maybe the fact that his mother finally cut him off financially, or maybe just hearing Dr. Sam's voice on the radio again. That squares with what Norm Stowell said.' Bentz took another look at the accident scene. 'Looks like we may never know for certain what pushed him over the edge.'

'He left something,' Montoya said.

'What?'

'I don't know . . . looks like a recorder, one of those handheld jobs.' Carefully Montoya used his handkerchief and picked it up. Beneath the recorder were a set of keys.

'What the hell are these?' Bentz's sense that something was wrong heightened. Using the same handkerchief he'd used for the recorder, Montoya picked up the keys.

'You think they're Kent's?'

Bentz glanced from the phone booth to the ambulance as it began to roll through the crowd, lights flashing, siren wailing, then back to the keys.

'I doubt it . . . Look at this.' Under the streetlamp he spread the keys with one of his own. The key ring was shaped in the form of an oversize heart. 'Unless I miss my guess, these keys belong to a woman.'

'Who?'

Bentz flipped through the keys carefully until he found a miniature Louisiana license plate with the raised letters spelling Melanie.

'Shit,' Montoya whispered. 'Dr. Sam's assistant.'

A rock settled in the pit of Bentz's stomach. 'According to Dorothy Hodges, Melanie Davis got pissed and quit the show today. Didn't show up for work.'

Montoya's jaw tightened. 'Maybe because she couldn't.'

'Maybe.' Bentz whipped out his cell phone, called the dispatcher and ordered a unit sent to Melanie Davis's home. 'I want the officers to call me back as soon as they locate her,' he said. 'Page me.' He clicked off, then gazed at the recorder still sitting on the tiny shelf in the phone booth. 'Let's see if John left us a message.'

Careful not to wipe any prints off the recorder, Bentz pressed the play button with one of his keys. The tape started instantly and over the commotion outside the booth a woman's breathy voice was audible from the single speaker on the tiny machine.

'This is Annie and I'd like to speak to Dr. Sam about my ex-mother-in-law. I was hoping she could help.' Then a long pause and finally, in a higher-pitched voice, *'Annie,'* and a pause. *'Don't you remember me?'*

'He did tape her,' Montoya said, as another pause ensued.

'I called you before . . . Thursday's my birthday. I would be twenty-five.'

'Son of a bitch,' Montoya muttered as they listened to all of the tape, hoping that at the end of the short one-sided conversation they would hear more and clear up the woman's identity, but the rest of the tape was blank. 'Do you think that Melanie was involved, that she's the person on the tape, that she screened her own damned call?' Montoya asked, pulling at his goatee.

'It would explain a lot, wouldn't it? Someone was working on the inside, unlocked the door for the cake to be delivered, gave out the private number.' Bentz ached for a smoke. 'Why aren't they calling me back?'

'You think she's dead.'

Bentz nodded curtly. 'There's a damned good chance.'

'Shit.' Montoya glared through the smudged glass of the phone booth to the street and the dented minivan. 'So you think John left all this stuff here and when he was running away he got hit?' Montoya asked.

'Do you?'

'It looks that way.' He frowned. 'So what's going down, Bentz?'

'Nothin' good, Reuben. Nothin' good.' Bentz's pager went off. 'Have this booth gone over with a fine-toothed comb,' he said, 'and have crews sweep the street – look for anything out of the ordinary.' He pulled his cell phone from his jacket pocket, dialed the number on his pager's display and took the message.

It was short and simple. Bentz's jaw grew tight. His gut twisted. He hung up and swore, then met the questions in his partner's eyes. 'Melanie Davis is dead. Strangled. Odd ligature around her neck. Probably a rosary.'

36

Sam stroked Charon's black coat as she sat in the deck chair and twilight darkened the sky. So it was over. Finally. But the effects would last forever. So many people she knew were dead, the last being Melanie Davis . . . the woman the police decided had posed as Annie. The story was still fragmented, but it seemed that Melanie had been dating Kent Seger – he'd been the new boyfriend, 'the one' she'd told Sam about.

'It makes you wonder,' she said to the cat. Kent was still barely alive, under police guard at the hospital, and the press was everywhere, trying to get a story. Sam had taken her own phone off the hook and refused to answer her door. She needed time to pull herself together, to sort things out, to figure out what she was going to do with the rest of her life.

If Kent survived, maybe they'd learn the answers and he'd go to prison forever; if he died, the world was probably better off. Sam had never really believed in the death penalty but when she thought of the women he'd killed, starting with his own sister and unborn baby, she decided he deserved whatever fate God or the courts meted out. It was lucky that he'd been caught, but the drugs in his system, a combination of angel dust and crack, had made him hallucinate and reel into the path of an oncoming car after getting off the phone with Sam.

Which was odd. He didn't sound out of control when he'd called. But then he hadn't said much.

She stretched the muscles in the back of her neck and watched a butterfly flit over the grass near the water.

So what about you, Sam? What're you going to do?

Maybe she should take the job in LA. 'How about that,' she said to Charon, who arched his back under her fingers. 'You could be a Hollywood cat.'

She would be closer to her father – away from all the pain here. Through it all, she hadn't heard from Peter. She'd half expected to get a call from him when the news had broken, but there had been no messages either here or with her dad. Some things just didn't change.

Could you possibly leave Ty?

Her heart filled at the thought of him. Shading her eyes with her hand, she stared out at the lake and saw his boat, the *Bright Angel*, skimming across the water. She should have gone with him, she supposed, but she needed a little time alone, to think, and he'd just decided to pick up Sasquatch from his house and bring him back by boat. They planned to cook dinner together, right after she took a shower. She smiled a little as she saw Ty's dog sitting nose to the wind on the deck.

It had only been eighteen hours since she'd signed off the air last night, and in that time her life had changed.

Melanie was dead.

Like Leanne.

Like Annie.

Like all the others who had the misfortune to run into Kent Seger.

Her heart ached for the ambitious girl who had, the police suspected, gone along with Kent in the hopes of somehow snagging Sam's job. Melanie had always been too ambitious, and in the end it had cost her. She stood and waved and Ty, from the helm, waved back. Had it only been a few weeks since she'd thought she'd spied the *Bright Angel* bobbing on the night-darkened waves, a dark stranger at her helm?

Several publishers had shown some interest in Ty's story, and his agent was shopping the idea around. There was talk of an auction.

A lot had happened in the span of eighteen hours.

Carrying Charon, Sam walked into the house, locked the door from habit, and climbed the stairs to her bedroom, leaving the door ajar so that the cat could go in and out rather than cry and paw at the door. A pair of Ty's slacks were slung over the end of the bed. He hadn't moved out yet, and Sam wasn't sure she wanted him to. They were good together, she told herself as she stripped out of her sundress and underwear, made her way to the bathroom and turned on the shower's spray. Through a window she'd cracked to let out steam, she heard the familiar sound of Hannibal barking – ever ready to start a ruckus – ever vigilant for squirrels or all manner of other critters. She flipped on the radio to WSLJ and heard the rough sound of Ramblin' Rob's voice as he told the audience that he was going to check the library and come back with a Patsy Cline hit. The first caller to name the year the song was popular would receive a WSLJ mug.

Sam wrapped a towel over her head, then stepped under the pulsing spray. Closing her eyes, she tried to chase the demons away. How could she have not known that Melanie was jealous of her? How had she worked with the girl night after night and even trusted her to watch her house and cat . . . and David? His betrayal was worse. He'd planned to use the situation with 'John,' hoping to force her back into his arms. She'd even gotten a call from her ex – Jeremy Leeds, Ph.D., telling her he was sorry for what she was going through.

She doubted Jeremy had ever been sorry in his life.

She lathered her body, hearing Patsy Cline's clear melancholy voice over the spray. But the worst was Kent Seger, a man obsessed with his sister and then Samantha. He blamed Sam for taking Annie's life, but had actually killed his sister, making it look like a suicide, because he was jealous of Ryan Zimmerman, a boy he didn't know was his half brother.

Sick, it was all sick.

Rinsing, she thought of Estelle, found yesterday morning facedown in her pool, unable to face another scandal. Her first husband, Annie's father Wally, had been shocked when Ty had called him. He blamed himself.

A lot of people around here were taking long guilt trips these day.

Twisting off the spigots, she heard the back door open. Ty must've docked. She whipped the towel off her head and stepped into her robe. 'I haven't started dinner yet, so pour yourself a drink,' she yelled down the stairs as she cinched the belt and glanced out the window where, on the horizon, she saw the familiar masts and sails of the *Bright Angel*.

But that was impossible. Why would the sloop be in the water when she was certain she'd heard a door open? A *locked* door open. The hairs lifted on the back of her neck. 'Ty?' she called, and told herself she was being a fool. Kent Seger was in the hospital, barely clinging to his life. Her brother and Ryan Zimmerman had been cleared of any crimes. And besides, *no one* was in the house but her.

Then she heard the footsteps. Heavy and quick, mounting the stairs. Oh, God. Her heart pounded. Panic rose in her throat. She glanced through the window, saw the sailboat heading inland, Ty at the helm, Sasquatch at his side. Hissing, Charon streaked through the open bedroom door and slunk under the bed.

Sam searched the room wildly for a weapon – the window. If she could just flag Ty down. She flung the sash open and heard the door creak.

'You bitch!'

John's voice. No!

'Ty!' she screamed, then turned as the intruder reached her – a tall man in dark glasses and a cold, angry leer.

'Who are you?'

'Your worst nightmare,' he said, and she noticed a handkerchief in his hand.

A sickly smell surrounded him. 'Get out!' she yelled, her blood cold as ice. She searched wildly for a weapon and saw the lamp. Before she could grab it, he was on her. Holding her fast, trying to force the horrid gag to her face.

She kicked, clawed and screamed, fought like a tiger, but he was so big that he wrapped an arm around her and pushed the cloth into her face. She couldn't breathe, the smell, that horrid smell of ether, filled her nostrils and burned down her throat. Her eyes watered, she coughed, couldn't breathe.

The smell was overpowering.

She tried to scream but dragged in more of the drug. Blackness pulled at the edges of her consciousness. She clawed at his face and he laughed. The darkness came and went. Her arms and legs were so heavy, she couldn't keep her eyes open and the fight left her.

She saw his smile and from the corner of her eye the twinkle of light, blood-red light cast by a string of beads.

'We've got the wrong guy!' Bentz stared at the medical chart hanging from the end of Kent Seger's bed, then swore a blue streak. A uniformed guard was posted at the door of this private room, plainclothes officers situated at other points in the hospital, but it didn't matter. The guy in the bed with all the tubes and wires poking in and out of his damned body wasn't Kent Seger.

'The wrong guy?' Montoya was eating from a bag of chips he'd bought at a machine in the cafeteria.

'Look at his blood type.'

'But—'

'I don't know who the hell he is but the guy's not Kent Seger and he's not John. It was a setup.' Bentz was running out of the room. 'Stay put,' he told the guard. 'Don't let anyone in or out. Not even a doctor.'

'But—'

'Why the hell didn't anyone check his blood type?' Bentz yanked his cell phone from his pocket and found the nearest exit. Montoya was only a step behind.

'So who is he?' Montoya asked as ran to his car and reached inside for his cell phone.

'It doesn't matter. What does is that our boy is still on the loose.'

Bentz punched out the numbers for the dispatcher. 'Call the Cambrai police. Send someone out to Samantha Leeds's house on Lake View Drive, pronto.' He climbed behind the wheel.

'I'll drive,' Montoya offered.

'No way. You're too slow. Get in.'

Montoya hadn't even strapped himself in when Bentz switched on the ignition and floored it, driving like holy hell through the parking lot and flipping on his siren as the cruiser bucked onto the street. He tossed Montoya the cell phone. 'Call Samantha Leeds. Tell her what's up.'

While Montoya tried to get through, Bentz was on the police band, instructing other units on what was happening.

'No one answers,' Montoya said.

'Damn it all to hell. Then try Ty Wheeler . . . at home or on his cell. Call information, just get the hell through!'

He took a corner too fast and the tires squealed. The drive to Cambrai usually took twenty minutes. If he was lucky, he could make it in fifteen.

He only hoped he wasn't too late.

Ty saw Sam in the window. She was waving. No . . . she flung the sash open and called to him. Then he saw the shadow – someone was in the bedroom with her. Someone dressed in black. Someone wearing dark sunglasses. She was struggling. Screaming. Being attacked right before his eyes. And he couldn't reach her. Knowing he'd never make it in time, he lowered the sails, started the engine and pushed the throttle open full bore.

He stared at the window, caught only glimpses of a horror he'd thought was behind them and knew that the monster was loose. Somehow the animal had escaped, and he was killing Samantha right in front of Ty's eyes.

'You won't get away with it, you bastard,' Ty vowed, his hands gripping the wheel, the sloop cutting through the water. 'I'll kill you first.'

It was dark . . . so dark – she could tell even though her eyes were closed. And there were sounds . . . strange sounds . . . a deep rumbling hum. Her head pounded.

She wanted to fall back to sleep, but something forced her to inch open her eyelids. The darkness persisted. She felt motion and realized she was moving, but . . . Her head ached and she felt like she might throw up. Where was she? She tried to sit up and felt woozy. For a second she thought she might pass out again and then she started to remember. Flashes of bright images. She'd been in her bedroom and she'd been attacked by a man in dark glasses . . . oh, God . . . John, somehow he'd escaped.

She felt with her hands, took in deep lungfuls of air and smelled gasoline. She was riding in something, the trunk of a vehicle . . . no, there was too much room . . . she was in the bed of a pickup with one of those canopies over it, and John was driving, taking her somewhere . . . but where?

He slowed and her heart, already racing miles a minute, went into overtime. She didn't doubt for a second that he was going to kill her. He just wanted to do it privately, so he could have more time. She thought of his victims, the torture they'd been through and knew she would endure the same hideous pain.

If she could only get her bearings, and think . . . this was a truck . . . there could be tools. He turned quickly and she slid to one side . . . rolling against the wheel well, banging her head again. *Think, Sam, think, where's he taking you?* Somewhere remote. But he usually kills women in their rooms with a rosary . . . the police had finally made some of the details of the crimes public. She felt around, her fingers sliding over the bed of the truck until she came upon something . . . a toolbox. Could she be so lucky? She tried to open it, but it was locked. *Don't panic, just think.* She tried to force the lid open, but it wouldn't budge.

Tires crunched on gravel. The truck was barely moving now. The tire jack! Where was it? Could she pry it loose? She went over every inch of the bed and along the wheel wells. All she found was a fishing rod. Nothing heavy. Just bamboo. Locked in place along one side of the canopy. Damn!

The truck slid to a stop. She weighed her options. She could spring at him when he opened the back, but he'd probably be expecting that, no, it was better to play as if she was still unconscious and then if he tried to slip anything over her head, she'd react.

It was all she could do to lie still, to try and relax, to make it look like her muscles and bones had melted when she was really so tense she was having trouble breathing.

The engine died.

Oh, God, help me.

She heard the creak of the driver's door open, then the sound of footsteps crunching gravel.

Stay calm. She lay still, breathed slowly, closed her eyes but didn't squeeze them, appeared to relax when all of her nerve endings were stretched taut.

The back of the truck opened, warm fetid air wafted in and the sounds of bullfrogs croaking and insects thrumming through the night met her ears.

Bayou country. Oh, God they'd never be found.

'You awake yet?' he said in his seductive tone. 'Dr. Sam? He wiggled her bare foot, a hot hand on her toes. She didn't react. 'Hell, wake up would ya?' His voice was more agitated. Still she didn't stir. 'You'd better not be playin' possum.' He tickled the bottom of her foot and she forced herself to stay limp. 'Come on.' He pulled her out of the back of the truck and she slumped against him, her legs dragging. It took all of her willpower not to kick him, but she let her toes scrape against the ground. He packed her across the gravel road for a few feet before the crunching beneath his feet changed to a hollow ring, like boots on bare wood.

She slitted her eye open just a bit and caught a glimpse of the bleached boards of a dock.

'Maybe it's better you sleep,' he said, as if to himself. 'Because we're going to have a party later.' He dropped her into a small boat tied to the dock. She crumpled into a boneless heap, though she was scared to death. 'Kinda like the party I had with

Melanie . . . only this time we won't be listening to you on the radio. No, we'll have to play a tape. And I've got them, all your shows. I've brought one along.'

She thought she might be sick. This monster actually planned to kill her while they were listening to her voice as she took calls on the airwaves. *No way in hell*, she thought as he began untying the small boat from its moorings. She needed a weapon, any kind of weapon. As his back was turned she let her eyes open just a hair and began to search the sides of the tiny craft for something . . . anything. Through the slits she noticed a fishing creel tucked under the bench but that wouldn't do . . . then she saw the oar. If she moved quickly, she could reach it, whack him on the back and slide into the swamp.

In that split-second she thought of the creatures of the bayou – alligators, snakes, bats . . . but which was worse? Nature or this unnatural monster? Her mind was still fuzzy. Sluggish.

He began to shove off.

Now!

She sprang, stumbled, grabbed the oar and swung hard.

Crack!

The oar smacked the back of his head.

He roared in pain, stumbled forward. She whacked him again, but he turned on the third attempt.

'You bitch.' Grabbing her makeshift club, he ripped it from her hands. 'You stupid, stupid cunt!' He lunged at her and she dived over the side. Thick water submerged her and she tried to swim, but she was caught. He'd snagged the hem of her robe, dragging her back. She tried to loosen the knot of the tie, but it was cinched tight. Wet.

Swearing loudly he yanked her backward to certain death. She kicked, tried to hold her breath, worked the damned knot, but she was losing ground. His fingers scraped against her ankle.

No! No! NO!

Her lungs were aching, her head cloudy, her fingers fumbling with the damned tie.

He pulled hard. Again reached for her leg. She kicked. The

knot came free. Driven by terror she slid out of the robe's arms and dived fast. Deep. Swimming naked through the thick water far under the surface. Her lungs burned but she ignored the fire, kicking hard, sliding farther from the dock until she thought she would explode.

In a splash, she broke surface, barely twenty feet from him. Gasping for air, she dived again, but not before he cast the beam of a spotlight upon her and spun the damned boat in her direction.

How could she outmaneuver him? How could she save herself? She dived into the sluggish, murky water again, kicking hard, swimming blindly away from the light. *Faster, Sam, go faster. Get away!* Her lungs were about to burst when she scraped her fingers on the roots of a cypress tree and pulled herself to the far side. Slowly she surfaced and took in long, deep breaths while trying to remain silent and get her bearings. *God help me*, she thought desperately, then knew she had to help herself. No one was out here. This was pure, raw, Louisiana wilderness.

She had to escape somehow or kill him.

Either way would do.

Naked and shivering, her head finally clearing, she could barely hear over the drumming of her heart and had trouble tamping down the sheer panic sending adrenalin through her blood. She felt something slippery brush against her leg, but she didn't move, didn't cry out, didn't dare. The smell of the swamp was heavy in her nostrils, the feel of the sultry air cool against her skin. She heard the sound of his oars slicing through the water, watched as the spotlight flickered on, then quickly off again, teasing her, causing her pupils to dilate and narrow, making it more difficult to see.

'You're not going to get away, you know,' he drawled, his voice low and sexy and far too close. Where was he? *Where?*

Then the light flared again barely five feet away. Silently she slid under the water, swam stealthily beneath the lily pads and surfaced in a grove of tall, skeletal trees and flattened against one bleached cypress.

'You can't last long. The gators will get you. Or somethin' else. Come on out, Samantha,' his voice was coaxing, meant to be seductive over the drone of insects, but she heard the edge of frustration in his words, the hint of his psychosis. 'You started this, you know. You told Annie to confide in someone and she told Mother.' He clicked his tongue. 'Mother didn't believe her, though. No, she didn't think I would actually fuck my little sister.' He laughed. 'And Annie . . . she liked it, whether she admitted it or not. She got wet for me . . . just like you're going to.'

Terror struck deep in her heart. She had to get out of here. Now. Before he found her. Before exhaustion overtook her. Before her luck ran out. She managed a peek around the bole of the tree and caught a glimpse of the outline of his truck, the metal shining in the moonlight. It was her only chance.

Noiselessly Sam slipped beneath the surface again. She swam silently away from his voice, toward the dock. Had he left his keys in the truck's ignition? Or had he pocketed them? Had he locked the doors?

She needed some means of escape, some kind of transportation. How far could she get, naked and barefoot?

Just swim. Get to the shore. Get away.

Her lungs were burning, threatening to burst as she propelled herself through the slimy duckweed. Finally, she surfaced, silently dragging in air.

The spotlight flashed on.

The beam caught her square in its hideous brilliance. Somehow he'd been tracking her and realized she'd double back to the dock!

Quickly she slid underneath the water again, swimming frantically, seeking cover beneath the dock, and surfacing on the far side. Peering over the edge of the rotted wood, she saw the spotlight glowing eerily through the rising mist. The boat hadn't moved. Was it possible that she'd lost him? Would he give up so easily? Not unless she'd hurt him when she'd hit him with the oars.

Carefully she edged toward the shore and saw a flash through the trees – headlights? Her heart leapt. Was it possible? Oh, God, could someone be traveling down these deserted roads? Could she be somewhere near a main road? She moved more quickly, her toes searching for purchase in the muddy bottom. Again she felt something brush against her. Fish? Alligator? Snake?

She stepped forward.

Steely fingers clamped around her ankle.

No!

Oh, God, he'd found her. She kicked but it was no use.

He was on her then. His hard body bent on dragging her under. He'd left the spotlight turned on and let the boat drift as he'd slipped under the surface and swum unerringly to her.

The hand was a manacle, pulling her under, into deeper water. She thrashed and kicked, gasping for air. Her heel connected with something solid. He burst to the surface and dragged her with him. 'You fucking bitch,' he swore, naked from the waist up, his skin white in the dark night, the dark glasses gone and wide eyes with pale irises glowering down at her. 'You're gonna pay,' he said, water dripping from his dark hair and down his face. He was standing, his head above water, she, shorter, couldn't touch ground. Angrily, he yanked her down, jerked her under the surface. She gasped, caught a mouthful of stagnant water and came up coughing and spitting.

Kicking and slapping, she aimed for his testicles, but he pulled her under again. Again she gulped water. She bobbed up. Gasped. Coughing, sputtering, choking. He grabbed her hair with his free hand. 'Now Dr. Sam, repent,'

'Wh – what?'

'Repent for your sins.'

He dunked her again, holding her down in the sluggish water, robbing her of air until she couldn't breathe, saw images in the darkness, murky shapes moving near his legs.

With a hard pull, he yanked her up and she could barely move. 'Go ahead play dead. See what good it does you,' he said, and dragged her closer to the shore. Her toes touched now, and she tried to run, but he held her fast and fumbled beneath the water, reaching into his pocket, withdrawing his wicked weapon. In the darkness she saw the beads – his rosary.

She struggled, but it was no use. He was so much stronger. So much bigger. Knew the swamp. If only she had a weapon, a stick, a rock, anything! In the distance she saw headlights, growing nearer, flashing through the trees.

'Say your prayers, Dr. Sam,' Kent ordered as he slipped the noose over her head. The beads were cold as death. Sharp. Hard. Brittle. He twisted the garrotte, and she gasped. Pain seared through her neck. Her leaned forward. 'Repent and kiss me, you miserable bitch,' he ordered, and she lunged forward, teeth bared, and bit hard into his cheek.

He yowled, let go for just a second and she swam under the dock, tore the wicked rosary from her neck and came up on the other side. She heard him splashing behind her, but she swam to the boat, grabbed the spotlight and moved it frantically toward the headlights cutting through the darkness. She heard a car's engine, the grind of tires spinning on gravel.

Her feet touched and she started for the shore, hoping that whoever was coming could reach her in time. 'Here!' she screamed. 'Help!' But Kent was behind her and lunged forward just as the car ground to a stop.

Doors opened. Two men and a dog flew out of the car.

'Police, Seger! Give it up!' a voice boomed.

Kent's hand clamped over her shoulder. She dived into the shallow water.

Crack!

A rifle report echoed through the bayou.

Kent squealed and fell back into the water. Splashing. Flailing. His blood flowing into the dark ripples. 'God damn it,' he cried, but his voice was fading, gurgling.

Gasping and shaking, Sam lunged toward the shore, frantically slogging through the water lilies and vines, sobbing and shaking, certain he would reappear and drag her under again.

'Samantha!' Ty's voice rang across the swamp, through the trees.

Sam nearly crumbled into a thousand pieces.

'Here!' she tried to scream, but her words were only a whisper. She pushed herself forward, feeling as if she was running in slow motion.

She saw him silhouetted by the headlights, racing toward her, the dog at his heels. She started sobbing wildly and couldn't stop when he wrapped his arms around her and held her body to his. 'Sam . . . Sam . . . oh, God, are you all right?'

'Yes . . . no . . . yes . . .' She was holding him, trying to regain some kind of composure and falling into a million pieces.

'Over here,' Ty yelled, turning his head toward the sniper. 'Bring a blanket.' He turned back to her. 'Jesus, Samantha, I shouldn't have let you out of my sight. I'm sorry, I'm so, so sorry . . . what the hell have you got?'

Only then did she realize she was still holding the damned rosary. As if it were truly evil, she let it slide through her fingers to drop onto the soggy ground. She was trembling and shivering and on the verge of passing out. Through her fog, she felt someone throw a blanket over her nakedness and realized it was Detective Bentz.

'I'll need some kind of statement,' he said, averting his eyes as she wrapped the thin blanket around her.

'Later,' Ty said.

In the distance she saw other headlights.

'The cavalry,' Bentz explained, as an owl hooted from a nearby branch. 'I figured we could use some backup.' He looked at the swamp and reached into the pocket of his jacket, retrieving an unopened pack of cigarettes. 'I suppose I should go retrieve the son of a bitch,' he said. 'Right after I have a smoke. If I'm lucky, maybe the gators will do my work for me.' Then he lit up and, gun still in hand, slowly walked onto the dock, searching the dark water while the tip of his cigarette glowed red in the misty darkness.

'How – how did you find me?' Sam asked, her mind still foggy.

'Navarrone knew that Kent had a place here – the only thing his mother had given him when she cut him off. Basically we got lucky.'

'Lucky? I was hoping you would say it was all because of brilliant police work.'

'There was a little of that, but luck played a major part.'

'That's so reassuring,' she said, shaking her head and holding the blanket tight around her shivering body.

'It's meant to be.'

'God help us.' She felt the streaks of mud on her skin and saw, in the headlights, drips of red. Blood. Not hers but Kent's. Diluted with swamp water, but still running down her legs. Shuddering, she wiped the vile fluid from her skin. 'Can we get out of here?' she asked.

'You bet.' Ty whistled to the dog and kissed the top of her head. 'Let's go home.'

Epilogue

'So it's "case closed,"' Montoya said as he walked into Bentz's office and sat on the corner of his desk. Ever cool, Montoya was in his signature leather coat, some dark slacks and a white T-shirt. He'd traded in the goatee for a moustache and instead of one earring, he sported two.

Through the open window, the sounds of the night seeped into the building – a solitary riff from a saxophonist, the hum of traffic, the buzz of laughter. It was night in the city of New Orleans.

'The case is closed except for the fact that we never found Kent Seger's body.'

'You figure he got out alive?'

'With all those gators? Nope.' Bentz leaned back in his desk chair and found a piece of gum in his desk. 'I think he got what he deserved.'

'You give up smokin' again?'

'For the time being.'

'Probably a mistake.'

'Probably.'

'So what's happening with Dr. Sam?'

'All good things,' Bentz said with a grin. He'd talked to Dr. Sam and was surprised at how well she'd survived her ordeal. She was one tough cookie and now she was calling the shots. 'The way I hear it she's got a new assistant and refused to expand the program to seven days a week. George Hannah's going along with it, because he's afraid to lose her. And he would. There are other bigger stations who would hire her in an instant. One as far away as Chicago.'

'So why's she stayin'?'

'One reason is Ty Wheeler.' Reaching behind him, he flipped on the fan and the hot air blew from one end of the tiny office to the other.

'Thought you didn't like him?'

'I don't. Anyone who gives up being a cop to write books is a candy-ass.'

'Or smart. You let him and that dog ride with you,' Montoya reminded him.

'The dog, I like.'

'So Kent Seger was just one messed-up mother.'

'Yeah, I've seen some hospital records. Depression, drug use, violence.'

'And what about Ryan Zimmerman?' Montoya asked.

Bentz frowned. 'He'll probably try to patch things up with his wife if he ever gets out of the hospital. The story is that he ran into Kent one night in the bars – he'd just lost his job and been kicked out of the house. Kent was an old friend, or so he thought and Kent was connected, had a virtual candy store of drugs. They hooked up and once Ryan was out of it, Kent took him hostage. Held him prisoner. Tortured him in that lair of his.'

'The one Navarrone discovered.'

'Yeah. Where we found the trophies.' Bentz chewed hard on his gum. Seeing the jewelry had gotten to him – everything from earring studs to ankle bracelets and a locket with Kent and Annie's picture inside – probably taken off his sister on the night she'd died, though no one had mentioned it. The way Bentz figured it, Kent had swapped Ryan's picture for his own. The world was no worse without Kent Seger.

'So Zimmerman's sworn off drugs, for good, or so he claims. You can't trust junkies,' Bentz said. 'The combination of drugs Kent gave him the night Melanie was killed messed him up bad enough that Kent had no problem setting him up. Kent made the call to the station the night Melanie was killed, then pushed Zimmerman into the street. He just happened to get hit by the car. That wasn't necessarily planned. If the hospital hadn't pumped his stomach, he would have died.'

'As would have Samantha Leeds.'

Bentz scowled. 'She nearly did anyway.' He glanced out the open window to the city lights and remembered how Kent Seger had gotten past her security, with the one key she didn't duplicate when she changed the locks, a small key she'd rarely used, the one to the trap door under her stairs. All Kent had to do was slip under the verandah, make his way to the trap door and let himself into the house. Easy as pie. What a bastard. And his body had never been recovered from the swamp, as if the dark vile water had claimed one of its own.

Montoya leaned against the file cabinet and crossed his booted feet in front of him. 'So what happened to that brother of hers. Pete or Peter or whatever he went by? I thought he might have been involved.'

'From all I know he's as elusive as ever. Hasn't surfaced. He worked for a cell phone company for a while, but quit his job. No one's heard from him. Not Sam, not her father, not even the damned IRS.'

'What's up with that?'

'Maybe he's just a private person.'

'Or a junkie.'

'A lot of those out there.' Bentz glanced into the night. 'My guess is that Samantha and her father won't hear from him until the coroner comes knocking – if then.'

'So that's it,' Montoya said. 'The case is closed.'

'There're a few loose ends,' Bentz allowed. 'I still want to talk to some people who conveniently dropped out of sight when the bodies started piling up. Roommates, exes, pimps and the like, but I think they're all clean, probably just had other issues with the law that they didn't want to go into and decided it was time to disappear.' He thought of Marc Duvall, the pimp and Sweet Cindy AKA Sweet Sin, to name a couple persons of interest who had conveniently turned up missing. Sooner or later he'd track them down. Especially Duvall. 'But yeah, for all intents and purposes it's over.'

'Good.' Reuben snapped to attention. 'Then we're done. Right? Maybe you should celebrate with one of those near-beers.'

'We still have a couple of murders that haven't been solved,' Bentz reminded him, and glanced at the computer screen where images of two dead women, one Jane Doe burned and left in front of the statue of Joan of Arc, the other, Cathy Adams, the stripper/student/prostitute who had been found with her head shaved in her apartment.

So close in age to his own daughter. The only kid he'd ever raise. That thought bothered him, but, hell, it was working out. She was a great kid. A great kid.

'We'll figure the other murders out,' Montoya said, never doubting himself for a minute.

'I hope so.' But Bentz wasn't convinced. In his gut he knew another serial killer was stalking the streets of his city. Another sick bastard with strange rituals. A signature? God, he hoped not. Maybe the two cases on his desk weren't related. And yet . . . he sensed they were.

Damn it all to hell.

'Well, I don't know about you, but I'm definitely celebrating tonight. Definitely.'

'Probably a good idea,' Montoya agreed.

'A damned good one. Hey – what time is it?' He looked at his watch, a knock off of a Rolex, then walked over to the file cabinet and switched on the radio just as the first few strains of 'A Hard Day's Night' faded away and Samantha Leeds's sultry voice floated from the speakers.

'Good evening New Orleans, this is Dr. Sam at WSLJ. You're listening to *Midnight Confessions*, and tonight we're going to be talking about luck . . .'